Garbhan Downey cut his [...] College Galway's student [...] qualified, he worked as a [...] regional and national newspapers. He then spent several years as a reporter, producer and presenter with the BBC, in Derry and Belfast, before becoming editor of the *Derry News* in 2001. During his three years there, the paper doubled its circulation, won two Newspaper Society (UK) awards, and started a second edition. Now writing fiction full-time, he has published four books including *The Private Diary of a Suspended MLA* – which was described by the *Sunday Times* as 'the best Northern Ireland political novel of the century' – and *Off Broadway*, which 'Dickens would have been proud to have created' (*Irish News*). He is editor of Ireland's new literary magazine, *Verbal*, and is completing another novel.

RUNNING MATES
GARBHAN DOWNEY

BLACKSTAFF
PRESS

BELFAST

Many thanks for their expertise, time and support to: Des
Doherty; Patsy Horton, Helen Wright and all at Blackstaff Press;
Áine McCarthy and Ita O'Driscoll of Font International; John
McCloskey; Keith Munro M.B.; Dr Niall Ó Dochartaigh,
Politics Department, NUI Galway; Pat O'Flaherty; Damian
Smyth, Arts Council of Northern Ireland; and Cecelia Taaffe.
May they forgive me for taking liberties with their better advice.
A special mention also to my family and friends for their
continued encouragement – and particularly to the book's first
reader, my uncle Kevin Downey.

First published in 2007 by
Blackstaff Press
4c Heron Wharf, Sydenham Business Park
Belfast BT3 9LE
with the assistance of
The Arts Council of Northern Ireland

Garbhan Downey has asserted his right under
the Copyright, Designs and Patents Act 1988
to be identified as the author of this work.

Typeset by CJWT Solutions, St. Helens, England

Printed in England by Cox and Wyman

A CIP catalogue record for this book is available from the British Library

ISBN 978-0-85640-799-4

www.blackstaffpress.com
www.garbhandowney.com

To Úna –
for the best years
of my life

Key Players

POLITICOS

'Rubber' John Blake	Irish Taoiseach (premier), Fianna Fáil party
Sonny Waterhouse	Meath parliamentarian, Blake's double agent in the far right
Louise Johnston ('Letemout' Lou)	young Derry judge with a tongue like a docker's and the body of a goddess
Stan Stevenson	politically savvy newspaper man
John 'Joxer' O'Duffy	nasty-minded posterboy of the far right
Jim Wynne	O'Duffy's sycophantic deputy
Mark Blake	Taoiseach's cousin and confidant, Chief Whip

THE BACKROOM BOYS

Tommy 'Bowtie' McGinlay	hapless lawyer with chronic irritable bowel syndrome
Bartholomew 'King Size' Barkley	ruthless, morally bankrupt millionaire
Eva 'Ready' Given	drop-dead gorgeous film student, part-time working girl

Barry Magee	photographer by profession, blackmailer by vocation
Mary Slavin	hardbitten, brutally frank, fifty-something newspaper editor
Harry 'the Hurler' Hurley	mellowing former leader of anti-British paramilitary group
Jimmy 'Fidget' Hurley	Harry's handsome but damaged little brother
Uncle Hugo Stevenson	gentlemanly newspaper proprietor; Stan's uncle and Mary Slavin's paramour
Susie 'Short Shorts' Barkley	glamorous hotel manager with an eye for Stan
Gráinne Gael McCormack (Gigi)	photographer with the best legs in Derry
Audrey Grafton	liberal-minded police chief
Monsignor George 'Bend'em-Back' Behan	psychiatrist and pal of Joxer O'Duffy

PROLOGUE

'**N**o offence, Taoiseach,' said the dumpy red-headed man, 'but you're talking out of your hole. If you give speaking rights to Northerners, the entire fucking chamber will walk out. Bad enough we're stuck living next door to the whinging bastards without having to listen to them day in, day out in our own parliament. Next thing you know, they'll be looking for votes. Then your arse'll really be in a sling.'

Rubber John Blake, leader of Ireland's newest government, smiled over his blasted-oak desk and wistfully recalled the days when he surrounded himself with yes-men. 'You're not lish'ning to what I'm telling you, Sonny,' he sighed, his Galway brogue broadening as ever when he was trying to placate his straight-shooting advisor. 'I'm saying we should proposhe the idea, that's all. Ara, I know there's not a shnowball's chance in hell of it going through. Not with that bollix O'Duffy about. But sometimes there's no harm wrapping an oul flag round you and throwing a nod to the North. Keeps the poor saps up there happy – not to mention our own hardliners.'

Sonny Waterhouse, who'd just been returned as TD for North Meath for the fourth time, shook his head defiantly at the curly-haired bear of a man opposite. The possible reunification of Northern Ireland with the Republic had been an academic debate, at strongest, in the South for almost a century. And there was no way – strike that, no fucking way whatsoever – that he was going to let Rubber John steer it into the mainstream.

'O'Duffy's going to run for president next year,' he insisted, 'and you're handing him his manifesto on a plate. He's already hammering you on immigration, tax and tribunals. You make the North an issue and he can start picking out the curtains for Phoenix Park right now.'

'Which is precisely,' interrupted the Taoiseach, 'why I need your help ...'

Sonny stopped abruptly and glared across at his boss. Rubber John had done it again. The cunning hoor had thrown out a rope and let Sonny tie himself up with it. Sonny shook his head again, though this time slowly in disbelief. 'You're a fucking reptile,' he said at last. 'What do you need?'

'Well, Sonny,' grinned the Taoiseach, 'you're my only real friend on the right of the party. You're the only person I know – and can trusht – who understands how Joxer O'Duffy operates. And we can't have him holding the highest office in the country – even if it is an honorary one. Not for our party. Not for Fianna Fáil. So I want you to, ah, get close to him and report back.'

'You want me to spy for you?' protested Sonny, his voice rising in outrage.

'No, no, no. Think of it more as representing my interests within his little fringe group.'

'Say it. It's spying.'

'Think of it more as intelligence-gathering ...'

'And you seem to be gathering that I don't have any,' retorted Sonny. 'Admit that it's spying and I'll do it for you ...'

'Of course it's fucking spying, Sonny,' smirked Rubber John. 'But show me a man who's never been a spy, and I'll show you a man who's never been in politics.'

The Taoiseach crossed the massive room to the corner bar and lifted a new bottle of Paddy off the counter. He searched the little press underneath for glasses, and stood up clutching two half-pint beakers, which he filled with whiskey. Water was for Dubliners and other pansies. He handed a glass to Sonny and sat down again in his leather E-Z-Boy. 'It means that you have to fall out with me, Sonny. Publicly.'

'I figured that,' nodded the TD. 'You're not going to give me the junior ministry you promised me, so I'm going to storm out of here in a huff.'

'More or less. I'm really sorry ...'

'Fuck you.'

'That's it. Method acting will help.'

Sonny laughed in spite of himself and sipped his drink.

'Look,' said the Taoiseach. 'This is really important. And you'll be back in the fold by November next year, after the election, at the very latest. Stop him, and you'll get a full seat at the table. No messing. Tourism, maybe. I hear you just love those trips abroad ...'

'You've met my wife, then.'

Rubber John chuckled warmly. He had a deal. 'Okay so,' he continued, 'on to part two of your new job.'

Sonny sat forward and placed his drink on the desk. 'No problem,' he sniffed, 'I'll just run upstairs and get the Vaseline right away ...'

The Taoiseach gave him a don't-be-like-that look and gestured to him to sit back into his armchair. 'We need to get some Northerners into the party,' he said. 'Decent ones. And I'd like you to keep your ears and eyes open. Particularly for people Joxer mightn't like ...'

Sonny stared at him, puzzled. 'Now you've totally fucking lost me,' he said. 'Whatever about putting up a façade that you're interested in the Six Counties, you can't start recruiting up there. Jesus, they'll be looking for you to fix things for them. Represent them even ...'

'Hear me out,' explained the Taoiseach, holding his hand up protectively. 'We have to do this. It's in our own selfish interest. We're leaking republican votes to Sinn Féin every day. They're the only party operating both sides of the border, and we have to show there's an alternative. And, more important, we have to show there's an alternative that we control – and will bring about in our own time. Please God, on the never-never, just like our fathers and forefathers before us. But what we absolutely cannot do is let some Northern fucking headcases set us a five-year agenda ...'

'You're looking for puppy dogs so,' smiled Sonny, cottoning on.

'Think of them more as realists,' smiled the Taoiseach. He reached into his desk drawer for an A4 sheet of paper, which he passed to the North Meath TD. 'Now here's a list to get started with. Softly does it.'

I

She had him exactly where she wanted him – deep in shit and begging for help. His big, smart mouth had walked him right into court again.

'This is particularly stupid – even for you,' she told him. 'You should have called me before you published.'

Most lawyers aren't normally so blunt with their clients, but then the *Derry Standard*'s legal advisor was no ordinary lawyer. Nor was the newspaper editor Stan Stevenson shy about giving it back.

'What would you know?' he retorted. 'If I rang you every time I was worried about a story, I couldn't print a parish bulletin – never mind a hundred-page newspaper. You're so damn prissy. Every time I ask your advice for a story, it's: "*Don't put that in*"; "*What's that doing there?*"; and "*Oh Lord, I would never touch that*". Christ, it's worse than Friday nights when we first started dating.'

Letemout Lou Johnston, the North's youngest High Court judge – and indeed the only judge ever to have been called a 'fit-looking bitch' by a murder defendant in open court – laughed. 'Problem is, Stan,' she said, 'you're expecting me to bail you out after the damage is done. It's a clear-cut libel, and you would have known that if you'd called. You're just lucky I'll not be hearing it. But you're right. It's exactly like when we started dating – I'm no use to you any more, once your horse has bolted …'

'Ouch.' Stan grinned. 'But seriously, can you get me off?'

'Possibly,' she replied, raising her eyebrows. 'But almost certainly not in any legal sense.'

Stan Stevenson had never wanted to edit the *Derry Standard* in the first place. His passion in life was politics. Not feelgood stories or song contests, or flower shows, or, Jesus help us, bridge notes. No. For him, there was one subject and one subject only. Politics. The eternal war to determine who owns society. Politics. The poisoned milk that flows through our every vein to assure us that we are always better than the next guy. Politics. The anti-sex – it doesn't matter who you screw just as long as you come first. The problem with living in the North was that serious people like Stan didn't do politics. Not as players at least. They realised the futility of it. The Brits, cynical bastards, had devised the perfect system to cope with the natives: give them all the responsibility and none of the power. So the smart money had all opted out of the process and stood at the sidelines making smart remarks, while the lower orders fucked everything up.

Stan, needless to say, had become a master of the smart remark. If anything, he was too good at his job as chief political writer and leader writer for the *Standard*. So when the editor's job suddenly became available, Stan's Uncle Hugo, who owned the paper, squeezed him into the round hole.

The previous chair-holder had been Mary Slavin, a fiery, foul-mouthed veteran, who was a walking testament to the link between red hair and bad temper. Mary had stormed out after a furious row with Hugo at the Christmas party. The pair had got drunk and begun an 'I'm the Cleverest' contest, which Hugo unfortunately then went and won by asking Mary if she were so bright, how come she wasn't signing *his* cheques. Hugo, while he'd been sharp enough to inherit money, was too old-school to apologise to the help. So Mary departed, and Stan took over the chair.

Stan's two years as editor had seen no fewer than nine separate libel writs land on Hugo's desk, including the now infamous case of Mayor Lucky Tucker and the malicious proofreader. Thanks to Letemout Lou, however, the *Standard* managed to knock the first eight claims back into touch. But when the letter from Tommy Bowtie McGinlay arrived the day before Christmas Eve, it seemed that this time they were in trouble. Six-figure trouble.

This wasn't what Stan had signed up for. Thirty-six years

old and he was going grey worrying about crooked lawyers. And, most important, he missed his politics. So when Uncle Hugo had come into Stan's office earlier that New Year's Day and busted him back to the newsdesk, he offered precisely just enough argument to make sure his pay cheque wouldn't be sliced. Stan was a thirty per cent shareholder in the paper and Hugo's sole heir, so whoever got the big job wasn't going to present him with any headaches anyway.

Newspapers work largely on the basis that if something is of public interest, it should be written down. Solicitors, on the other hand, work on the principle that there is nothing that will hang you quicker than the printed word – and they will only resort to paper and ink in an outright emergency. It is not by sheer dint of coincidence that the lawyers swan off to court in their brand new Beamers while the hacks shuffle about in second-hand Volvos.

Most newspapers know, however, that while publishing stories about ordinary punters carries a certain degree of risk, publishing anything remotely critical about solicitors is suicide. Even if, as sports editor Mike Harrison would say, you are 110 per cent certain of it. Because although you might think all the *i*s are dotted and the *t*s are crossed, if a lawyer finds even the most tenuous reason to haul you into court for defamation, all of a sudden you're in his patch, playing by his rules and being judged by his friends. And, unless you're airtight, you're going to leave the courtroom very much the good-looking cellmate.

That the solicitor Tommy Bowtie fell on his mouth while staggering home from the Jack Kennedy Inn is beyond dispute – the incident was caught on CCTV and is still played nightly on the Bloopers tape in the police social club. Likewise, there is no doubting that he had to get four stitches in his left nostril where his index finger had been stationed immediately prior to the fall, and another eight in his upper lip – this is documented in the hospital notes. Nor indeed is there any argument that Tommy Bowtie then filed a false claim for £10K in compensation, alleging he had been 'savagely assaulted' by a gang of hoods. All this is a matter of public record.

Sadly for Tommy, however, the scumbag police have long memories – and didn't tell him about the CCTV footage until they got him into the dock. He was laughed out of court – and was only allowed to keep his licence after a shrink convinced the judge that the knock might have brought on False Memory Syndrome.

And it is at this point precisely that Stan should have stopped writing his report. But, despite being close pals, in days gone by, Tommy had irked Stan with so many threats, letters and writs that the editor couldn't resist one final victory dig. And so he headlined the court report, 'Drunk lawyer admits he wasn't mugged', and stuck it on the front page.

The only difficulty was, for once in his life Tommy Bowtie wasn't drunk leaving the Jack Kennedy. In fact, he hadn't been drinking at all, as he was on a course of penicillin for what was termed an 'ongoing personal condition'. And Tommy had been falling all over the road because the antibiotic had reacted badly with his late-evening Prozac. Other than that, the hospital test had shown his blood was cleaner than the Virgin Mary's.

Stan's sacking was one of the conditions of Tommy Bowtie's new letter, along with a full apology, a modest donation to charity – to show the public what a caring sort of fellow Tommy actually is – and Tommy's own legal expenses. Which is where the fun started.

The day Tommy's office opened after the holidays, Lou rang him to get the bottom line and then relayed the news to Hugo.

'One hundred grand,' screamed Hugo. 'I'd sooner bankrupt the paper than give that fat, thieving wino a cent.'

'Alternatively,' said Lou slowly, 'he'll take a ten per cent share of the *Standard*.'

'No way,' said Hugo. 'For Christ's sake, he's already got Stan's nuts in a jar – he's not getting mine.'

'Stan's assets are still fully attached and in perfect working order,' chuckled Lou, 'as will yours be if you'll just listen up. You're going to have to pay him money – Stan made sure of that with the "drunk" gibe. Big money. Unless of course, you manage to prove fair comment ...'

'And how could I do that?' asked Hugo.

'Personally,' said Letemout, 'I'd just wait until Tommy gets blind drunk again and get someone to take a bunch of photos of him. Only one problem there, though.'

'What's that?'

'You might have to hang on until the weekend,' quipped Letemout, and hung up.

For the first time since Christmas, Hugo smiled. He picked up the phone and buzzed upstairs for his number one cameraman, Barry Magee.

Hugo wasn't the only one tying up a noose for Tommy Bowtie. At the exact same time that Lou was handing Hugo his lifeline, Tommy's Dunavady office was being ransacked by the CID and Inland Revenue as part of a joint anti-fraud inquiry. The warrant was deliberately vague but did mention all files relating to the Dunavady Improvement Agency. Files that were, fortuitously, locked in another office two doors down.

Tommy Bowtie was secretary of the DIA and had been involved in drawing down three million pounds in government grants to develop a business park outside the town. All legitimate and above board. But the fact that the thirty-acre site for the park had been bought by Tommy and his associate Bartholomew King Size Barkley as farmland just a year ago – and then sold on by them to the DIA, as zoned land, at four times the price in November, was upsetting the local Luddites. Hence the raid.

In fairness, this was such small beer that ninety-nine per cent of the time, the cops and Revenue wouldn't have bothered with it. But Tommy had committed the cardinal error of disgracing his profession, or rather of being caught disgracing his profession, over his false compensation claim. So his old comrades, it seems, were determined to deliver him a sound smack in the mouth.

And a happy fucking New Year to you too.

2

Harry the Hurler Hurley, the retired chief executive of all the Boys in Derry, had adapted well to the end of the old order. He had inherited his mother's head for business and had taken the money 'entrusted' to him and invested it wisely in property and bars. This had included buying out the Jack Kennedy Inn, a mock seventeenth-century carriage house overlooking the Foyle, from his former front man Danny Boy Gillespie. And it was here that he established a suite of offices on the second floor, to run all his legitimate operations. Clearly, he was never going to be Mary Poppins. But, as his brother-in-law Sergeant Jack Gilmore said, in five years' time he might be as clean as Michael Corleone.

A tall bull of a man who could have passed for Gene Hackman in dim light, Harry had started to bulge in the middle after he'd got his own restaurant. But the genes were good, so he'd a few years left before he started to waddle.

At forty-eight, Harry was the eldest of the late republican patriarch Dominic Hurley's four children. Gerry, the next, had got himself a late-learner's degree and transferred into politics about a decade back. Donna, the only girl, had opted for civilian life before bringing eternal shame on the family by marrying Sergeant Jack the Black. And then you had the youngest, and Old Ma Hurley's favourite, Jimmy Fidget. And Jimmy, not to put too fine a point on it, was on a one-man mission to fuck up Harry's life.

To the outsider, Jimmy Fidget was a charming rogue. Dark and good-looking, with that dangerous streak that breaks smart women's hearts, he liked to think of himself as the archetypal Provo Laughing Boy. The trouble was, Jimmy had spent one too many years in jail, alone with the memory of what he'd done in the war. And ten years on, he was chewing more tablets than Tony Soprano. The wider public, however, knew little of this. If pushed, Old Ma would tell you in hushed whispers, Jimmy was sometimes 'a bit on edge'. Dom, God rest him, would have privately conceded that Jimmy was occasionally 'bad with his nerves'. Harry, however, had long given up on the euphemisms. A spade was a spade, and his brother was a fucking psycho.

Harry had attempted to ease Jimmy into the new era by appointing him Head of Retail for his Cut-price Cigarettes and DVDs sector. He installed him in an old factory warehouse on Bishop Street and got him a trader's licence to sell furnishings and bed linen. 'Blankets conceal a multitude of sins,' he told Jimmy with a smirk. But the joke whizzed right over Jimmy's head.

The problems began more or less immediately, when Jimmy – who could only do things his own way – decided to switch suppliers. Harry's guy had been based in Belfast and, all things considered, was very reliable for an out-and-out thief. But Jimmy had been in prison with a South Armagh man, Jolly Roger Logue, who convinced Jimmy he was paying about a third over the odds, and so a new alliance was born: Cheap Incorporated.

For the first few weeks, everything was going well and the profits were higher than the tar count in Jolly Roger's fags. But where Jimmy's thinking fell down was that being the scariest man in Derry no longer counted for anything in business. The whole town knew he wouldn't dare touch them, as the parole people would haul him back to jail. And so, if the customers' Marlboro tasted of camel shit, as can happen when you import from Tunisia, they would insist on getting their money back. Likewise, when they found out that their five pound copy of *Shrek 3* was in German with Japanese subtitles, they would think nothing of reporting him to the Trading Standards Agency.

Soon the ship was starting to leak. But instead of manning the lifebelts, Jimmy decided to steer straight into the iceberg and began diversifying into bootleg hooch. Harry had warned him not to sell it – begged him even. But Jimmy didn't share

Harry's new-found aversion to dealing in anything that could actually kill somebody. And within a couple of weeks the casualty department at Altnagelvin Hospital was busier than Baghdad Central.

Jack Gilmore warned Jimmy a raid was coming. But the youngest Hurley was too busy collecting money to take any notice, and so on 23 December – the busiest shopping day of the year – Jimmy was stunned to see twenty members of the new Police Service of Northern Ireland, and a similar number of customs officers, burst through the door. The subsequent charge list was longer than a five-decade Rosary – and, worst of all for Jimmy, it was Harry's name as owner, and not his, that appeared on all the paperwork.

Suffice it to say that Christmas festivities at the Hurleys were very muted, and the New Year was toasted in with Coca-Cola, as Harry wouldn't allow Jimmy to bring booze, of any sort, into the house.

The Friday after New Year Letemout Lou was at her desk in her private office above the Jack Kennedy Inn, when the love of her life came in. He sat down opposite, silently watching her, as she finished reading the sheaf of indictments Harry had left on her desk. She was sitting in her leather armchair, feet tucked under her, wearing a pair of ten-year-old jeans and a T-shirt that had been washed so many times the visitor couldn't read the logo. No socks, no makeup, and no frills – and yet if you'd taken her into the restaurant downstairs, she'd have turned every head in the place. Maybe it was the sleek coal-black hair, currently tied up in a bundle to reveal her long, slender neck. Equally well it could have been the bright, disbelieving eyes – or the generous, smiling mouth. Personally, Stan put it down to the natural confidence that exudes from a beautiful woman who'd think nothing of banging you into a twelve-by-eight cell for twenty years. Add all this to the fact that she wasn't wearing a bra, and Stan was finding it difficult to concentrate.

Stan was about to head off on his stag night to Dublin. And, although he was still kidding himself he wasn't whipped, he was in to seek special dispensation to get drunk and sing rebel songs in Slattery's Bar.

Like Lou, Stan had never been short of admirers. He'd been doubly lucky in his ancestry – which was allowing him to inherit all his uncle's money and none of his looks. While Hugo was bald and bulbous, Stan was six foot tall, slim and fair-haired. He'd also acquired his mother's baby-blue eyes and a mouth that was never done smiling. Of course, it helped that Stan almost always looked unbothered – largely because he was. Not that any of this mattered, though – he only had eyes for Lou.

'You have fun, handsome,' Lou told him with a wicked grin. 'Course if you so much as look at another girl, you know I'll find out. Then I'll hunt you down and ruin you for any other woman – or indeed man.'

'That's rich coming from you,' said Stan, 'considering what Alice Springs told me about your hen weekend in Amsterdam.'

'You're bluffing,' replied Lou cautiously.

'Am I?' smiled Stan. 'So it isn't true then, that you were the first people ever to be thrown out of the Anything Goes adult entertainment complex for rude and unacceptable behaviour? And it was nothing to do with the quarter-bottle of vodka in your handbag …'

'You've got nothing on me, Stevenson, and you know it,' countered Lou smugly.

'Nor is it true,' he retorted, 'that the customs men seized twenty-seven pairs of furry handcuffs from your group – a set in every suitcase – after you set the metal detectors off in Dublin. According to Alice, you even tried to pull rank and told them that you were a judge researching more humane methods of restraining prisoners. And when that failed you even gave the poor guy a big wink and offered to demonstrate.'

Lou felt her cheeks flushing. Jesus, she thought to herself, you can't trust anyone.

'That bitch.' She grinned at last. 'Typical Provo wife. All *omerta* and loyalty to the cause until you pour three Bacardi Breezers down her neck. I'm sure she told you all about

Jumbo, the stripper they got me, as well. Talk about false advertising ...'

'No,' said Stan, 'actually, she forgot about that one ... But don't worry about me, I'll behave. Unlike some, I purged all my sleazy fantasies long ago – well, apart from the ones you know about. And believe it or not, I'm also head over heels in love with the girl I'm marrying.'

'You're a living saint,' laughed Lou, putting her arms around him. 'And you know I love you too. Now, could you ever come down off the high moral ground long enough to give me a proper goodbye?'

'That depends,' said Stan.

'Depends on what?'

'On if you tell me the real reason you were so disappointed with Jumbo ...'

Stan had been gang leader since the age of five, and had a knack for not losing friends, so the forty-four-seater bus they'd hired for the trip to Dublin for his bash was full. They were splitting into two camps – Stan and the Thursday-night indoor footballers were staying at the Gresham, while the journalists and lesser mortals were for the Shelbourne.

Barry Magee, Stan's wedding photographer, was being forced to miss the weekend, however, as he was on Tommy Bowtie duty for the *Derry Standard*. Not that he minded too much. Stag parties always ended in tears. Invariably, the lads would invoke a 'no talking when we get home' pact before start of play. And invariably, at least one of the squad would let everybody down and confess all to his wife within five minutes of landing back in Derry. It was part of the ritual – as predictable as Danny Boy getting thrown out of Abra Kebabra on O'Connell Street for flashing his arse at passing buses.

Two years ago, at Gerry Hurley's last hurrah, three of the squad had scored at the late-night disco on Dame Street. And this time, Barry recalled, the touts didn't even have the decency to wait until they got home. So by the time the bus arrived back to Foyle Street, there was an angry posse waiting for the three young Lochinvars, consisting of not only their girlfriends, but their wives as well.

No. Derry men couldn't hold their water. Barry Magee, however, was a blow-in from north Wales, who preferred to enjoy his indiscretions a lot more discreetly. Like his friends, Barry had a taste for women. But it went largely unreciprocated. His shyness tended to go against him – as indeed did the fact that he was small, stubby, pink and hairless. So, somewhere in the throes of his ten years as a lensman, he'd developed a little fetish for voyeurism. Of course, he never talked about it – nor indeed any of his personal matters – and could never understand those who did. Though, for all that, he did enjoy listening. And you'd be surprised how many people, who should have known better, wanted to chat about this sort of stuff. Which is pretty much why Barry decided to combine his talents and start up a sideline in professional blackmail.

Tonight, however, it was business first. A true craftsman, Barry's plan was to produce for the newspaper a secret 'Clockwatch' of Tommy getting drunk, drunker and then incapable in the Jack Kennedy. If all went according to plan, Mr Bowtie would be struck off the lawyers' register before the month was out.

Barry might even make a few quid on the q.t. from other solicitors looking for prints, particularly if Tommy tried to cop off with a barmaid. Though not even Barry could have predicted how explosive the results were going to be.

3

Hugo Stevenson would never give you the impression of being the brightest bulb on the tree. But that was all part of the façade. He had survived – no, thrived – for fifty years in the newspaper industry by letting people underestimate him. Truth is, Hugo was shrewder than any of them – and richer too.

Where Hugo fell down, was in making tough decisions. Or rather following through on them. He was a gentle old soul, who looked and talked like something out of P.G. Wodehouse, and couldn't abide social awkwardness of any sort. It was fair to say he'd agonised over the sacking of his nephew. It took him three days to work up the nerve to speak to Stanley, despite the fact that anyone – particularly Stan – could have told him it was inevitable.

Stan's appointment had been, at best, a quick-fix solution after Mary Slavin walked out. He said on the first day that he didn't want the job, and he had asked Hugo a dozen times to release him. Hugo had refused each time, however, and Stan had remained as loyal as a dog all the while. But at long last, Hugo had taken Old Shep out to the barn.

As far as Stan was concerned, his sacking was entirely victimless. The real problem stemmed not from him, but from his uncle, who'd refused to bite the bit and say sorry to Mary Slavin two years ago. On that occasion, Hugo ducked the hard decision.

He should never have let her go – he knew that from the minute Mary threw the gin and tonic in his face. A veteran of thirty-five years' service, Mary was better connected than anyone in the business. She could also manage a newsroom full of egos without a daily riot and wrote sharper headlines than God. Most important, she was the only person who ever stood up to Hugo and his money. And it didn't hurt either that she looked great for a woman of fifty-three – or indeed forty-six, which was her official age.

Ultimately, Hugo knew he couldn't blame Stan. No. If he'd been more of a man, he would have gone down on his bended knees after the first week and begged Mary to come back.

Which is what he was going to do now.

By 11 p.m. on Friday night, Tommy Bowtie's legal action against the *Derry Standard* was effectively over. Barry Magee had managed to position himself so he could get pictures of Tommy and the bar clock in the one frame. So, on Monday morning readers would be able to make up their own minds as to whether nine pints and eight shorts constituted drunkenness. Tommy's three falls from the barstool (9.48 p.m., 10.10 p.m. and 10.11 p.m.) and the big kiss on the barman's cheek (10.28 p.m.) would obviously add to the debate. As would the big damp patch on his trousers after Tommy's eighth visit to the Gents (10.32 p.m.).

Indeed, Barry was about to head into the sunset when he overheard Michelle, the day waitress, say she'd walk up home with Tommy to make sure he was safe. Now, Tommy had been cut off and living in the back bedroom since child number four had arrived over a year ago – and was a known ladies' man – so there was a chance this could prove very interesting. And Barry, for one, was going to be there to record it for posterity. And more than a little pin money.

First, however, he had to give Hugo the good news: he could tell him to put the chequebook back in the safe. So he stepped out to his car and rang the boss from his mobile.

'Mission accomplished,' he said. 'The eagle is loaded.'

'You're a magician, dear boy,' replied Hugo. 'Give Stan a buzz to let him know. And many thanks.'

There was still no sign of Tommy and Michelle at the doorway, so Barry rang Stan who was busy knocking back stout in Doheny & Nesbitt's on Lower Baggot Street.

'Poor sod,' sighed Stan, when Barry told him. 'But I suppose people living in glass houses shouldn't wet their pants.'

The photographer laughed and rang off. And so, his professional day over, Barry Magee, master blackmailer, sat on in the Jack Kennedy car park to wait for Tommy Bowtie, Michelle the femme fatale, and a big fat payday.

Hugo was so buoyed up by Barry's news that he decided to seize the initiative and ring Mary at once. Since the split, Mary had been making a shedload of money in PR and freelancing for RTÉ, but she missed the status of running her own paper. Hugo was aware, however, that Mary would never admit this and that if he wanted her back he was going to have to grovel.

He still had the number of her riverfront flat on speed dial, so he lifted the receiver, pressed the digit '1' and waited.

'Took you fucking long enough,' growled the voice, before Hugo had uttered a word.

'I'm sorry?' he replied, puzzled.

'Yes, you are sorry, you donkey,' said Mary. 'Really fucking sorry. And it's taken you two years to say it.'

'You're right, Mary. I am really sorry. I'm prostrating myself here on the carpet pleading with you to come back … and to forgive me. Will you?'

'Of course I will,' replied Mary. 'Now, just shut the fuck up and I'll give you the terms. Double my last salary, a five per cent sharehold, plus full hiring and firing powers.'

'Ah, Mary, you can't sack Stan,' protested Hugo. 'He pulled me out of a terrible hole, when you walked out on me … because of my awfulness. Besides, he's the best political writer in the town – if only we could rein him in a little.'

'I'm not talking about Stan,' said Mary. 'For better or worse, he's my own protégé. And he'll be no worse an MD than you, whenever your liver gives out. At least Stan understands how things work at the sharp end of journalism. No. It's that greedy little Welsh prick Barry Magee. He's been taking dirty pictures of half the town and selling them off to the highest bidder. If you want me back on board – he has to go.'

'Can it wait a day or two?' asked Hugo. 'He's involved in an undercover assignment. Something rather important.'

'No doubt,' retorted Mary. 'I bet you've got him tailing

Tommy Bowtie as we speak – I heard he wanted you to donate a hundred grand to charity.'

'Christ, Mary. You're a witch.'

'Yes, I am, Hugo. But I'm your witch now.'

'You were always my witch, Mary,' continued Hugo slowly.

'I know, Hugo, I know,' murmured Mary. 'And for what it's worth, I'm really sorry too. It was way, way too long. It should never have happened. Let's not do this again.'

'Okay, Mary,' said Hugo, with a chuckle, 'you can stop there. You had me at "took you fucking long enough".'

Upstairs in the Jack Kennedy Inn, Letemout Lou was looking out the darkened window of her office at Barry Magee, skulking down in the back seat of his car with the lens pointed towards the bar door. Some poor sap who'd spent all week looking forward to their Friday night out was going to wake up to the mother of all comeuppances. But if you're going to cheat, be discreet, as Harry the Hurler always said.

With Stan off in Dublin, Lou had been spending the evening preparing a defence of sorts for Harry against the smuggling and piracy charges. It amounted to putting his hands up, taking his oil and sacking Jimmy Fidget. As a practising High Court judge, Lou could take no money for her consultations with Harry, something he resented greatly. So he was insisting on laying on the Valentine's Day wedding reception at the Jack Kennedy for free gratis, and he'd gifted them a one-acre site overlooking Lough Swilly at Fahan, which would have come in at £250,000 on the open market. Tax people wouldn't like it, of course, but Harry's late father Dom had been her godfather, so they could go whistle up a rope.

Harry had actually been partly responsible for bringing Stan and Lou back together. The pair had known one another from when they were children at Bogside Infants', more than twenty-five years ago. She was the fat girl in the front row with no friends, while Stan was the guy in the back corner working the crowd. Unusually, Stan had resisted the temptation to torment the weakest link and instead adopted Lou as his enforcer. Physically there wasn't an eight-year-old in the city – boy or girl – who could touch her, and verbally she was so sharp and so sarcastic that even the teachers left her alone. There was never any doubt she was going to be a lawyer.

Stan and Lou became inseparable. Then, in their teens, they began a tentative adolescent courtship after Lou lost half her body weight and Stan took her to the school formal. Truth is, he wouldn't have noticed if she were eight stone or eighty. By that stage, they were two halves of the one sentence.

In the late 1980s, however, Lou went off to study and, as can happen, the two drifted in different directions. Lou became the rising star of the Belfast legal set while Stan assumed his role as heir apparent at the uncle's paper. Both, unsurprisingly, developed a keen interest in politics. Stan, who had trained as a hack right out of school, took the more pragmatic approach, as was reflected by his straight-shooting commentary and reportage for the *Derry Standard*. Lou was more idealistic and took a year out from her degree to serve as a particularly vocal students' union president at Queen's. 'It was,' the vice-chancellor said later, 'the happiest fucking day of my life, bar none, when Ms Johnston decided not to run for a second term.'

After Lou qualified, she returned to Derry to serve as Harry the Hurler's personal lawyer. But it was a post she vacated after just twelve months, when the Crown Prosecution Service pressed her to become the North's youngest magistrate. The CPS had quickly realised that she was far too dangerous in the private sector. So they leaned on her by threatening to open an old file on her brother, who'd been a demolition consultant for the Boys during the early part of the revolution. Her court appointment also meant knocking her politics on the head, another small victory for the Empire.

After two years on the bench, Lou was fast-tracked to the High Court, and it was from there that Harry prevailed on her to preside over a private libel dispute he was involved in back in Derry. And when she arrived into the nightclub basement for the 'hearing', who was sitting in the reporters' dock grinning up at her, only Stan Stevenson. By the end of the week, the pair were tighter than skin on a stick again. And now, six years on, they were finally heading up the aisle.

And no, if we're to be honest, it wasn't the first private tribunal Lou had chaired for Harry. Nor would it be the last. And not all of them were for libel either.

4

Back in Dublin, the remains of the stag party were inching their way slowly towards Leeson Street but at the insistence of Skidmark Gormley, the retired bank robber, had pulled in for a pit stop at the Haughey Arms on Fitzwilliam Square. The upstairs lounge was booked for some private meeting, so the twelve-strong group squeezed into the downstairs bar, where Danny Boy Gillespie called for a quick-and-easy dozen stout.

Stan had never been in Fitzwilliam Square before, so he was very charmed when a gorgeous blonde girl of about twenty, wearing a miniskirt you hardly could floss your teeth with, sat beside him at the bar and produced a pack of cigarettes.

'Got a light?' she asked with the hint of a Cork brogue.

'Don't smoke,' grinned Stan innocently. 'Besides, it's illegal here now, isn't it?'

'Lots of things are illegal here,' countered the girl, 'but it doesn't mean you can't enjoy them, now does it?'

'I'll buy you a drink though,' said Stan, still oblivious. 'We're all down from Derry on my stag night – I'm sure the kitty can handle it. My name's Stanley, by the way – Stan to my friends.'

'One drink'll not get you far,' replied the girl with a cheeky wink. 'Oh, and my name's Eva. My friends call me Eva Ready …'

'Good one,' chuckled Stan. 'Like the bunny rabbit.'

'Exactly like the bunny rabbit,' laughed Eva, wondering just exactly when the light was going to go on in the bumpkin's head.

'You've a little sticker on the sole of your shoe,' said Stan, handing her a tonic water that had appeared on the counter.

'Hold on and I'll get it. Christ, two hundred and fifty euro. That's one dear pair of shoes.'

'I hate to break this to you, Stanley,' whispered Eva, conspiratorially, 'but that's not the price of the shoes ...'

There was silence for about ten seconds while the penny slowly dropped.

'Oh dear Lord,' said Stan, shaking his head at his innocence. And the table behind him erupted with long laughter.

'So tell me about this kitty, then,' continued Eva, flashing her eyes back at Stan. 'Just how big is it?'

Stan was outvoted eleven to one. And for a flat fee of seven hundred and fifty pounds sterling, Eva Ready was appointed Entertainments Advisor to the Gresham team of the stag party for the weekend. The deal, naturally enough, was conducted by King Size Barkley, the crooked jockey turned crooked businessman, who was richer even than Stan, and was their banker for the weekend.

Upstairs in the Haughey Arms, negotiations of a very different sort were under way – negotiations that would have far-reaching consequences for everyone in the country, and Stan Stevenson in particular.

Exactly forty men were in the upstairs lounge. The Committee of Eight – all disaffected Fianna Fáil TDs – had each agreed to bring four trusted associates to the gathering. Included among the guests were two newspaper owners, three judges, a university president, a Garda superintendent, a retired army general, four or five top bankers and about half a dozen of the biggest landowners in the Free State.

They were determined men, men of common purpose, men who would style themselves men of honour. And their aim was simple – to bring down the government and get the Celtic Tiger back up on all four paws.

The chairman of the Committee of Eight was the darling of the right, John Joxer O'Duffy, who'd been sacked as a minister five years before. A white-haired, expensively tailored man in his early sixties, Joxer still had the menacing physique and huge shovels of hands that had made him one of the most feared members of the Garda's 'heavy gang' in the seventies. Indeed it was one of these shovels that had clipped the Taoiseach on the ear during a heated Cabinet discussion on immigration, and ultimately led to his dismissal. They'd been rowing about Joxer's column in the *Daily Irishman*, in which he had called on the government to stop non-Caucasians and 'suspiciously tanned' Europeans automatically at all the Republic's ports. He'd also suggested building a 'dirty big fucking wall' right along the border with the Six Counties – to keep out 'Northern hoors' as well. The article, as you'd expect, didn't go down too well with Rubber John and the party's lily-livered intelligentsia. But ultimately it had earned Joxer huge popularity with the grassroots. And despite his sacking, at the last election O'Duffy, J. had been swept back into Leinster House with the highest vote ever recorded in Dún Laoghaire East.

Joxer had been responsible for drawing up the schedule for the meeting in the Haughey Arms, in conjunction with his right-hand man, the North Meath TD Sonny Waterhouse.

Items one to three presented very little debate. The room agreed, with virtually no discussion, to launch a stalking-horse challenge to Rubber John's leadership at the Easter Ard Fheis. The trick was to find a soldier who didn't have any designs on the crown but who could wound the king just enough to allow a more serious swordsman to step in. A number of names were mooted, but there was time to narrow it down.

Next, there was almost unanimous agreement on Joxer's proposal to freeze the state pension, which in turn could generate enough revenue to annihilate corporation tax completely. A rider to this stipulated that all benefits to non-residents would be stopped immediately. And all capital freed up would then be used to provide incentives to US investors.

The discussion on Northern representation in the Dáil was a little more tricky. As 'the Republican Party', Fianna Fáil always liked to talk the talk – though up until now, no one had seriously expected them to walk the walk. But Sinn Féin's rapid emergence as an all-Ireland party was changing things, and Rubber John and some of his liberal colleagues were looking towards a possible merger with the SDLP – and even giving Northerners some minor foothold in the Southern Cabinet, way down the line.

The Committee of Eight and friends, however, were all agreed that it would be a cold day in Ballymun before they would allow Six-County madmen to dictate to them. And it would be a colder day still before their government would take any fiscal or political responsibility for what was a money-sapping cancer. Their problem was the traditional Fianna Fáil voter, who loved to wrap the green flag round himself when he'd a few drinks in him. So all in the room were of a mind that they should proceed with caution.

'Why don't we get a few donkeys and headcases to stand for us across the North,' suggested the Garda superintendent. 'All it would take would be a series of fuck-ups, a couple of scandals, and the party could dump the idea as a dead loss.'

'Not a bad idea,' said Joxer. 'Not bad at all.'

Matters of great importance were also being settled downstairs in the Haughey Arms. King Size Barkley had worked out a sure-fire way of ensuring that, when they got home, no one would rat to their wife about their private Entertainments Advisor. Each of the team had to get photographed while Eva was giving them a little one-on-one counsel.

King Size, however, was no match for Stan, being a scrawny little midget with a big red beak of a nose, who'd no natural authority other than his money.

'No way,' Stan told him flatly. 'The rest of you can do what you want. But I'm warning you now, I'll walk away from my own stag night.'

'Ah sure, no one will ever find out, Stan,' pleaded King Size.

'It's not about that,' said Stan. 'There's no way I'm going to let down Lou now. And besides, I wouldn't be married five minutes before the pictures would be posted all over the internet. It's not your fault – you can't help yourself, King Size. You were born to mix shit.'

'Let Stan out of it,' interrupted Dumpy Doherty, who didn't like where this was going. 'There'll be all the more for the rest of us …'

King Size nodded okay. 'Any other virgins want out?' he
asked. But there were none.

His point made, Stan headed for the jacks, congratulating
himself on a job well avoided. King Size sat in the corner,
glaring after him.

'What's going on upstairs then?' said Stan to the tired-looking
guy at the urinal beside him.

'A long boring political discussion,' replied Sonny
Waterhouse. 'A bunch of rich guys want to depose the
Taoiseach because he's a redneck in a flat cap with cowshit on
his boots.'

'Typical Friday night out in Dublin so,' laughed Stan.

'Not really,' said Sonny. He glanced over at his smartly
dressed neighbour with the Derry lilt and grinned. 'These guys
are off their bleeding heads. They reckon they can eradicate
poverty by starving all the poor people to death. They want all
immigrants shipped back to Africa – even the Eastern
Europeans. Oh, and they're going to set up machine-gun nests
at the border to keep you lot from the North from coming
down here and contaminating our good country.'

'So what are you doing with them?' asked Stan.

'Keeping an eye on things, son,' said Sonny. 'A tight
fucking eye on things.'

Stan went over to the sink to wash his hands, glanced
sideways in the mirror at the moustachioed, red-haired man
and smiled in eventual recognition.

'You're Waterhouse, the Meath TD,' he said triumphantly.

'Not bad for a Northerner,' Sonny replied, turning his head
round and smiling back.

'Committee of Eight?' continued Stan. 'You lot think
anyone born north of Monaghan should get numbers tattooed
on their arms …'

'Behind their ears, actually. Though we'll include
Monaghan people as well, if you like.'

'You'll be telling me now you're one of the good guys,'
smirked Stan.

'I just might be,' replied Sonny, looking directly at him.
'Why don't you let me buy you a jar?'

'Jesus Christ, what is this place?' laughed Stan. 'I'm just after escaping from the Happy Hooker out in the bar – and now a strange man in the toilets wants to get me drunk.'

'Welcome to the capital, handsome,' laughed Sonny. 'Now let me wash my hands, and I'll get the stout in. You might be interested in what I've got to say.'

King Size spotted Stan having a pint with the little fat ginger chap at the bar and was doubly irked. Bad enough that the guest of honour was too high and mighty to enjoy his pre-nuptial treat, he was now bailing out to talk to a complete stranger. A politician, no doubt. Stan was an addict.

'Well, fuck that,' said King Size to the rest of the group. 'I'm damned if I'm travelling three hundred miles just to watch him schmooze. Time Mr Stevenson got down and dirty with the rest of us. We'll wait until he's asleep and Eva can hop into the bed alongside of him so.'

Up at the counter, Stan was trying to suss out what exactly Sonny Waterhouse was at. But it was a two-way game.

'You're not exactly comfortable with Joxer's politics so?' asked the Derryman.

'You know an awful lot about the business yourself,' replied Sonny. 'You wouldn't be a journalist, would you?'

Stan laughed and took a healthy slug of Coldflow. 'Okay, you got me. But we're all off the record. I'm here on my stag night. I'm Stan Stevenson, part-owner and ex-editor of the *Derry Standard*. We've also a little radio station in the city. Though it's still just semi-legal so we don't talk too much about it.'

'You'll be a connection of Hugo's so?'

'Yes, his nephew.'

'Hugo was one smart operator. Soft as shit to look at, but sharp as a splinter underneath. He still in politics?'

'Not really,' answered Stan, impressed. 'He stayed chairman of the Independence Party till it broke up. But he hasn't been a councillor for more than a decade. He still advises both the SDLP and the Shinners though. I think he talks to your lot as well. Well mainstream Fianna Fáil, at least. I'm not sure he's much time for your little happy-clappy wing.'

'Me neither,' muttered Sonny, drawing deep on his pint.

Stan eyed the Meath man cautiously. 'You're testing me, aren't you?' he said.

'Sort of,' conceded Sonny. 'What do you think of the idea of Joxer for president?'

'Appalling,' tutted Stan. 'I'd sooner have Dana ... Fuck it, I'd rather have herpes.' He paused. 'Is that where Joxer's headed?'

'Unless someone stops him, that is.'

'So what are you doing about it? You personally, Sonny?'

'Okay so.' Sonny nodded, deciding to take a chance. He was drunk, bored and, most important of all, Uncle Hugo had been third on the list the Taoiseach had given him the day he'd appointed him recruiting officer. 'Let me give you a hypothesis here – and then, maybe, you ask a few questions. Imagine if the Taoiseach – who is one conniving bastard, and never forget that – planted someone in Joxer's inner circle to keep an eye on things. Imagine if that guy were also charged with doing everything he could to disrupt Joxer from within. Imagine, then, if that guy met a guy in a bar that he thought could help him. A guy who might actually want to help him. Should the first guy maybe let down his guard a little and chat to the second guy? How would he know he could trust him?'

'The short answer is he couldn't.' Stan grinned, enjoying the double-play. 'I'd say it's far, far too big a risk for the first guy to show his hand like that. But ...' He paused.

'But what?' pressed Sonny.

'But,' continued Stan slowly, 'as long as it were all hypothetical, I'd say the second guy would be very interested in hearing what the first guy had to say. And that might give the first guy enough time to figure out that the second guy is probably the type of guy who can keep his mouth shut. What I can't figure, Sonny, is why you think the second guy would be able to help you. Bottom line is, he's probably just small potatoes compared to a man like, say, yourself.'

'Actually,' replied Sonny, 'the second guy is far too modest. He owns half a newspaper and, between you and me, he seems like a pretty smart cookie to boot.'

'Smart enough to realise when he's being played ...?' countered Stan.

'Certainly,' replied Sonny. 'But he's also smart enough to realise that he can turn the play to his advantage. The first guy is reaching out for a hand-up. And if he gets a hand-up, he'd be very happy to return the favour.'

'So, back to my first question, then,' interrupted Stan. 'What are you personally doing to stop Joxer O'Duffy?'

'Publicly nothing,' said Sonny. 'I'm still in the Committee of Eight, for reasons I'm not going to go into right now. But privately, and I mean just between us – or should I say the first guy and the second guy – I'll not be there much longer. Also, and again privately, I happen to know that there's a big campaign about to begin in mainstream Fianna Fáil to allow Northerners to vote in this year's presidential elections. It's one sure way of helping to shaft Joxer. And Rubber John – the Taoiseach that is – is looking for people up in the Six Counties to champion it. People of influence – like you, Stanley. There'd be great benefits for you in it. Real political gains for the North. You'd be pushing on an open door.'

Stan set his empty pint glass on the counter and shook his head cynically at Sonny. 'You guys are great ones for talking,' he smiled, turning to walk away. 'We've spent the last ninety years waiting for you. But now, all of a sudden, you tell me you're ready to welcome us back with open arms. And all we have to do is kill your king. Jesus, at least the Brits are honest when they're screwing us.' He glanced at his watch. 'Look, I have a stag night to go to ...'

Sonny stopped Stan with a light touch on his arm and signalled to the barman for two more pints of Coldflow. 'One more drink,' he said. 'Look, Stan, you can't be a hurler on the ditch all your life ...'

'What do you mean?' asked Stan, facing him again.

Sonny shrugged as if the answer were obvious. 'It's easy to snipe from the sidelines. To remain aloof from it all. And to be honest, if I'd your money and ability, politics is the last thing I'd be mixing in. But if you – and by *you*, I also mean you personally – refuse to take part in the process, then you can't condemn everyone else when it all goes arseways. Who are you going to blame when Joxer's crowned president? You had your shot to stop him. Who are you going to call when they come knocking on your door to take you away?'

Stan couldn't help grinning. Flattery, threats and guilt, all in the one sentence. This guy was a natural. He should be recruiting for the IRA.

But Stan had one more ball he wanted to pitch at Sonny. 'Problem with all this is that it's not real politics,' he said. 'The Irish people don't care who's president. It's an office for amateurs, not serious politicians. No executive power. No advisory role. Just sign the bill where we tell you, and shut the fuck up. Let's face it, half of Leinster House couldn't tell Cearbhall Ó Dálaigh from the drunk at the gate.'

Sonny raised his finger to interrupt, but Stan wasn't finished. 'Look at the calibre of some of the people who run for president. Most of them couldn't get elected to the parish council – never mind the Dáil. No. Really. Why should I be one damn bit interested in you giving us votes – just to stop Joxer O'Duffy?'

'Because,' said Sonny quietly, 'it's a start, Stan. It's a start.'

5

In what he would later discover was probably the most pleasant moment of his day, Tommy Bowtie woke in the back bedroom with a stabbing pain in his gut. His Rapid Irritable Bowel Syndrome – or 'Ribs' as the doctor now called it – had returned with a vengeance the minute the cops had raided his office, and was showing no signs of abating. He quickly slipped out of the room, managing not to wake his four-year-old son who'd joined him at around 4 a.m., and made it to the bog just in time. Tears rolled down his big purple cheeks as the remnants of last night's Guinness and chilli lamb kebabs left his system in a boiling, black cascade. He reached over to turn on the bidet, but it was a false dawn. He was back splattering the bowl again before the first wave of fire had fully subsided.

It was the combination, of course, that had wrecked his stomach. He was almost as addicted to Tabasco sauce as he was to stout. Twenty-five years of necking back heroic levels of both had brought on the first attack about a year ago. But the doctor told him that it would regress as long as he could avoid undue stress. As if.

Undue stress? He was a lawyer for fuck's sake – and in bed with King Size Barkley, the biggest gangster in North Derry. Undue stress? Four squalling youngsters under the age of six, and a wife who'd made it clear that he was never getting near her again until she had both bollocks in a steel box and a framed 'Snipped' certificate on the mantelpiece. Undue stress? The Law Society threatening to strike him off over his false compensation claim?

What was he thinking of listening to King Size? This was the same guy who'd advised him to go off Prozac cold turkey. And then threatening to sue the *Derry Standard*? Jesus, was he losing the run of himself entirely? Again that was King Size's doing – the little runt had been angling for ages to get a slice of the paper.

No, the only way Tommy could avoid undue stress was to suck hard on a gas pipe. But even then, he couldn't give Dora the satisfaction of saying he'd taken the easy way out.

So here he was, stuck with his Ribs. For the past week, he hadn't been able to stray more than twenty yards from his office toilet, and his hole was redder than a pope's hat. Worse again, who could he tell? If word got out about his condition, he'd be laughed out of the city. They'd be calling him Tommy Bisto.

Settle yourself, Tommy. Think of your happy place. The Jack Kennedy on a Saturday night before the crowd lands in. The first pint of the night. Cold, creamy, not too sour, not too sweet. That's better.

After five minutes' happy-time, Tommy felt well enough to try to make it to the kitchen for a Nurofen Resolve. He handled the stairs well enough, but disaster was lurking in the hall. For there on the mat was a letter from Stormont addressed to Mr Thomas McGinlay, BCL, MA. He knew immediately it wasn't a cheque. God doesn't operate like that. It was a day, like every other, for getting slapped in the teeth. So, never a man to delay the inevitable, he ripped open the envelope and started reading.

Dear Mr McGinlay

Further to our initial investigations, the Northern Ireland Office would like to invite you to take part in a public inquiry into the activities of the Dunavady Improvement Agency.

The aim of the inquiry, which will be chaired by Dunavady Town Council, is to establish if applications made by you, as Secretary of the DIA, for funding from the Government's Prosperity Fund were fraudulent. It will also examine if the dispersal of said funding to individuals and groups in the Dunavady area was fraudulent.

The tribunal will begin its hearings in March and is expected to last two years. For its duration, counsel for the

NIO will be proposing the voluntary suspension of your
licence to practise law …

Christ. Christ. Christ. But before Tommy could read another
word, a sudden spasm in the belly doubled him over and sent
him lurching towards the downstairs jacks. Good job his
jogging bottoms had elasticated ankles.

Back in the Gresham, Stan Stevenson woke up in much better
form. He'd stopped drinking early on, as he wanted to make
sure he could outrun his team-mates whenever they tried to
tie him naked to the lamppost outside Trinity College. They'd
chased him as far as the Harp Bar at O'Connell Bridge, before
the gardaí intervened and gave him a lift to the hotel.

Afterwards, in the residents' lounge, Stan gamely fought off
the lads' attempts to hook him up with Eva Ready by
producing a stun gun that Harry the Hurler had loaned him.
Skidmark Gormley had been the only one foolish enough to
suggest it was a bluff – and ended the night with an icepack on
his groin and the promise of a part refund from Eva.

At about four bells, he left them at it and went upstairs
to sleep the deep sleep of the just. So, by the time Lou rang at
10.30, Stan was up, showered, breakfasted and raring to go again.

'You've a new editor,' announced Lou when they'd got last
night's body count out of the way. 'Hugo rang me about half
an hour ago.'

'I hope he crawled back to Mary,' replied Stan.

'Of course he did,' said Lou. 'Jesus, if he'd had any sense
he'd have married her twenty years ago.'

'But then they would have had children,' countered Stan,
'and I wouldn't be a media tycoon.'

'Some tycoon,' Lou laughed, 'you're as cheap as a walk in
the rain.'

'Oy,' protested Stan, 'I resent that remark.'

'Stanley, darling,' said Lou. 'I love you more than life. But
you're the guy who heard there was no such thing as a free
lunch and turned it into a lifelong challenge.'

'Somebody has to be frugal,' sniffed Stan. 'We can't all have
four pairs of shoes.'

Lou laughed again. 'But there's bad news as well,' she continued.

'And what's that?'

'Well, I rang Mary to congratulate her, and she says she's got clearance from Hugo to sack your pal Barry Magee. Proper order if you ask me. He should be in jail.'

'But he's the photographer for our wedding,' protested Stan.

'Only because he threatened to report you to Harry for stealing a bottle of fifty-year-old brandy from the Jack Kennedy off-licence.'

'I know, I know,' said Stan. 'But if he does the pictures, it'll save us about seven hundred quid.'

'Yeah, yeah, he's all heart,' retorted Lou. 'You can be sure he'll make twice that back in extortion before the day's out.'

'He sorted out Tommy Bowtie last night though,' Stan pointed out.

'He did that,' conceded Lou. 'But I have to say, I feel very sorry for Tommy. He's weak, not bad. That evil little shit King Size is pulling all the strings there. Just like his evil little uncle, Sparkly, did before him. Rot his soul ... Anyway, I have to run. How's your room?'

'All right – I had to share with King Size,' said Stan. 'He's out getting some breakfast at the minute. Very comfortable bed. Funny smell off the pillow though. Almost like perfume. Must be whatever conditioner they use.'

'Either that, or you were drinking Grand Marnier again.' Lou laughed. 'I'm away. I love you, pet.'

'Love you too, Your Honour,' said Stan, grinning to himself.

He hung up and looked over to King Size's bed, where Eva, the twenty-year-old prostitute, was still flaked out. Naked, skinny as a child, and exhausted.

Christ, for a man with so much money, Barkley had damn all class.

'Mornin', Sonny,' said the voice on the phone.

'Good morning yourself, Taoiseach,' said Sonny Waterhouse, who'd been pacing the floor of his living room for the past ten minutes waiting for the call.

'So what are they up to?'

'Same old shite,' he sighed. 'The immigrants are stealing all our houses and infecting us all with TB – so we should pack them all into crates and send them home. After that, they're going to get a stalking horse to take you on at the Ard Fheis. And they want to wreck your chances of starting up in the North by picking the village idiots for candidates.'

'What about the tribunals so?'

'As in your plan to cut the legal fees to defendants by two-thirds?'

'That's right.'

'It went down like a fart on a first date,' said Sonny. 'The Committee say it's a tax on successful businessmen and want the lawyers' scale upped to three grand a day.'

'What about the judges? I can't see them backin' that.'

'Yeah, well they liked your cuts at first – there's no way they want barristers earning more money than them. So Joxer then proposed that the tribunal panel should get paid twenty per cent more than senior counsel.'

'The clever bashtard.' Rubber John laughed.

'He has his moments,' agreed Sonny. 'Thankfully, they're few and far between. But there's better news on the other matter, Taoiseach. I met up with this Derryman, in the Haughey Arms last night, guy by the name of Stevenson. He's actually Hugo Stevenson's nephew. Shrewd too. Says it's time to give Northerners seats in the Dáil. Even if they are Shinners. But he himself reckons that if people in the North get the chance, they'll vote for Fianna Fáilers and an all-Ireland government rather than Sinn Féin and an all-Ireland opposition.'

'What's he do, this guy?'

'He's Hugo's heir apparent,' replied Sonny. 'He's the news editor at the *Derry Standard* – owns a big whack of the paper as well.'

'Sounds exactly what we need,' said Rubber John. 'Nail him down.'

'What about Joxer then?' Sonny asked. 'How long do I have to stick this Committee of Eight? I'm running out of friends. This is doing me serious damage.'

'I'll not forget you,' promised the Taoiseach. 'But for the minute, he's the most dangerous fuckin' man in the country. You're all that's standin' between us and 1930s Alabama. Hang in there and keep doing our work. We should count ourselves lucky that Joxer forgot the first rule of politics.'

'And what's that?' said Sonny.

'Well,' said Rubber John, 'where two or more are gathered in my name, always remember — one of them's a spy.'

Tommy was still hosing off the backs of his legs in the shower when the phone rang.

'It's Hugo Stevenson,' shouted in Dora. 'Can you take it?'

'I'll be out now,' yelled Tommy, and quickly pulled a towel round him. He lumbered down the stairs and picked up the receiver on the hall table.

'Checkmate, Tommy,' said Hugo. 'I'm afraid our man Barry acquired a most unfortunate set of photographs of you debasing yourself in the Jack Kennedy last night. It appears you took three separate tumbles from your barstool. And then, how can I put this delicately, you tucked up the little chap a bit too early after you went to the lavatory ... I take it you'll fuck off now like a good fellow?'

'Sorry, Hugo,' said Tommy, utterly deflated. 'Yes, of course, I'll fuck off so. Nothing personal.'

Tommy sat for a minute staring into the handset after Hugo rang off. If Barry had the pictures of him inside the bar, it was odds on he'd followed him outside. With Michelle. And then the trip home.

No. No. No. No. No.

He clicked the receiver into place and the phone rang again instantly. He didn't have to ask.

'I was just trying to get you,' said Barry happily, 'but you were engaged.'

'How much?' asked Tommy.

'What, no foreplay?' Barry laughed.

'I'm not in the form, Barry,' replied Tommy. 'How much?'

'Well, it's hot stuff,' said the cameraman. 'Career-stopping even. Tell you what so, give me fifteen for the pictures of you trying to get your hand inside Michelle's shirt and her slapping you in the mouth. We'll talk about the good stuff later.'

'Fifteen hundred quid, for that,' spat Tommy. 'Jesus, that's extortion.'

'Fifteen thousand, actually,' countered Barry coolly. 'It's about a tenth what it would cost you if Missus Bowtie got the pictures.'

'You're a wicked, wicked man, Magee,' hissed Tommy.

'And we haven't even got to the rest yet,' interrupted Barry with a chuckle. 'I'll be hard pressed to put a figure on them. They're priceless. Just get me the fifteen grand for the moment, and I'll be in touch within the week.'

As Tommy reached over to hang up the receiver, his towel came loose and fell to the floor. As he stooped naked to pick it up, a fresh cramp paralysed his colon and, oh fuck, Dora's new mauve carpet ...

6

King Size Barkley was deleting the three images of himself and Eva Ready from his digital camera, while he waited for Stan to come up from the gift shop. Whatever about the rest of the gang, there was no way he was getting caught playing away from home. Not again.

About a year previously, he'd taken his personal secretary to a conference at the Glasgow Hilton. He'd only been married six months and it was his first attempted dalliance. God, she was a tidy wee thing. Bobbed blonde hair and a tight little ass you could have bounced a handball off. And, most important of all, up for anything.

About half an hour after they checked in, however, Patsy, King Size's wife, had rung through to reception and asked to be put through to his room.

'I'm sorry,' the receptionist told her, 'but I think Mr and Mrs Barkley have just popped into the bar for a drink …'

That had set him back a £122,000 Lamborghini Gallardo – the most he'd ever paid for no sex – and made him the laughing stock of the Brooke Park changing room for an entire year.

King Size had been a flat-racer in his former life – and quite a successful one when he wasn't suspended pending investigations. He'd come home after his Uncle Sparkly's career in high finance was abruptly ended by some bullet-hole brain surgery. King Size had never liked his uncle but was only too happy to inherit the farm and take up where Sparkly had left off.

He had got to know Tommy Bowtie during his days across the water, when the young lawyer used to ring him up for hush-hush tips about who would and who wouldn't be trying in the next day's races. These calls were mostly at the behest of other citizens, such as Harry the Hurler, whose own phone had more taps than the City Baths.

Nonetheless, King Size and Tommy developed quite a rapport, so when the jockey returned to Derry after a decade in England, Tommy became his lawyer and business advisor. But given the Barkley genes, it was only a matter of months before the pupil outstripped the master – and Tommy was relegated to the role of respectable front man.

This was particularly important given the new Dunavady Inquiry. Sure, King Size might take a financial hit – he'd invested two million of his and Harry the Hurler's capital in the agency. But if anyone were going to jail, it would be Tommy Bowtie. That's what they paid him for.

The phone in the hotel bedroom rang. It was him, of course.

'Are you alone?' asked Tommy, in a ridiculously furtive voice.

'More or less.' King Size laughed, glancing over at Eva still asleep on the next pillow.

'The inquiry's going to start in March,' said Tommy, 'and it looks like I have to surrender my licence till it's over.'

'Fuck.' King Size sighed. That was a complication. Tommy was company secretary to most of his businesses, and there was no way he would get another solicitor to step in now – not with the new anti-racketeering legislation.

'Who's chairing the inquiry?' he asked, immediately wondering if they could buy their way out.

'Dunavady council,' replied Tommy.

'So, we'll get Shay Gallagher on the panel, and he'll look after you.'

'He's barred,' said Tommy. 'I was his election agent – and you were his chief funder. I was thinking maybe about one of the Shinners …'

King Size frowned and stroked his chin. 'No way they'll put their necks out,' he replied. 'Not even for Harry. They're far too cute. But maybe if we'd someone else in the chair making the recommendations, they'd weigh in behind them.'

'So who'll we get then – the SDLP will never bail us out,'

argued Tommy. 'They think we screwed them royally over the land sale. And all the unionists out these parts are too straight and God-fearing.'

'Okay so,' said King Size, 'we're going to have to get someone new onto the council, who'll go on to chair the inquiry. I'll talk to Harry about it … Anything else?'

'I have to drop the case against the *Standard*,' said Tommy quietly. 'Barry Magee got a bunch of bad photos of me last night. Twisted little bastard.'

'I warned you.' King Size sighed again. 'All you had to do was watch yourself for a few weeks. But you wouldn't listen.'

'Fuck's sake, King Size. I have four screaming youngsters and a wife who hates the sight of me. And it was you who put me off the fucking Prozac. If I didn't get out of the house for a drink at night, I'd be in the clinic eating dinner with a rubber spoon.'

'Jesus, Tommy,' groaned King Size, 'we were counting on a tame press. But now old Hugo's going to nail us to the wall.'

'I know. But maybe if you'd listened to me in the first place, we could have gone to Hugo cap in hand, instead of threatening him.'

'It wouldn't have worked. Not with Stan there. For a start he's too honest, and secondly we've pissed him off too many times.'

'Funny thing is,' replied Tommy, 'before you came back, Stan and I used to be good pals. If only we could get him back onside.'

'I just might have an idea,' said King Size, suddenly looking down at his digital camera.

'Okay, then,' said Tommy, sensing a sudden stomach tremor, 'you work on it. I have to run. It's urgent. Bye.'

And he was gone.

King Size smirked broadly as he flicked through the previews on the Nikon. Sure enough, there it was. Stanley Stevenson, groom-to-be, sleeping like a baby. Wonder what Letemout Lou would say about the naked hooker draped around him …

'So what are we going to do with this fella, Lou?' asked Harry, pointing over at Jimmy Fidget.

Letemout Lou had long understood that the downside of having a free office over the Jack Kennedy Inn was that her former number one client could drop in any time for private consultations. She'd snuck in quietly to get on with some paperwork when the Hurley brothers arrived.

'You could kick his hole for a start,' said Lou, eyeing the youngest Hurley coldly. 'Jesus, Jimmy, you'd a tidy little number, making a tidy little profit, but you had to be the bigshot. On your first day, you thought you knew more than your brother – who'd been running the show for twenty years. And now the whole thing's gone belly up, and we've the entire cast of *NYPD Blue* parked outside this office seven days a week.'

Jimmy flashed her an innocent smile. 'I just wanted to prove myself, Lou,' he said coyly. 'I mean, those are some very big shoes I have to fill.'

'Sucking up's not going to work either,' sniffed Lou, trying to stop a grin. She'd always found Jimmy a right charmer, but she knew he needed watching. 'You forgot the golden rule.'

'Which is?' Jimmy smiled.

'Which is, a small fire will keep you warm, but a big one will burn the arse off you. You're totally tainted now, Jimmy – so whatever you do next has to be one hundred per cent legitimate.'

'Oh,' interrupted Harry, disappointed. 'I was hoping that Jimmy might take over on the supply end of things.'

'Are you off your head?' yelled Lou. 'You want him to smuggle in cigarettes from your timeshare in Lanzarote? They'd be on him quicker than a rat on a warm shite.'

'But if, but if …' began Harry.

'But if, but if, but if,' mocked Lou. 'If my aunt had balls she'd be my uncle … All it takes is for a public figure like Jimmy to be caught with a suitcase full of fags, and the papers would go to town on you, Harry, for months. Jesus, they'd be trying to bring down Stormont over it. No, Jimmy goes legit. No other option.'

This is why Harry loved Lou. She was the only one who ever faced him down, other than maybe Old Ma. She'd impressed him from day one, when she defended him on a trumped-up assault charge. He'd wanted to get up in court to challenge some crown lawyer, but Lou had grabbed him by the wrist, pointed her finger dead into his face and warned him: 'This is my ballpark now, son. You sit there and shut your fat mouth, and I'll get you out of here. Say another word, and I'll walk out and leave you.'

Simple truth was, she scared him to death – and everyone, even Harry the Hurler, needed people like that around.

'So who's going to look after the retail end of things now?' asked Lou.

'Dumpy Doherty will handle the fags, and Skidmark Gormley the DVDs and all the rest,' replied Harry slowly, hoping he'd got it right.

'Fair enough,' said Lou, nodding. 'They both know what they're doing and are far enough away from you to give you deniability. That just leaves us him …' She stared over at Jimmy, who was busy pulling little pieces off a polystyrene cup.

'What else can you do?' she asked him.

'Well, I got a couple of A Levels when I was in jail,' he retorted. 'So I suppose I can write a bit. I wouldn't be as brainy as our Gerard though.'

They all laughed. Gerry Hurley had become a renowned authority on every subject under the sun since he got his BA in War Trauma Studies.

'All right so,' said Lou, 'we'll see if we can get you a job doing some writing, Jimmy. I'll ring Hugo and see if he can maybe find some room for you at the *Standard*. Though he's probably a bit overstaffed now he's got Mary back.'

'Oh, is Mary back?' interrupted Harry. 'I'm thrilled for him. They should have got married twenty years ago.'

'You're right,' said Lou, 'but then, as Stan says, I wouldn't be marrying a media tycoon. No. Between Stan and Hugo, I'll fix it for Jim. I'm family now, so I'm pretty hard to turn down.'

'Thanks, Lou,' said Harry, relieved. 'Now what about this Dunavady business? We need to protect this investment. Jesus, the inquiry's looking for the deeds of the hotel.'

'I spoke to King Size earlier this morning,' answered Lou,

'and of course, the little weasel has already got a plan. You have to square the inquiry panel.'

'But the party will never go for that,' protested Harry.

'I know,' said Lou. 'Someone else is going to have to chair it. Shay Gallagher was your best hope, but he's disqualified because of Tommy Bowtie. So you'll have to find someone else and get them co-opted onto the council as an independent. It won't be easy, but you've done it before.'

'So how do we get someone to retire from the council?' asked Harry.

'No way, kid,' grinned Lou, pointing him towards the door. 'No way. No way. No way. That's your problem – not mine. Now fuck off and let me do some real work.'

Less than half an hour later, Harry poked his head in the door again, eyes lowered by way of apology.

'I thought I told you to fuck off and leave me in peace,' snapped Lou, without looking up from her file.

'Two minutes,' pleaded Harry. 'I've just had a thought.'

'Okay so,' she replied, looking up. 'I've set my watch. You've one minute fifty seconds left. Make your pitch.'

Harry took a breath. 'Why don't you chair it?'

'Chair what?'

'The inquiry. I could fix it for you to join the council. No one's going to question your integrity. You're a judge for Chrissake.'

'No can do, Harry. Nice try, though. No, I can't hold public office while I'm in the High Court.'

'Could you resign for the duration?'

'And give up one hundred grand a year for a four-thousand-pound council allowance? Are you insane? Who's going to pay my mortgage?'

'I will. And your salary.'

'Get out. Get out now.'

'But really. You've often talked about going into politics before … Jesus, Lou, with your brains and that smart mouth you could be president of Ireland if you put your mind to it.'

Lou smiled at the inverted compliment. But she wasn't for

bending. 'I'm interested in real politics, Harry,' she said. 'Like the Assembly, or Westminster, or the Dáil. Where I could make a difference. Legislate even. Not some hole-in-the-hedge parish, where my only job would be to bury your bodies.'

Harry grinned and threw his hands up, as he backed out of the room. 'Worth a shot,' he said. 'What if I got you an Assembly seat as well?'

'Seriously?' she replied, looking at him quizzically.

'Anything's possible,' said Harry. 'Though it'll probably not come to that. We'll sort something out.'

7

Their departure from the Gresham was unremarkable but for two things. First, King Size tried to rip off Eva Ready before they left the bedroom.

'No way,' she yelled, pretty green eyes cold with rage. 'You agreed seven-fifty sterling. Cash. Now pay up.'

'But I've only five hundred left,' he sneered. 'And sure, that's plenty for two days' work.'

'You cheap little man,' hissed Eva.

'Pay the lady,' interrupted Stan fiercely. 'Pay her now, or I promise you, Patsy will be getting a new Porsche.'

'All I wanted was one little favour,' pleaded King Size. 'A little, how shall we say, unfettered access? But Eva won't play unless I'm Michelin Man.'

'Tell you what, so,' said Eva, suddenly tired. 'Put the other two-fifty on that dresser there, and you'll get your access as a special treat. How's that?'

'That's a deal,' declared King Size. 'Wait for me in the lobby, Stan, I'll not be long.'

'There's an understatement,' quipped Eva, and Stan laughed.

'Tell you what, King Size,' said Stan, thinking ahead, 'give me the money first. I'll hold it for Eva.'

'Thanks, Stanley,' replied Eva. 'You're a gentleman – no matter what company you keep. And you're the only guy I ever met who turned down a freebie on his stag night.'

'They can put it on my tombstone,' grinned Stan, disappearing out the door.

The second incident of note came about half an hour later. The group settled their accounts after some minor squabbles over minibar and TV porn bills and then headed down O'Connell Street, towards Burgh Quay, where their coach was to pick them up. Eva, her long green Burberry coat draped over her shoulders like a cloak, walked with them as far as Talbot Street where she flagged a taxi.

'I'm sorry, Stanley,' she said to him as he opened the door for her. 'I'm really sorry. He made me do it.'

'Don't worry about it,' said Stan, wondering why the hell she was apologising to him for making an honest living. She'd no need to – Christ, it's not as if she were a lawyer.

Eva threw her coat into the back seat of the car and stood shivering for a moment in her T-shirt and miniskirt beside Stan. 'Thanks,' she whispered, putting her hand to his cheek. He bent down to hug her and then he saw them.

Needle marks on her thighs.

Oh shit. Oh shit. Oh shit. Bigshot Barkley was in trouble. This could be serious. Very serious indeed.

Worse again, he was going to have to tell him. If only for Patsy's sake.

Back in Derry, Mary Slavin couldn't wait to get back to her old desk, so she got her old key back from Hugo and let herself into the *Standard* building on William Street.

Sunday afternoons were the perfect time to get organised. No one about, no distractions. No fights over who's going to tonight's match, who's going to court and who has to go to the Technical Fucking Services meeting. No cranks ringing in to complain that their photo wasn't in – or indeed that it was in, but the photographer had got the name wrong in the caption. Profuse apologies, Mister MacHarsehole. And yes, we'll be sure and get both aitches in next time.

God she'd missed it. Not as much as she'd missed Hugo though. The stupid big gulpin. He'd appointed her himself, just a month or so after he'd succeeded his late father as chairman thirty-five years ago. She'd come in as an eager young junior straight out of school, and only eighteen months later was in charge of the newsdesk. She was that sharp. By the time she was twenty-six, she was editor.

There'd been a spark between her and Hugo from day one.

The whole town knew it. But because he was fifteen years older and was her employer, neither of them felt it was right. So instead, they spent thirty years wasting their time with strangers and no-hopers. Pair of fucking idiots.

Then, Christmas two years ago, Hugo decided to make a move. They'd both got to the point where they didn't care what other people thought. They spent all their days chatting in Mary's office and all their evenings drinking gin in Charlie's Bar. They ate together, went to parties together, ran a business together – did everything but live together. And both of them knew it was time.

But, typically, they'd fucked it up. Hugo had bought her a magnificent ruby ring from Hastings' Jewellers. She, of course, had heard about it before it left the shop – and the fact that he was planning to spring it on her at the Christmas party. It should have been magical – a night to savour. But instead, the two of them had got so nervous that they started fighting and she, the fucking pigheaded bint, had stormed out in a huff. And he, the fucking pigheaded bollix, had let her go.

Now she was home – and determined not to blow it again.

She was standing at the shelf behind her desk, arranging a few books, when there was a knock on the door. And who was standing there, in a cheap pair of jeans and a cheaper polyester shirt, only Barry Magee. He looked for all the world like a badly dressed serial killer.

'You're very welcome back,' he smiled, holding out his hand.

'And you're fucking lying, as always,' replied Mary, ignoring it. There was only one side to her – head on.

'Have you those images of Tommy Bowtie in the system?' she asked perfunctorily.

'Yes, boss.'

'And have you made prints for Mr Stevenson?' she pressed.

'They're on the desk in that envelope in front of you.'

'Are they the only pictures you took of Tommy?'

'What do you mean?'

'Are they the only pictures you took?' she growled through gritted teeth.

'Yes.'

'Are you sure?'

'Yes, I'm absolutely certain.'

'That's odd,' said Mary, 'because Letemout Lou was talking to Tommy this morning. And she says you're demanding fifteen grand, or you'll shop him to his wife for trying to wrestle with a waitress.'

'No way, not true,' protested Barry quickly.

'So I rang Tommy myself,' continued Mary, 'and after some arm-twisting, he admitted that yes, he'd been very drunk and very foolish and that yes, you were putting the bite on him.'

'He's clearly lost his mind with drink, he doesn't know what he's saying,' said Barry, who'd graduated with honours from the School of Deny, Deny, Deny. 'I can prove it too – I can show you photos of him from later on that night, and you wouldn't believe what he's doing in them. He should be in an institution.'

'Let me see them, now,' snapped Mary, a little curious.

So Barry went out to the newsroom and came in with six separate prints, which he handed to his new editor in silence. He was right. They were unbelievable. Unless Barry Magee had somehow doctored the photos, on his way home on Friday night, Tommy Bowtie, solicitor at law, had stopped at a full half-dozen of his neighbours' gardens and defecated into their hedges.

'I thought you hadn't taken any more pictures then,' grinned Mary.

'Well, you know yourself,' said Barry, smiling back. 'You follow the story.'

'Pity,' sighed Mary. 'You were a damn good cameraman.'

'What do you mean?' asked Barry, suddenly wrong-footed.

'I mean I'm sacking you, Barry,' replied Mary. 'As of this very moment. Summary dismissal for gross misconduct. You abused your position with us to commit serious criminal acts. Under the terms of your contract, you'll be paid up until the end of today and receive no further remuneration. I've already cleared it with Hugo. And if you try to appeal, we will be forced to disclose everything to the police.'

'You bastard,' yelled Barry, firing up. 'I'll do the lot of you.'

'No you won't,' said Mary calmly. 'If you ever cross anyone

connected with this paper again, I will tell Harry the Hurler how you sold off the photos of him handling weapons in the early days. He'll not be a bit pleased to hear how he did two months on remand because his bosom buddy thought he could make five hundred quid off the national press.

'And by the way, just in case you think of running crying and lying to Harry, I should warn you that his brother Jimmy Fidget is starting in here tomorrow. A vacancy just came up for a trainee photojournalist.

'Now fuck off out that door, and never come back.'

Back in Dublin, Eva got the taxi to take her to the Jervis Shopping Centre and wait for her while she ran inside to collect her drugs.

She hated herself for posing with Stan and hoped that he wouldn't hold it against her when King Size showed him the photo. Not that she'd ever see any of them again, mind. But still. Stan was a rare item – a genuine good guy.

'There's your insulin, Miss,' said the chemist.

Eva had been a diabetic since she was twelve – it was in the genes. She was normally very smart about it, took her injections on time, and stayed clear of all other drugs, apart from maybe a cigarette or two. But her blood sugar was badly screwed up because she'd been partying with the Derry boys, missed her jags, and now she urgently needed to get stabilised. In fact, she'd nearly fallen asleep in the cab on the way over, she felt so weak. The guys, God love them, thought they'd worn her out.

King Size Barkley? Now, there was fucking irony.

8

S tan waited until they got back to Foyle Street bus station in Derry before telling him. As the others headed off towards the Gainsborough Bar for one last pint, he pulled King Size aside and suggested that they hang back a couple of minutes for a private chat.

King Size immediately assumed that Eva Ready had told Stan about posing for the photo – and that the journalist was about to appeal to his sense of decency. Poor fucker.

'It's about Eva,' said Stan sombrely.

King Size gave a big Cheshire cat grin. 'She told you so?' he asked.

'She told me nothing,' replied Stan. 'I saw for myself.'

'What the fuck are you talking about?' pressed King Size, certain he had never left his camera out of his sight for one second.

'The track marks.'

'What track marks?' said King Size.

'The needle marks on her thighs, King Size,' retorted Stan, 'the ones you quite obviously didn't see. I noticed them when I bent down to hug her at the taxi. The poor girl was a junkie.'

'No way,' protested King Size hoarsely. 'You're winding me up.'

'You know me,' said Stan, 'I wouldn't do that. I couldn't do it. I don't have it in me to lie about something like that. That's more your angle. I saw what I saw and the reason I'm telling you is, well, because of Patsy.'

'Oh Christ Almighty, Patsy,' pleaded King Size. 'You're wrong. You must be wrong ...'

'Think back,' said Stan. 'She spent half the time asleep. She threw up in the sink this morning – despite the fact she didn't touch a drink all weekend. And she was white as a ghost when she left the hotel today. Plus, King Size. I saw the needle marks. They were on her thighs, clear as day. And as she was leaving, she repeated two or three times how she tried to stop you. But you, you dopey little bollix, had to get your money's worth and wouldn't listen to her.'

'Don't you presume to lecture me,' snapped King Size, getting redder. 'Who do you think you are – Snow Fucking White? If you open your mouth about this to anyone …'

'Don't worry,' retorted Stan. 'I know how to keep it zipped – unlike some round here.'

'Watch what you're saying, Stanley,' warned King Size. 'You wouldn't want to fall out with me.'

'I've been a messenger all my life,' quipped Stan, trying to take some of the heat out of things. 'I'm used to getting shot.'

'I'm telling you one last time, Stan,' said King Size, menacingly. 'Nobody likes a smart git.'

'So what did you bring me back?' Lou shouted out from the kitchen, as she heard Stan bang the door of their flat above the marina.

'I brought you myself, *virgo intacta*, isn't that enough?' laughed Stan, as she ran down the hall to hug him.

'We'll have to see what we can do about that then,' Lou giggled. 'How was your weekend?'

'All right,' said Stan unconvincingly. 'I had a big fight with King Size when we landed at the station …'

'What happened?' inquired Lou, worried.

'I'm not allowed to tell you,' said Stan, shaking his head ruefully. 'It's one of these pact things. You'll hear about it soon enough, I'm sure. Suffice it to say, just when you thought a man couldn't sink any deeper in your esteem, King Size goes and lowers the bar.'

'Okay, I'll leave it so,' said Lou judiciously. She'd been around Stan long enough to know when to pick her moment. 'So, really, what did you bring me back?'

'Well,' said Stan, producing a gift box, which was about six inches cubed, 'I went shopping on Grafton Street early this afternoon and found this beautiful little jewellery shop …'

'Oh, I love you, I love you,' grinned Lou, snatching the present and tearing at the paper excitedly. She opened the package quickly, tossed out a ream of tissue, and then suddenly let out a loud shriek of laughter.

There, in a leather box, sitting on top of a velvet jeweller's cushion, was a pair of furry handcuffs.

King Size Barkley spent the night on the old Chesterfield couch in his private study – tossing and turning between fear and anger. Yes, it was the stupidest thing he'd ever done in his life. But somebody should have warned him. Stan should have warned him. Jesus, how could he tell Patsy? They'd been married for less than two years, and she was not only the most beautiful girl in the town, but she was also, by a mile, the biggest-hearted. Christ, she put up with him, for fuck's sake. He sometimes reckoned that she'd been an angel sent to save him. She'd even forgiven him when she caught him trying to play that away fixture in Glasgow. The car, contrary to popular belief, had been an apology and not a pay-off.

He just couldn't help himself. He simply craved women. All women. He needed their attention. Their validation. Their approval. Just like his Uncle Sparkly had before him. Maybe Tommy Bowtie was right – maybe it was a shortarse thing.

Patsy had come down in her babydoll at about midnight looking to entice him up to bed – but he couldn't take the chance. He told her his stomach was wrecked with too much bad drink – and spent the next hour going out every five minutes to flush the toilet, until he was sure she was asleep.

No. Stanley should have warned him. He knew beforehand. That's why he'd had nothing to do with Eva. Sly bastard. Well, if King Size Barkley were going down, Stan Stevenson would be down a long time before him. He'd make sure of it.

In the early hours, the beginnings of a plan began to formulate in King Size's mind. It wouldn't help as regards the Eva situation – but at least this way, he'd get to screw somebody.

First thing in the morning, he rang Barry Magee to come over to make prints of the photos of Stan and Eva Ready.

'You heard I resigned from the *Standard*?' said Barry, as King Size ushered him into the study.

'No you didn't,' sniffed King Size. 'You got fired. Letemout Lou rang Stan on the bus to gloat.'

'Bastards,' said Barry, looking down at the two images, which King Size had already uploaded to his computer. 'Still, they'll be a lot less high and mighty when these hit the streets. Stan, the hypocrite, is always harping on about how he's a one-woman man.' Barry switched on the printer, which he was certain had never been used. It was a state-of-the-art model – an improved version of the one he'd been using at the *Derry Standard*. King Size, naturally, couldn't work it.

'So, how did you get on with Stan as your boss?' inquired King Size.

'Actually, he was quite sound, you know,' replied Barry, with just a tinge of regret. 'Very fair. Good about time off – and if you did your work, he didn't bother you.'

'Would you work for him again?'

'I suppose I would,' said Barry, 'but Jesus, I can't see the *Standard* ever having me back – not after what I said to Mary yesterday.'

'I'm not talking about the *Standard*,' continued King Size. 'What about if we set up a new paper. I've been thinking about it for years. I've got the money, and if I'd the right personnel, there's no reason it couldn't work. I mean, Derry already has about twenty-five papers – some of them must be making money.'

'Ah,' grinned Barry. 'And you reckon it might help you with this Dunavady problem too. Because, of course, Hugo and the *Standard* are ready to go for your jugular.'

King Size smirked and gave his visitor a mock bow. 'You're very perceptive. That's what I like about you, Barry. That and the fact that you refuse to waste any money on clothes …'

Barry laughed.

'And just like yourself,' King Size continued, 'I wouldn't mind taking the Stevenson connection down a peg or two. So, can I count you in?'

'Are you serious?' laughed Barry. 'Of course, I'm in. Who the fuck else would ever hire me? I thought I was going to end my days back on the dole in Wrexham … But what are you going to do about an editor?'

'Well,' said King Size smoothly, 'I think Stanley might be open to offers.'

'How's that?' said Barry, a little puzzled. 'Sure, he already owns the *Standard* – or he will do as soon as the drink catches up with Hugo.'

'I think you may just have the answer in your hand,' grinned King Size, pointing at the ten-by-eight glossy Barry was pulling from the printer. 'There's no way the big sap's going to let me show these to his bride-to-be. Now is there? No, I think Stan could just be our man. Here's to the city's newest paper – the *North-West Standard*.'

The two men clinked imaginary glasses and bent over the desk to get a better look at Stan's picture. Barry had made a beautiful job of the print – so beautiful in fact that if you studied it closely, you could just about make out two puncture wounds on Eva's right thigh and another pair on her left.

King Size saw the marks, rushed out to the downstairs toilet and vomited.

'Must be all that invisible champagne,' muttered Barry.

9

All told, Monday was the worst possible day Mary Slavin could have picked to lay down the law with Stan. He was knackered after his weekend in Dublin. And while he bore absolutely no resentment to his new editor, there were always going to be a few run-ins until the proper pecking order was re-established.

Mary needed to prove to the other reporters that there would be no favouritism. So, just as they were about to shut the office for the day, she asked Stan if he would head out to that night's council meeting in Dunavady. Stan, however, had far too many stripes on his sleeve for that sort of nonsense, so he suggested, less than politely, that Mary go and perform her toilet in a large bag.

'Don't make me order you, Stanley,' Mary yelled, silencing an office full of chattering hacks and production staff.

'Look Mary,' countered Stan, 'we all know you're a hardass. And we all know you're my boss now. You've nothing to prove. But I've spent two years editing this paper and I'm still in charge of the newsdesk. I don't do courts, councils and football matches – we've a full panel of people for that.'

'You'll do exactly what I tell you,' said Mary. 'And you will go to Dunavady tonight or you can fuck right off out the door.'

'Maybe I'll just do that,' said Stan quietly, picking up his mobile from the desk. 'See you around, Mary.'

He was bluffing, of course. And so was she. He'd be back the following morning, and the incident would never be mentioned again. No one would lose face, and everyone would have made their point.

Unfortunately, however, King Size got wind of the fight within minutes and decided to strike while the anger was hot. Only that lunchtime, Spike O'Kelly, the *Standard*'s senior graphic designer, had privately agreed to jump ship to the new paper – for a thirty per cent raise. And he was on the blower to his next paymaster as soon as Stan walked out the door.

Lou was away for the week hearing a case in Belfast, so Stan was left pretty much to his devices. On a good day, this would entail a big meal at the City Hotel and lashings of drink. On a bad day, just lashings of drink. And today was turning into an exceptionally bad day. He'd barely got his coat over the stool in the lobby bar when the mobile rang.

'Hi, Stan,' said King Size. 'I just wanted to say sorry for our little misunderstanding last night.'

'No problem,' replied Stan, curiously pleased that someone thought enough of him to apologise.

'Any chance you could come over to my house this evening?' asked King Size, sounding concerned. 'I could do with a bit of advice. About the weekend. Patsy will be out. You know where we are?'

'Yeah,' laughed Stan. 'You're the only house on the Culmore Road with a life-size model of the Trevi fountain in your front garden. No problem, King Size, I'll be there in an hour. Misery loves company and all that.'

King Size figured if he played it properly, he might never even have to use the picture. But he wasn't counting on Stan's loyalty.

'No chance,' Stan said, when the plan was put to him. 'I really appreciate you making me this offer. But it would kill Hugo – and then Lou would kill me.'

'You're sure I can't tempt you?' asked King Size. 'I'll give you a twenty per cent salary bump – and a forty per cent share of the company. That's ten more than you get from Hugo. Full editorial control ...'

'I can't do it,' replied Stan. 'I'm very flattered, but I can't turn my back on my family.'

'But maybe if you don't do it, your family will turn their back on you,' countered King Size with his trademark smirk.

'I don't follow,' said Stan, confused.

King Size produced an A4 envelope from his bureau and handed it across. Stan pulled the picture about halfway out then froze.

'You can't be serious?' he gasped.

'Deadly,' said King Size, his voice ice-cold.

Stan glared at him, his eyes narrowing with rage. 'I'll see you in hell for this.'

'No you won't,' smirked King Size. 'There are too many copies of it in safe places, along with sworn statements from me and Danny Boy Gillespie – both eye-witnesses.'

'But Danny Boy's one of my best friends,' protested Stan, froth flying from his lips. He stopped, then added, 'What have you got on him?'

'Much the same,' smiled King Size. 'Except the prints that I have for his lovely wife, Jilly, weren't quite, how would I put it, quite as staged. And they leave a lot less to the imagination … Look Stan, you're not happy where you are at the *Standard*. And you've nothing left to challenge you there. This way, you get more money, a new challenge and, most important of all, you get to hang on to your fiancée – oh, and your dignity.'

'Are you sure you want a man who hates you running a business for you?' interrupted Stan. 'I promise you now, I'm going to knife you as soon as I get a chance.'

'Keep your friends close, Stan …' said King Size, grinning at his victory.

'One question,' demanded Stan. 'How long before I get the prints back?'

'Two years, maximum,' said King Size. 'As soon as the Dunavady Inquiry is over.'

'Shit,' swore Stan. 'I should have worked it out. You're going to write yourself up whiter than white.'

'No,' laughed King Size. 'You're going to.'

If Stan had gone ballistic when he saw the photo, it was nothing compared to how Lou reacted later that night, when he told her he was leaving the *Standard*.

'I forbid it,' she screamed down the phone. 'I absolutely forbid it. Here we are finally settled, finally happy, less than six weeks from the wedding – and you decide to fuck it all up. All over one stupid fight with Mary Slavin? Have you lost your mind?'

'It doesn't change anything,' said Stan quietly. 'We're still getting married.'

'Do you really think I could marry a guy who's going to be a paid liar for King Size Barkley?' she yelled. 'Do you have any idea what you're doing? He's the most malevolent, poisonous little fucker in all of Derry. If you want to give up your family and friends, and leave maybe the cushiest job in Derry to hook up with that evil bastard – all because Mary Slavin clips your wings a little, you do it. But I'm not going to be there with you.'

With that the line went dead. Stan decided to give her a few minutes to cool down before calling back. But it wasn't enough. She was too wound up.

'You're copping out, you gutless bastard,' she roared. 'Don't try and tell me that you're leaving because Mary's going to usurp you as Hugo's next-in-line. That's a flat lie. You know it – and I know it. Who do you think draws up all Hugo's contracts? …You're just another dirty money-grabber, who couldn't resist the lure of King Size's wallet. Okay, if you want to waste the rest of your life as a bagman for that little hood, do it on your own. But I'll not be about. I'll send a van round for my stuff at the weekend. Don't try to keep any of my things – and don't ever try to contact me again.'

Stan was shaking as he put down the phone. In one evening, he'd managed to cut himself off from his family, his friends and his wife-to-be.

He was heartsick. Devastated. Empty. But most crucial of all, he was absolutely determined to make King Size Barkley rue the day he ever fucking met him.

'I can't interfere, Lou,' Harry told her, when she rang him at the Jack Kennedy an hour later. 'And it's certainly not in my interests to. Hugo had already made it clear he'd do us no favours over the inquiry. And after Tommy's intervention, the *Standard* are going to nail us to a cross. So, bottom line, we need the new paper. There's far too much at stake.'

Lou wasn't buying. 'You're going to sit and watch King Size drive a wedge between Stanley and his family? Just to protect dirty money you're probably going to lose anyway? You can't wash this one all away.'

'It's not just about money,' sighed Harry. 'If you hadn't noticed, Lou, I now live and die in the field of public opinion … And besides, no one's holding a gun to Stan's head.'

'That's not true, Harry,' snapped Lou. 'I'm pretty certain King Size is. And I think you, you rotten bastard, know all about it.'

'You're being hysterical, Lou. You're seeing things that aren't there.'

'Funny, Harry. That's exactly what you told Lorna when you were running round behind her back with Susie Short Shorts. But let me tell you this – if you call me hysterical one more time, I'll come round to your office and cut your heart out with a rusty nail. In cold fucking blood. Do you understand?'

Harry took a deep breath. He'd overstepped the line. Time to reel back in a bit. 'I'm sorry, Lou. Really. But let's be honest here. Stan is wasted as Mary's number two. He needs a challenge. Otherwise, he's going to grow fat as Hugo and drink himself to death. He's far too good to sit where he is – I know that, you know that. So maybe this might be an opportunity for him. And second, Lou – and much more important – no one is forcing you to walk out on Stan. You took that decision yourself. But one of the problems with marriage, as you will someday find out, is that you have to back your other half up even when they've totally gone off the rails.'

'I suppose you're right, Harry,' said Lou, a bit calmer. 'And I'm sorry too. It wasn't you who let me down, it was him. I don't care what pressure he was under, he shut me out. It doesn't matter about anything else. He shut me out, Harry – and that's unforgivable.'

Back at the apartment, Tommy Bowtie had called in to do a little repair work of his own with Stan. Tommy, above all people, knew what it was like to be owned by King Size –

and, despite his legal training, he was a nice guy who wanted to reach out to his old adversary.

'Maybe she'll come back,' said Tommy, watching Stan mope into a huge gin.

'No chance,' declared Stan abruptly. 'I shut her out. It doesn't matter about anything else. I shut her out, Tommy – and that's unforgivable.'

10

Despite his genial manner, Hugo hadn't survived a lifetime in business by being sentimental. He could do nothing about the thirty per cent share in the company that he'd already signed over to his nephew – but if Stan was going to canoodle about with the opposition, he was damned if he was getting the other seventy per cent from the will.

Mary Slavin was doing her best to take some of the steam out of Hugo by refusing point blank to become his beneficiary. Indeed, she was insisting that if he changed his will, she'd hand every cent back to Stan before Hugo's organs had been surreptitiously removed from his warm body.

'He'll be back, Hugo,' she told him, as he paced up and down on her office floor. Privately, though, Mary was worried. It was a week to the day since Stan had walked out of the *Standard*. And all attempts at conciliation had failed. Hugo wasn't sleeping and had started drinking before lunch again. Her only consolation was that Letemout was just as bad.

'What did he say when you called at the flat last night?' asked Hugo.

'He lied his arse off. He said that it was nothing to do with our fight, which is only partly true. And that he really needed a new challenge. Which is bullshit. If Stan needed a challenge, he could try finding a matching pair of socks – now that Letemout's not dressing him in the morning … He also said the money King Size was paying him was better – and he'd negotiated a fifty per cent share of the paper, which again is a big fat lie. He's only got forty, because Tommy Bowtie drew up the contract and told me himself.'

Hugo sat down in the chair opposite Mary and started drumming his fingers on the desk. 'So what's really happening?' he asked distractedly. 'Has King Size got the goods on him?'

'Almost certainly,' answered Mary. 'I think Stan cut a bit too loose on the stag weekend, and King Size threatened to tell teacher.'

'Little bastard,' said Hugo. 'Is there no chance Harry the Hurler could straighten him out? He did before, the last time King Size tried to sue me. I seem to remember Harry very successfully argued that it wasn't in the wider public interest.'

On that occasion Harry, it was alleged, had given greater weight to his argument by suspending King Size out his office window, seventy-five feet above Butcher Street pavement.

'Harry can't repeat the favour, I'm afraid,' replied Mary. 'He's too much money invested with King Size in Dunavady for him to go playing ankles again …'

Hugo gave a humourless laugh. 'So how was Stan looking?' he continued, trying not to appear too concerned.

'Shattered,' replied Mary. 'His face was longer than a Latin Mass. He's worse than you were when I walked out two years ago.'

Hugo smiled – grateful for Mary's attempts to lift him.

'The floor of the flat was a mess of pizza boxes and beer cans,' she continued. 'And the place smelt worse than Tommy Bowtie's office toilet … Oh, and Lou took all the furniture except the two metal chairs from the balcony and a portable TV.'

'All right, all right,' grinned Hugo, 'you're breaking my heart here. I'll hold fire on cutting him off for the minute. But why are you so confident he'll be back so?'

'Because he promised me he would be,' replied Mary. 'Just as soon as he sorts out that quote unquote "twisted little fucker King Size Barkley". But there's very little chance we'll see Stan back before the Dunavady Inquiry is over. And that could last anything between three months and two years.'

Hugo nodded. The most damaging thing about the inquiry – as with any court case – would be the write-up in the paper afterwards.

'Don't worry,' said Mary, reading his thought. 'We'll have a reporter at the inquiry every day. And the first chance we get, we will slice Mr Barkley's bollocks off and feed them to our readers on the front page.'

'What about Letemout?' Hugo asked. 'Any chance she'll let Stan off the hook?'

'Absolutely none,' said Mary, shaking her head. 'There's a better chance of Harry the Hurler getting laid on the Shankill Road. I went down to the Jack Kennedy myself on Saturday and told her to get off her judicial high horse and wind her honourable neck down. But Stan's kept her waiting for almost twenty years now – and even the most patient of women have their limits. If you follow what I'm saying – Hugo.'

'Only too clearly, pet,' laughed Hugo. 'Only too clearly.'

Harry had given Letemout Lou the Presidential Suite above her office at the Jack Kennedy Inn for as long as she needed it. But while she was very grateful, it meant that as long as she was in Derry, she was now on twenty-four-hour call.

Harry had two problems in particular that were irking him – and hence Lou. He had to find a way to reclaim the pile of old money he'd laundered into the Dunavady Investment Agency. And, second, he needed to straighten out his brother Jimmy before he wound up back in jail again – this time for something socially unacceptable.

Tonight it was business first.

'Effectively you control Dunavady council,' Lou told him, as she folded her blouses into a drawer. 'You've already got six seats out of the thirteen – and Shay Gallagher, the independent, will fall in behind you. Why not just appoint your own man to chair the inquiry?'

'I'd love to,' Harry sighed, 'but the boys in Belfast are afraid we could be tainted by allegations of corruption. Ever since the Yanks threatened to ban us, they're all born-again virgins.'

'Okay so,' she replied. 'It's back to getting one of your boys to step down and replacing him with an independent. Why not ask Chris Caddle to retire – I'm sure he's a bit old-school for some of the new young doves that have swooped in recently?'

'No way,' said Harry. 'He's our main attraction out there since Barney Joyce went to the Assembly. And besides, I need a few hard men. We've more than our quota of doves – I've never met so many people who'll lay down their life for Ireland, now there's a truce.'

'What about Sammy Muir then?' pressed Lou. 'Sure, no one can stick him. And if I remember, you were going to kneecap him for stealing from the POW fund in the mid-nineties.'

'I have to say, I wouldn't miss Sammy the Squint, myself,' answered Harry slowly. 'Why did we forgive him, again?'

'Because he knew where your bodies were buried,' smirked Lou. 'Literally.'

'Aha,' grinned Harry. 'But maybe if we could persuade him that it was for the common good, he might listen to reason.'

'I don't want to hear any more,' smiled Lou.

'Don't worry,' said Harry. 'I'll be as quiet as the grave.'

Harry the Hurler put his hand on the door to leave, and then turned awkwardly back to face Lou. 'Can I ask you one more favour?' he said.

'If it means me getting a room to myself for half an hour, I suppose you can.'

'You need to get back out into the world,' said Harry. 'Why don't you let Jimmy take you to dinner?'

'Jimmy Fidget?' exclaimed Lou. 'You want to fix me up with your brother?'

'I know, I know,' said Harry. 'But he's crazy about you – ever since you handled his appeal. And he's a good-looking guy. And you might talk a little sense into him.'

'Jesus, Harry,' said Lou, 'Stan'll go clean demented.'

'Precisely,' smiled Harry. 'Precisely …'

Patsy Barkley, sporting one of the legendary minidresses that Father Shaw had quietly asked her not to wear to eleven o'clock Mass, showed Stan into the living room. Without asking, she poured him a large Hennessy.

'You look like hell,' she said. 'It must have been something you boys picked up when you went away on your weekend. King Size is still wrecked with cramps. The doctor says it's probably a vicious stomach flu – and could take three months to work its way through his system.'

Stan took the drink, trying valiantly not to stare at the legs that had carried Patsy to the Miss Foyle Banker title three times. Instead he concentrated on the fresh young face that was smiling out from under a mop of long, curly, auburn hair. Patsy was so far out of King Size's league, it was a crime against taste.

'This flu,' asked Stan, innocently, 'is it contagious?'

'Possibly,' sniffed Patsy, rolling her big brown eyes. 'Suffice to say, we're not allowed to take any chances ...'

'You should offer it up for the Holy Souls,' laughed Stan.

'I'd offer it up for much less than that,' grinned Patsy, giving him a dirty wink.

'You're only saying that because you know I never would,' retorted Stan.

'You're right,' smiled Patsy, 'and nor would I. I know you've no time for my Bart – and I can't understand what you're doing with him. But, he has a good streak in him too – and maybe I'm the only one who gets to see it, but it's worth hanging on for.'

Stan stared into his glass and said nothing. She needed him to believe her. It was all she had.

'What about this new paper so?' she said breezily. 'When's it starting?'

'Saturday week,' replied Stan. 'The personnel and money are all in place. And the printers are ready to go. Fianna Fáil in Dublin are giving us some political support – albeit a bit guarded. But we've an interview with the Taoiseach lined up for the first edition. All we need now is for the Mayor to be caught in bed with a naked hooker about an hour before deadline, and we'll be laughing. And Barry Magee is working on that as we speak.'

'I'll bet,' laughed Patsy. 'And sure if that fails, Barry can always raid his own private collection.'

Stan heard a phone being clicked into place upstairs and rapid footsteps coming down the stairs. Seconds later, King Size burst in the door grinning from ear to ear.

'Councillor Stevenson, you're very welcome,' said King Size, shaking his editor's hand.

'I'm sorry,' replied Stan, puzzled.

'Haven't you heard?' laughed King Size. 'Poor Sammy Muir was killed in a car crash out in Drumbridge this morning. You remember him – he was a Shinner councillor in Dunavady for years. They used to call him Sammy the Squint. Brakes failed on the mountain brae, I think.

'Anyway, the Shinners met with the unionists about an hour ago, and the DUP are refusing to allow them to co-opt a replacement. And no one wants a by-election. So all parties have agreed to draft in a new independent councillor – as long as it's …'

'You're joking,' said Stan, astounded that Barkley would try a stroke like this.

'Yep,' grinned King Size. 'Congratulations. I'm sure you'll be very good at it. You've been pulling strings in politics for years. And don't worry about the local nutters out there. Shay Gallagher will keep you right … Oh, and one more thing.'

'What's that?' sighed Stan.

'Next week you're going to be proposed as chairman of the Dunavady Inquiry,' said King Size very pointedly. 'Do not even fucking dream of turning it down.'

11

After twenty years in charge of The Boys Inc., Harry the Hurler had acquired a reputation for ruthlessness that was second to none. This was a man who would snuff out your lights and come back for the candles. And yet, those who knew him well – and they were few enough – were aware that he hadn't remained Derry's largest (unregistered) employer by dint of terror alone. He was also astute, compassionate, and, like all good managers, knew how to get the best out of his players. Some you praise, some you browbeat. Some you cajole – some you threaten. Some you just keep busy and out of harm's way. And of course, there are those you'll always have to beat around the back room with the butt of a rifle.

Stan Stevenson had never lined out for Harry's team. While he accepted that it was important to win the game, he never had the stomach for their tactics. For all that, however, the journalist had a great rapport with the older man and would often use him as a sounding board. And just occasionally he would ask him for a favour. Like he was doing now.

He'd called Harry on his mobile and arranged to meet him at the Four Green Fields Bar on Waterloo Street – he didn't want to go down to the Jack Kennedy in case he bumped into Lou. By the time Stan arrived, Harry had already bagged a snug and was sitting with two pints of Coldflow in front of him.

'I'm being blackmailed,' Stan said simply, as he sat down.

'I know,' replied Harry. 'King Size has a picture of you and a girl ...'

'I didn't touch her,' interrupted Stan. 'They staged it when I was asleep.'

'So you say,' said Harry coldly, raising his hand to stop Stan.

'But that's your affair and not mine. I'm not getting involved. Sort it out yourself.'

Stan shook his head half in anger, half in disbelief. 'I went on my stag night, refused to sleep with a prostitute, and now I've no friends left. Is that how it's going to be? Well, fuck you too Harry.'

Harry leaned across the table and grabbed Stan's wrist with brutal strength. 'Don't blame me for your fucking mess,' he spat. 'You should be more careful with the company you keep.'

Stan pulled himself free of the grip and stood up to leave.

'I'm not finished with you yet,' snapped Harry. 'Sit fucking down till I tell you to go.'

Stan caught one glimpse of the cold, soulless eyes and knew not to take another step. He was beaten and there was nowhere left to go. He slumped back on the wooden bench and dropped his head into his heads. 'I can't stick it any more, Harry,' he said. 'King Size is going to make me join Dunavady council and fix the inquiry for him. I'm not able for that. That's not what I do. That's not what the press do. We're the watchdog.'

Harry shook his head slowly and grinned back across the table. 'You really think you're above it all, don't you?' he said. 'You and your ilk sit in judgement on all the rest of us and never get your hands dirty. Never contribute a thing. Heaven forbid you'd take any responsibility for the state of the country.'

He stopped to take a long slug of Coldflow and let Stan sweat a little. He had him. It was time to introduce a little sugar.

'The bottom line, Stan,' he continued softly, 'is that you know politics better than anyone in this city. You've spent fifteen years writing the sharpest commentary I've ever read. You've provided leadership through your columns – real leadership – and provided inspiration for people like me to go out and make change. The only damn reason you're not in politics already is that you're a coward. You're afraid you'll be found out. Trust me. You won't. You hit the ball too damn straight – just like your uncle … Truth is, I need you out in Dunavady as well. I've money invested out there. Legitimately invested. And I want it protected. We'll sort this out first, and then we'll deal with that little bastard King Size.'

Stan nodded his head in agreement. It was the best deal he was going to leave the room with – and he was flattered that Harry thought so much of his columns.

'So I work for you now?' he asked, matter-of-factly.

'Bollocks,' snapped Harry, angry again. 'You're your own man, Stan – never forget that. I've enough damn yes-men who can do fuck all but rhyme off the party mantra. Christ knows, we need people in this world who can think for themselves. But I do hope that you'll work *with* me. All we expect of you here is a fair job – not a King Size fix. If you have to rough him up a bit, don't worry. I'll not let him publish that damn photo. But it won't come to that. Use your head, and take the breaks that come your way, and it'll all work out.'

'You're very confident,' said Stan.

'Yes,' replied Harry, 'in your ability. Stan, this could be your chance to challenge yourself. You can sit and grow fat like Hugo, and drink yourself into a clinic. Or you can start dreaming dreams – and maybe use the gifts God gave you.'

'Start chasing rainbows, you mean,' retorted Stan.

'It sure beats chasing hookers,' grinned Harry. And they both laughed. Stan drained the last couple of inches of his pint, grabbed his coat, and pushed open the door of the snug.

'Thanks,' he said quietly.

'Pleasure was all mine,' answered Harry. And Stan headed off through the bar towards the front door.

Yes, mused Harry, studying the remains of his stout. Some need a carrot and some the stick. And some you have to throw your whole fucking armoury at.

'Did he accept the appointment?' Rubber John asked Sonny Waterhouse the next day.

'He did indeed, Taoiseach,' said Sonny. 'Shay Gallagher, our man in Dunavady, rang me last night to say it had all been squared.'

'And what about this inquiry, will he chair it properly?'

'I'd say he intends to – but it's fuck-all odds. We'll just make sure he doesn't get hung out to dry and embarrass us.'

'Are ya sure he's our man?'

'Oh yes, he's young, good-looking, speaks well – but not so bright that you'd have to watch him. Harry says he's as good as they've got up there – that's not in his camp.'

'What about King Size Barkley – could he be any use to us? I mean, Chrisht, he's loaded.'

'Nope. He's far too bent. Even for the good old days. And besides, Stan's going to cut his throat as soon as he gets an in. In fact, the real reason he took the council job is so that when he finally shites on Barkley, he's going to do it from as great a height as possible.'

'Welcome to the party,' laughed the boss.

12

Shay Gallagher, the independent Assemblyman for North Derry, was guest speaker at the launch of the *North-West Standard*, while Monsignor Noel 'Know-All' Giddens was drafted in to provide the blessing. The priest's inclusion was an astute piece of politics on Stan's part, as it meant it would be at least a month before the good father could reasonably start bad-mouthing the new paper all over the county.

Father K, not surprisingly, refused to pose for a picture with a copy of the first edition. He'd never been entirely comfortable with breast-feeding, even as an infant. And he certainly didn't approve of the senior vice-president of Dunavady Chamber of Commerce availing of the service during a weekend's 'fact-finding mission' in Amsterdam. Videophone cameras, as Barry Magee often said, are God's answer to those who think they're above the law.

The rag, as you'd expect, flew off the shelves 'faster than bog roll from Tommy Bowtie's corner shop', as King Size put it. The editor for one, however, would rather have wiped himself with the newspaper.

'It's truly repulsive,' he confessed to Tommy that night, when they met up in Stan's flat to swap notes on King Size. 'It's cheap, smutty and thoroughly disreputable. In fact, the only thing in the entire parish with less class is its owner.'

'Yeah,' agreed Tommy, 'but of course it's going to make him another fortune.'

Stan heaved a sigh, nodded down at the paper, which was lying on his living-room floor, and pointed at the front-page picture. 'I tried to talk him out of it on the grounds that Robert Fitzpatrick has four children. They'll never be able to put their noses out the door again. It's bad enough their Da's already known as Bertie the Bottle. But King Size just laughed and ordered me to caption it *A Milkman's Holiday*!'

Tommy winced. 'There but for the grace of God …' he said. He got up from his metal garden chair, lifted the brandy bottle from the windowsill and half-filled his cup. 'I've warned him,' he said. 'I told him that if you unleash this sort of a beast, it'll not be long before it'll turn round and bite the arse off you. But he won't be told. I just hope I'm around to see it … But as long as he has the prints of both of us, there's not much we can do. You're stuck peddling *Soft Porn for Good Catholics*, and I have to bend down and wait for the Dunavady Inquiry, with my bare ass in the air.'

Stan got up from his chair, took the bottle from under Tommy's feet and poured a home-made double into his beaker. The new furniture and kitchenware would be arriving at the weekend, please God.

'It's the inquiry that I wanted to talk to you about,' said Stan slowly. 'Look, if we play it straight, there's a chance we can get through it. But before it starts – and King Size starts burning files by the cartload – I need you to gather up every piece of paper you have about the Dunavady Improvement Agency.'

Tommy looked at him as if he wasn't entirely wise, but Stan ignored him.

'I want anything that can link King Size to improper grant applications,' he continued. 'Uncle Hugo said there's two million pounds' worth. And I want all the gen on that land deal where he bought very low and sold really high as soon as the council zoned it … I also want a full and detailed statement from you on any insider knowledge King Size was given by yourself or local councillors.'

Tommy stared into his drink thoughtfully, then drained the cup. 'There might be something we can do on the documents,' he said at last. 'But no statement. I'd go to jail.'

'Not if you do what I tell you,' said Stan. 'For a start, I'll be chairing the inquiry and will be very sympathetic to witnesses who have been coerced and threatened. And second, the Shinners could lose a chunk of money here – and they know it wasn't going into your pocket. So, when they get their chance, they're going to stick it to Mr Barkley.'

Tommy shook his head. 'But that doesn't change anything,' he sighed. 'King Size has it rigged so that I take the fall first.'

'What about the documents so?' asked Stan.

'Problem is,' explained Tommy, 'I can't hand them over to you without a court order – which you probably can't get in time – or King Size's express permission.'

'I didn't ask you to hand them over,' replied Stan with a grin. 'Just gather them up into one big bundle, and I'm going to steal them from you …'

13

Valentine's Day should have been the happiest day of Letemout Lou's life. But Stan had well and truly fucked that up. He'd left her no choice. None. If he'd held his hand up and admitted whatever it was King Size was holding over him, Lou would have had to give him a fool's pardon. At least until the wedding was over with, and there was absolutely no escape. She'd spent enough time on the bench to know that men – all men, that is – have no self-control. And while the whole notion of forgiving and forgetting ran totally contrary to her day job, she figured that everyone should be allowed one mad spell without it ruining their lives.

Stan, however, was too damned proud to say sorry and move on. And so instead of toasting two hundred guests with Veuve Clicquot at her reception in the Jack Kennedy ballroom, here she was sitting in one of the hotel's snugs knocking back gin and tonics with the city's number one sociopath, Jimmy Fidget Hurley.

They'd actually started the evening on vodka and Red Bull, but Lou had switched after four, when Jimmy suggested that the reason for the drink's popularity among clubbers was that it contained taurine – made from bulls' sperm. A total urban myth, of course, but try explaining that to the funny taste in your mouth.

Six G&Ts had come and gone since, and to her amazement Letemout was really enjoying herself. Jimmy was smart, funny and completely at ease with his own failings. He also possessed that black charm that comes with spending your entire life on the edge. And, unlike virtually every other man she'd met, he had absolutely no respect for Lou's profession.

'Truth is, you scared Stan off,' he told her, slugging back a mouthful of gin. 'You're so wrapped up in what's right and who's guilty, that you forget that not everybody is always able to play by your rules. Your standards are far too high. You should maybe drop them a bit – enjoy yourself a little.'

'What?' laughed Lou. 'With you, you mean?'

'Why not?' grinned Jimmy. 'It wouldn't do you any harm to be a little less anal. You're too demanding – no one could live up to you … I shouldn't say this, given that I would love nothing better than to wipe his eye, but Stan is the most straight-up guy I have ever met. I don't believe for one minute what they're saying about him.'

'What do you mean?' said Lou soberly.

Jimmy saw his chance and put it away with the precision of a man who had spent his formative years detonating bombs. 'Well, I certainly don't believe he went near that girl in Dublin,' he said. 'No matter what it looks like in King Size's photograph …'

'What girl?' interrupted Lou, furious. 'And what photograph?'

'The one King Size used to force Stan to leave the *Standard*,' said Jimmy apologetically. 'I haven't seen it myself, but I hear it's pretty self-explanatory. And you can be sure Barry Magee has more than one print.'

'That bastard,' groaned Lou, closing her eyes slowly. 'I knew it.'

'I'm sorry, Lou,' whispered Jimmy, putting his arm around her shoulder and kissing her hair gently. 'I thought you knew.'

Valentine's Day should have been the happiest day of Stan's life. Better even than that day, twelve years ago, when Lou finally overcame her Catholic guilt up in Benevenagh Mountain Car Park. Four times. But instead of taking to the floor for his first tango as a married man, he was sitting alone in the bar of the Jack Kennedy, watching a karaoke compere in a shrunken tux serenade a hundred smooching couples, who frankly were too horny to care.

The hotel manager Susan Barkley, better known as Susie Short Shorts, was keeping a close eye on Stan from across the room. Tall, blonde and very, very brainy, Susie was her father's pride and joy. So naturally as soon as she was twenty-one and got her first-class honours degree from Trinity, she ran off with the biggest lowlife in Derry – King Size's late Uncle Sparkly. She'd stuck with him right up until he was gunned down by his mistress about four years ago. But Stan had taken great pains to ensure that no one, above all the press, learned the full story. And it was written off as a sectarian shooting.

Susie had already warned the barmaids not to serve Stan double brandies – unless they were from the watered-down bottle she saved for the frisky Culmore Road drunks. He was too good a guy to go hitting the self-destruct button – in public at least.

And she'd also alerted all the staff not to allow him into the lounge until they'd packed that uptight, self-righteous bitch Letemout Lou into a taxi. And preferably alone, if they could prise Jimmy Fidget's tongue out of her ear. Susie had warned Harry the Hurler that hooking Lou up with Jimmy was a bad, bad idea. She knew Jimmy well and despite all his charm, he was always going to come off the rails again. And they couldn't afford to let him take Lou down with him the next time. But Harry couldn't see beyond the quick fix.

As Susie looked over at Stan, he necked his drink and eased himself down from his high stool to head for the jacks. He slipped slightly as he descended, but quickly steadied himself. Susie caught the head barmaid's eye and made a cutting motion with her finger – he'd had his quota.

As he came out of the toilets, Susie was waiting in the little hallway, excuse right at the ready. 'Stanley,' she gushed, 'I need a favour. The alarm has just gone off at my house – and I could do with someone to head up with me, in case it's for real.'

'Sure thing,' replied Stan automatically. 'But Jesus, Susie, you've twenty bouncers in this place who'd be a lot more useful than me ...'

'True', sighed Susie, 'but the last time I did that, they wrote stories on the toilet walls about my erotic art collection.'

'No appreciation for rubber masks and leather horsewhips.'

'None whatsoever,' laughed Susie flirtatiously. 'But really, would you mind? We're just about to close here anyway.'

'You're giving me the bum's rush here, aren't you?' said Stan, catching on.

'Sorry, Stan, but it's for your own good.'

'No problem, Susie,' smiled Stan, nodding slowly. 'It's the kindest anyone's been to me in months.'

Timing in life is everything. And Letemout Lou's couldn't have been worse. Stan had been waiting less than thirty seconds at the Jack Kennedy main entrance while Susie got the keys to run him home, when Lou and Jimmy Fidget lurched out of the lounge, arm in arm, giggling dirty big giggles of foreplay.

'I'm sorry,' said Stan, standing aside to let them out. 'I appear to have walked into the middle of my worst nightmare.'

Lou stopped and glared back at him coldly. 'At least I didn't sleep with a twenty-year-old prostitute on my stag night,' she hissed.

'Nor did I,' said Stan, shaking his head over at Jimmy. 'But by the looks of things, the judge has already decided to hang me anyway. Happy wedding day, Your Honour.'

Lou was suddenly overwhelmed with grief and remorse. And she was finding it difficult to breathe. 'Go fuck yourself, you hypocrite,' she retorted quickly. But the tears were already forming in her eyes and she couldn't get out the door quick enough.

14

Stan was to be co-opted onto the council on his birthday, 25 February. So the night beforehand, Susie Short Shorts went to Harry the Hurler's office on the first floor and asked her boss if she could accompany the new member to his first meeting. Stan had a real weakness for bossy women and had always harboured a furtive notion for her, so she figured it was about time he acted on it.

Susie had two reasons for approaching Harry. For one, she had enjoyed a brief affair with him back when Sparkly was alive – and ever since her rotten little bastard of a husband got plugged, Harry had been looking out for her in a guilt-ridden, paternal sort of way. And second, and more important, she wanted to find out if Lou was in any way serious about Jimmy Fidget, or if she was using him as bait to bring Stan swimming back.

The answer, however, was just as Susie had feared. 'No way,' declared Harry. 'You can't go. Lou would tie me to that desk and beat me to death with her gavel.'

'From what I hear,' retorted Susie, 'Lou's in no position to complain. Word is, she's spending all her time, how will we put this, giving one-on-one law grinds to your little brother. In fact there's a strong rumour that she actually dropped her hankerchief in the restaurant a few nights ago and gave him an oral exam …'

'Didn't hear that myself,' grinned Harry sheepishly. 'Though I do hear she's the first person ever to get Jimmy into a pair of handcuffs voluntarily …'

'So, can I go?' pleaded Susie, giving him her big doe eyes. 'Jesus, Harry, Stan's totally on his own. His entire family have cut him off, and you set your own brother up with his fiancée.

Other than Tommy Bowtie, I'm all he's got. It'd mean a lot to him to look up and see a friendly face in the gallery – particularly with Lou gone and all.'

Harry winced. Susie was pushing all the right buttons and truth is, he did feel sorry for Stan. What a fucking time to get a conscience. 'Lou won't wear Jimmy for too long,' he said quietly. 'We all know that – Jimmy included. It's no secret he's not well. Most of the time he's plausible, but the bottom line is that he's still eaten up by what he did when he was a young buck. And sooner or later, the mask slips, and Jimmy the Headcase jumps out and starts talking to God and all manner of dead people. I hate to say this, him being my brother, but Lou deserves a whole lot better.'

'So why does that rule me going out with Stan then?' pressed Susie.

'Because,' sighed Harry, 'you're a nice girl, Stan's a nice lad, and the pair of you could actually click. Look, if you really want to go, I can't stop you. But please don't tell anyone we had this chat.'

'We never met,' winked Susie.

'Oh and one more thing,' said Harry, looking at her legs with a forlorn pang.

'What's that?' replied Susie.

'For God's sake, wear a pair of long trousers out to Dunavady tomorrow night. Four of the councillors out there are in their seventies. The last time Shay Gallagher's fiancée, Sue Mack, appeared in a miniskirt, they had to call a cardiac ambulance.'

Susie's dream of witnessing a night of quiet triumph for Stan in Dunavady lasted precisely thirty minutes. The DUP and the UUP briefly welcomed his co-option at the start of the council's monthly meeting, trumpeting it as a victory for themselves in ridding the council of a Sinn Féiner. But when Shay Gallagher proposed him to chair the Dunavady Inquiry – with the support of both the Shinners and the independents – the unionist bloc realised they'd been shafted.

Tony Blunt of the DUP was first to cotton on. 'With all due respect to the chair,' he told the mayor, 'you're all a bunch of lying scoundrels. Stan Stevenson is blatantly in the pocket of the man he's supposed to be investigating. He even works for him.'

'Actually, I don't,' retorted Stan. 'Mr Barkley is an investor in the *North-West Standard*, of which I'm an executive director. But I'm telling you now, if there is any impropriety on his part, he will feel the full weight of the inquiry. In fact, I personally assure you of it.'

The Ulster Unionist leader on Council, Dexter Hart, snorted loudly and shook an imaginary can of Coca-Cola in Stan's direction. 'It's a fix,' he declared. 'You've come in here to cover the whole thing up. We'll not even get a fair report of it in the media – given that you now have shares in two papers and own half a radio station to boot. I never thought of you as shady, Stanley. You were always decent when you worked out here before. But you've just proved what I've always believed: money beats integrity every single time.'

Stan winced at the gibe, coming as it did from an old friend. 'If Mr Barkley is guilty of fraud, I'll recommend criminal prosecution,' he said quietly. 'You can count on it. But nothing's been proved yet.'

'You're a liar,' interjected Tony Blunt. 'A low-down, cowardly liar who has been bought and paid for. The people of this borough have been ripped off to the tune of three million quid by the IRA and their criminal front man Barkley. And you're going to wash them whiter than white.'

'Fuck, and you say the Brits are crooked?' quipped Dexter Hart. And the unionist benches, to a man, laughed in approval.

Under the current law, Letemout Lou was saying, journalists covering council meetings in the North of Ireland are free to report on anything said in the chamber. More or less. Councillors are protected by 'qualified privilege', which – while not as strong as the 'absolute privilege' enjoyed by MPs – allows them a lot more leeway than they get outside the chamber. So if you want to call someone a thieving bastard, just step inside the door and wait until the mayor takes his seat.

A key difference between the Commons and a town hall, however, is that while an MP is protected even if he makes *dishonest* or *malicious* statements in Parliament, a councillor isn't necessarily covered in a council chamber. And the only person who can fairly say what is malicious or dishonest is the High Court judge hearing the libel case – or at least that's the only person that counts.

'So what you're saying,' said Mary Slavin, 'is that if we report what the unionist councillors said about Stan, he can sue our arses off.'

'Not *can*,' sniffed Lou, who was sitting in Mary's chair deleting chunks of text from her computer screen. 'The word you're looking for is *will*.'

'So what exactly can we say?' asked Mary. 'I was thinking of a big picture of Stan with the headline "Crooked as the Brits".'

'I love it,' laughed Lou. 'But no fucking way. Never forget that more people wind up in court because of smart remarks than for robbing banks. Get a bad judge on a bad day, and Stan could close you down … Seriously. Don't mess about with this. You can note that the unionists objected to the appointment of the inquiry chairman, and leave it at that. Oh, and you can leave in the bit where Dexter called Stan a self-abuser. I'd love to see him trying to challenge that one in court.'

'Fair enough,' tutted Mary. 'We'll wait until the inquiry starts and get them then. Thanks for dropping in, Lou.'

'Pleasure was mine, Mary,' said Lou. 'And I love the ring by the way – a ruby is such a passionate stone.'

Mary gazed down at her Valentine's Day present for the hundredth time that day and beamed. 'He'd carried it around in his pocket for two full years.' She smiled. 'God love him.'

'The last of the great romantics,' said Lou. 'If you could only bottle Hugo and feed him to the nephew.'

'That chapter's not finished yet, and well you know it,' laughed the older woman. 'Susie is no threat to you. She's just scratching an itch for him until you take the poker out of your arse and forgive him.'

'But she's gorgeous,' groaned Lou. 'And when she gets her hooks into a man, she's hard to shake off. And my Stanley is a sucker for long legs …'

'Except, of course,' interrupted Mary, 'he's not your Stanley any more. And you, from what I hear, are not his either – by a long chalk. Not if what the maître d' in the Jack Kennedy is telling everyone is true.'

'That big-mouthed bastard,' hissed Lou, firing up. 'I've a good mind to drive straight down there and have Harry fire him ...'

'But then Susie might have some objections – after all she's his boss,' grinned Mary, raising her eyebrows. 'Gets complicated, doesn't it?'

'Things used to be a lot simpler, all right,' agreed Lou, rising from the editor's seat. She picked up her suede jacket from the back and walked across to the door. 'You know, Mary,' she sighed, 'I love Stan, I miss him so much I can't sleep, and there'll never be anyone like him in my life again. But at the minute, it's almost like we're out to see who can inflict the most damage on the other. I've a terrible feeling it's not going to happen again for us.'

'Course it will, Lou,' grinned Mary. 'He can't stop it. It's in the genes. Didn't I tell you? Two years that daft bastard of an uncle of his had the ring in his pocket.'

Any worries Mary Slavin had about whether her heavily edited piece would incur the legal wrath of Stan and King Size were allayed two days later when she read her rival paper. Indeed, when she saw the front page, she laughed out loud. Stan had hung the little fucker out to dry.

'NEWBOY STAN IS A LYING CROOK' announced the North-West Standard's banner headline. Pages two and three, meanwhile, followed the theme with: 'KING SIZE BUYS HIS OWN TRIBUNAL'.

King Size, it transpired, had actually left the paper's offices an hour before production, with the front page still reading 'NEW CHAIRMAN PROMISES FAIR INQUIRY'. But Stan felt it lacked a little punch. So he decided to deliver one. Just below King Size's trouser button.

The paper's owner jumped up and down when he saw it – and even threatened to sue his own editor for slander. But then two very peculiar things happened. First the paper sold out, and then Dexter Hart went on Radio Foyle to apologise to Stan Stevenson for doubting him and to commend him for his ruthlessly impartial reportage.

By the end of the day, Stan was the big dog's bollix again, and the NWS was the only honest paper in town.

'You're one lucky individual,' sniffed King Size, when he called round at Stan's flat to return his office keys. 'But the next time you send a paper to the printers without my say-so, you'll wake up in a binbag in a Donegal bog. Capeesh?'

'*Capisco*,' said Stan, grinning at the bad Mafia impression. 'But you'll agree, I owed you at least one good kick in the *pomodori* ...'

'Okay, *caro mio*,' laughed King Size. 'We'll call it quits.'

'My arse we will,' replied Stan softly. But only after King Size's Lexus had pulled out of the car park.

15

Sonny Waterhouse was very alarmed – and just a little impressed – when Stan Stevenson faxed him down the headlines from the *NWS*. Sonny had assured Rubber John that Stan was a stable force and a possible standard-bearer for when the party organised officially in the North. They'd even permitted Stan to designate himself as a Fianna Fáil councillor – the first in the Six Counties. The last thing they needed was a maverick.

As soon as Stan got back to the flat that night, he'd rung Sonny to explain. If the inquiry was to have any integrity at all, he had to pre-empt right away any allegations of a cover-up.

'One thing I discovered in my time as a reporter is this,' said Stan, 'no one gets away with a damn thing. You'll always be caught. You'll always be found out. It's like the old French cardinal used to say at the time of the Inquisition – give me six lines written by any man and I'll find enough in there to hang him. In today's language: if you wait about long enough, you can get to boot anyone in the balls.

'There's no point in me trying to hide the fact I'm Barkley's bagman – the whole country knows it. But what they're now wondering is if I'm crazy enough to turn on him.'

'And are you?' asked Sonny.

'You bet your bad moustache I am,' laughed Stan. 'But I'm not crazy enough to go down with him. I'll fuck up my own life for myself, thank you very much.'

'The boss is worried you could embarrass the party …' continued Sonny.

'I won't,' replied Stan abruptly. 'And, sure if I do, he can cut me loose any time. Listen Sonny. I've no intention of messing up. It mightn't be how I envisaged starting a new career – but this is my life now. And I'm going to make a damn good job of it.'

Stan sounded convincing, but Sonny had to check. 'I hate to be blunt here,' he said, 'but what's in it for you?'

It was a good question and a fair one. Stan was loaded, already had a great career, and didn't need the hassle. 'Truth is, I'm bored,' he confessed. 'And this is the most excitement I've had in years. For the first time, I actually believe I'm being useful. You need a man up here – and I think we need a man down there. More than one man. We need the Northern voice to be heard in Dublin. Not just over tea in the Áras – but in the Dáil and in the Senate. The unionists can promote and defend their union in the House of Commons – why can't we do the same for ours at Leinster House?'

Sonny laughed. 'I don't know whether to admire you or pity you,' he declared. 'Jesus, are you in for a wake-up call.'

Stan took a small sip of his Powers and sighed into the phone. 'Look, Sonny,' he said, 'I'm no innocent. I know most of you guys down there would like to tie a big plastic bag around the Six Counties and hold it till our feet stop kicking. Let's face it, we're the child you gave up for adoption when you got knocked up too young. But like it or not, the secret's out now – and we want our mummy.'

Fair comment, thought Sonny, chuckling to himself. 'Well, actually, Stan,' he said, 'Joxer O'Duffy and the Committee of Eight reckon you're the best thing that's ever happened to the North. Joxer's certain you're just the man to fuck up the Taoiseach's recruitment drive. He's even going to ask the Boss to nominate you for the Senate. There's a vacancy after old Danny O'Hanlon died.'

'Wasn't he the old civil rights guy from Enniskillen?' asked Stan. 'He couldn't hold his beer. They used to call him Whole Hanlon?'

'One and the same,' replied Sonny. 'His kidneys dissolved about a month ago, and his heart finally gave up last week. Now, the Taoiseach wants another Northerner – a safe one, and a popular one. And Joxer's suggesting you. He's going to sign you up to his cause, parade you as his token Northerner – then watch you make a complete idiot of yourself and hang you out to dry … But we're not going to let him. You'd be the original double agent in the Senate. What do you reckon?'

'Are you serious?'

'Deadly,' said Sonny, sipping determinedly on his own drink. 'Stan, this Joxer business will, at most, be a brief blip at the start of your political career. But in the long run, you've a real chance of better things. You're great with people, mostly honest and you know your way about. You're also so good-looking, I actually hate you for it. But your big strength is that you're completely aware of your limitations. You're exactly bright enough to realise that you're not really that smart. And that works for us. We can do without another clever bastard that we'd have to watch twenty-four hours a day.'

'Very flattering,' laughed Stan. And he was very impressed with the offer. Unlike Dunavady council, the Senate was serious politics. 'Would I have to move to Dublin?' he asked.

'Not at all,' explained Sonny. 'Many senators hold down day jobs – so you could still edit the paper. And no one would expect you to attend any debates until the inquiry's over.'

'Okay so,' said Stan, delighted. 'Stick my name in.'

'Magic,' laughed Sonny. 'You'll get a call from Rubber John tomorrow. Try not to correct his grammar.'

'I won't.' Stan put down the phone and beamed with pride. He looked down at Speed Dial 1 – Lou's office – and lifted the receiver. He was sorely tempted.

'No,' he said softly to himself. 'Let's finish tidying up this mess first.'

Down at the Jack Kennedy, Letemout Lou was sitting deep in thought at the mahogany bureau in her suite when Harry the Hurler rapped on the door. Lou had been trying hopelessly to fabricate an explanation for the two thousand bottles of homemade vodka that had just been seized from a van being driven by her new boyfriend. And she'd already chewed her way through a pen top in frustration.

'Come in, Harry – it's open,' she yelled without looking up from her file pad.

'The little bastard,' he said, heading straight for a leather armchair. 'I thought you were going to straighten him out …'

'I've had him thirty days – you had him thirty years,' snapped Lou. 'And by the way, Harry, and let's be clear about this, I don't have him any more. I'm not going to risk my career on him ... And besides, you do know he's off his fucking head. Don't you?'

'Busted,' grinned Harry, holding out his hands sheepishly. 'Seriously though, thanks Lou.'

Lou pointed to the Paddy bottle on the sideboard and Harry poured out two large glasses.

'Did you hear the evening news?' he asked.

'No,' she replied. 'I was stuck at the Strand Road police station with your brother until twenty minutes ago.'

'According to the forensics,' continued Harry, 'Sammy Muir's death wasn't an accident.'

'There's a shocker,' sniffed Lou, raising her finger sharply to warn Harry to be really careful.

'Someone cut the brakes in his car,' he said. 'By the time the cross-eyed little thief crashed at the bottom of Drumbridge Bray he was hitting close to eighty-five miles an hour.'

'That's awful,' replied Lou.

'Terrible,' said Harry. 'We issued a statement an hour ago condemning the murder as a blatant breach of the ceasefire and warning all our people to take extra care, as the loyalists are back targeting us.'

'You must be very shocked,' said Lou, her voice cynical.

'I am,' said Harry. And even if there had been a mike in the room, it would never have picked up the twinkle in his eye.

Next morning on her way to court in Belfast, Lou asked her driver to stop at Tommy Bowtie's Dunavady office. It was just possible she'd thought of a way to prevent him taking the full hit for King Size at the inquiry and she wanted to run it by him. But they had barely turned the corner onto Main Street, when they spotted the posse of four police jeeps parked outside his door.

'What's happened?' Lou asked Tommy, who was pacing up and down in a state of panic in the hallway.

'Burglary,' he replied quickly, clutching his gut. 'Excuse me, I have to run.'

A tall, good-looking young inspector was standing at the reception desk checking a clipboard.

'It's not a raid so,' joked Lou.

'No, that was next week.' He laughed. 'And, by sheer coincidence, it seems they've taken all the stuff we were coming to collect on Monday.'

'Like anything with Bartholomew Barkley's name on it?' pressed Lou.

'Got it in one, Your Honour,' said the inspector.

'The crafty little git,' muttered Lou.

'My words precisely,' grinned the cop.

'Was Tommy in on it?' asked Lou.

'No idea,' said the inspector. 'I haven't been able to question him yet. Every time I say, "Could I have a minute, Mr McGinlay?" he runs off to the privy again. But, whoever did it was cute enough to steal a whole swathe of other files – and a small bagful of cash. I don't think we'll be able to pin this on anyone.'

'What about the CCTV camera from Shay Gallagher's office next door?' said Lou, thinking out loud. 'Did that pick up anything?'

'Fuck, I never thought of that,' replied the cop. 'I must go check.' He caught himself, then added quickly, 'Apologies for the language, Miss Johnston.'

'And proper fucking order too,' grinned Her Honour.

16

The decision to arrest Stan Stevenson for the break-in at Tommy Bowtie's offices was a very simple one for the police. The CCTV footage from the office next door had shown a hooded man similar in shape and size to Stan opening Tommy's door with a set of keys that had been reported stolen a day before. Then, when you ran the tape forward twelve minutes, the intruder could be seen taking off his balaclava on his way out of the building, so absolutely confirming himself as the newly installed chairman of the Dunavady Inquiry. And finally, just to ensure he had no defence whatsoever, the camera panned to capture Stan throwing the box of files into a black sports car indistinguishable in make, model and registration from the Mercedes coupé he had bought himself only three months previously. And which had not been reported stolen. Not never.

Stan the bagman had been caught stealing to order for his paymaster. It was open and shut. The only other suspect the police looked at was Tommy Bowtie himself. But while everyone was certain he gave Stan the keys, there was no witness to the handover. So unless Stan turned him in, Tommy was home and dry, and smelling of roses. Or not, in Tommy Bowtie's case.

Yes, it was all open and shut. Apart from two things. First – when the police told King Size that Stan had stolen the files, he was totally and utterly inconsolable. Indeed, according to one constable's note, Mr Barkley replied, 'Oh Jesus, no. I didn't tell him to do that. That fucker's getting ready to shaft me.'

And, second, the police had forgotten to ask Shay Gallagher's permission to take the CCTV film. Moreover, they'd browbeaten his secretary into giving them access to his machine without even telling him. So all evidence arising from the tape was suppressed. Indeed, before Stan had even had a chance to finish the cup of tea PSNI Superintendent Audrey Grafton had brought him, Tommy Bowtie had got the cassette returned by High Court order and issued lawsuits against the eighteen PSNI officers who had illegally detained his client.

Letemout, who had spent the past day telling everyone how she had outsmarted the cops by spotting the CCTV camera, was spitting tacks when she found out she'd been used as a patsy.

'I hear Stan's threatening to cite me for abuse of process,' she told Tommy Bowtie when he called into her chambers at the Jack Kennedy for a drink later than evening.

'That depends,' said Tommy slowly.

'On what?' Lou asked.

'On whether you trust Stan's doing the right thing.'

'And if I don't?'

Tommy shook his head in frustration. 'Why don't you just stop interfering and let him do his job?' He sighed. 'He knows what he's doing. King Size ruined his life. He made him lose you, his uncle and that crappy little newspaper of Hugo's – which by the way is worse than nothing without Stan. Everyone in the county now knows just how far Stan will go to expose Barkley. And, better again, he wants everyone to know that it's him that's doing it. That's precisely why he took his mask off, Lou.'

Lou rolled her Paddy slowly around in her mouth and nodded. 'Okay so, I'll stay out of the way,' she said quietly.

Tommy drained his drink and headed for the door. Lou bade him goodnight. 'Pity no one would sort it all out for us,' she laughed. 'Maybe send King Size the way of his uncle Sparkly. Two little bullets, and we're all right as rain again.'

'Jesus, Lou,' replied Tommy, shocked. 'Don't ever say anything like that out loud. Not in Harry the Hurler's hotel.'

The following morning when Tommy Bowtie arrived in Dunavady for work, there was a box sitting on the office doorstep. A note, written in block capitals, had been taped to the top.

Dear Mr McGinlay

Enclosed find every document pertaining to the Dunavady
Inquiry that I stole during the burglary. While I would never
voluntarily make public the content of these files, I have
made copies of them. So, if you don't hand them over to the
inquiry – I will. And you and Mr Barkley will be prosecuted
for obstructing the tribunal besides everything else.

Yours, Concerned Citizen.

Typical Stan, grinned Tommy. He was even thoughtful
enough to break a window so I'd have to call the police. King
Size wouldn't like it, but he could go pee up a very small rope.

Just one thing to check though. 'Hey Shay,' he shouted,
opening his next-door neighbour's foyer door.

'That you, Tommy?' came the voice from the back room.

'Yeah,' replied the lawyer. 'Was your CCTV on last night?'

'Nah,' said Shay. 'The whole system's banjaxed since the
cops took it apart.'

''Bout time you got it fixed again,' shouted in Tommy.

'I'll look after that today,' called out Shay.

The lawyer disappeared back to his own offices again,
happier than he'd been in weeks.

Stan Stevenson was also having a pretty good day. After he'd
dropped the box off at Tommy Bowtie's on Main Street, he'd
headed straight to the offices of the *North-West Standard* in the
industrial estate just outside the town. And there was a message
to ring Sonny.

'You're to ring Rubber John at his office at exactly quarter
past ten this morning,' sniffed Sonny officiously when Stan
finally tracked him.

'Do you think he's heard about the little incident in
Dunavady the other day?' asked Stan, sensing the coolness.

'What the fuck do you think?' snapped Sonny sarcastically.
'Our number one contender for a Senate appointment is
arrested for a felony? How would we hear something like that?
No. Not only do we not read the papers down here, we also
don't listen to the radio or watch TV. We're all fucking
culchies with straw behind our ears …'.

Stan blanched with embarrassment and fear. But Sonny wasn't finished and was intent on proving every cliché about red hair and bad temper. 'Of course he heard, you fucking bollix,' he yelled. 'And he was going to fuck you back into the pond, on my advice. Except then Joxer O'Duffy threatened a rebellion if you weren't confirmed. So, as and from twenty minutes' time, if you can stay out of jail that long, you waste of fucking space, you will be our new appointee for the Senate. They'll make the announcement at lunchtime, and you'll come down on Monday week for the swearing in. Oh, and on behalf of the party, I'd like to formally congratulate you, Senator, yada, yada, yada ...'

Stan grinned and silently punched the air.

'And don't forget,' warned Sonny, 'any interviews you're doing, always mention Rubber John's commitment to the North. He likes that. And this is the most republican thing he's done since he's taken office, so let him warm himself in the flag for a couple of hours.'

'At least Haughey sent up guns,' retorted Stan, anxious to break the ice again.

'Maybe,' retorted Sonny. 'But if you'd ever broken into Charlie's private office looking for dodgy files, you'd have needed a dirty big bastard of an articulated lorry to get them all out. Now fuck off, stop annoying me, and ring back at ten-fifteen.'

Sonny had deliberately roughed Stan so the Taoiseach wouldn't have to. Rubber John's chat with Stan was a lot more pleasant.

'Stanley,' he declared when the call was put through, 'how are they hanging?'

'Well actually, Taoiseach, it's me they're trying to hang,' laughed Stan.

'So I hear,' said Rubber John. 'Jesus, you're only in Fianna Fáil a fortnight and you've pulled more strokes than a convent schoolgirl on Debs night. Slow down, man – or I'll be sticking you on my Clever Bastard lists.'

'It's called survival up here,' said Stan. 'But I really hope there shouldn't be any more trouble.'

'You know what we need you to do for us?' asked the Taoiseach, serious again.

'Yes,' replied Stan soberly. 'Join the Committee of Eight and report back.'

'Correct,' said the Boss. 'When two or more are gathered together in my name, I'd like at least one of them to be working for me.'

'And in turn,' said Stan, 'I'll have free rein to introduce new policy on the North in the Senate ...'

'What?' interrupted Rubber John. 'You will in your arse. Who told you that?' Then he realised what Stan had done and laughed. 'I've just walked into a haymaker, haven't I? You're making a point, aren't you?'

'Sorry about that,' chuckled Stan, 'but at least you know where I'm coming from now. I'm not a nodding dog.'

'I never thought for a minute you were, Stanley,' said Rubber John.

'Other than that – any tips?' asked Stan.

'Yeah,' laughed Rubber John. 'Don't take your mask off in front of the video camera. And next time, use someone else's car ...'

On a normal newsday, Stan Stevenson's appointment as a Fianna Fáil senator would probably have been the main lunchtime news story on Radio Foyle. And the fact that An Taoiseach had given the station a pre-recorded interview on the nomination would undoubtedly have sealed the top billing.

But this was no ordinary day. Somebody else had nipped in at the last minute to steal the limelight. King Size Barkley, typical of the selfish little runt, just couldn't let Stan have his moment in the sun on his own.

Not that King Size would have been too keen to be hogging the news cycle on this particular occasion, however. Nor, indeed, did he know much about it. The two little bullets in his rotten little heart had put paid to that. And, no, the bullet through his right eye wouldn't have helped much either. Bam, bam, bam. Dead as a louse.

17

King Size had been driving along the Strand Road towards the embankment, just before noon, when a motorcyclist pulled up beside his purple Lexus at traffic lights. According to eyewitnesses, the biker knocked on the driver's window and, when King Size looked round, fired three times. The bike then sped off around the corner and into the Quayside multi-storey car park, where it was recovered on Level Two about three hours later.

The murder drew an instantaneous but identical response from hundreds of men and women right across the city. And it was this: who can vouch for where I was when the little shit got plugged?

Stan Stevenson had a cast-iron alibi. He was standing on the Radio Foyle roof terrace, recording a thirty-second TV clip on his appointment as senator, when the three bangs rang out in the distance. Stan even had the presence of mind to say to the cameraman, 'I think that sounded like shooting. Better redo the clip, just in case.'

Harry the Hurler likewise was pretty fireproof. He was in court along with a judge, twelve jurors, two prosecutors, seventy-one state witnesses and two defence counsel explaining how he actively tried to dissuade Jimmy Fidget from distilling his own hooch.

Down at the *Derry Standard* offices, Hugo and Mary, meanwhile, were hosting a pre-Patrick's Day reception for the city's thirty councillors – at least three or four of whom were particularly glad to have taken up the invite.

Also in the clear was Letemout Lou, who'd been up in Belfast hearing a libel case, and who, coincidentally, had shared the car journey up with the new Widow Barkley. Patsy had just been awarded a £20,000 shopping spree as a result of what was to be her husband's last serious bout of guilt.

King Size's only other living relative – his step-aunt Susie Short Shorts – was another name police were eager to rule out. She'd been lucky to hold on to her home after King Size tried to hoover up the last remaining crumbs from Sparkly's will. Fortunately for her, she was in the Radio Foyle car park at the time, waiting for Stan to take her for an early lunch. Though the ever-fiery Susie did tell detectives she would be happy to take credit for stiffing the little fucker, if no one else would.

That only left Tommy Bowtie, who had been in the car in front of King Size, but was indignantly refusing to discuss why he'd sped off from the scene. So in line with police procedure, they called up the TV crews, slapped him in handcuffs and hauled him in.

Father Noel Giddens, who was press-ganged by the bishop into coming in from Dunavady to perform the funeral Mass, did an admirable job under the circumstances. The first task had been to get the deceased's best buddy out of jail. The front three rows of the chapel were for direct relatives and good friends of the deceased. And without Tommy Bowtie, Patsy Barkley would have cut a lone figure up at the altar rails.

'Chrissake, Audrey,' Father Know-All told the city's police chief, 'you know he couldn't have done it. Let him go.'

'Tommy saw the whole thing in his mirror,' retorted Superintendent Audrey Grafton. 'Unless he starts to clue us in, we'll hold him as an accessory.'

The lawyer had readily confirmed that when the shooting took place, he and King Size had been on their way out to Dunavady for a pre-inquiry briefing with their barrister. They were using two cars as always. King Size liked to smoke when he was driving, while Tommy insisted on having the two windows wide open.

On the face of things, the CCTV footage the cops had grabbed had tallied with Tommy's account. What they couldn't figure was why he had fled the scene – and then had his car valeted.

'But he's already told you everything he saw,' replied Father Know-All. 'And you know as well as I do why he dashed off to get the car cleaned. It was nothing to do with evidence. The man wasn't going have your knuckle-draggers telling the whole world how the tough-guy lawyer shat in his trousers while his buddy was being shot.'

Audrey lowered her face to hide an embarrassed grin.

'Okay so,' continued the priest. 'What if I get Doc Clancy to release the file that shows Tommy suffers from Rapid Irritable Bowel Syndrome? Would that do? But it'll not go into the record for your end-of-year Let's Make Fun Of The Punters party. The file will go to you personally. And you'll be responsible for its safe return.'

'Give me a look, and I'll see what I can do,' sighed Audrey. 'But I still want more on the gunman.'

'What's Tommy saying?' asked Father Know-All.

'Damn all,' said Audrey. 'He couldn't even tell if the shooter was a man or a woman. Whoever it was was wearing racing leathers and a helmet. You'd almost think they didn't want to be recognised ...'

The priest's next job was to arrange for four pallbearers. In a worst-case scenario, the undertakers would provide men for the job. But given that the funeral would be on TV, decorum insisted that there should be grieving faces propping up the corpse. Like the rest of the world, Father Know-All could operate pretty well on blackmail when he had to. So after considerable arm-twisting, Harry the Hurler agreed to carry the front end of the coffin along with Tommy Bowtie. Father K assured Harry that his altruism would mean that the police would never get to hear how he had once taken King Size on a boat trip on the Foyle, stuffed a grenade into his trunks and thrown the pin into the river. King Size was never slow paying his fifteen per cent after that – though in fairness, Harry knew all along that it was only a smoke bomb.

Barry Magee then allowed his name to go down for back left. This was settled after Father Know-All got a commitment from Tommy Bowtie that the *North-West Standard* would stay open for at least another three months — so guaranteeing Barry's meal ticket.

This left just one position. And there was only one man who could fill it.

'Senator Stevenson,' said Father K, 'I need your help.'

Stan gave the priest the finger before taking the phone off the speaker. He knew what was coming.

'I'm not a hypocrite, Father,' he replied before the question was even asked. 'I won't do it.'

'Hear me out, son,' said Father K. 'Funerals are the life blood of politics. For most politicians, the best they can do is to arrive halfway through the ceremony and stomp up to the front of the chapel so that everyone can see them. I'm offering you a place at centre stage.'

'I'm not interested,' retorted Stan. 'The man was scum. He blackmailed me, threatened my friends, and threatened my family. Up until yesterday, my only abiding interest in life was to ruin him. I normally never gloat at misfortune — but in this case I'll make an exception.'

'I'm not asking you to do the eulogy,' chuckled the priest, 'I need you for lifting, pure and simple. We want some political muscle. Shay Gallagher has slipped a disc — so he can't do it. Besides, you worked with King Size for the past three months, so you're the closest thing he's got to an ally.'

'I'm not sure about Gallagher,' sniffed Stan. 'He slips that same disc any time a Provo dies in Derry, Drumbridge or Dunavady.'

'Maybe,' said the priest, 'but then he's a lot longer in the game than you are. Tell you what so, do this for me, and I'll make Gallagher write the obituary.'

'You're one bad bastard,' Stan grinned, weighing up his options. 'Okay so. You've got a deal …'

Father K's own tribute to King Size was short and sweet. He told the half-empty church that violence solved nothing, it was a sin against God to cut any life short, and anyone who knew anything about this brutal slaying should not take the law into their own hands but contact instead the 'relevant' authorities.

Truth was, Father K was stretching to get that much. But luckily he'd had the presence of mind to revisit his file labelled 'G' – for Gangsters – and hoke out the sermon he'd given for a Drumbridge drug dealer who'd got whacked in a Belfast nightclub two years ago. Only difference was, this time the grieving widow would be worth a lottery cheque. Which, as Tommy Bowtie pointed out, begged another question.

18

'Theoretically, she could have done it,' said Tommy. 'You left her at the Europa at half-nine, King Size was shot in Derry at noon. And we couldn't contact Patsy until 3 p.m. at CastleCourt because her mobile was off. She had enough time to scoot back to Derry, shoot her husband, and get back up to Belfast, before giving an Oscar-winning performance as the devastated widow. Better again, she has no witnesses in Belfast. Not a single one. None of the shop assistants remember her — nor does the lady in Waterstone's café where she's supposed to have had lunch.'

Letemout just shook her head slowly, and poured herself another drink from the complimentary bottle on top of her filing cabinet. 'Only problem with your theory,' she said, 'is that Patsy is the only person on earth who didn't want King Size dead. The poor child loved him.'

'Maybe,' countered Tommy, 'but she's now going to inherit twenty-five million pounds in cash and property, and another bundle of businesses — including the country's fastest-growing newspaper ...'

'No,' interrupted Lou, impatiently. 'It wasn't her. She'd never pull it off. To tell you the truth, if I were to be completely impartial, I'd put my own money on Stan. Don't know how he arranged it — but I do know he's a whole lot smarter than you give him credit for.'

Tommy eyed her quizzically across the desk. He was pretty sure she was just fishing — shopping for the latest gossip on the love of her life. But he'd been a lawyer way too long to start playing this particular game with a High Court judge.

'It absolutely wasn't Stan,' he asserted. 'For a start, he was gearing up to screw King Size at the inquiry. That's why he was so keen to get all the documents from my office. You're just sore because he won't come crawling back to you.'

Lou bit her lip to stop a grin. 'I don't know what you're talking about,' she said. 'But seriously. What if Stan figured that King Size was going to buy his way out of jail? He'd done it before. Maybe Stan couldn't face the thought of him getting the all clear from the inquiry. Why wouldn't he bury the little shit properly if he got the chance?'

'Quite simple,' responded Tommy. 'As you and I are both aware, Stanley is a lifelong believer in the Fuck-up Factor. He knows that if you do something bad, you're going to get caught. No matter how clever you are or how many angles you close down, your inner idiot will always escape. And Stan wouldn't risk going to jail for King Size.'

'You're wrong,' countered Lou. 'I think the only thing holding Stan up at the moment is bitterness – I'm next door to him on that one. I think he was determined to get even. So he got one of his new Dublin buddies in to plug King Size. The entire town is convinced of it.'

'So,' mused Tommy, 'why hasn't he fucked up yet then?'

Tommy had been visiting Lou's suite at the Kennedy to submit an application to delay the start of the Dunavady Inquiry. As Derry's only resident High Court judge, she was normally happy to handle paperwork on behalf of the Belfast bench if it meant saving the court service a few pounds in travel and *per diem* expenses. And she was always particularly happy to see Tommy Bowtie, as he was her one remaining link to the no-good bastard who broke her heart.

After Tommy left, she sat finishing her drink and wondering if maybe, just maybe, she should maybe just pick up the phone and call him, when as if by a miracle her mobile started ringing.

'Hello, hello,' she gushed, seeing the number.

'Hello, hello yourself,' replied Harry the Hurler, pleased at the warmth of the greeting. 'Sorry to bother you this late, but Jimmy's just been arrested again. I'm just out of the station – and didn't want to use the mobile, so I called in to Stan's flat to use his phone … It's the worst yet.'

'Come straight down to the suite,' sighed Lou, 'I'm still up.'

Harry was right. It was the worst yet. By a country fucking mile.

'I spoke to the cops when you were on your way over,' she told Harry. 'He's going to jail this time. Almost certainly. They smuggled sixty trailerloads of cigarettes into the North from a bonded warehouse in Dublin. Fags made in the Republic that were to be sent to Africa – no duty on them. You're talking a three million pound fraud here. And your brother's fingerprints are, quite literally, all over it.'

'It'll wreck us,' groaned Harry. 'Politically, they'll hammer me. And on a personal level, it'll probably kill my mother.'

Lou handed him a drink and refilled her own glass. 'With all due respect Harry,' she said, 'if you could go to God now and tell him that the worst thing you ever did was move some fags, you'd be doing rightly. In fact, I think I represented you in relation to fourteen separate crimes that were a lot more politically damaging than what Jimmy's facing – including, if I remember correctly, the suspected murder of two of your political opponents and the clandestine disposal of their earthly remains.'

Harry motioned to butt in, but Lou raised a warning finger.

'Second,' she went on, 'your mother, my godmother Brigid, is one of the hardest bitches ever to draw breath. And you're not one damn bit afraid of her dropping dead. What you're really afraid of is what's she's going to do to you when you go in and tell her that Jimmy slipped the leash again …'

Harry grinned at his most trusted advisor and nodded sheepishly. 'You're right about the political embarrassment,' he nodded, 'we'll get over it. And about my mother … God, you're very like her.'

After Harry had left his flat, Stan had to fight the urge to press Redial on the phone. He hadn't spoken to Lou in more than a month now – two months if you didn't count the train wreck at the Jack Kennedy Inn on Valentine's Night. They'd passed one another in the small line at King Size's graveside, but Stan had been with Susie, and Lou appeared to be in a hurry anywhere else, so they'd just nodded.

Susie was becoming an issue. She'd asked to come to his swearing-in at Leinster House. He'd already got the ceremony put back to the start of April, but it would have to be rescheduled again because of the shooting and the inquiry.

'Probably best head down to Dublin the next day you're free and get stuck in,' Tommy Bowtie advised him. 'Never mind the fancy tails. It might also allow you to let Susie down a little more gently.'

So Stan sat and stared at the handset and tried to dream up ten logical reasons not to call Lou, when, all of a sudden, the phone rang.

It was Sonny.

'Senator Stevenson,' he began very formally, 'you mightn't remember me, but my name is Sonny Waterhouse and I'm ringing on behalf of Joxer O'Duffy.'

'Nice to hear from you, Mr Waterhouse,' replied Stan, playing the game. 'I'm a big fan of Mr O'Duffy. As you might know, we have a desperate problem with immigrants up here in the north-west of the island, and I'd be keen to highlight the issue in the Seanad – with his help of course.'

'Mr Stevenson, delighted to meet you,' interrupted O'Duffy, with a big throaty laugh. 'I'm sitting here right beside Mr Waterhouse. We're using a speakerphone.'

You don't say, smirked Stan to himself.

'We're hoping you might come and meet with us in Dún Laoghaire at the weekend,' continued O'Duffy. 'I run a small focus group in the Oireachtas and wonder if you might like to consider joining us. I understand that Rubber John has given you a key role in Northern policy in the Seanad – I've got some very wise advisors who could be a great help to you.'

'I'd be delighted, Mr O'Duffy,' said Stan, relieved that Joxer was going to try and butter him up first, rather than shoot him straight out of the trap.

'I don't really know an awful lot about the logistics of policy-making,' Stan continued. 'And to be honest, while I've a few ideas on Northern policies, they're probably very raw and unpolished. So any help you can give me will be greatly appreciated.'

I'm a virgin, Stan grinned to himself, come gobble me up.

'Shall we say the Forty Foot Restaurant on Saturday evening at about seven?' asked O'Duffy.

'Why not?' Stan replied. 'And I hope to see you there too, Mr Waterhouse.'

Sonny rang back ten minutes later. 'Well played, Stan,' he started.

'I just decided to throw in the racist card on the hoof,' laughed Stan. 'Jesus, it was like he'd found a brother ...'

'He's already talking about getting you to run his deportation bill through the Senate,' said Sonny. 'If you're off-white, you're off the island ... But be careful. Remember: don't get too caught up in your role-play here. You're there to bury him – not to praise him.'

'I'll not forget,' replied Stan. 'We Derrymen have long memories. He's the fucker who said, "The only thing worse than a black Taoiseach would be a Northern Taoiseach." ... Anyway, how long am I to be his guy, then?'

'Just long enough till Rubber John can sink him,' said Sonny.

'And after that, how long until they rehabilitate us?' asked Stan. 'Won't we be tainted by association?'

'God, I hope not,' replied Sonny. 'The Taoiseach says he'll make a big push to reunify the party and come offering us his hand – maybe a Cabinet seat. Just don't say anything that's going to come back and bite you on the arse in the meantime.'

'I'm not sure this is altogether wise,' responded Stan.

'Of course, it's not fucking wise,' laughed Sonny. 'Welcome to politics.'

19

With King Size out of the picture, the smart money reckoned that the *North-West Standard* would trundle along for at best a couple of months, before the editor would agree to merge with his Uncle Hugo.

But, as Mary Slavin often said, when it comes to running newspapers, the smart money wouldn't know its arse from a hole in the ground. The new *NWS*, not to overstate the point, was making money by the bagful. Readers loved its rude and abrasive style, and advertisers loved the fact that it was selling quicker than free beer.

The paper's success was due in no small part to Barry Magee's standards of decency and integrity. He had none whatsoever. To him, human frailty was a commodity to be exposed and ridiculed. And the public were lapping it up. Which is why – despite the fortune waiting for him in the wings – Stan intended to sell off the *NWS* just as soon as he could square things with his photographer. That and the fact that Uncle Hugo's *Derry Standard* was going down the tubes quicker than last night's curry.

Barry, however, saw things differently. And when Stan called him into the office a fortnight to the day after King Size's funeral, the Welshman blew up like a mid-summer riot.

'Don't even fucking dream of putting it on the market,' he started. 'You've given me a six-month guarantee.'

'And I will pay you the full term. Every cent you're owed.'

'But who's going to hire me?' yelled Barry. 'There's no way Hugo would take me back as part of any merger.'

'True,' said Stan, 'but then no one asked you to go round burning all your boats.'

'So it's like that, is it?' snapped Barry. 'You're just going to throw me out, you asshole?'

Stan momentarily considered bouncing his coffee mug off Barry's head but instead grabbed hard onto the edge of his seat. 'I'm giving you half a year's salary as a payoff – not bad after just three months' work,' he retorted through gritted teeth. 'And besides, no one twisted your arm to join us here. It's not as if anyone was blackmailing you now … was it?'

Barry gave a derisive smirk, then sat back casually into his chair. 'I get you now,' he said. 'So what you're really saying is that if I don't go quietly, you'll blow the whistle.'

'I'm sorry,' said Stan, 'it was a very ill-judged remark and I take it back.'

'Your arse you do,' sneered Barry. 'Let me tell you this, Mister Bigshot Senator. Your paper thrives on blackmail – as does your politics. But this time, you're messing with the wrong guy. I knew you'd pull a stunt like this. Do you really think I wouldn't have any insurance? Just so that everything's on the table now, let me remind you that I still have the picture that will end your career – King Size, the stupid little prick, didn't even notice while I copied it onto a disc right in front of him.'

Stan watched Barry's little piggy eyes gleam with triumph. He'd always figured Barry was a step ahead of King Size.

'And by the way,' continued the photographer, 'just in case you're ever tempted to fall on your sword, I've also got a lovely set of twelve-by-eight glossies of a certain High Court judge and Jimmy Fidget down at the Jack Kennedy restaurant. Who'd have thought an under-table camera could pick up so much? Let's just say, Lou's developed a very novel way of flossing between courses …'

Stan's face remained impassive, but his hands were shaking so badly he had to sit on them. There was no way this little hood was going to know how rattled he was. 'Okay,' he nodded slowly. And he pointed over to the Paddy bottle on top of his bookshelves. 'Let's talk some more.'

Back at the offices of the *Derry Standard*, Harry the Hurler was also fighting an uphill battle – to keep his brother in a job.

Even Hugo's legendary tolerance had reached its limit.

'I have been retaining the services of James for a little more than three months now,' explained Hugo nervously. 'During that time he has spent four weeks off on what you euphemistically call "the sick". And he has wasted another fortnight languishing in either the police cells or court. Jimmy is precisely the reason I introduced a six-month probation period for all new recruits. In common parlance, Harry, he's a total fucking liability.'

'But if you fire him now,' argued Harry, 'he'll get jail. No option. We can't even argue that he's a good employee with a secure job.'

'That's because he's not – and he hasn't,' declared Hugo.

'I'll pay his wages,' offered Harry.

'I hate to refuse you,' replied Hugo, 'but only because I'm terrified of you. Listen, Harry, one of the reasons the paper is doing so badly at the moment is because our clientele cannot abide Jimmy. When he's out taking photographs – which granted is rare – he loses us readers by the bagful. He treats the punters like his personal prisoners – abuses them, swears at them and sometimes even strikes them. I sometimes wonder if he thinks he's a cop ...'

Harry laughed, but his old friend wasn't finished.

'When people ring up for a cameraman they specifically ask that we do NOT send Jimmy. But, what we're discovering is that most people don't ring up at all any more. They don't want to take the chance. Your brother, I hate to say this, Harold, is a card-carrying bedlamite. And I don't want him in here. You couldn't pay me to keep him.'

'I've another idea,' grinned Mary Slavin, who'd been sitting quietly nursing her coffee until now. 'Why not offer Jimmy to Stanley out in Dunavady? He seems to have been getting it all his own way for the last few months ...'

'No way,' laughed Stan. 'No way. No way. No way. No way.'

Barry just sat back in the chair opposite his boss and waited, staring at him over his folded hands.

'You want me to give you a year's redundancy from here,' said Stan, 'and then persuade Mary Slavin to take you back into the Derry paper? Plus, you hold onto the negatives. Why shouldn't I just give Harry the money – and get you whacked?'

'Because,' explained Barry carefully, 'there are little packages left, which will be opened immediately in the case of that very eventuality.'

'For the benefit of the tape,' said Stan, thinking ahead, 'I'm not being serious. Nor am I threatening you. I don't get people shot, Barry – contrary to what you've been putting about on your Derry Exposed website. Look, I'll talk to Mary – but I wouldn't hold out any hope.'

'I'm only doing what King Size would have wanted,' smiled Barry. 'Preserving his memory.'

'Be careful what you pray for,' quipped Stan.

'I don't follow,' said Barry.

'Well, you're so wrapped up in your admiration for King Size,' said Stan, 'that you forget how it all worked out for him. Let's face it, Barry, you've got a King Size Barkley complex. You'd love to be just like him. Your car has a personalised number plate, just like his did. You've even got the same make of Ray-Ban glasses that he used to wear and the same type of mobile. In fact the only reason you don't wear Gucci shoes and Armani sports jackets like him is that, when it comes to the push, you're too cheap. But now you figure you're going to make a fortune in business by screwing everyone around you – just like your late great mentor. The problem is, you're missing the sting in the tail.'

'And what's that?' sniffed Barry.

'Actually there are two.'

'And they are?'

'One – everyone hated King Size,' said Stan. 'So much so, someone shot him dead, and when the police went to round up the usual suspects, they had to use the Brandywell stadium.'

'And second?' pressed Barry.

'Second, there are no pockets on a shroud.'

'What do you mean by that?'

'What I mean,' said Stan, 'is that you can't take it with you.'

'Oh,' replied Barry, 'for a second there, I thought you were threatening me again.'

'Not at all,' countered Stan. 'The thing about me, Barry, is that I believe in karma – and I know that you'll eventually get yours without my help ...'

'Stanley won't go for it at all,' declared Hugo, placing his cup carefully on the coaster on Mary's desk. 'Not after that carry-on between Jimmy and Louise. He won't want to be near him. And anyway, I don't want to start more fisticuffs with Stan – not now when there's a chance of a détente.'

'Stan's not coming back, Hugo,' interrupted Mary. 'Well, at least not yet.'

'And why do you say that?' pressed Hugo.

'Because Barry Magee won't let him,' said Mary. 'Stan is his banker – and Barry still has a gun pointed to his head.'

'Why don't you offer to swap Jimmy for Barry, then?' asked Harry. 'Stan will be so happy to get rid of Dirty Dai, he might be prepared to stomach Jimmy – at least until the case is over.'

'Barry Magee makes my skin crawl,' replied Mary abruptly.

'On the other hand,' said Hugo, stroking his chin, 'there's no doubt his vulgar little pictures are selling papers – which, no offence, Mary, we aren't. And furthermore, if Barry's inside the tent, we can keep a better eye on where he's peeing. And maybe even, long term, we can cut off his little waterpipe.'

Harry the Hurler grinned over at the editor, who shook her head in exasperation. 'Sorry, Mary,' he said. 'But it's your own fault for suggesting Jimmy should go to Dunavady. Now all we have to do is explain to the Revenue Commissioners what he was doing with thirty million cigarettes in the boot of his car.'

20

The next morning, Tommy Bowtie rang Harry the Hurler and insisted that he needed to see him in person. So Harry drove out to the lawyer's Dunavady offices, to find his old pal in disconcertingly good form.

'Stan's offered us a deal,' began Tommy, as Harry pulled a green leather swivel-chair up to the desk.

'Go ahead,' nodded Harry.

'The Dunavady Improvement Trust, which operated as the holding company for the Agency, will be fined two million pounds,' said Tommy.

Harry winced.

'This fine, however,' smiled Tommy, 'will be paid out from King Size's estate. Patsy knows that's precisely what he made from the grants and the land deals, so she won't oppose it. You and I, Harry, as the only other named trustees of the DIT, will be asked to pay personal levies of one hundred thousand pounds each, in cognisance of our failure to alert. In return, all threats of criminal charges will be dropped.'

'Christ, that's steep,' groaned Harry.

'Look,' said Tommy softly, 'we're getting out with our trousers on. We'd be crazy to throw it back. I would be struck off if I told you to refuse this deal.'

'But we control the panel,' persisted Harry. 'If we wanted to, we could drop the fines altogether. My councillors will never vote against me.'

'They will if they're directed to from Belfast,' countered Tommy sharply. 'And they will be. It's enough of an embarrassment to the party that you're being hauled before an inquiry. But they'd never forgive you if you were caught trying to fix it for a lousy hundred grand. The inquiry is making sure that King Size – and he alone – takes the full hit. The Boys' capital investment is safe. Besides, everyone in town reckons that a hundred Gs is exactly what you stuck in your own pocket, for brokerage fees.'

Harry chewed hard on a thumbnail, before exhaling deeply in agreement. 'And what about you?' he asked Tommy. 'Where are you going to get that sort of cash?'

'Coincidentally,' said Tommy, 'a hundred grand is pretty much to the penny what I'll get when I cash in my various directorships of the late Mr Barkley's companies.'

'Wow,' sighed Harry. 'It's almost like Stan's got a camera planted in both our wallets and has worked out exactly what we can pay.'

'No doubt about it,' replied Tommy. 'He knows what we can afford – and he knows exactly the lowest number the inquiry will settle for.'

'No liability – no bad press?' asked Harry.

'Absolutely none,' asserted Tommy. 'It all dies a death as soon as we admit our negligence and pay the fines. He has all the documents ready to hang the whole lot on King Size. Quote, unquote: "I'll make heroes of the pair of you".'

'And what of Stan?' asked Harry.

'Well,' said Tommy, 'Senator Stevenson recoups two-point-two million pounds for the Exchequer and saves about four times that much in inquiry fees. He'll be the greatest thing since the see-through bra.'

'Jesus,' grinned Harry, 'who'd have thought it? Stan's got a real knack for this politics stuff.'

'Truth is,' said Tommy, 'he was very worried about all the witnesses to the tribunal developing CRAFT syndrome. Apparently, it's become very common at all the other inquiries …'

'CRAFT syndrome – what's that?'

'Can't Remember A Fucking Thing.'

'Okay so,' laughed Harry. 'Well, I suppose we better pay the man before he changes his mind.'

Superintendent Audrey Grafton wasn't normally one for social calls, but when a senior judge rings up and asks to meet you for a coffee and a chat, you tend to put on your best coat and hat. There's no saying when you might need a friend in court.

The pair had bagged a window seat in Scott's café. Four floors up, they had a panoramic view of the city, the river, and about a dozen little lowlifes who were buying and selling drugs at the war memorial below.

Audrey still preferred to dress in civvies when she was doing business about the town – officially because it was less conspicuous. Unofficially, however, she was well aware that there wasn't another forty-year-old in the country who looked as well in a Roland Mouret pinstripe suit. Letemout Lou, on the other hand, only ever dressed up for court, and was sitting opposite her in a plain white T-shirt and blue Levi jeans. A pair of Jimmy Choo ankle boots was her only concession to fashion.

'Can I cut to the chase?' asked Lou as Audrey took the two little coffeepots from the tray and set them on the table.

'You want to know if he did it,' replied the policewoman evenly.

Lou looked sharply across at her companion, not knowing whether to be offended or burst out laughing. So she chose the latter. 'Men must love you,' she grinned.

'Why's that?' asked Audrey.

'You just sail through foreplay, right into the game.'

Audrey held up her hands in acknowledgement. 'Most men find me a little intimidating.' She sighed. 'They don't appreciate the direct approach ... Anyhow, as regards whether the senator plugged King Size, truth is – I'm not sure. I know now it wasn't Mrs Barkley – or I'm fairly certain at least. We've just found a witness putting her in a bakery in Belfast an hour and fifteen minutes after the shooting. Now it's still just about possible, if you're a rally driver. But she's not. Nor has she the connections to organise something like this. Between ourselves, she couldn't organise a dozen stout ...'

Lou chuckled at the apt description of King Size's stunningly dim wife.

'I'm also pretty confident it wasn't Harry and the Boys,' continued Audrey. 'I'm not saying they mightn't benefit – they're already moving in on King Size's street-market franchise. But politically, it's far too delicate. To be honest, if

I were putting money on Harry to whack anyone at the moment, it would be his own brother.'

'So that brings us back to Stan,' replied Lou, looking down into her mug. 'Could he have got someone up from Dublin to do the dirty work while he was up at Radio Foyle broadcasting to the nation?'

'It's possible,' answered Audrey. 'But again, if I'm to be brutally honest with you, Lou, this isn't what you might term a priority case. I'm only sorry we didn't get a chance to hang King Size with due process. But for the minute there's no one down in Strand Road who's missing him — and there's no outcry for a full investigation, so I'm not going to lose any sleep over it. We've damn all evidence pointing to anybody, so the case is as good as closed.'

'But you can't go around just killing people,' protested Lou. 'You of all people, Audrey, must know that.'

'Yeah,' said Audrey, 'but just imagine if they'd taken out Hitler ten years earlier. I'll level with you, Lou, if I had seen Stanley whacking King Size, I'm not sure I would have tried to stop him.'

'But it's not in his nature,' insisted Lou a little too quickly.

'Aha,' grinned Audrey, who'd been waiting for the chink. 'You're of course worried it might be hereditary ...'

'I've nothing to do with him,' sniffed Lou.

'Twenty-five years is a lot of nothing,' said the older woman softly. 'Look, for what it's worth, I think Stan is a great guy. But equally, I cannot sit here and tell you he absolutely did not do it. Why don't you ask him?'

Lou chewed on her lip pensively, then looked directly at Audrey. 'I can't ask him,' she sighed. 'If he did it, and he told me, it's the end of everything. And if he didn't do it, and I can't believe him, it's the end of everything.'

'So, what if he tells you he didn't do it, and you just believe him anyway?' grinned Audrey. 'After all, it's what ninety-nine per cent of marriages are built on.'

'How's the new job?' Harry the Hurler asked his brother, as Jimmy pulled up a high stool beside him at the Jack Kennedy bar.

'Christ but they're tough operators,' said Jimmy, motioning to the barmaid for a pint of what Harry was having. 'They remind me of the time you and Teddy Bigmouth, God rest his soul, ran that wee training camp down the Poison Glen. One smart remark and Teddy would crack you on the jaw with the butt of a rifle. Jesus, is it any wonder we were queuing up to nut him, the day we finally caught him touting.'

Harry quickly looked around to see who was behind him, but there was nobody.

Jimmy watched the panic leave his brother's face and smiled. 'Seriously though, they've no mercy out there,' he continued. 'There's days I think I'm back in prison – but at least there, the guards had manners. Stan spoke to me just once, the day I started. Nine words: "Fuck up one time, and you go to jail". I suppose at least he's not a hypocrite ... He's away to Dublin tomorrow – getting ready for his inception. But Ivan Coultron, the news editor, is even worse. A total bastard. They say he's the only man ever thrown out of the BBC for being too unpleasant. He told me, straight out, I was a lowlife gangster and he didn't want me in the newsroom. He said Stan had only taken me in because he owed Mary Slavin a bagful of favours. But he warned me if he had one complaint about me, he had Stan's full permission to kick my arse out the door.' He shucked back a mouthful of stout and heaved a big sigh. 'They're not going to give me a contract – ever. And if I take off any time at all, they're going to dock it from my wages.'

Harry nodded sympathetically. 'Welcome to the real world, Jimmy,' he said. 'I'm afraid your long and glorious career as a hero of the revolution is over. You've no weight to throw around any more. So suck it up and do your job. You might even enjoy it. You had your chances, and you blew them. Same as you did with Letemout Lou.'

Jimmy lowered his head and massaged his brow with his right hand, like he was trying to rub away a migraine. 'You know I can't help myself sometimes, Harry,' he said.

'I know, son,' replied his brother gently. 'I know only too well. Look, we all got hurt ...'

'But she was only a little girl,' said Jimmy. 'Eight years old, and we – or, I should say, *I* – sent a mortar right through her bedroom window.'

'You've paid your dues, Jimmy,' said Harry. 'Fourteen years of them – and then you made peace with her family. Or as much as they'd let you. It's time to let it go. The war's over, Jimmy. Time to make a new start.'

'But I keep messing up everything,' snapped Jimmy. 'Just like you say. Losing jobs, losing friends – losing women.'

'Lou was never for you,' grinned Harry. 'You knew it was only to slow you down a little. And besides, there's only one man for her – God love her wit. But you have to keep trying, Jimmy. Keep taking the knocks. The only time you really lose is when you don't get up again. If I were you, I might just start flashing my baby-blues at Susie Short Shorts. She's a fine-looking woman, but she likes her men to have a few rough edges. And she's always had a thing for you …'

Jimmy looked sideways at Harry, then smiled. 'Stan Stevenson is looking for a parachute, isn't he?' he mused.

'I don't know that for sure,' laughed Harry, 'but I do think that this time you'd be doing your new boss a big favour …'

21

Sonny booked Stan into the Herbert Park Hotel to give him a chance to unwind the night before his inauguration. Susie Short Shorts would be driving down in the morning, after Stan told her he needed some time alone to get his head together. Susie knew that she'd been working on borrowed time since Letemout Lou disposed of Jimmy Fidget. But there was no damn way she was missing her chance to meet the Taoiseach.

Inside the presidential suite, Sonny was pacing up and down irritably in the living room, while Stan lay back on the Manhattan four-seater sofa, sipping too much brandy and asking too many questions.

'So,' he said, 'what you're telling me, Sonny, is that I should sign in on Wednesday and Thursday mornings, spend a couple of hours reading the newspapers, keep my mouth shut, and they'll send me out eight hundred quid pay and expenses on a Friday evening?'

Sonny put his head in his hands as if he were about to weep. 'Stop it,' he snapped. 'You're fucking torturing me here, Stan. I know you're wound up, but could you ever stop with the sarcastic remarks and listen for a minute.'

'I'm sorry, Sonny,' grinned the senator. 'Christ, I really wish Lou were here with me. She's the only one who's able to take the edge off me when I'm nervous …'

Sonny glanced at him sideways, paused, then shook his head: 'Not even for you, Stan.'

They both laughed.

'Basically,' explained Sonny. 'The Senate is a watchdog body – but you can instigate new bills as well, as long as they don't cost the Treasury money. There are sixty senators in all – forty-nine elected from vocational panels and eleven appointees, such as yourself. Your real influence comes in the Joint Committees where you work with the deputies from the Dáil, tailoring and refining legislation. You're privileged and are going to be appointed to two. Rubber John is going to stick you on the Foreign Affairs Committee and Joxer wants you on the Family Matters group. So you'll be as busy as you want.'

'What about bringing in new legislation?' interrupted Stan.

'As regards the law-making side of things, there might be an opportunity for you to introduce the issue of giving Northerners votes in the presidential election,' replied Sonny noncommittally. 'That's if the Taoiseach decides not to take it to the Dáil first. Which is looking more and more likely.'

Stan smirked. 'Jesus. Votes for Northerners. That could be dangerous – they could elect someone like me.'

'We don't care,' smiled his friend. 'As long as it's not Joxer.' Sonny looked at his watch and nodded towards the door. 'I've a paper to finish reading for the morning, so if you don't mind I'm going to leave you with your drinking. Why don't you do yourself a favour and ring Lou?'

Stan looked at him soberly. 'I just wish I could, Sonny. But tonight, I don't think she'd thank me. Next time. I promise.'

Stan wasn't the only one in need of cheering up. Back in Derry, Harry was calling up to Lou's suite in the Jack Kennedy to try and put her nose back into joint. If only Cinderella hadn't told the prince to go fuck himself.

'Come in, Harry,' she yelled, as he rapped gently on the door. 'I'd cut you a key, except you already have one.'

Lou was slumped in her brown leather recliner, pretending to read a brief. There was a forty-ounce flagon of Paddy, half empty, on the coffee table at her elbow. Lou had already announced her intentions by throwing the bottle-top into the waste-paper bin.

'It's only the Senate,' said Harry, sitting tentatively on the armchair opposite. 'They've no power. It's not as if it's real politics.'

'Don't try and soft-soap me, Harry,' snorted Lou. 'Two

senators, Hyde and Robinson, went on to be president.'

'So what?' retorted Harry contemptuously. 'You know as
well as I do that the real pros go into the Dáil. Your problem,
Lou, is that you don't know whether to be proud of Stan or
jealous of him. But trust me – you've a much bigger future
than the Senate, whenever you get into the game.'

Lou pulled herself up to a sitting position and proffered
Harry the bottle, gesturing towards some tumblers on the
bureau. Harry poured himself close to half a pint, figuring that
his friend's liver could do with all the help it could get.

'You do know, by the way,' he went on, 'that Hyde was
lacerated when he was in the Senate. He was hit so badly by
smears that he lost his seat. The Catholic Truth Society, lying
bastards, told everyone he was pro-divorce, because he was a
Prod ... It's a dirty game, Lou. Stan's welcome to it.'

Lou just shook her head sadly. 'It's not any of that, Harry,'
she said quietly. 'Truth is, I'm so proud of him and I just wish
I was standing beside him tomorrow when he takes his bows.
I hate to miss it. Hate it. There's a real finality to all this.'

'The show's not over till Oprah sings,' answered Harry
with a soft grin. 'There'll be other days for you and Stan, Lou.
I promise.'

As things turned out, Stan's debut at the Seanad was a quiet
affair. Senator Jim Wynne, a dwarfish, rabbit-toothed
Corkonian who was O'Duffy's Finance spokesman, met Stan
and Susie at the Kildare Street entrance and quickly brought
them into the entrance hall. The lobby featured portraits of
Collins and Cathal Brugha – and an original copy of the Easter
Proclamation – but they had barely time to look at them
before they were whisked upstairs, through the Seanad ante-
room and into the chamber. 'It used to be a ballroom, when
the Duke of Leinster had the house,' explained Wynne. 'Now,
when we've a full house, you'll find there is no ball room. Ha!
Ha!' Stan blushed with embarrassment for the man.

Senators began drifting in from the coffee dock, and a bell
was rung calling the room to order. As business began, the
chairman briefly welcomed the new member 'Stanley
MacStiofáin from Derry'. But there was no swearing-in

ceremony and, after a nod from Jim Wynne, Stan was nominated on to his two committees without a vote.

The new senator then made a brief maiden speech proposing a cross-border school dental survey. The Committee of Eight had baulked at the idea initially, until Sonny Waterhouse pointed out that tooth decay in the North was so bad, the survey would make it much easier for them to retain fluoridation in the South.

'It'll stop those lefty environmentalists from whingeing on again,' he told Joxer, who eventually assented.

After about an hour of speeches – none of which appeared to relate to one another – the chairman announced a smoke break, and the members dived for the door.

'We need you to be a good strong voice on these joint committees,' declared Wynne, as he left the room with Stan. 'Too many damn pinkos and Fenian-lovers about. No offence, senator.'

'None taken,' grinned Stan.

After a whistle-stop tour of the Leinster House committee rooms, and a thirty-second meet, greet and photo with Rubber John, it was time for lunch. Susie wanted to try the Members' Restaurant, but Joxer had offered Stan a table at the Shelbourne Hotel around the corner, so he felt obliged to make good on the offer. But just as he and Susie were rounding the corner on to Stephen's Green at the top of Kildare Street, they heard a girl hollering after them from the direction of Grafton Street.

'Stanley Stevenson, get over here, you big rip,' yelled the happy voice. And Susie gawped as a very expensively dressed young woman ran towards the senator and flung her arms around him.

'Eva – is that you?' grinned Stan, wondering how the hell he was going to start explaining this twenty-year-old blonde model to Susie.

He needn't have worried.

'I heard you'd been nominated,' said Eva, 'and I just wished to pass on congratulations on behalf of everyone at Dublin South West.'

She turned to Susie and explained, 'We were having our annual constituency dinner at the Gresham Hotel the weekend of Stan's stag night ...You must be the lucky woman?'

'Ouch,' said Stan with a grin, 'and you were doing so well, Eva. No. This is my friend Susie. I'm afraid the wedding thing didn't work out.'

'Jesus that's a shame, Stan,' said Eva, disoriented. 'I don't think I ever met a man as serious about his fiancée before ... All you did was talk about her all night.'

'You're absolutely killing me here, Eva,' laughed Stan, trying to shut her up. 'What about yourself? What are you at? You look a whole lot better than the last time I saw you ...'

'Yeah,' she smiled. 'But I've the diabetes back in check now. Late nights and messed-up sugar levels leave me looking like shit. Not to mention the moodiness from aggressive hypoglycaemia – worse than PMT. God knows what I'd be like if I took a drink ...'

Diabetes. It hit him like a shot. The needle marks. Jesus, poor King Size died after the longest dry spell of his life and it was all because of Eva's insulin deficiency. Stan couldn't help grinning.

'What about work?' he asked her mischievously.

'I'm still working full-time for the party,' she smiled, giving him a mock salute. 'Though actually, I'm doing more and more acting in my free time. I've done a couple of TV commercials – mostly this side of the border. Though we shot one in Derry a couple of months back. I've an agent now who reckons he can get me some film work. Good stuff too.'

'You've certainly got the looks for it,' said Susie, eager to forgive Eva for the New Bride fiasco.

'The hard part was breaking into the agencies,' explained Eva. 'I spent thousands on portfolios and getting into the shop window. But, touch wood, I'm pretty much there now. All being well, I'll be able to give up my office job in about three months' time.

'Look Stan, if you're going to be in Dublin, here's my card. And be sure and use it. And don't worry, Susie, I'll not let him near any of those young Dublin vamps ... Anyway, I must fly. Bye.'

Stan looked at the card, memorised the number quickly, and put it in the pocket of his Crombie. It was just as well.

'Give it to me,' said Susie as they went into the foyer of the Shelbourne.

'No,' said Stan.

'Give me the card,' repeated Susie.

'But I might need it,' he protested. 'She's a party officer.'

'No she's not,' retorted Susie. 'She's the prostitute you slept with on your stag night. King Size was showing the photos of her with Danny Boy Gillespie around the bar one night after you shafted him over the inquiry story.'

'Ah,' said Stan quietly. 'But you're wrong, you know. I didn't sleep with her.'

'Tell it to the judge,' quipped Susie. And they both laughed.

22

Stan's appointment to the all-Ireland Sexual Health Awareness Group had, of course, been Joxer's idea. The Dún Laoghaire deputy summoned the new man to his Dáil office the Wednesday after the Easter break to deliver the news.

'There's too much left-wing bullshit on this committee,' explained Joxer. 'SHAG wants to give every student a packet of condoms when they start college, and another pack every rag week. They've also produced a little booklet for young couples – complete with diagrams – called *50 Things You Can Try and Still Not Get Pregnant.*'

'Where were you all my life?' muttered Stan. Though not loud enough for Joxer to hear.

'What we need from you, Senator Stevenson,' continued Joxer, 'is someone to promote good family values on the committee. You Northerners have a reputation of being upright and moral people. It's the influence of all the Prods, no doubt. And I need someone who can go on the committee and talk passionately about our three core values – marriage, abstinence and the rhythm method.'

Nought for three there, thought Stan.

'I'm not quite sure I'm your man, Joxer,' said Stan, making a pained face. 'I've always been a bit of a fun-loving bachelor. I'd hate for you to wind up with egg on your face …'

Joxer groaned. 'We're talking skeletons here?' he asked.

'I'm afraid so,' replied Stan, grimacing.

'How bad?'

'Bad as it goes,' sighed Stan. 'A picture of me in bed with a naked hooker on my stag night – but on my word of honour, I didn't touch her. The guys waited till I was asleep and snuck her into my bed. Was the end of the wedding though.'

'Hmmm,' said Joxer, thinking hard. 'Well, we've no option then. You'll have to play the convert. A man on the road to ruin who saw the light. A sinner who fought the temptations of the flesh and ultimately overcame them … Course, you'll have to announce your intentions towards that new lady friend of yours – and quickly. Shouldn't be a problem though. She looks like she can't wait to get a ring on her finger.'

This is not going well, thought Stan. Time to be a bit creative.

'There's another little snag, Joxer,' he confessed. 'I'm afraid, well, I'm afraid I can't marry her …'

'Why not?' asked Joxer.

'Because I don't love her.'

'But sure what's that got to do with anything?'

'Well, it's the reason I don't love her.'

'And what's that?'

'You want the truth?'

'Oh yes,' said Joxer, 'I need the truth.'

Stan took a deep breath. 'Well,' he answered, 'strictly between ourselves, Joxer … I prefer men.'

Joxer gasped in disbelief. 'You're an arse-bandit?' he whispered.

Stan bowed his head in shame. 'I'm afraid so,' he said.

'Well, that's just fucking perfect.'

'The good news, though,' continued Stan quickly, 'is that nobody knows. Not a single person other than you, me and a Croatian friend I go on cruises with every September.'

'What about Susie – and your ex-fiancée?' protested Joxer.

'Not a clue,' sighed Stan. 'I even go through some of the motions for them, but my heart's never been in it … Look, Joxer, I've hidden it now for fifteen years – and I'm fighting it all the time. The only reason I told you, well, is because I don't want to let you down. I'd prefer to be up front with you from the start. And I can assure you that no one, I repeat no one, will ever suspect that I'm anything but a happy-go-lucky ladies' man playing the field.'

'Jesus, Stan, it's an awful cross you have to carry,' said Joxer, shaking his head sympathetically. 'But if it's any consolation, you're not the first man I met who's wrestling with this demon. And I may just be able to help you. There's a friend of mine, Monsignor George Behan, who trained with the Jesuits in New York. He's done some work for me before – and come up trumps every time. I'll fix you up with an appointment with him for next week.'

'What exactly does he do?' asked Stan, a little baffled.

'Oh don't worry,' replied Joxer, 'he's a qualified psychiatrist.'

'A psychiatrist?' interjected Stan.

'That's right.' Joxer nodded. 'A psychiatrist, who specialises in curing arse-bandits …'

Sonny Waterhouse couldn't wait to tell Rubber John. When Stan had recounted what Joxer had arranged, Sonny had laughed so hard the Guinness ran out his nose. He'd met Stan for teatime stout in Doheny & Nesbitt's – and, immediately he heard the story, dialled the boss on his mobile.

'Jesus,' chuckled Rubber John, 'I've heard about this guy. Bend'em-Back Behan, they call him. He wires up your bits and then shows you pictures of the Chippendales. If anything moves, you get twenty thousand volts right through your charlie.'

'I'm not going,' declared Stan, snatching the phone from Sonny. 'I'm going to see Joxer tomorrow and confess everything.'

'What are you going to do, Stan?' retorted the Taoiseach. 'Fall on your sword? He'll be very disappointed – he'll be expecting you to fall on his.'

'That's it,' snapped Stan. 'I resign. I'm off to join the fucking PDs.'

'Not a bad idea,' laughed the Taoiseach. 'Plenty of opportunities there for an uptight single man …'

'I mean it,' said Stan. 'Nobody is wiring me up to anything.'

'Stanley, Stanley, I'm only codding,' replied the Taoiseach softly. 'And anyway, Monsignor Behan's not too bad … Besides, electric shock treatment went out with the ark.'

'Glad to hear it,' declared Stan.

'Yeah,' said Rubber John, 'but watch out for his big wooden hammer …'

Stan laughed in spite of himself.

'The one good thing about all this,' the Taoiseach went on, 'is that Joxer won't breathe a word of this to anyone. You're now established as his protégé – and he'd be absolutely terrified of becoming a bandit by association. So, settle yourself, and have a pint on me. Better make it a glass actually – given your condition, and all.'

'Bastard,' laughed Stan. But he was gone.

23

One of the benefits of the new political dispensation in the North was that Superintendent Audrey Grafton could now meet publicly with Harry the Hurler without anyone assuming there was a conspiracy afoot. Truth was, they were old associates – friends, nearly. Many years ago, Harry's sister Donna had married a cop – Jack Gilmore – and over time the Hurleys had become quite fond of him. Began to trust him too. So if there were ever very delicate matters that could be squared quickly and privately, instead of wasting everybody's time in courts, Jack would arrange for Audrey and Harry to get together for a private confab. Like, for example, the time Jimmy Fidget was snagged at a checkpoint with an unlicensed gun in his car. On this occasion, Audrey was able to assure her commanders that she had given the wink to the Boys' pro-truce lobby to carry pistols as personal protection. In turn, Harry would, equally quietly, give the odd nod to Audrey as to where the anti-truce brigade were stashing their blow-pipes. So her strike rate tended to be just that little bit better than the other regional commanders'.

They were very alike, Harry and Audrey. They were both in their forties – Audrey just entering, Harry just departing – both had strong good looks, and they both conducted themselves with the easy authority of born leaders. Needless to say, there was a spark there too, but one they never talked about. Harry's wife Lorna had spotted it the first day and warned him if he acted on it, Audrey would become the first copper to investigate her own homicide.

This meeting today was on Audrey's nickel. She wanted to do a little fishing for Letemout Lou and, truth be known, for herself.

'You're looking super, Super,' smiled Harry as Audrey – wearing a sleek silk trouser suit – came into the big snug at the back of the Jack Kennedy lounge.

She took his outstretched hand and kissed him flirtatiously on the cheek. 'No eyeing up the goods, until you can afford to cash that cheque,' she grinned.

Harry handed her a lunch menu and sat back onto the couch. 'You want to talk about King Size,' he began.

'What, straight to business?' Audrey replied, raising her eyes disappointedly.

'Yeah,' sighed Harry. 'But sure, you don't do small talk …'

'You mean you're not allowed,' sniffed Audrey. And they both laughed.

'Okay,' she went on. 'Tell me, who shot the little toad?'

'I don't honestly know,' answered Harry. 'It wasn't us – and the reason you can be sure it wasn't is that he was worth more to us alive than dead. Pure and simple. We had a nice stake in several of his companies, which the new Widow Barkley is not too keen to honour. Fair enough, we got the street markets, but Patsy shut down a few of his other sidelines – despite the fact that they were damn good earners.'

'Okay,' said Audrey. 'But what about this idea it could have been pros from Dublin?'

'I'm not gone on that theory either,' Harry replied. 'We've our own network down there, and we'd have heard something. So if Stan did it, he kept it very tight. Besides, Stanley is very straight-laced. Back in the old days, he always made it very clear to me he didn't approve of our non-political activities. I can't see him suddenly turning rogue.'

'What about Letemout Lou?' Audrey pressed. 'Could she have done it?'

'No chance,' declared Harry. 'She hated King Size with a vengeance all right. But there's a malevolent streak in Lou, and she'd much rather have seen him rot in jail.'

The waitress knocked on the snug door to take their orders. They both plumped for the club sandwich with a glass of white.

'If only I could explain those last two bullets,' said Audrey as the door swung closed again.

'Why's that?' inquired Harry.

'Well,' replied Audrey, 'other than that, it's the clearest case of suicide I've ever seen.'

Harry laughed. 'You're forgetting one person,' he said.

'Who's that?' asked Audrey, puzzled.

'Barry Magee. His little sideline is starting to pay out bucks. Big bucks. But the word is that it was cutting a little too close to some of King Size's business, and Mr Barkley was about to shut him down.'

'Barry wouldn't have the nerve,' countered Audrey, daring Harry to produce more.

'Why not shake the tree and see what drops?' said Harry. 'The very least you're going to get is a stack of dirty pictures of the great and the good.'

'And what use are they to me?' retorted the policewoman.

'Jesus, I'm disappointed in you, Audrey,' laughed Harry. 'The man's a professional shakedown artist. Let's just say that once you get your hands on Barry's portfolio, you'll get a lot less bother from all those sore-heads on the Police Liaison Committee. Excuse me, councillor, is that you in the fishnets with the four-foot rubber attachment – or have you just withdrawn your stupid fucking question …?'

An hour later, Jimmy Fidget was having a sandwich and a glass of milk on his own at the bar counter (drinking on duty being a no-no at the new office) when Susie Short Shorts came in to start her shift. She hadn't seen him since the cops released him, so she greeted him with a big hug.

Jimmy had been her late husband's chief aide and collector for a year. But he'd made it clear from the off that he wouldn't cover for Sparkly when he was running around behind Susie's back. Which was often. As far as Jimmy was concerned, Mrs B was his friend and if anyone crossed her, he'd deal with them just as surely and as thoroughly as he'd deal with anyone who crossed his brother. So Sparkly kept his indiscretions away from Jimmy, and they got along just fine.

Susie, in turn, liked the fact that Jimmy was always straight with her – he must have told her to leave her no-good thief of a husband about a thousand times. Even when Sparkly was in the room. Jimmy never dressed things up. He shot from the hip. It was the same with his illness – he knew he was cracked and didn't try and pretend otherwise. 'It's like this, Suze,' he used to say to her, 'we all have our own wee ways of going mad. It's just some of us aren't as good at hiding them.'

The lunchtime crowd had mostly drifted off, so Susie poured herself a coffee from the glass pot and sat down on the empty barstool beside Jimmy.

'How's things with yourself and the senator?' he asked her.

'He's looking for a soft landing.' She shrugged matter-of-factly. 'Not his fault. He's still hung up on Letemout. I keep telling myself I'm wasting my time. But I'm having a lot of fun. Even if there's no future in it.'

'He's a fool who doesn't know when he's well off,' grinned Jimmy. 'Maybe it's not you at all. Maybe now he's in Dublin every week, some of those big-city ways are rubbing off on him – if you follow my drift. You never know with these sensitive types …'

'Not Stanley,' laughed Susie. 'In fact it's my only consolation. And a very regular consolation at that.'

'Yeah, I suppose,' smiled Jimmy. 'I mean, would you date Letemout Lou if you'd a valid excuse not to?'

'You're one to talk,' countered Susie, slapping his arm. 'From what I hear, Barry Magee's got a stack of photos of you and Her Honour, how will I put this, swapping oral arguments *in camera*.'

'Really?' said Jimmy, surprised. 'I didn't know that.' He was silent for a moment, and then frowned. 'The little bastard,' he said, shaking his head. 'It doesn't surprise me. Barry's probably looking for a little judicial leverage down the road. He shouldn't involve me in it though. I don't like that sort of thing at all. Maybe I'll go and talk to him.'

'No don't,' insisted Susie. 'Let it be. Stan said he's going to sort him out.'

'I wouldn't count on it,' said Jimmy, smiling again. 'But I'll leave it for the moment – if you say so.'

Tommy Bowtie was particularly thrilled to be in Letemout Lou's office that same evening. It wasn't that she was pouring the whiskey with reckless abandon; this was par for the course for Lou in recent weeks. Nor was it that she was telling a whole range of scurrilous stories about hardman Jimmy Fidget and his off-stage nervous breakdowns. These yarns had been doing the rounds for years – though, in fairness, Lou did have the personal insight.

No, Lou's generosity had always been legendary, and her conversation had always been sparkling. But tonight, Tommy had an exceptionally good reason to be glad of her company. And it was this. Ten minutes before he had gone upstairs to meet Lou, he'd come across Barry Magee in the downstairs lobby of the Jack Kennedy. And, other than the funeral, it was the first time he'd seen the little shit since he tried to blackmail him. So Tommy had snuck up behind him while he was taking a picture of a group of business leaders and punched him as hard as he could on the back of the head, catapulting him into the stone pillar at reception.

As Barry was lying bleeding on the marble floor, Tommy spat on him and, in front of the entire Chamber of Commerce, told him, 'Next time I see you, I'll fucking kill you.'

Tommy then fixed his tie and bounded up the stairs towards Lou's office on the first floor. Which is where he was an hour later, when he and Lou heard the shots. Two minutes later and their pagers beeped at almost exactly the same time – Hugo had texted them both. 'Barry M's just been stiffed,' read the message.

Thank God, thought Tommy.

If there was ever a time to be caught having a drink with a High Court judge, this was it.

24

This time there wasn't even a discussion; the undertakers had to carry the coffin themselves. Stan – who had been in Dublin when Barry got shot – refused to attend any part of the funeral, as did Harry and the Boys. Uncle Hugo was obliged to attend, as officially Barry had been out on a job for him when he was killed.

But what no one was saying publicly was that Barry had been making one of his regular house calls to the city's favourite dogging spot, at the Baywater Industrial Estate, when he got caught – literally – with his trousers down.

Other than that, the m.o. was virtually identical to King Size's: two bullets in the heart and one in the right eye. Though this time, the killer or killers had a bit of time, and scattered a thousand pounds in ten-pound notes around the inside of the car – £940 of which had been recovered.

A week to the day after the murder, Audrey Grafton had broadcast a renewed radio appeal for anyone who might have been in the Baywater area at the time to contact the police. She wasn't holding out any hope.

'You can just picture it now,' she sighed. '"You know when I was out getting the milk last night, dearest? Well, on my way home, I just called past Baywater to get some air, and some no-strings-attached sex. And now the police want to talk to me. What do you think I should do?"'

Tommy Bowtie smirked the smirk of the guy with the best alibi in the city and poured out two cups of tea from the pot his secretary had just left on the desk.

'So, Tommy, what did you want to see me for anyway?' said Audrey, cutting as ever to the chase.

Tommy unlocked his desk drawer and produced an

unmarked file, which he handed across to Audrey. She opened it and stopped abruptly. It contained just one item and one item only: an eight-by-six glossy of herself and Harry the Hurler. And it appeared to show Audrey leaning over to kiss the chief executive of the Boys affectionately on the cheek, while he patted her backside goodbye.

'Barry took that the day he was killed,' said Tommy. 'He'd a remote spy camera set up in the Jack Kennedy snug ... He could have got ten grand for it off a national – or maybe a little more from yourself and Harry. But, thank God, someone with a bit of sense broke into Barry's flat and emptied all his files before your lot got in.'

The Superintendent was outraged. 'Jesus Christ,' she protested. 'You and I both know, Tommy, this is totally innocent ....'

'Tell that to Lorna Hurley,' retorted Tommy. And his eyes danced as Audrey's face lit up like a furnace.

'Don't worry,' he continued. 'I have the negative safely stored away ... One more thing though. Over the next couple of weeks, you'll probably get a few letters from Barry – from beyond the grave. He wrote them to be sent in the event of his sudden death – he even stashed one with me for a time.'

'I'd heard that,' replied Audrey carefully.

'Well,' said Tommy, 'both you and I know that these letters will contain wild accusations – and nothing remotely amounting to proof.'

'Maybe,' answered Audrey, not liking where this was going.

'At the very best,' said Tommy, 'they're going to cause considerable embarrassment to some people who you know for certain, Audrey, had nothing to do with this awful crime. And all of us, Audrey, could do without that sort of embarrassment.'

The Superintendent quickly mulled over the deal Tommy was putting to her and nodded. 'Fair enough,' she told him, 'each of us will look after our own dirty linen privately. And I'll stick to the facts. But let me tell you this, Tommy. I've now had two murders on my patch in the past month, and nothing remotely approaching anybody's arse in a sling. If I catch this Dirty Harry, I'll bang him up for good – even if he is a senator …'

'Understood,' said Tommy, and he handed her an envelope for her photograph.

Two days later, Hugo Stevenson convened an emergency meeting of the *Derry Standard*'s board of directors in the upstairs conference room of the paper's William Street offices. There was only one item for discussion. The *North-West Standard* was looking for a new owner, and Tommy Bowtie, as the paper's company secretary, had rung Hugo to alert him.

Mary Slavin and Letemout Lou arrived bang on time at 7.30 p.m., Mary letting in Lou at the front door. Hugo was already inside. As a matter of form, he'd invited Stan as well – the only other shareholder. But according to Stan's secretary, he was still in Dublin attending a late session of a joint committee. And besides, Stan hadn't set foot in the offices in more than three months.

'He's not coming?' asked Lou, as she picked up the minute pad.

'No,' replied Hugo, shaking his head sadly. 'Senate business. The Sexual Health Action Group – of all things. I've tried him three or four times, but he's not returning my calls.'

'What's his problem?' asked Lou. 'Does he not like the colour of our money? Is he expecting us to apologise before he'll do business with us again?'

'No,' replied Mary quietly. 'He doesn't want us to apologise – just you, Lou.'

'Well he can go whistle,' snapped the judge. 'He left us. Not the other way about.

'How much is he looking for anyway? What'll it take to buy him out?'

Hugo paused, folded his hands on the mahogany table in front of him and glanced briefly at each of his two colleagues. 'Not a damn thing,' he said. 'He's offering us the whole thing, free gratis – as long as we guarantee to maintain it, and the staff, as a going concern for two years.'

'Jesus,' said Lou, 'but the Irish Media Institute valued it only last week at three million. It's the hottest new start in a decade. Stan's pulling in advertising hand over fist – and sales are going through the roof.'

'I know,' nodded Hugo. 'But Tommy Bowtie says Stan is becoming more and more involved in his political career and doesn't want the new paper to suffer. He knows that both titles are going to come his way, anyway, as soon as the gin does its job on me. So this will do away with a whole lot of paperwork. The way I see it, we can run our own paper as the city edition and Stan's as a county edition. We'll even have the office in Dunavady.'

'What about Patsy Barkley's share?' pressed Lou.

'She signed it over to Stan for a peppercorn fee,' explained Hugo. 'She knew King Size had been extorting him, and wanted to make it up to him. Besides, she has absolutely no interest in the media. If it's not in *Hello!*, she doesn't want to know.'

'One thing we'll need, though, and urgently,' interrupted Mary.

'What's that?' asked Hugo.

'A new photographer,' she replied. 'We can leave Jimmy Fidget out in Dunavady – Ivan's got him on a very tight leash. But we've been finding ourselves very stretched here in Derry – ever since Barry got what was coming to him.'

'Are you going to advertise?' asked Lou.

'Not on your life,' laughed Mary. 'The last time we did that, I spent a month looking through two thousand out-of-focus portfolios, and about the same number of family albums. And I still wound up with Barry Fucking Magee. No, Gigi McCormack – Switchblade Vic's daughter – is back in town and she's looking for a job.'

Hugo and Mary both looked over at Lou. It didn't have to be said. Stan had made the suggestion via Tommy, and it was a done deal.

'But isn't she a physiotherapist?' asked Lou.

'Yep,' said Mary, 'but she was also head of the Londonderry Camera Society – and used to do a lot of freelance work for me at football matches. She's very good – plus, whisper it carefully, she's a Planter, so she'll make a little hole in our Unfair Employment figures.'

'Okay so,' said Hugo, 'let's try her out. Start her on a junior wage and we'll see how it goes.'

'You're all heart,' laughed Mary. 'But I'll start her as a senior – to give us a decent chance of hanging on to her.'

'Any other business so?' said Hugo, closing up his file.

'Just one thing,' boomed a voice from the hall. 'Do you not think it's about time you changed the locks downstairs? All sorts of lowlifes have got keys ...'

And with that Senator Stan Stevenson strode through the doorway, walked to the end of the table, bent down and hugged his uncle.

'I'm sorry I'm late,' he declared when Hugo released him. 'But I've spent the past hour on the phone trying to persuade the House Chairman that I'm not quite the right man to head up the new All-Ireland Pre-Marital Chastity Drive.'

Hugo laughed. 'Maybe if you're a very good boy,' he grinned, 'Letemout Lou will ring him up later and explain ...'

25

One of the problems with being a member of the judiciary is that, unlike the rest of society, you never develop the capacity to put the past behind you. It is foreign to your processes. First there must be investigation, then determination, and finally recrimination. There is very little room in your thinking for forgiving, forgetting and moving on.

Letemout Lou, of course, couldn't let it go. Not with two warm bodies in the City Cemetery. There had to be resolution. But Stan either couldn't – or wouldn't – provide her with what she needed. Lou knew she was in danger of wrecking the fragile peace if she didn't let up, but she couldn't physically stop herself.

Stan, on the other hand, was testing Lou's faith. He'd told her before she'd asked that he had clean hands for both killings, and if she couldn't believe him, then there was no point in discussing the matter any more. And this is precisely where things stood a fortnight after the family reunion.

'Why don't you just park it and start afresh?' suggested Harry the Hurler, as he helped Lou pack the last of her books into boxes.

'I can't,' Lou said. 'It's too big.'

'Running away to Belfast's not going to help,' he countered.

'How would you feel if it turned out the love of your life was a cold-blooded psycho?' declared Lou.

'I take it you've met my wife,' laughed Harry. 'Look, theoretically, Stan might have been involved – but it's highly unlikely. And the odds are you'll never know for sure anyway. So, take it from an old-timer, stop torturing yourself and let it go. I really think you should give him another chance before you skip town.'

'It's only a six-month placement,' said Lou. 'I could well be home in three.'

'What department?'

'Racketeering,' replied Lou with a malicious smirk.

A look of complete horror flashed across Harry's face and she burst out laughing.

'Don't worry, pet,' she said. 'It's all drugs and building sites. I'll not be bearing down on you or Jimmy Fidget just yet.'

'That sounds all right then,' grinned Harry. 'Though could you ever just give me a day or two till I go through our books …?'

Strand Road PSNI station would probably win the award for Derry's ugliest building – but for two very important considerations. First, it lies hidden behind huge stone walls, erected to surround the old lunatic asylum which sat on the site until the 1960s. And, second, the station is only two hundred yards away from the new Riverview shopping centre, which is now accepted as the most hideous piece of architecture on the entire island.

Superintendent Audrey Grafton's office, on the top floor of the police station, had one of the most stunning views of the river that Tommy Bowtie had ever seen. It put him in mind of Oscar Wilde's line about why he liked to eat lunch at the Eiffel Tower – 'because it's the only place in Paris where I don't have to look at the fucking thing'. But Tommy was not in Audrey's office in his capacity as connoisseur of river views, nor indeed as an aficionado of literary maxims. He was there because Audrey wanted to talk to him, on the record, about his client Senator Stanley Stevenson.

'We need Stan to explain a few phone calls,' said Audrey, passing an A4 computer printout over the desk to Tommy. 'According to these records of his cellphone, he made two calls to a Southern mobile the day King Size was shot. One of those calls was made ten minutes before the shooting, the other an hour afterwards … By sheer quirk of fate, Stan also called this same number twice on the day that Barry Magee was topped.

And again it was about ten minutes before and one hour afterwards.'

'Fuck me,' said Tommy quietly. 'There's a coincidence.'

'It gets better,' continued Audrey. 'We've talked to the gardaí, and they say the Southern mobile he was calling is government-issue, though they can't tell us any more unless we can give them specific proof of any wrongdoing.'

'They're right too,' said Tommy. 'It's all very circumstantial – and it proves nothing. He was probably ringing some buddy in the Senate to go for a drink, or some civil servant to get somebody's drain fixed.'

'Possibly,' replied Audrey. 'But I'd like to talk to the senator regardless.'

'Have you been talking to Letemout Lou?' asked Tommy suddenly.

'What if I have?' responded Audrey defensively.

'It's starting to rub off on you,' said Tommy, returning to full lawyer mode. 'Look, Stan Stevenson killed no one. He's a good man, who doesn't have it in him. You're asking him to prove his innocence. But at the same time, you have absolutely no proof linking him to anything. I'm certainly not going to let him talk to you. You think I'd let a couple of your trickiest bastards take him into an interview room and start shining lights in his eyes? Come on now, Audrey. This is a member of the Irish Senate. Stop wasting everybody's time, or we'll haul your arse before the Anglo-Irish Secretariat.'

'Alternatively,' said Audrey, 'you could bring Stan in quietly, and we could have him issued with his It Wasn't Me certificate by teatime.'

'I'll talk to him,' replied Tommy. 'But I wouldn't hold out any hope … Now, would you mind if I use your bathroom before I go?'

Stan, however, was unavailable for interview in Derry as he'd a prior engagement in Dublin with Monsignor Behan. He'd already cancelled his first appointment twice – and was toying with the idea of ringing in sick today, when the priest appeared at his office door. Stan recognised him immediately from the Saving Ireland from Sodomy website – and there being nothing else for it, stood up and shook his hand.

'You're not a homosexual,' said Monsignor Behan, eyeballing him closely.

'Glad to hear you say it, I'm trying very hard not to be, Father,' replied Stan, referring to the cleric by the more familiar title. Monsignor was quite a mouthful. He pointed the priest to a leather armchair.

'Don't get cute with me son,' said Father Behan. 'I'm a qualified doctor, and I can tell a bluffer when I see one. You only think you're a deviant because you don't want to disappoint your mother.'

'What?' Stan exclaimed.

'You're a classic case,' said the priest. 'Look, I can tell by the cut of you, you're no nancy-boy. You don't gel your hair, you bite your nails, and your socks and tie don't match your suit ... What you are, is afraid of marrying a girl your mother wouldn't approve of. Maybe you never got over your little crush on your mother as a child – and no woman's ever matched her in your mind. So, instead, you reckon that maybe a man could fill the gap. Take it from me, he can't.'

'My mother's dead thirty years,' said Stan. 'I was six when she died. I'm now thirty-six, unmarried, with no children. Women just don't do it for me – and with all due respect, I have no interest in celibacy.'

'Trust me,' said the priest. 'You're not a homo. This is just a minor wiring problem in your head. You've blown a little fuse – and I'm the electrician who's going to fix it. From my experience, only about one per cent of all men I treat are genuine, unsavable poofters. The rest are just ordinary people like you who have a little fault on the circuit board.'

'I'm not sure it's that simple,' said Stan.

'Oh but it is,' said Father Behan. 'We're going to work through this together using a series of exercises I'll be giving you for homework. I have here two booklets I'd like you to take back to your flat. The first is a little magazine called *Readers' Wives*. And I'd like you to study it carefully, and as you're doing so – how can I put this delicately – pick one of the prettier ladies and pretend to yourself that you're married to her.'

'No offence, Father,' smiled Stan, 'but it sounds the sort of thing I might have done twenty years ago.'

'Don't be flippant,' snapped the priest. 'You will do this exercise, twice a night every night for a full week – or until you find yourself enjoying it.'

'Okay so,' said Stan, 'and what's the second booklet.'

'This second booklet is what's called a Log of Lust,' replied Father Behan. 'I need you to fill it in every night and record every erotic fantasy – involving male, female or other – that you've had throughout the day. You don't have to be too graphic – but obviously if we want to make progress, you're going to have to be completely honest.'

'Can I be completely honest now, doctor?' asked Stan.

'Certainly, senator,' replied the priest.

'I'll take the *Readers' Wives*, but I'm not filling in that fucking log ever.'

26

Stan had long been a great believer in telling the worst stories against yourself first – that way nobody got a chance to beat you to it. So, after his first session with the good Father, he figured he'd better meet Sonny quickly and confess all. This way, when Rubber John got to hear about it, at least the new senator would seem like a good sport.

Sonny suggested hooking up for a pint at the Henry Grattan on Baggot Street, and was already there when Stan arrived – sitting with two pints of stout in front of him. 'Drink up,' he said to his colleague, as he squatted onto the stool opposite. 'By Christ, you deserve it.'

It was a four-pint story, punctuated with two calls to the Taoiseach: the first when Stan had finished telling his version – and the second half an hour later, when Sonny suddenly got the idea that his pal had made the whole thing up and demanded proof. Suffice to say, he nearly fell off his chair when Stan produced a dog-eared dirty book bearing the sticker 'Property of the Saving Ireland from Sodomy Association'.

'I'll be damned,' laughed Rubber John, when Sonny rang him again. 'Homework was never that much fun when I was a lad.'

After the bar kicked them out, the pair crossed the street to Stan's apartment in Lad Lane for a nightcap. He'd been subletting the flat for a knockdown rent from a Munster TD, Mikey Cadden, who'd bought it before he acquired a mistress in Foxrock. The only condition was that Stan had to clear out his stuff before Mikey's wife made her annual shopping trips to the capital.

Stan handed Sonny a very large Paddy and pointed him to

the leather recliner. 'So why did you get into this game?' he asked the Meath man.

'Same as yourself,' sighed his friend, chugging back the guts of a measure. 'I looked around, saw the quality of the arseholes representing me and thought to myself, I can't have that. So I joined the party, spent three terms on the backbenches, and after I got elected last time out, Rubber John asked me if I fancied a special assignment. So next thing you know, I was underboss to Attila the Dub … Worst thing about it is, it'll do my vote no harm at all, back home. The more extreme Joxer gets, the more calls I get telling me what a great job we're doing. The Church are praising us from the altar, the guards think we're the best thing since CS gas, and the wee woman who runs the corner shop can't thank us enough for standing up to all those thieving darkies and Dublin shirt-lifters. No offence, Stan.'

'None taken,' smiled Stan. He knew well that if he showed so much as the mildest annoyance the stick would get worse and worse.

'But do you never feel guilty that you're as much to blame as Joxer?' he asked Sonny. 'I know I get sick to the stomach every time some journalist describes me as the new voice of the New Right.'

Sonny took another draught of his whiskey and nodded. 'You suck it up for the greater good, Stan,' he said. 'Joxer's shelf life is about another six months – a year tops. But when we pull the plug on him, we're going to make sure he goes down the drain completely. Without a trace. No residue … And you should never worry about what they write about you. You of all people should know that. The whole notion of your political identity, it's bullshit.'

'I don't follow you,' interrupted Stan. 'Are you saying it doesn't matter what party you're in?'

'Pretty much so,' replied Sonny. 'Politics is a very simple business – it's about making your friends rich. Nothing more, nothing less. It doesn't matter if you're on the right or the left, you're only going to succeed if you put money in people's pockets. The left think everyone should get the same amount; the right think the size of your wallet should be decided on merit. But ultimately, all we're doing – right and left alike – is making as many people as we can fat enough so we can get elected again next time ... That's what you're hoping to do by getting funding and representation for the North. And it's what I want to do, by building a motorway from my hometown to Dublin Central.'

Stan drained his drink and shook his head. 'Jesus, that's a very black view of the job.'

'You're part of it now,' grinned Sonny. 'You've taken the money, so lie down on the bed like a good girl and stop complaining. And you're right – it is black. Which is why it's important that we stop people like Joxer – who only want a very select few to get very rich – from abusing the process.'

Back in Dunavady, Tommy Bowtie had spent the evening in the Castle Inn with two North Derry MLAs, the nominally independent Shay Gallagher and Sinn Féin's Barney Joyce.

Barney, who'd been as tight as two teeth with Stan Stevenson when the senator had worked in Dunavady, was aghast at his old pal's sudden lurch into the mainstream.

'Joxer O'Duffy is bad news,' he sniffed. 'Stan's better off away from him. O'Duffy was the man who said that if every single Northerner was fucked into the middle of the Atlantic Ocean – the only person who'd miss them would be guy who got to drown them.'

Tommy Bowtie laughed in spite of himself.

'Yeah,' added Shay Gallagher, 'and what's more worrying again is that the day after Joxer said that, an *Irish Star* poll showed that ninety-two per cent of the public in the Free State agree with him.'

'Stan's just being cute,' Tommy cut in. 'He knows that Joxer has a committee chairmanship in his gift – and he's got his eyes set on it ... And he's already made it clear that he has no time for Joxer's attitude to the Six Counties. In fact, he spoke against him at the Foreign Affairs Committee.'

'That was a set-up,' countered Barney Joyce. 'To cover up the fact he's selling out.'

'No he's not,' said Tommy. 'Stan's a businessman, just like he's always been. That's why the Soldiers of Destiny love him.

And if he gets twenty cents of Free State money pumped into Dunavady in the next five years, that's twenty cents more than you, or your cohorts, Barney, have managed to get in the last fifty.'

Barney raised his fists and pretended to square up to Tommy. 'You're a lucky man I've been stood down, Bowtie,' he warned.

'Seriously,' continued Tommy, 'your lot might have a handful of seats, Barney, but the big parties are still keeping you at the end of a very long bargepole. The South has had its fill of *Shadow of a Gunman* politics. The Workers' Party wrecked it for everybody. You're going nowhere till you wash the smell of cordite off your hands. And until the bigger parties work with you – you'll have damn all influence.'

'Join the real republican party, Barney,' quipped Shay Gallagher, who got his money from Fianna Fáil. 'You know it makes sense.'

Barney told Shay to fuck off, then grinned and drained his pint. 'I'm away home in a huff,' he laughed. 'Anybody want a lift?'

'Fuck no,' replied Gallagher, 'you've had six pints. I'm getting a taxi.'

'I'm going to crash over in the office,' said Tommy.

'Your funeral,' said Barney, as he headed for the door. But he was wrong.

It was, in fact, his.

Five miles out the Drumbridge Road, about twenty yards away from where Sammy Muir's brakes had failed, Barney Joyce smacked his Mondeo into a tractor that had been badly parked at a farm gateway. His car, which the traffic police believe was travelling at approximately eighty-two miles an hour, flipped six times on the road before bursting into flames.

Barney, mercifully, was dead on arrival at Altnagelvin Hospital. And all of a sudden, the Shinners had an Assembly seat to fill.

Officially, Dunavady wasn't Harry the Hurler's patch, though, of course, he still had the call. There were a few councillors who felt they deserved a trip to the big school, but when Harry announced the candidate ten days after the tragedy, there were no arguments. Not a cheep. Rather, there was all-round delight at what the national press were hailing as a political masterstroke.

It had taken Harry less than thirty seconds to convince his nominee.

'You're on,' she said. 'If that big useless donkey can do it, so can I. Where do I sign?'

Harry produced a pen, pointed to the sheet, and Letemout Lou Johnston, High Court judge and former fiancée of Senator Stanley Stevenson, became the newest Member of the Legislative Assembly for North Derry.

Lou crossed the suite to her filing cabinet and produced from the bottom drawer a bottle of Veuve Clicquot 1998 Reserve. 'I'd intended to send it to Stan when he was appointed to the Senate,' she explained, a little despondently. 'But then he went and took that slapper to his inauguration …'

Harry ignored the gibe and passed her two wine glasses from the little corner bar. 'That's all over now, you know,' he said. 'What with all the travelling and everything, they weren't really compatible … Susie was a little upset, but she's promised me there'll be no bunny-boiling business like there was with, ah, other people.'

'Yeah,' sniffed Lou disapprovingly. 'Like other people in this room. When incidentally, both she and that other person were still married to other people …'

Harry winced in embarrassment as Her Honour carefully poured out the champagne.

'Let's have a toast,' he said, raising his glass. 'To the end of a magnificent career in the High Court. The only way they'll get you back in there again is when they're indicting you for vote fraud.'

'*Sláinte*,' replied Lou, returning the toast. 'May you be in heaven half an hour before Joxer O'Duffy knows you're dead …'

Harry laughed. 'Next stop Westminster,' he declared, 'or even the Dáil.'

'Thanks, Harry,' said Lou. 'And what's wrong with the Áras …?'

'Jesus, now you're talking, Lou,' retorted Harry. 'You know you could do it if you set your mind to it. President of Ireland. Christ, you'd be Stan's boss. He wouldn't like that at all.'

'Why wouldn't he?' grinned Lou, as she sipped the champagne. 'Sure, he's had twenty-five years to get used to it.'

Stan laughed out loud when he heard. 'She's coming after me,' he told Tommy, when the solicitor rang to break the news. 'I've got my very own smart-mouthed, political stalker. I just hope Harry the Hurler knows what he's doing. Christ help him if he thinks he's going to have any control over her.'

'Take it from one who knows, eh?' grinned Tommy. 'You know, they've already nominated her for the All-Ireland Sexual Health Action Group.'

'Oh fuck no,' groaned Stan. 'I've been bitching at Joxer for over a month now to give me a committee. And you'll never guess what I'm taking over next week …'

Tommy chuckled. 'You and Lou arguing over who's on top,' he said. 'It'll be just like old times.'

'Maybe,' sighed Stan. 'Though I suppose at least this time, I'll get to sit in the big chair and bang the gavel …'

27

It was only a fortnight before Stan and Lou met up, and sure enough there was blood on the carpet. The May meeting of the All-Ireland Sexual Health Action Group took place at the Four Seasons Hotel in Monaghan on the tenth of the month. And it reminded Lou – who to be honest shouldn't have needed reminding – why she should never underestimate Stan.

As the newest member of the eleven-man committee – or eleven-*person* committee as it now was – Lou was keen to make her presence felt. But her appointment had come too late for her to get anything listed on the agenda. So, at the start of the meeting, she asked the chair if she would be able to raise an item under Any Other Business at the end. And Stan told her to make herself at home.

The meeting itself was pretty tame by the group's standards. The main topic for discussion had been the ethical difficulty of accepting sponsorship from a drinks company for an STD awareness campaign. The group wrestled with their consciences for an hour but, as expected, lost unanimously. Half a million euro bought a lot of posters.

As always, AOB – or Headcase Hour as Stan privately referred to it – was a bit livelier. Fine Gael and the DUP were attempting to table a thirty-two-county ban on fruit-flavoured condoms for under-twenty-ones, after two cases of suspected latex poisoning: one at Queen's in Belfast, the other at Galway MIT. But this was defeated when the UUP and Fianna Fáil tabled a tongue-in-cheek amendment demanding an all-out ban on all other products students liked to chew on, including biro tops and plastic rulers. There then followed a twenty-minute dispute on whether it was appropriate for the University of Ulster Students' Union to include a box of chocolate fingers in their Freshers' Welcome To Sex pack. But again, this was eventually kicked for touch, when the chairman pointed out that at least the youngsters wouldn't be keeling over from rubber pollution.

Finally came Lou's turn. 'With the indulgence of Senator Stevenson,' she began, 'I would like on behalf of my party to raise the prohibition on pregnancy termination in both parts of the island. My party would like to propose that this committee sets a lead, by developing a progressive policy on this issue – and would sponsor bills in both parliaments on the island introducing the same legislation that exists across the water in Britain.'

Stan looked at the nine other faces on the committee – whom, of course, he'd already primed – and called for discussion. No one spoke. Not a one. The group had spent the entire previous year devising a strategy, which amounted to For Christ's Sake Don't Drop This One In Our Lap – and eventually kicked it to the Family Affairs Committee. And there was not a hope of them readopting it now – and certainly not at some Shinner lawyer's behest.

The room was silent for a full thirty seconds.

'Okay so,' said Stan, eventually, 'let's go straight to a vote … I make that nine votes to one. I myself only vote in the event of a tie. I'm afraid Ms Johnston your motion is defeated.'

Lou lowered her head. She'd pitched like a wide-eyed amateur, and Stan had knocked her into the stands.

As the other committee members filed out of the hotel boardroom, she stood at the door and waited for her ex. 'I deserved that,' she told him, nodding her head. 'I tried to embarrass you, but I never got near you.'

'Sure, you'll get me next time,' grinned Stan. 'Let me buy you a drink to make it up to you …'

Audrey Grafton resisted making a habit of anything. It went against everything in her training. Criminals got caught because of their habits; they repeated patterns and repeated mistakes. In the bad old days, cops had got killed because of their habits – even today the Superintendent never drove the same way to work twice in the one week. So what was she doing having lunch for the fourth Friday in a row with Harry the Hurler? Anyone would think she was putting it out there for him on a tray.

In mitigation, she'd decided not to wear a skirt today. There was too much business to get through, and she needed Harry's full attention. So she settled instead on a deep-red Ralph Lauren trouser suit and a black silk crêpe-de-Chine chemise. The girl at Colour-Me-Beautiful assured her that the combination would bring out the new dark-plum shade in her hair. The effect was completely wasted on Harry, though, who as yet had not lifted his eyes from the top button of her blouse.

'Two specials and a nice bottle of Chardonnay,' said Harry, gesturing to the waitress to shut the snug door.

They were at the Jack Kennedy, of course – in a booth that Harry's man had swept carefully that morning, and that he would sweep every week thereafter. Though of course, this man was not using a brush.

'Barney Joyce was a right fella,' began Audrey conversationally. 'And a total democrat, of course. He never met a single one of my officers he wouldn't have shot on sight.'

'It takes time to teach old dogs new tricks,' agreed Harry.

'So is that why you killed him?' she asked. 'The same way you did Sammy Muir …'

Harry chewed slowly on his breadstick and grinned at her. Her deep brown eyes were soft and seductive. She was just having a bit of fun with him. Teasing him. And God, her perfume was really something: Obsession, he'd bet. He should really explain to her …

Suddenly the light went back on in his head. 'Jesus, Superintendent,' he laughed, 'I invite you out for lunch and you accuse me of double murder. Look. Barney was my top guy in Dunavady and one of my best friends. But he had absolutely no sense when he was drinking. Shay and Tommy tried to talk him out of driving that night – but he wouldn't listen. Sure, you lot had done him twice for DUI – and from what I heard, he had four times the quota in his body when he died.'

'Closer to five,' nodded Audrey. 'Okay, I'll give you that one. So what about Sammy the Squint?'

'I wouldn't know anything about that,' replied Harry, his sharp blue eyes mocking her. 'Maybe Special Branch did it. After all, they'd been running him for years. Maybe they were afraid he was going to turn tail – and decided to shut him up.'

'You're a little too smart for your own good, Mr Hurley,' sniffed Audrey primly. 'I suppose you're going to tell me now that Senator Stan had nothing to do with those three holes in Barry Magee.'

'Interesting you mention that,' said Harry. 'But even Letemout Lou's beginning to give him the benefit of the doubt now. She met him in Monaghan last week and asked him about the phone calls. And he told her straight out they were government business – and that he'd be able to prove it if he had to. But he said there's no way he'd release any details unless he got clearance from the very top.'

'Handy enough for him,' said Audrey. 'But I'm not convinced.'

'I know Stan a lifetime,' replied Harry. 'It wasn't him. He's just too damned straight. And even if it had been him, you can be sure he'd have messed it up.' He paused to refill their glasses.

'Well that presents me with two problems, Harry,' said Audrey. 'The first is that we've now cast-iron proof that Stan wasn't in Leinster House at the time Barry got whacked. Indeed, his security fob records show he left the building at 3 p.m. – the shooting was at eight.'

'And the second problem?' asked Harry, not really wanting an answer.

'The second problem,' said Audrey, 'is that if Stan isn't in the frame, as you suggest, the only other person we're looking at is your little brother Jimmy.'

'Oh no, no, no, no, no,' replied Harry, shaking his head beseechingly. 'Don't say that. Please don't say that. My mother will kill me.'

'Well tell her from me, if she wants to do it cleanly she should take you for a drive out Drumbridge mountain brae,'

grinned the police chief. 'The clear-up rate is really lousy …
Now, where's our pasta, I'm starving.'

'So is it all rosy in the garden again for Stan and Lou?' asked
Jimmy.

'Not even remotely,' replied Susie. 'Lou, the prissy little
madam, had more preconditions than the DUP …'

'What? Is she looking for photographic evidence?' smiled
Jimmy. 'I thought she already had that.'

'As does Stan – of your good self and Lou,' sniped Susie,
flicking the switch. 'Clear as day, under the table of the Jack
Kennedy. And let me tell you, if you ever try any of that crack
in my restaurant again, you'll be banned for life.'

'I'll only have to eat elsewhere,' laughed Jimmy, rinsing the
toothpaste out of the sink.

'Talking of which,' said Susie, stepping past him into the
shower, 'what has a girl to do to get her back scrubbed round
here …?'

28

'So, you want to make a new law, Senator,' said Sonny. 'Glad to see you're keen – but let me warn you, it's virtually impossible to get a private member's bill through the Seanad without full government support.'

'He knows that already, you jumped-up little prick,' interrupted Letemout Lou. 'That's why he's here talking to you.'

'Deputy Waterhouse meet Assemblywoman Johnston,' grinned Stan.

Stan had arranged to meet Sonny at his constituency office in Navan's new interpretive centre and Lou, who was en route to Dublin for a Sinn Féin Ard Comhairle meeting, had come along to help. So, naturally, Stan hadn't clued her in.

'It's a joint initiative,' explained Stan, flicking Sonny the eyebrow. 'It's taking the presidential votes for Northerners idea and developing it a little. Lou here wants to propose that Southern TDs and senators get speaking rights in the Assembly. And I'm going to call for MLAs to get speaking rights in Leinster House.'

Sonny smirked. Memo to Rubber John: Never give a Northerner an inch. 'Why don't we just pull out an envelope and draft up a new constitution,' he said. 'Or even better, two new constitutions.'

'If you don't want to help us,' snapped Lou, 'maybe we'll go and talk to some real politicians – instead of a bagman for a racist thug.'

'That's a racist thug with a seventy-five per cent approval rating,' retorted Sonny. 'Now, listen, little Miss Angry, you came to me for advice. Not the other way about. So if you just remove the hair from out of your ass for one minute, I just might be of some use to you.'

Stan covered his mouth to suppress a smirk and made a mental note of the insults for the car ride back into Dublin.

'Okay,' said Sonny. 'The Committee of Eight – of which, Stan, I'd remind you, you are a signed-up member – won't back this motion. But you knew that anyway. But we're not going to give you too hard a time about it either. You've got your council elections in Dunavady next month and you're wrapping the flag around you, which is perfectly understandable. We do it ourselves all the time …'

Stan nodded to the Meath man to carry on.

'Second,' said Sonny, 'nobody in the party is going to like the fact that you're teaming up with the likes of Lou Johnston. If there's one thing that Fianna Fáilers are more scared of than an IRA gunman with tattoos on his knuckles, it's a smartarse IRA intellectual with a postgraduate degree. No offence, Miss.'

'None taken,' laughed Letemout, who was warming to Sonny's bluntness. 'And call me Lou.'

'The silver lining here, Lou,' Sonny continued, 'is that everyone knows you and Stanley have, how will we put this, a very strong non-political connection.'

'Not for a while now,' interjected Stan, raising a finger. 'Miss Johnston has some issues …'

'Okay so,' said Sonny, 'but the point is that we can explain that this joint approach derives from your personal relationship – rather than the parties linking up. But Stan has to take the lead on it. If it's seen as a Shinner bill, it won't even get to discussion.'

Lou tutted loudly but she knew better than to argue. And besides, as she always said herself, there's little point in asking for advice if you're not going to take it.

'Your next problem,' Sonny went on, 'is getting four other senators to co-sign the bill. You need five signatures to get it discussed in the Seanad. Your best bet here will be with the border people. I think we have two from Monaghan, two from Louth, one from Cavan and two from Donegal. Lobby them hard – and if they won't bite, warn them that you personally, Stan, will issue press releases to every one of their local papers condemning them as West Brits or whatever. Again, you stay out of that one, Lou.'

Lou nodded grumpily.

'After you introduce the bill, there are four more stages before it becomes law. The next hurdle is the house debate – which, I'll be honest, is as far as you're going to go. We – that is the government – have pretty much absolute control in the Seanad. But at least, there you'll get to make your points.'

'What happens next?' asked Lou.

'Well,' replied Sonny, 'it falls on its hole. You're not going to get it to committee stage. You'd need our full backing.'

'What if we do?' pressed Stan. 'Humour us.'

'Okay,' smiled Sonny. 'The relevant committee will give the bill full consideration and then suggest amendments. After that, the amendments will be considered at the report stage. And then, the amended bill will be voted on in the Seanad. If, by a miracle, the Seanad passes it, the bill will go to the Dáil. And if they pass it, the president will sign it into law.'

'As easy as that,' grinned Stan. 'Okay so, let's give it a shot. What odds will you give me on getting it passed?'

'Hmmm.' Sonny mused. 'About ten thousand to one.'

'Okay,' said Stan. 'I'll have a tenner on that. As witnessed by a High Court judge …'

'You will in your fuck,' laughed Sonny. 'Go to Paddy Power.'

'So why did you bring it to him?' inquired Lou on the way to the car park.

'Because in spite of his friends, he's actually a very decent man,' replied Stan. 'And I like him.'

'So do I,' said Lou.

Stan put his key in the passenger door and opened it for her. 'So do you still like me?' he asked, shooting her a sideways glance.

She stood motionless for a second at the open door and looked directly into his face. 'Of course I do,' she said sharply. 'You of all people should know that. I've spent more than half my life with you. But as regards you and me becoming *us* again? There's no chance. You blew that when you shut me out. The one thing in life I was always certain of was you. You were the one decent thing in a rotten fucking world. But you let me down wholescale, you rat bastard. And I'm never going to let you do it again.'

'Your loss,' he sniffed and opened his own door.

He sat at the steering wheel, staring ahead for a minute, and adjusted his mirror before turning round to face her. Her cheeks were flushed and her eyes were starting to well up. He knew that she was trying desperately to hold herself together.

'Lou,' he said gently, 'I'm not strong enough to keep fighting with you. You have to know that without you, I'm nothing. Everything I do, without you in my world, is pointless. And I think – though I don't know it for sure – that you feel the same. It's been too long. We can't wait until the world is perfect. You can't just pick a date out of the air and say, Happy Ever After will begin here.'

She took his hand and cupped it between hers. 'Nice words, Stan,' she replied, avoiding his look. 'And you're dead right. Without you, most things seem pointless. But it's also pointless me even trying to start my Happy Ever Afters while I'm wondering who you are any more. '

'I'm the same guy you used to beat up until he'd carry your books to school,' said Stan, giving her his most boyish smile.

'It won't wash, Stan,' she retorted, releasing his hand. 'You can still play the wide-eyed innocent with others, but I know you. I see right through you. You've changed. Really changed. Look at your career. In the past four or five months, you've gone from being an honest defender of the public interest to brawling in the bearpit.'

'Jesus, you're one to talk,' said Stan. 'There's two of us in it. And besides, that's the nature of politics.'

'But the problem is,' Lou countered, 'you're better than any of them. It's like you've unleashed a whole new you. A tough new you. And …'

She let it hang.

'And what?' he said.

'And I'm not sure that this new you wouldn't knock down people who were standing in his way.'

The journey back to Dublin passed in almost complete silence. Stan didn't even have the heart to repeat Sonny's insults.

29

It was another chance blown, and both Stan and Lou knew it. Even their friends were starting to worry about them. So the next day, after spending the night on the phone to a ranting and raving Stan, Tommy Bowtie was going to try a last-ditch Hail Mary for the senator.

Tommy had fixed Lou up with a constituency office in Dunavady, four terraced houses down from Shay Gallagher's and five doors down from his own HQ. The locals, as you'd expect, had already rechristened the street Liars Row.

Harry the Hurler had agreed to accompany Tommy to visit the new Assemblywoman, ostensibly so she could brief him on how the meeting with Waterhouse had gone. But after ten minutes hearing what they already knew from Stan anyway, they cut straight to the chase.

'It's time to cut him some slack, Lou,' warned Tommy, helping himself to a pre-prandial brandy and soda from the little cabinet in the corner of her office. 'If only to give the rest of us some peace.'

'Listen to Tommy, Lou,' said Harry. 'It's only a matter of time before Stan gets himself into bother. He has no one talking any sense to him. He's far too pally with that Committee of Eight, and he's going to harm himself politically. And the way he's drinking, it's only a matter of time before some pretty little vulture in a see-through top is selling her story to the Dublin rags. He needs you, Lou. And, by the way, we haven't even started on how much you need him …'

Lou stroked her chin dispassionately, as if she were considering for how many years to bang up a particularly choice villain, then shook her head. No.

'Where was he when Barry was killed?' she asked.

'He'd a doctor's appointment in north Dublin,' replied Tommy.

'Will he prove it?' pressed Lou.

'He's tired proving himself,' sighed Tommy. 'He didn't do anything wrong and is sick of having to account for himself. Whether to you, the Taoiseach or the cops. Audrey Grafton called him up last week for an off-the-record chat, and he told her if she'd any evidence to come and arrest him. He said he didn't care if she was Harry the Hurler's girlfriend, if she so much as rang him again, he'd sue her for harassment.'

Harry winced.

'I'm sorry,' said Lou. 'But I'm not convinced.'

'But you're a Shinner, now,' declared Harry in mock protest. 'What's a couple of dead bodies you can't explain?'

Lou smiled sadly at the attempt at levity and shook her head. 'Maybe that's the way things operate for you, Harry, but not him. Stanley, well, he's my baby. And when I go home at night, I don't want to be cuddling up to him and wondering if there's an axe under the bed. No offence, Harry, but I just don't know how Lorna puts up with it.'

'Take it from me,' grunted Harry, 'Lorna's got a sharp enough axe of her own ...'

This was the second time that Stan had set off for Monsignor Behan's office on Dominick Street, but the first time he was actually going to enter the building. The last day he'd got as far as Parnell Street before losing his nerve and ducking into Conway's Pub. That was the day Barry Magee had got shot in Derry.

This time, however, he was going to go through with it. Largely because he was too weary to care. Tommy had rung after lunch to tell him, very kindly but very firmly, that Lou had bolted the door and it was time to move on.

He reached Dominick Street, went up to the big Georgian door, pressed the SIS button, composed himself and stepped through the threshold at the sound of the buzzer.

'Made it up the stairs this time,' smiled the priest, shaking his guest's hand. 'Now sit over on that couch, till we get a bit of a chat.'

'I've only got ten minutes,' replied Stan pointedly. 'I have to be back for a vote. It's the Internet Child Safety Bill. Very important, as you can gather.'

'So it is,' said Father Behan, pursing his lips. 'Okay, we'll do the pared-down version so. I've two pieces of homework for you for the next week. First of all, I want you to take another little booklet home.'

The priest put a key in a little one-drawer filing cabinet and produced another magazine, which he handed down to Stan. Again it was immediately apparent that it was a flesh rag. But when Stan saw the title, he couldn't stop the smirk. Just what the fuck was he supposed to do with *Bangor Boy-Bang*?

'Now,' said Father Behan. 'Listen to me very carefully here – I want you to leave this book in a very easily accessible place. But under no circumstances are you to open it. You are absolutely forbidden from peeking inside. And if you do, have no doubt about it, I will find out. It will be written all over your face ...'

And printed indelibly into my mind, thought Stan.

'There'll be no peeking, I promise,' he asserted.

'It's all about temptation, Stanley,' explained the priest. 'If you can keep this book in your apartment for a fortnight, totally untouched, you're halfway cured. There is a danger of lapsing. But, let's face it, there's no point in being a reformed alcoholic if you can't handle the sight of anyone having a drink.'

'I understand entirely.' Stan nodded, anxious to move on. 'Good thinking. And what's the second piece of homework I have to do.'

'Ah,' said Father Behan. 'Well this might be a little more difficult. And I appreciate you mightn't feel entirely up to it just yet. But over the next fourteen days, I want you to endeavour, as hard as you can ... to get yourself a new girlfriend.'

Now that, thought Stan to himself, is a task I might just rise to. 'I'll do what I can,' he nodded soberly. 'But don't expect any miracles, Father.'

'I won't,' said the priest. 'But I will pray for you. God bless you.'

158

'Thank you, and God bless you too,' replied Stan, standing up to leave.

I knew it, said Stan to himself as he skipped happily down the stairs. If you hang around with anyone long enough, they're bound to make sense eventually.

30

Gráinne Gael McCormack, in the words of her father, was as pretty as a poem. Her father Victor, for the record, was not. Switchblade Vic, as his business associates referred to him, often joked that he married outside his species. And it was a good job for Gráinne too.

Vic had met Gráinne's mother, Maria, a Spanish model, while he was on a trip to London to purchase equipment for his company. C Company. Vic was the managing director of the Planters' Independence Group, or as one paper put it, 'Harry the Hurler in red, white and blue stripes'. And he ended up staying a little longer in London than intended, while the police tried to prove that the twenty-four Luger pistols in the crate in his van were his. Ultimately, they couldn't, however, and Vic returned to the east bank of the Foyle with a new bride in tow.

Truth be known, he was so smitten that he totally forgave the fact that Maria was a Romanist – just so long as she promised never to bring it up in polite company. He even let his wife name their daughter Gráinne Gael in honour of the famous fourteenth-century buccaneer. 'If you're going to behave like a damn Irish pirate,' Maria had said, 'we should name our daughter after one as well.' To Vic, however, his daughter would always be known as Gigi.

Gigi, by the luck of God, had inherited her mother's gorgeous Catalan looks: dark eyes, raven-black hair, sallow olive skin, and teeth as straight and white as a row of little fridges. But, try as she might, she couldn't escape her father's genes entirely – and, like him, she had acquired an early reputation for being extremely single-minded. People who didn't know her could find her terrifying, as indeed did some who knew her well. Her ex-husband, Diarmuid Dee-Dee Dunne, had put up with her bossiness for just a year before finally putting his foot down and running away.

Not that Stan Stevenson was too worried, mind. He was used to terrifying women. Bossy ones too. Indeed, if he were to be honest, he liked them that way. He loved directness. Nothing made him happier than a stroppy lady in a hot temper slapping him around like a mischievous little boy. So when he bounced into the *Derry Standard* photographic department to congratulate his new camerawoman on her appointment, he was thrilled with her response.

'Shut the fuck up,' she snapped, 'till I sort out the mayor's red-eye.'

'Been on the sauce again, has he?' Stan laughed.

'What are you, deaf as well as stupid?' retorted Gigi, not lifting her eyes from the computer screen.

There being nothing else for it, Stan shut the fuck up and waited. He'd known Gigi for years – and had actually recruited her as a freelance for the *Derry Standard* many moons ago. And no, despite what Hugo said, it wasn't true that he'd only interviewed her legs.

About two minutes later, Gigi finished up with the image she was working on, turned round to him and grinned. It was worth the wait. 'You took your time,' she said. 'I've been here three weeks and finally the high-flying senator deigns to visit me.'

'Good to have you back in town, Gigi,' replied Stan. 'Sorry it's taken me so long – and I'm sorry to hear about Dee-Dee.'

'You shouldn't be,' said Gigi, glaring at him directly with her big brown-black eyes. 'It clears the field.'

'What do you mean?' asked Stan.

'Well Stan,' she began, 'the short version is this. I'm twenty-seven years old and I gave up being coy a long time ago. I'm more than acceptable-looking, I'm looking for a new man, and I'm just about at the height of my sexual peak. Oh, and I like you.'

Stan swallowed nervously. This was going a lot better – and quicker – than he'd hoped.

'Now, the reason you hadn't come to see me yet,' she said

coolly, 'is that you've spent the past two months playing the odds with Letemout Lou. But you've finally worked out what everybody else knew a long time ago – she's not coming back …'

He grimaced. Caught.

'So you came in here today, ostensibly to say hello,' she went on. 'But really you were hoping to find out if I would maybe like to go for a drink with you later, just as friends. And then maybe in about three weeks' time, you'll take me to the pictures, hold my hand and give me a peck on the cheek on the way home.'

She'd read his CV, he'd swear it.

'Truth is, Stan,' she said, 'I've no interest in that. I don't want the hassle of another long, protracted courtship – and you haven't got the time for it. But let's face it, you're one babe of a man, and you're in serious need of female company. Jesus, your hands are shaking as I'm talking to you. And yes, I do want to go to bed with you. And yes, just as soon as we can arrange it. So if you call at my flat at about half-eight tonight, we'll take it from there. Oh, and bring a tooth-brush …'

'Jesus Christ, Gigi.' laughed Stan. 'What do you do for an encore?'

'Come early and find out.' She grinned.

I can't wait to tell Monsignor Behan, thought Stan.

Letemout Lou wasn't at all pleased when she heard about Stan's new distraction. But as Harry the Hurler said, if you won't feed them at home, you can't complain when they eat out.

Harry and Jimmy had called out to her Dunavady office to discuss a possible no-jail deal Jimmy was being offered if he held his hand up to the cigarette fraud. The case was now being tried in the South after some jurisdictional to-ing and fro-ing, so Lou could advise them openly without fear of prejudice. And, frank as ever, she told Jimmy to pay the two hundred thousand pound fine before the day was out and thank the Lord for his lucky break.

'Easy for you to say, Lou,' said Harry. 'We've just lost a shedload in the inquiry.'

'You got away light,' snapped Lou. 'You lost the interest on your money – and not a cent more. I did the numbers myself – and gave them to Tommy. He passed them on to Stan.'

'Still, Lou,' sighed Harry, 'this is another damn hit.'

'Forget about it,' said Lou unsympathetically. 'It's done. Now I wanted to talk to you about this amendment to our bill. The Taoiseach might be prepared to let the presidential-votes-for-Northerners part through – which could mean we'd have the vote in time for the November election. But there's no way he's going to give us speaking rights just yet.'

'We didn't expect him to,' nodded Harry. 'It's simple horse-trading. We get what we really wanted all along, while he looks like he's beating our price down.'

'Except for one thing,' said Lou.

'What's that?' asked Harry.

'No one's told Stanley,' she replied, 'and he's working night and day to push the whole damn thing through.'

'The big idiot,' grinned Harry. 'Don't worry, he'll soon learn.'

'Don't underestimate him,' retorted Lou. 'I've watched him in action down there – it's like he's been doing it all his life. He's one hell of an operator.'

'It's not the only thing he's operating on at the moment,' quipped Jimmy.

'So you tell me,' replied Lou frostily. 'But to take Harry's analogy to its conclusion, it's all very well to snack at the burger bar now and again. But you'll always go home for your big steak dinner ...'

Even Lou was impressed by what happened next. Four days before their bill was due to be heard in the Seanad, Switchblade Vic McCormack – the North's most senior loyalist hardman – came out and gave it his backing in the *Irish Times*.

'The all-Ireland dimension to the Agreement is just as important to shore up as the British one,' he told the paper. 'We want Dublin to be aware of our concerns and to address them if they can. And we are happy to listen to their advice on our internal arrangements. Though, of course, there's no question of it going beyond that. It's about being good neighbours – not brothers-in-arms.'

Lou read on in disbelief.

'As for the presidential votes,' Vic was saying, 'why shouldn't we get them? There are those who say he or she won't represent them. That's okay. The president has no authority here any way. But the vote allows our Roman Catholic friends to maintain their all-Ireland aspirations without in any way jeopardising the unionist position ...'

She finished the piece and rang Stan in Dublin to congratulate him. 'Bugger me,' she said. 'How did you get him to write that?'

'Well, actually,' said Stan sheepishly, 'and you cannot under any circumstances repeat this, he didn't write it. His daughter did. And her mother made Vic put his name to it.'

Lou laughed out loud.

'Regardless,' said Stan, 'it means I'm ending this campaign with one hell of a bang.'

'Unfortunate turn of phrase, Stanley,' sniffed Lou, 'but I'll let it go.'

Dexter Hart, the UUP on Dunavady Council, was next to weigh in behind the bill. The following morning, he told the Belfast *News Letter* that observer status for Northerners in the Seanad would cement the 'hand-holding' relationship between the two parts of the island – without necessarily leading to any improper intercourse. The paper, of course, only printed the first bit.

The only publicly dissenting voice was the DUP's, but even that was fairly muted. Tony Blunt, the party's 'International Affairs' spokesman, knew that Stan was running far too far ahead of the Southern government and that Rubber John would sooner put vinegar on his piles than give Northerners speaking rights. But Blunt was also bright enough to work out that if he and the other Righteous Brothers made too much noise, the Taoiseach might be obliged to step in to protect Stan. So he didn't throw the rattle too far out of the pram.

Thus, the night before the bill's first hearing in the Seanad, it looked like Stan was facing an honourable defeat. A few of the party faithful would vote with him to make it look decent – as would a swathe of the independents and one or two of Fine Gael's border troops. But even the most optimistic poll had him losing by forty votes to twenty. Then, however, Stan pulled the stroke of his life. He got himself arrested.

31

Stan was sitting in the City of Derry Airport lounge, waiting for the Dublin plane to appear on the runway, when Audrey Grafton sat down beside him, put her hand on his shoulder and began reading him his rights. She was holding a copy of the previous night's *Belfast Telegraph*, which had been leaked details of Stan's phone records from the times of the murders and which was demanding an explanation.

It was 7.45 a.m., two and a half hours before the senator was due to introduce his bill. And he was being charged with obstructing a police investigation.

'Do I get a call?' he asked the Superintendent.

Audrey nodded okay, thinking that Tommy Bowtie might as well enjoy the early start too. So Stan pulled his mobile phone out of his pocket and dialled the BBC Radio Foyle newsroom. 'Start taping this call,' he said to the reporter immediately, 'it'll be your lead story at eight o'clock.'

Audrey chuckled to herself, then thought, What the hell, and let the senator rattle off his spiel.

Five minutes later, Stan clicked his phone off again. 'You know you'll be out again in half an hour,' the policewoman said to him. 'It's not as if you're going to Castlereagh.'

'Maybe,' snapped Stan, 'but it's a damn sight harder to drum up outrage when you're back out on the streets ... Besides, you're going to hold me for the day. I'm going to make sure of it.'

Within an hour, the entire country had heard how the British state was trying to stop the senator from introducing his bill. His interview with BBC Radio Foyle had been immediately relayed to BBC Radio Ulster, which in turn sent it on to RTÉ radio. They ran it as soon as they got it, at 8.20 a.m., and again after the Nine O'Clock News in case anyone missed it first time. As far as PR disasters go, the PSNI might as well have impounded the Taoiseach's car and shat in the ashtrays.

In Stan's absence, Fianna Fáil immediately imposed a three-line whip on all its senators telling them to get into their chamber and vote *en bloc* for the Good Neighbour Bill, immediately and without debate. Rubber John then issued an APB instructing all his TDs to drop whatever they were doing and return to the Dáil, as he was going to fast-track the bill through both houses. Finally, he rang the Anglo-Irish Secretariat in Belfast and ordered them to 'move fucking mountains' to get Stan out of his holding cell.

It didn't take Fine Gael long, either, to decide what side of the kicking they wanted to be on. They issued a statement condemning the Northern police's 'draconian interference' in Southern governmental affairs, and called the Northern Secretary direct to demand Stan's release. The Blueshirts then said they were allowing all their people a free vote on the bill. And to a man, their senators and deputies lined up to back what the media were now terming 'The Stan Plan'.

Indeed, by close of business, the only votes against the bill were from two non-party fascists, who'd got into the Senate on the university ballot, and a reformed Stick from Dublin 4, who told the Dáil that Stan was an 'IRA wolf' in sheep's clothing.

Stanley himself wasn't going anywhere. Not until Audrey Grafton – and the Chief Constable, who had personally signed off on his arrest warrant – apologised to him publicly.

'They humiliated my client in full view,' Tommy Bowtie told the Six O'Clock News, 'so they can say they're sorry in full view.'

Harry the Hurler and Letemout, who'd both flown down to Leinster House for what they thought was going to be a near miss, had been astonished to witness the bill go through both houses in record time. And they were now watching the débâcle continue on teatime TV in the Shelbourne Hotel.

'Hats off to him,' said Harry, toasting the screen with his

stout. 'He's a complete master. But I still don't quite get why Fianna Fáil are parading him as such a martyr.'

'It's simple,' replied Lou. 'The cops were demanding to know who Stan was ringing when King Size and Barry got whacked. But he wouldn't tell them — because it was a private Irish government number. And he didn't want to embarrass the contact. So by Audrey putting the squeeze on him, she's implying that the South were in some way involved in the shootings.'

'Even so,' continued Harry, 'why did they all line out to push through his bill?'

'Two reasons, I suspect,' answered Lou. 'First — they wanted to hit the Brits a good Stay-Out-Of-Our-Fucking-Business slap. And second, I think it's now pretty apparent who Stan had been talking to — and is refusing to give up.'

'And who might that be?' asked Harry, puzzled.

'The man who told his party to vote *en bloc* for the Stan Plan or he'd cut their bollocks off,' declared Lou.

'I will prostrate myself on the ground in front of all the cameras in the world if you just take him out of here,' a harassed Audrey Grafton told Tommy Bowtie.

The three of them were sitting in her sixth-floor office, sipping glasses of Paddy and watching the live feed of the police station on Channel 9 news. There were fourteen TV crews and four satellite vans parked on the Strand Road below them. Stan hadn't enjoyed himself so much since the night Letemout thanked him for the furry handcuffs.

'What about the Chief Constable?' he asked her.

'Not going to happen, Stanley,' replied the Superintendent. 'Until we find who shot the Shakedown Sisters, he cannot and will not rule you out definitively … I on the other hand will swear that you are cleaner than God's shirts, if you just get the hell out of my station and take your big fucking bandwagon along with you.'

'I'm not going anywhere,' said the senator calmly.

'That's it,' snapped Audrey, picking up a phone. 'I'm putting an end to this now.' She dialled a long number, waited for about thirty seconds and then spoke. 'Harry? I'm calling in a marker. Will you please tell Mother Ireland here that she's made her point?'

Audrey handed Stan the phone.

'You can do no more, Stan,' laughed Harry. 'You led the news cycle from morning to night. Your bill went through to a band playing. And when the British PM tried to downplay your arrest as a storm in a teacup, the Taoiseach, fair play to him, called him a "know-nothing fuckwit". On live TV. For God's sake, quit now man. The only way you can go is down.'

'Put Lou on,' said Stan.

There was a brief pause while Harry passed Lou the phone.

'Let Audrey off the hook, Stan,' she told him. 'We're going to need her again before this is over.'

'Still don't believe me so,' he sighed. 'Even the leader of the country does …'

'I need a higher standard of proof,' sniffed Lou. 'Now say goodnight to Audrey, and go off and play in the darkroom with your little Proddy dolly bird.'

'I'd much rather be playing Judges and Jailbirds with you.'

'Next time I get you in chains I might never let you out,' laughed Lou. And the phone went click.

Stan turned to Audrey and smiled. 'Okay so,' he said, 'let's go out and tell all the cameras how you got the wrong guy.'

Harold Wilson once said that a week was a long time in politics; Stan Stevenson had cemented his reputation in just one day. The following morning, the Southern papers were trumpeting him as the new Mandela and lauding the Stan Plan as a vital safeguard against 'Northern oppression'. Well, except for the *Dublin Daily*, which led with the headline: 'PM a f★ckwit'.

Virtually all of the press carried lengthy profiles of the Derry senator, most of them with dramatic photos of his late-night release. Many of the papers also referred to his 'sparky' relationship with the Sinn Féin MLA Louise Johnston. It was a term Stan himself had once used, so they were on safe ground there. But even the tabloids knew better than to speculate any further. No one wants to take on a former High Court judge in a libel court.

The *Irish Times*, however, stole a march on the rest of the pack by snaring an off-the-record briefing with a senior government source, who confirmed that the senator had been giving regular private briefings on Northern affairs to the Taoiseach's department. 'I think it's highly likely that Stan had rung in the aftermath of the shootings to assure the government that the murders weren't politically related,' explained the source.

Interestingly, the paper made no reference to the two calls made by Stan to the same number immediately prior to the murders.

On his return to Dublin the afternoon after his arrest, Stan was invited to a private reception at Rubber John's office. Sonny Waterhouse was also there – as was the Taoiseach's cousin, Mark Blake, the Chief Whip. The Whip, who was better known as Marky Choo-Choo from his days with the Railworkers' Union, stood up from the leather settee and shook Stan's hand warmly.

'Home is the hero,' he declared. 'You handled it like a veteran.'

'Thanks, Marky,' said Stan, sitting down. 'We still haven't explained the two earlier calls, though. And some tricky reporter's going to be asking questions about them before the end of the day. I know I would.'

'Here's the thing,' interrupted the Taoiseach, handing Stan a glass of Paddy. 'You won't have to. We're going to come clean. I'm making to move against Joxer O'Duffy and the Committee of Eight today. RTÉ did a snap poll last night and my numbers have shot through the roof. Apparently, I should have called that bollix across the water a fuckwit a long time ago.

'But it means we're now strong enough to take Joxer on. And I'm going to make an announcement at five o'clock today that yes, you had been ringing me, personally, with updates on the murders. But I'm also going to say that you'd called me, by sheer coincidence, in the hour before both killings to raise your concerns about Joxer's mental health.'

'Doesn't it still look a bit strange?' asked Stan.

'That's because it is a bit strange,' replied Rubber John. 'But it's also pretty much what happened … And I'm also going to reveal how Sonny there had privately contacted me, independently of you, Stan, to say that he was worried Joxer was coming off the rails. Particularly after his No Darkies in Dún Laoghaire campaign didn't get off the ground.'

'But you could risk losing the entire committee by that reckoning,' interjected Stan.

'Actually there's no risk at all.' The Chief Whip grinned. 'We're going to expel them all – apart from Sonny. He's actually getting promoted to Minister for State for his loyalty. But we've already met with the seven independent TDs who are sitting as the Rainbow Group, and they've agreed to back us for the rest of the session – in return for kicking out the committee.'

'Jesus,' laughed Stan. 'Talk about win–win.'

'Not entirely,' sniffed Rubber John.

'What do you mean?' asked the senator for Derry.

'Well,' grinned the Taoiseach, 'thanks to you and your Stan Plan, Leinster House is going to be full of whingeing fucking Northerners. The resht of us will never get a word in edgewise.'

'Suck it up,' grinned Stan. 'You've had eighty years to get ready for it.'

32

Now it was Lou's turn. And while Stan's task had been tough, hers was damn near impossible. Harry had warned her. She had a better chance of dancing a three-hand reel in an Orange Hall than getting the Stan Plan past the Northern Assembly. There was no way the unionist majority would countenance Southern speakers now – not if they were going to call the country's proper leader a 'fuckwit'. But your first couple of years in politics are all about profile, so if Lou was going down, she was determined to go down in a blaze of headlines.

She'd managed to secure the votes of forty-eight of the one hundred and ten Assembly members. The combined nationalist and republican vote, and all but one of the Alliance Party, had already committed themselves. And she was confident that both the independent nationalist Shay Gallagher and his fiancée, the independent unionist Sue McEwan, would weigh in behind her. But because of the Assembly's weighted voting system, unless Lou could get forty per cent of the combined unionist vote – that is, the support of twenty-five UUP or DUP members – she was stuffed.

The hardline DUP had already shown their intentions by tabling an amendment changing the name of Lou's paper to the Keep Your Nose Over the Border and the Assembly Fenian Free Bill – or the Knob Aff Bill for short. And despite the UUP's earlier indication that they might be prepared to hold out the hand of friendship, even lily-livered liberals were now running back into their bunkers.

There was one remote possibility, however. Cyril Murnay, a moderate unionist, who'd run as a friendly stalking-horse against the previous UUP leader and accidentally deposed him, had been at Queen's at the same time as Lou. And while the pair had never exactly swapped spit – most likely because Cyril never had much interest in swapping spit with girls – they were at least on nodding terms. So when Lou rang and asked could she come to his Glengall Street office to talk about the vote, Cyril agreed to give her fifteen minutes.

Lou knew it was a high-risk strategy. She was going in there with only one card in her hand, and she wasn't at all keen to play it. But, after Stan had pulled off the impossible in Dublin, she had no other option.

'I need a favour, Cyril,' she told him, as she sat down in the beige PVC armchair opposite his desk.

'And what's that, Lou?' he replied. 'You want me to tear up the Ulster Covenant, pack one million Prods into boats and set sail back to the mainland?'

'Jesus, Cyril,' laughed Lou, 'that's very generous indeed. I'd settle for half a million Prods – if you give us all of our land back. But that's not why I'm here. No, I need you to help me put the Good Neighbour Bill through – in its original form. Put some clear water between yourselves and your good friends over there in the Third Reich. Sell it as cementing the peace, that last bit of the jigsaw, a progressive European initiative. Stan'll get Rubber John to nominate you for a Nobel Prize. Just think, five hundred grand untaxed – and you'll not even have to share it with our lot.'

Cyril stared at her over his leather-lined desk and folded his hands self-importantly. He had never liked her from her days in Queen's Students' Union – she'd been loud, aggressive and too hard to beat. Now, however, she was just wasting his time – trying to oil him up like some virgin. 'That's not your best pitch or even near it,' he said coldly. 'What else have you got?'

Lou glared over the desk at him, ruffled by his abruptness.

'I'm sorry?' she said.

'Stop wasting my time,' snapped Murnay. 'I said, what else have you got?''

'Nothing but my silence,' retorted Lou, staring directly into his eyes. 'Oh, and one question. Why did you pay your sixteen-year-old cousin Darryl ten thousand pounds, back when you were a final-year law student?'

A big smirk appeared on Cyril's face. She was putting all her threats in the one basket.

'Speak softly and carry a big stick,' he sighed. 'What you're doing is extortion, Lou – you do know that?'

'Be careful what you accuse a judge of, Cyril,' snapped Lou. 'I prefer to think of it as a matter of public interest.'

'Okay,' replied Cyril, still smirking. 'If you want to fight with the big boys, let's go. My cousin Darryl, who incidentally was certified as mentally incompetent, made a series of false allegations about me more than ten years ago. Nothing ever came of them – because there was no truth in them. A long, long time afterwards, my father then gave Darryl's mother Edith – his own sister – money for private health care for Darryl. Edith could corroborate this, except she's dead, as sadly is Darryl. He hanged himself in the grounds of a clinic two years ago.'

Lou swallowed uncomfortably and held up her hands to signal stop, but Murnay wasn't finished.

'For your information, Lou,' he smiled, 'I now have a girlfriend. And let me tell you, she is one randy article. Almost as much of a goer as you yourself were back in the day – according, that is, to my many, many friends in the Queen's Soccer Club ...'

Lou got up from her seat angrily, and began rounding up her coat and bag.

'Climb off your high horse and sit down,' commanded Murnay. 'We're not done yet.'

There was something in his look that frightened Lou, so she stopped mid-tracks and waited for him to continue.

'Two other things I also remember from our university time together, Lou,' he said. 'First is that when you were a law student, while the rest of us were sitting in on the magistrates' court it was widely reported that you sat in on private tribunals being conducted by Harry the Hurler. The story goes that, even after you became a judge, you chaired two different in-house inquiries for the Boys – one into an informer, who was subsequently shot dead and left on the border in a binbag. But the other trial – if you can call it that – was of a cop who accidentally knocked down and killed Harry's senile old father. The word is that this same cop subsequently gave a full account of the quote, unquote trial to his solicitor, just in case the Boys went back on your decision to dismiss the case – and whacked him anyway. Oh, and the word is that I myself was the solicitor that he gave his statement to.'

'You're a bluffer,' said Lou, praying she wouldn't go red.

'And the second thing I remember about you, Lou, from our student days, is your brother Michael,' continued Cyril. 'He's got a big, big job now out with Dunavady Council. Head engineer, is it? I wonder would his bosses like to see his police file from the seventies, when he was a specialist in another type of engineering entirely. Demolition, wasn't it? Unsolicited demolition to be precise. If memory serves correctly, they used to call him Mickey Bangers.'

'You bastard,' growled Lou. 'Leave my family out of this.'

'Now, now Louise,' said Cyril with a smooth, patronising smile, 'you were willing to malign the memory of my dead cousin and aunt. Why don't we just park our little game here and leave it as checkmate for me. And why don't you go off and learn not to be such a fucking amateur.'

And checkmate it would have remained, if Stan hadn't chanced to spot Cyril coming out of Monsignor Behan's office in Dublin the following day. The UUP man attempted to bury his head in his coat and duck down a nearby laneway, but the senator ran after him, grabbed him around the shoulder and hailed him like a long-lost brother.

'Cyril,' he chirped. 'Fancy meeting you here. What has you in Dublin?'

The UUP man nearly choked. 'My sister, my sister,' he stammered, pointing behind him. 'She works in that office.'

'Which office is that?' asked Stan. 'The Saving Ireland from Sodomy office or the one next door?'

'The one next door,' replied Cyril, collecting himself.

'Oh, I must have been mistaken – I thought you were in seeing Monsignor Behan,' laughed Stan. 'Heaven forbid. Jesus, your party would have you out the door quicker than shit from a soil pipe.'

'You saw me, didn't you?' said Cyril, closing his eyes as if in pain.

'Of course I saw you,' answered Stan amiably, 'and I could have taken a picture of you coming out the door on this new mobile phone I got. But I didn't, Cyril ... Look, your private life is your own business. It's nothing to do with me. As far as I'm concerned, you weren't here at all.'

'But Letemout Lou was in with me yesterday raking up muck,' said Cyril.

'So I believe,' said Stan. 'And you knocked the tar out of her, fair play to you. I warned her not to go there. But she's too damn determined. She doesn't realise that no one expects her to get this damn bill past you lot. I mean, with all due respect, you're not renowned for your forward thinking. In fact, I hear that the Taliban have asked to come to your party conference to learn a few moves.'

Cyril laughed and then thought to ask the obvious question.

'What are you doing here outside Monsignor Behan's anyway?' he inquired. 'Is he hiring you in as some kind of hetero role model?'

'Bit more complicated than that,' grimaced Stan. 'Short answer is Joxer O'Duffy was trying to get me married off, so I hatched a cunning plan. Now I'm paying for it.'

Cyril shook his head in disbelief. 'Jesus, he thinks you're ... Christ man, is he barking down the wrong hole.'

Stan winced at the pun.

'Did he give you the *Readers' Wives* magazine and tell you to pretend you were married to one of them?' Cyril asked.

'He did indeed,' laughed Stan. 'And by the way, wasn't the doll on the centrefold the spitting image of Dexter Hart's wife Julie?'

'Between you and me,' confessed Cyril sheepishly, 'I never opened it.'

'So what about *Bangor Boy-Bang*?' countered Stan. 'Did you peek?'

'No comment,' sniffed Cyril. 'But I'll tell you this, Stanley, and you didn't get this from me – if anybody should peek, you should. It could be very much to your advantage.'

'Not exactly my thing,' said Stan.

'Okay,' said Cyril slowly, 'so get Lou to do it ...'

'Someone we know?' asked Stan, suddenly curious. 'You mean it's not Bangor in New England?'

'Nor is it Bangor in Wales,' retorted Cyril. 'Just tell Lou to turn to page forty-eight and she'll get her votes.'

'That big?' said Stan.

'And bigger,' nodded Cyril.

'So why are you telling me this?' inquired Stan, a little baffled.

'Again between ourselves,' replied Cyril, 'I have no problems with your bill. We're giving away nothing – and we could even pick up a few quid from the South for playing ball. The righteous camp are just looking for a fight about anything. But ultimately, there's no principle here. It's just "Can't Share – Won't Share". And maybe it wouldn't do them any harm to lose one.'

'But why didn't you say this before now?' pressed Stan.

'Well I'd never been caught coming out of Father Behan's before,' chuckled Cyril. 'I'll be looking out for you in the Visitors' Gallery at Stormont next week.'

33

Shay Gallagher was going to be spending the entire day on the Assembly floor while the bill faced its various stages, so he loaned Stan his office. It was about twice the size of the senator's billet in Leinster House and much, much grander. Even the furniture – all culled from the top floor of Brown Thomas on Grafton Street – was a class apart.

Stan stretched himself out on the huge leather couch and asked Gigi to reach him over the order of business.

'What's the schedule so?' she asked.

'Well,' he said, 'if the bill gets through the Scrutiny Committee before lunchtime, they'll formally adopt it this afternoon. Shouldn't be any problems though. Lou did a deal with the DUP leader Duncan Hedges. She gets her votes as long as she accepts a unionist amendment that visiting speakers from the South could never have voting rights – for the lifetime of this Assembly, at the very least. So the hardliners can claim they're protecting their sovereignty, while Lou can chalk it up as stage one on the road to Dublin. The huns had a few problems with the idea of giving people here voting rights in the presidential election, but Lou managed to convince them that the *uachtarán* has about as much power as the Eurovision winner – and in some cases can be one and the same.'

Gigi raised one eyebrow at Stan to show him she didn't believe a word of it.

'Yeah, yeah,' she grinned. 'They just rolled over on their backs and asked Lou to tickle their bellies. How did you turn them round so quick? The way I hear it Duncan Hedges would have agreed to a united Ireland by the time Lou was finished with him.'

Stan laughed. 'Why, you little fox, what do you know?'

'Only,' she said, 'that Hedges's number one son, Dunky Junior, is being sent off to darkest Africa to work on the missions. Apparently it's a tragic loss to the Bangor club scene …'

'I've no idea what you're talking about,' Stan lied, flashing her a coy look. But he knew the game was up. Gigi's father, Switchblade Vic, got to hear about every fly that broke a wing in loyalist Ulster.

'Dad had actually given me a certain magazine for you,' she chuckled. 'But then he heard you'd found a copy yourself. I have to say I'm a little surprised at your bedside reading, senator …'

'Busted,' retorted Stan, with a big grin. 'My secret's out. Do you think you could ever cure me …?'

'We'll have to see if this bill goes through first,' sniffed Gigi. 'Now let's get down to the gallery and watch the debate.'

'Okay,' said the senator, sitting back up on the sofa. 'But I really think we should put some clothes on first …'

In a bid to be a little more discreet, Audrey had agreed to move their Friday lunch to the Holiday Inn in Dunavady. Susie Barkley kept a tight rein on the staff in the Kennedy, and Audrey always came in via the side door, but it was only a matter of time before one of the regulars twigged that the city's top cop had a weekly date in Harry's snug. And there was no way in hell Harry was going to have that conversation with Lorna.

So the Holiday Inn it was, with the pair arriving separately at their private booth. Harry landed first and ordered a bottle of Chardonnay and two house specials – garlic chicken tagliatelle with Waldorf salads. Eight minutes later, Audrey appeared, wearing a black Dolce & Gabbana miniskirted power suit and just a hint of Paris *parfum*. Her black satin blouse, which had been primly done up when she left the office, now had the first two buttons open. And her dark plum hair had been cut away from her face, to highlight those big hazel eyes. As she kissed him perfunctorily, but softly, on the cheek, Harry gripped the edge of the table tightly. This was getting far too dangerous.

'Caught any bad guys this week?' he asked her as she sat down.

'Close to getting one,' she replied, eyeing him directly. 'But he's still a little hard to pin down ...'

Harry chugged back half a glass of wine and coughed.

Her point made, Audrey grinned and switched tack to business.

'The *Derry Standard*,' she began, 'got a call yesterday from a woman who said she was a spokesperson for the Pure Republicans of Ireland Committee.'

'It's a wind-up,' laughed Harry. 'The PRICs? There's no such thing.'

'Our thoughts exactly,' said Audrey. 'But this lady – who incidentally was phoning from the South on a now-defunct mobile – claimed that her group had shot both King Size and Barry Magee.'

'Strongly doubt it,' declared Harry.

'Again, our very sentiments,' said Audrey. 'Except this lady knew the type of ammunition that we pulled out of both gentlemen.'

'And I take it you never gave this out?' asked Harry.

'I didn't even know it myself until about three days ago,' replied Audrey. 'They were obscure Russian bullets, from an obscure Russian pistol. We'd never seen them here before – and I'll tell you, that's saying something. Our first-time caller also knew that the killer had thrown a thousand pounds around the back seat of Barry Magee's car. Which again we'd never mentioned.'

'So how much was missing?' interrupted Harry.

'Sixty quid,' sighed Audrey, without missing a beat. 'I'll kill the Scene Of Crime Officer ...'

She looked across the table at Harry, closed her eyes and shook her head.

'So what else did this lady say?' pressed Harry.

'Most worryingly of all,' continued Audrey, 'Madame X claimed that her group intends to target all other people who are involved in blackmail, extortion and activities that harm the Derry community. She said, and I quote, that they are going to *prick* our consciences.'

'Oh God,' groaned Harry.

'Oh yes,' grinned Audrey. 'And they're going to single out, in particular, people who abuse the socially deprived by selling them homemade hooch, poisoned cigarettes and unwatchable DVDs.'

'Did they name anyone?' said Harry.

'Just the brother,' replied Audrey simply.

'Jesus,' replied Harry. 'As if I didn't have enough headcases of my own to watch out for. It's just one damn thing after another.'

'Never mind, Harry,' said Audrey, 'at least Letemout Lou got your bill through Stormont yesterday …'

Harry laughed. He wondered if Audrey knew about the Dunky Hedges angle, figured she did, and decided to give credit where credit was due. 'Yeah,' he said. 'Well actually, it was all down to some very clever behind-the-scenes work from Stan Stevenson – but never tell Lou that.'

'Christ, Harry,' laughed Audrey, 'I hope you'd never sell me out as quickly as you've just ratted out Stan.'

'I knew nothing about it,' he protested, holding up his hands. 'But I'll tell you better again. You'll never guess who wired Stan off …'

'Who?' asked Audrey, craning her neck forward.

'The Right Honourable Cyril Murnay,' smirked Harry.

'No honour among queens, then,' grinned Audrey.

'None indeed,' said Harry.

There was a rap on the door and the waiter brushed backwards into the snug. He set down the dishes of tagliatelle on the table and then looked up to greet his guests. 'Well, hello there, Harry,' he declared, delighted to see his old pal. 'And hello there, Superintendent.'

'Hi, Brendy,' said Harry and Audrey together. They shook their heads in mutual disbelief as Brendan Gallagher, first cousin of Shay Gallagher MLA – and owner of the biggest mouth in North Derry – began spooning out their salads.

'Next time,' said Harry after Brendy had bustled back into the kitchens, 'we'll go to Belfast.'

'Okay,' smiled Audrey, giving Harry another very direct look. 'And next time, we'll stay over …'

Mary Slavin was sitting at the desk in her William Street office, giving her final once-over to the front-page story for the Saturday *Derry Standard*, when Stan Stevenson bounded up the stairs.

'What are you leading with?' he asked her.

'The Stan Plan – as if you didn't know.' She grinned.

'And what way are you spinning it?'

'The bulk of the credit to your good self – with Lou getting a pretty decent sidebar for her speech on the floor,' said Mary. 'But you wrote the damn thing – and I happen to know that you did the musclework, so it's your glory.'

'I don't want it,' replied Stan. 'In fact I've got a much better story for you.'

'Jesus, Stanley,' exclaimed Mary, 'it's half-six on a Friday night. The production crew will gut me with their scalpels if I try to redo the front page.'

'It'll only mean switching your headline and your first couple of pars,' insisted her predecessor. 'And it'll be worth it.'

'Let me hear it so,' sighed Mary.

'Okay. I've just been talking to Harry the Hurler in the Jack Kennedy. It was just a friendly drink. He knows I go there the odd Friday evening to do a bit of glad-handing, so he was waiting for me on the off-chance. Anyway, I set him up a pint, and he started telling me this yarn that, I have to say, I'd have killed for when I was a hack.'

'Go on,' said Mary, warming up.

'The Boys,' continued Stan, 'are very impressed with how Louise has performed over the past month or so. Mightily impressed even. She speaks well, fears no one, looks damn good and, best of all, she's got the sharpest legal mind of her generation. So, Boys being Boys, they've got plans for her.'

'What sort of plans?'

'Let me on your machine,' said Stanley.

Mary got up out of her chair and gestured to Stan to work away. Quickly he erased the working headline 'Our Man Stan Gets His Plan' and began to type.

Mary looked over his shoulder, read the first seven words, then stepped quickly to her office door and gave a big wolf-whistle down to her three-man production team. 'Hold the front page,' she shouted.

Stanley looked up at her and winked. 'Atta girl.'

'Thirty years I'm working in journalism,' she grinned, 'and it's the first time I ever got to say that.'

34

'That dirty, stinking, lowlife bastard,' growled Harry, as he hurled his *Derry Standard* into the bin outside McCool's newsagent's on William Street. The banner headline, in screaming big 120-point type, had been enough: 'LETEMOUT LOU TO RUN FOR PRESIDENT – OFFICIAL.'

'I take it you're the official source, then?' asked Jimmy, trying desperately not to smirk.

'I'd a bottle and a half of white wine at lunch, and then maybe three or four pints in the Kennedy before Stan came in,' explained Harry as they hurried on their way towards the Guildhall. 'But that conniving fucking shitbag knew I was tanked up and should have checked back before he went to print … I'm a dead man, Jimmy. Lou is going to get out her spikiest pair of boots and play pin the toe on the donkey.'

Jimmy grinned. He had personal experience of Lou's softer side, albeit deliciously briefly, so he didn't share his brother's fear of her. 'Watch out for her teeth too,' he added.

'Don't worry,' said Harry. 'I saw the pictures …'

The younger Hurley bit his lower lip in mock embarrassment. 'It's all your own fault though, Harry,' he said. 'You should never have been off drinking in the middle of the day with your fancy woman …'

'Who told you that?' snapped Harry.

'Brendy Gallagher. He must have rung half the town by the time you and your mid-life crisis had landed back in from Dunavady. And what do you expect? It's like Al Capone hopping into bed with Mother Teresa.'

They passed by the market stalls on Waterloo Place, briefly acknowledging the salutes of Skidmark Gormley and Dumpy Doherty, and made their way across Guildhall Square.

Harry smiled in spite of himself. 'Stan should have known it was off the record,' he continued. 'Correction, he knew rightly it was off the record. I just didn't spell it out.'

Jimmy shook his head intently. 'It doesn't account for what you told him, Harry,' he said. 'Jesus, you of all people aren't a man for careless whispers. Twenty-seven times in Castlereagh Holding Centre and you never said a full sentence except "Get my fucking lawyer in here now".'

'I know,' sighed Harry. 'But, believe me, my lawyer is the last person on earth I want to run into today. Though, granted, the party selection committee would be a close second. They're going to bury me in the same bog as Woof-Woof Barker.'

'So just exactly what were you doing talking to a civilian like Stan, then?' pressed Jimmy.

'Truth is,' said Harry, 'I wanted to run it by him to see how it would fly. Like it or not, he has a damn fine political brain. Comes of years and years of doing nothing but sitting back and watching the rest of us fall on our arses. He also knows Lou better than anyone – and could give us the gen on how to handle her strengths and weaknesses.'

They walked up the steps into the Guildhall and Harry held the door open for his brother. 'But you forgot one thing,' said Jimmy as he stepped inside.

'I did indeed,' sighed Harry. 'Stanley, the clever git, has his own agenda …'

'Yeah,' replied Jimmy, 'and he's just shot your pigeon before it got out its box.'

'Maybe it's time for me to do a little shooting of my own,' said Harry ominously, as he ducked under the Guildhall's security scanner and turned right, towards his party office.

Letemout Lou wasn't sure who to kill first. But Mary Slavin and Harry the Hurler both had their mobiles off and were lying low as mice in a minefield, so it was always going to be Stanley. She got no reply from the phone in the apartment, so she drove round to his flat on spec, and sure enough his car was in the underground garage. It was the mercy of God that Gigi, who was making the coffee, had time to get a T-shirt over her head while Lou was letting herself in with her old key.

'Where is he?' she roared at Gigi.

'Away off to Dublin on the morning plane,' the terrified photographer lied.

Lou barged past the younger woman and tried the bathroom door. It was locked. A toilet flushed from inside, and thirty seconds later a smiling Stan appeared in the hall.

'I see the paper is touting you for great things.' He smiled at Lou.

'How fucking dare you?' she began. 'This could destroy me …'

Stan cut her short. 'I dare,' he said, pointing his finger into her face, 'because it's true. I dare because it is a matter of public interest. And I dare because I am your political opponent. And let me tell you, Lou, the next time you trespass on my property, I will dare to have your judicial arse hauled into the station. Now, leave that stolen key on the table, get out my door, and never come back.'

Lou had seen enough of these dramas replayed in front of her in the magistrates' court to know she didn't want to go there. So she gave Stan the finger and reached for the doorlatch.

'That reminds me,' said Stan, looking over at Gigi. 'The cleaning lady will be here at one – you'd better put some trousers on.'

The front door slammed shut with a huge bang, and Lou was gone.

Gigi had barely had a chance to get her breath back when the phone rang. The news had been picked up by RTÉ on their lunchtime bulletin, and Sonny Waterhouse was on the line for the inside track.

'Hang on a tick, Sonny,' said Gigi. 'He's back in the bathroom. Letemout Lou's just been round, and he's still hunting round for his testicles.'

Stanley laughed and snatched the phone out of her hand. 'I'm probably better off without them,' he told Sonny.

His friend sniggered. 'That was a great day's work, Stan,' he said. 'Seriously. You've announced the left's main candidate before they've had a chance to agree on her. So they're going to spend the next three months killing and blaming one another, while we can make hay.'

'You gotta put away your chances in this game,' replied Stan. 'Besides, it's good to put a little distance between myself and Lou – particularly after we worked so tightly together on the Good Neighbour Bill.'

'I take it Harry the Hurler was the source,' continued Sonny.

'He was indeed,' said Stan.

'He must be spitting tacks,' said Sonny. 'The Boys in Belfast won't like him bouncing the news out like that. Particularly before they've got their imprimatur on it.'

'Actually,' replied Stan, 'and strictly between ourselves, Harry begged me to run the story. He was afraid the Boys were going to blow the selection process – make it too democratic. Christ knows who they'd pick if you allowed the troops a free vote. But also, Harry wanted to get his candidate out before Labour got off the mark. Officially, he's outraged – and is going to fill me with more lead than Bonnie and Clyde. But privately, Harry is grinning all over his face.'

'He can't seriously think Lou has a chance,' interrupted Sonny. 'On the very best day, their vote's fifteen per cent across the island.'

'But Lou isn't them,' said Stan. 'She's totally untainted by all the non-political politics that went before. That's what they love about her – she's cleaner than a first date.'

Sonny grinned. 'But why did you run the story announcing her plans then?' he asked. 'I know she's the love of your life, but surely you're not switching over to help Harry out.'

'Not at all,' replied Stan. 'Harry was far too quick off the mark – and he completely lacks subtlety. What he forgets is that Lou's only in the party a wet week, and the story this morning makes her look like a power-mad queue-jumper. Which is why she came here this morning in search of all things circular.'

Sonny laughed again. 'Remind me never to fall out with you, Stan,' he said. 'And by the way. Rubber John is chuffed to bits. He wants to see you in Dublin tonight to tell you himself.'

At five o'clock that same evening, upstairs in the Jack

Kennedy, Harry poured himself a treble Paddy and sank back into his leather recliner. He toasted the empty office and grinned.

'*Sláinte*,' he declared to no one, just as his mobile rang.

Number withheld. Probably Audrey Grafton.

'Yep,' he said as he dropped the phone into the speaker set on the bureau beside him.

'My, you've been busy,' declared the Super.

'Why, what happened?' asked Harry, his eyes lighting up.

'Calls from three different national papers asking me if it's true that Senator Stanley Stevenson was actually in Derry when Barry Magee got killed,' said Audrey. 'Apparently a new eyewitness is putting him in a local hotel only half an hour before Barry was topped. And not in Dublin as Stan had previously stated.

'They also wanted to confirm if the senator was one of only two suspects we're looking at. And get this. They wanted to know if our investigation would be complete before the nominations close for the Irish presidential elections.'

'Why?' exclaimed Harry in mock shock. 'Is Stanley running for president as well?'

'Well, they seem to think he is,' laughed Audrey. 'Remind me never to fall out with you, Harry.'

And she clicked off.

Harry picked up the mobile and dialled a number.

'Senator,' he said when Stan picked up. 'Looks like we've set the world on fire. The Boys in Belfast actually wanted you whacked, but I've settled for kicking the shit out of you in tomorrow's papers.'

'I knew it was coming,' replied Stan. 'I take it you've announced I'm running as well?'

'I have indeed,' said Harry. 'Just as we discussed. Though I think, for your own sake, you'd better not shoot anybody else before your nomination is ratified.'

35

Stan and Harry had agreed that his status as darling boy of the Dublin liberals should be enough to protect him from the initial attacks on his candidacy. They realised that his character was going to be a central issue in the race and thought it made most sense to deal with it head on. It is one thing, however, to handle the man coming at you with a knife; it is another entirely to deal with the guy sneaking up behind you with a gun. And back in Dublin that same evening, as word was starting to filter out that Stan was going to enter the race, the senator's former mentor, Joxer O'Duffy, and his six fellow outcasts met in secret session to wreak their own revenge.

In the Dáil the expellees had adopted the working title Real Fianna Fáil, though they had quickly been rechristened The Magnificat Seven by their fellow TDs. They had assembled now in Monsignor Behan's offices on Dominick Street, with the good doctor acting – as he often did in times of crisis – as their spiritual advisor.

'Let's recap,' said the monsignor, looking around at the seven deputies, who were divided among three couches in the well-appointed room. 'Stan Stevenson convinced all of you that he would be the new champion of Christian ideals and family values. He also persuaded you, Joxer, that he would be a perfect watchdog for the right on the Sexual Health Action Group, and that he would adopt a moderate – i.e. anti-republican – stance while on the Joint Foreign Affairs Committee.'

Joxer nodded sheepishly, afraid to look directly at Father Behan.

'And yet,' continued the priest, 'just one phone call – one solitary phone call – to his former headmaster in Derry established that Stan Stevenson hasn't been inside a chapel since he was seventeen … Indeed, he was once barred from the city's cathedral for befouling four different holy water fonts on his way home from a drinking spree. According to the Derry police, who incidentally laughed out loud when they heard Stan had become a champion of moral values, an American TV company offered ten grand for the CCTV pictures. But the bishop was worried it would make the Church look bad. That and he was holding out for twenty …'

He paused to allow the group to smile uncomfortably. But they knew better than to laugh let alone speak.

'Another phone call,' Father Behan went on, 'this one to the Sisters of Mercy, who run a girls' school in Derry, ascertained that, far from being a paragon of sexual virtue – albeit in the form of a non-practising sodomite as he had you believe – the teenage senator was responsible for straddling more young fillies than Seabiscuit. And I quote Sister Brenda directly there. Jesus, and to think I gave him my last copy of *Bangor Boy-Bang* and told him not to open it …'

Joxer lowered his head, closed his eyes, and said a silent prayer the priest was winding up.

'Finally,' said Father Behan, 'as regards his politics, one call to Cyril Murnay of the Ulster Unionists, who I know, ahem, socially, confirmed that Stan Stevenson is a lifelong friend of one Harold Hurley. A name you may recognise from such soundbites as "the Republican leader Harry the Hurler is currently helping the RUC with their inquiries". Oh, and if you'd ever bothered doing a web search of the *Irish Times* archive, you'd have learned from the Social Announcements section of September two years ago that Mr Stevenson was once intending to marry Louise – Letemout Lou – Johnston, newly appointed Sinn Féin Assembly member for North Derry.'

This time, all seven heads dropped.

'Not to put too fine a point on it, Joxer,' the priest sighed, 'when you boys fuck up, you fuck up all over the place. This was amateur night. What the hell happened?'

Joxer stared at the floor, shaking his head, his face red with rage and embarrassment.

'Sonny Waterhouse,' he whispered, covering his eyes so he wouldn't have to look at his accuser.

'I don't follow,' said Father Behan.

'Sonny,' said Joxer, 'was in charge of recruiting a tame Northerner for us. Someone who on first appearances was reasonable – but would turn out to be a total disaster. Crooked maybe. But idiotic would be better still. The idea was we would look like we were extending the hand to the North – but when it fell apart, we could tar the whole lot of them with the same brush … Sonny was supposed to give the recruit a thorough P-check – personal history check – to make sure he'd broadly fit into our ideology. Instead, that treacherous Navan bastard went and double-crossed us.'

Joxer's new deputy, Jim Wynne, turned towards the monsignor and nodded his head sadly. 'Truth is, Father, Stan's just after doing to us what most of your clients would pay good money for.'

The joke got a few laughs so Father Behan let it go. 'Then we'll have to teach Mr Stevenson that we're not men to be trifled with,' said the priest.

'Agreed,' said Joxer ominously, 'but it's a lesson Mr Waterhouse is going to have to learn first.'

Across town, meanwhile, Rubber John was getting out of a plainclothes Ford Mondeo and slipping discreetly into a little apartment on Lad Lane. Stan had caught the late-evening plane down from Derry. And he, Sonny and Marky Choo-Choo the Chief Whip were sitting watching *Winning Streak* when the Taoiseach pounded on the door. Rubber John shook his Burberry coat off his shoulders and pinned it onto a peg behind the door before grabbing the proffered double Paddy.

'*Sláinte, a mhic,*' he grinned at Stan.

'*Sláinte, a Thaoisigh,*' the senator replied.

Rubber John drained his glass and handed it back to Stan with a same-again gesture. 'So they've bought it?' he asked.

'They have indeed,' nodded Stan unenthusiastically. 'At least four of tomorrow's nationals are leading with the fact that I'm going to run.'

'Good man,' replied Rubber John.

'The bad news, however,' continued Stan, 'is that, courtesy of Harry the Hurler, they're all going to claim that I'm a prime suspect in two murders. They're raking over the King Size Barkley and Barry Magee cases again. Harry told me he'd been forced to shaft me after his party cut up rough over us leaking Lou's candidacy.'

Rubber John glared at Stan over the top of his glass then necked the whiskey back in one.

'The bastards are out to drown you at birth,' he declared. 'Fuck 'em. We'll pound them into the dusht. There's nothing I enjoy better than a bare-knuckle fight at Ballinasloe fair.'

'Assuming, that is,' interrupted Sonny Waterhouse, 'that Stan didn't do anything wrong.'

'Granted,' grinned Rubber John. 'And, *ara*, sure even if he did, none of us is whiter than white ...'

The Chief Whip hadn't said anything and still looked a little uncertain.

'Out with it, man,' barked the Taoiseach.

'Well,' said his cousin. 'There are others who've given the party long service – and they mightn't be impressed by the new boy walking into the top job.'

'You're dead right, Marky,' said the Taoiseach, gesturing for another drink. 'But there's a couple of things you're forgetting. First, the presidency is not the top job – nor any way near it. With all due respect to Stan, the president has absolutely no power. Head of Ireland's armed forces? Fuck's sake, you'd do more damage as president of the Sisters of Mercy. Most parties select their candidates as a payoff or a retirement present. Either that or they want shot of them ... And, second, the other reason I think the party won't object is that I'm making my very best man Stan's campaign manager ...'

'Ah, you're jokin',' pleaded Marky.

'Get him elected in November,' said Rubber John, 'and you'll be Foreign Minister by the end of the year. And I'll feck that other, useless gobshite back to Mayo.'

'Well why didn't you say so before?' smirked his cousin. 'Now you're talkin' ...'

The four men stayed for another drink then left the flat in two groups of two. Rubber John and the Chief Whip drove back to Phibsboro together. Sonny, as was his habit on Saturday nights, headed for the Haughey Arms, dragging a reluctant Stan along.

'There's always fresh young talent in at the weekends,' promised Sonny as they walked up Baggot Street.

'I've seen your wife,' retorted Stan. 'Trust me – it's all relative.'

'What's the matter?' pressed Sonny. 'Afraid Gigi McCormack might have her spies in the pub?'

'No, it's not that,' replied Stan. 'It's just not my thing. If you only ever get to know one thing about me, Sonny, let it be this – I only ever take on one woman at a time. Two on the one page – no matter how far they are apart – is too much for me. I don't like being played for a sap, so I wouldn't do it to anyone else. But the bottom line is, if you do mess about, you always get caught. Even if they never find out about each other – which is rare – you'll always give yourself away. There'll come a point where you will get so fed up with one or other of them that you'll just have to tell her. To rub her nose in it. To show her how smart you are. And you can bet your eyeteeth she won't rest until the other one knows as well.'

Sonny gave Stan a Christ-Luck-To-You grin and shook his head in pity.

'Seriously,' said Stan, 'you shouldn't mock. I've watched better men than me fall on their arses because they thought they could whistle two tunes at the same time. And while I accept, Sonny, that you're a smart guy and know what you're doing, a man as prominent as you would really need to be careful … And besides, I need hardly remind you, I'm just about to run for president.'

Sonny laughed as he pulled open the side door to the pub. 'Jesus, Stan,' he said, 'you're like something out of the fourteenth century. Anyhow, the way my luck's been going over the past few months, the only fresh meat I'll be getting is from the kebab shop on my way home.'

But for once Sonny Waterhouse was wrong.

The pair fought their way through to the upstairs lounge,

which was slightly quieter, shouted two pints and grabbed a little table with three chairs by the frosted glass window. They weren't settled thirty seconds when a pretty blonde girl approached and asked if she could borrow the spare seat.

'Eva,' cried Stan, recognising her immediately.

'Senator,' exclaimed Eva, planting a kiss on his cheek. She looked stunning. Her miniskirt was precisely two inches higher than the shortest he'd ever seen − and if her blouse had been one inch lower, they'd have been drinking in a topless bar.

Stan figured she might have been out with friends. But instead of taking the seat away, she sat down and pulled out a cigarette.

'That's illegal here,' grinned Stan.

'It's okay,' replied Eva, 'I don't light them … And besides, lots of things are illegal here, but it doesn't mean you can't enjoy them now, does it?'

They both laughed, and then Eva turned to face Sonny Waterhouse.

'And who's your very handsome friend?' she asked Stan as she gave his pal a more than approving once-over.

'I'm Sonny,' replied the Meath shortarse with the 1970s moustache.

'They say small men are very durable, Sonny,' said Eva, lowering her voice and flicking her eyebrows just a notch. 'Would you say that's true?'

'Absolutely,' said Sonny, liking her style. 'When you're short on stature, you have to be durable. Extremely durable. You've got to make sure that anyone who ever tries to take advantage of you will never forget it.'

'I'm pretty durable myself,' continued Eva, looking him straight in the eye. 'In fact, my friends call me Eva Ready.'

Stan caught Eva's eye and quickly mouthed the words 'God no', but she was moving in for the kill.

'So what exactly is it you do, Eva?' pressed Sonny.

'I do lots of things,' replied Eva, as she slowly sucked on the straw that was sticking out of her Diet Coke bottle. 'But mostly, whatever comes into my head on the spur of the moment.'

'Good answer,' mumbled Sonny, suddenly unable to keep

up with the pace. 'Sorry, what I meant was how do you make your living?'

'I'm an actress,' said Eva. 'But you'll find, Sonny, that I'm also quite the performer off camera. I give private acting lessons – and I assure you my rates are quite reasonable.'

Sonny cottoned on and grinned back. The shock of it. The gorgeous woman had an ulterior motive.

'Watch her, Sonny, she's dangerous,' interrupted Stan with a not entirely sincere chuckle. But it was too late. Mister Durable was hooked.

'I'd say you've done a bit of acting in your time too, Sonny,' continued Eva. 'I mean, you've certainly got the looks for it. And I'd say you could manage as many takes as it needs to get the angle just perfect …'

'All down to durability,' retorted Sonny, reckoning what the hell.

'And boy do I like durable men,' smiled Eva, running her tongue slowly across her sharp white teeth.

Eva rose and made her way slowly to the Ladies, to give Sonny a better demonstration of what he could expect in his acting masterclass. The new minister was mightily impressed. And after about a minute, when she hadn't returned, he announced to Stan that the Guinness was shooting through him and he also disappeared.

Neither made it back to the table.

36

The BBC and RTÉ analysts don't always agree on Northern matters. But on this occasion they were singing note for note – Stan Stevenson's career in politics was over. It had been eight days since the Sundays had started wielding their knives, and the senator's reputation had been sliced up thinner than yellow-pack ham.

Rubber John, of course, wasn't a man to be caught wrong-footed. As a lifelong horse fancier, he was an expert in hedging his bets. So the Monday after the initial onslaught, he instructed the Chief Whip to put it about, quietly, that the nomination was by no means a done deal – despite his initial statement supporting Stan. There would, of course, be room for other would-be candidates to make their case to the party.

By Wednesday evening of the first week, only eighteen members of the Fianna Fáil parliamentary group were still openly prepared to support Stan's candidacy – as compared to the sixty-eight who'd backed him in the *Sunday Ireland* before they heard he was a double murderer. And an *Irish Times* poll on Thursday morning showed that just thirty-two per cent of the Southern electorate believed the senator was innocent, while sixty per cent thought he should be suspended from office until the police investigation into him was complete.

Sonny Waterhouse wasn't impressed with all the rushing for cover and told the Taoiseach so directly when they met briefly at the Mansion House May Ball.

'Why the fuck did you back him in the first place?' he asked Rubber John.

'Same reason Stan let his name go forward,' said the Taoiseach. 'Because he could win.'

'And now?'

'Two possibilities. He'll either die a thousand deaths in the papers and be in jail by the end of the month. Or the papers could be wrong – in which case he'll be the greatest martyr since Liam Mellows, and in November we'll romp home to a band playing.'

'But will it be Stan that is romping home, or will he be out of the picture by then?'

'That,' said the Taoiseach, 'remains to be seen.'

Harry the Hurler had warned Stan from the beginning that it would eventually emerge that he was in Derry at the time of Barry Magee's shooting. What Stan hadn't expected was that it would be Harry himself who would give him away. But after several sleepless nights, Harry had confided in Audrey Grafton, off the record, that the senator had called into his office in the Jack Kennedy thirty minutes before Barry got caught with his trousers down.

'I hate to do this to Stan,' he told her, 'but I have to take the heat off Jimmy. His nerves can't take it. The thought of him doing a stretch for something he didn't do would push him over.'

Stan had been expecting the onslaught, however, and was as ready as anyone could be. All questions about the murders were fielded by his solicitor Tommy Bowtie, who had already lodged libel writs against the four Sundays and the PSNI. This slowed up the worst excesses of the media's enthusiasm. Then on Thursday evening, Stan himself issued a brief denial of any wrongdoing and suggested that this was one witch-hunt that could turn against the Inquisition. But he refused point-blank to answer specifics – on legal advice. The message to the pack was simple. God help you all if you don't kill me outright.

By Monday of the second week, Stan's only priority was to stay in the presidential race till the weekend. The rule of thumb is that if a politician can survive an entire fortnight of a media-thrashing, he's pretty much made of Teflon and will scrub clean again.

There was, however, one practicality that Stan couldn't ignore. The nomination. And to secure his shot at the title, he needed the signatures of at least twenty TDs and senators. But without central party backing, he was in real trouble. Fine Gael, Labour, the Progressive Democrats and most of the independents wouldn't touch him with a Stinger missile. And the Shinners, of course, were backing Letemout Lou.

The only other avenue open to the senator was to persuade four county councils to nominate him. But that hadn't been tried since Dana's time. And, as the man in the *Irish Times* said, as soon as you go down that road, you may as well take out a marker and write 'Train Wreck' on your forehead.

But Tommy Bowtie and Sonny Waterhouse reckoned it was at least worth a shot, given that the Good Neighbour Act now allowed Northern councils to take part in the process as well. And so, on the eighth day, Stan Stevenson went home to ask the people of Dunavady if they wanted him to lead their country.

Six or seven camera crews and about a dozen journalists were stationed outside the town hall when Stan arrived, accompanied by Tommy Bowtie and Gigi McCormack. All the other councillors had already gone into the hall: five Sinn Féiners, two SDLP reps, one from the DUP, three Ulster Unionists and Shay Gallagher, the independent. A twelve-man jury. And not one of them had spoken to the mob on the way in.

The smart money, and the men from RTÉ and the BBC, were certain that it would be the senator's final humiliation. The council elections were only two weeks away and the parties would all want to deliver a resounding 'zero tolerance' message to their constituents. Shay Gallagher, they figured, was Stan's only possibility of a vote – and even that was watery. The only matter left to be decided was whether the Shinners would vote against him or abstain.

Inside the hall, the public gallery was packed, and a second desk had to be hoked out of storage for the media. Harry the Hurler, Letemout Lou, Jimmy Fidget, Sonny Waterhouse and Uncle Hugo had managed to get front-row seats, while Mary Slavin had come forty-five minutes early to bag a prime seat at the main press table. By the time Stan took his seat in the inner chamber, Tommy Bowtie and Gigi could only get standing spaces at the door.

The hall went silent as Chris Caddle, the Sinn Féin mayor, entered from the ante-room and took his seat. Nonetheless, he banged his gavel officiously on the rostrum, and called for order.

'Before we start normal council business tonight,' he began, 'we have agreed to suspend standing orders to discuss, and vote on, a motion calling on our council to nominate Senator Stanley Stevenson, a member of this authority, for the position of president of Ireland. Do I have a proposer?'

Dexter Hart, the pro-Agreement UUP man, put up his hand.

'That's odd,' muttered the man from RTÉ.

'And do I have a seconder?' continued the mayor.

Tony Blunt, the anti-Agreement DUP man from Drumbridge, stuck up a finger and announced, 'I second.'

'Well, fuck me,' whispered the man from BBC.

'Has anyone anything to say on the motion?' asked the chair.

'Just this,' announced Shay Gallagher. And with that he stood up from his seat and, at arm's length, brandished a copy of a Sunday broadsheet from eight days previously. The headline, which covered a full third of the page, read: 'DERRY SENATOR IS TWO TIMES KILLER'.

The councillor turned to face the public gallery and very slowly and very deliberately ripped the newspaper in two. He then scrunched up the two halves, spun round and hurled the ball of paper violently at the first press table.

The hacks, with the exception of Mary Slavin, ducked down and covered their heads as if it were raining rocks. There was some brief laughter from the gallery but it hushed quickly when Gallagher turned round and shook his head No. It wasn't the time.

'Okay,' he said, taking a breath and dusting his hands. 'That's all I've got. Let's put it to a vote.'

'All those for the motion,' called the mayor.

Eleven hands from the inner chamber shot up without hesitation — accompanied by Chris Caddle's from the chair. The press tables, to a reporter, sucked in air in shock.

'What's wrong, Mr Stevenson?' inquired the mayor with a grin. 'Are you not voting for yourself?'

'I'm not sure it would be appropriate,' replied Stan, wondering what the hell was going on.

The older man smiled down at him paternally. 'Well, Stanley, I think you should,' said Caddle. 'Otherwise those twisted vulture-bastards from Belfast and Dublin might try to convince us that it wasn't unanimous. Now, get your hand up before I go down to you.'

Stan nodded back at the mayor and raised his arm.

'Congratulations, senator,' grinned the mayor. 'You're the first man ever chosen by this council to run for president of Ireland. It goes without saying that we're very proud of you. Now, go off and win it – for all of us.'

Over in the public gallery, Harry the Hurler immediately stood up and shouted, 'Hear, hear'. Letemout Lou was right behind him, pounding her hands together joyously. Within seconds, they'd been joined by Uncle Hugo, Sonny Waterhouse, Jimmy Fidget, the entire row behind them and then the row behind that. And by the time the back row had all got to their feet, the noise inside the hall was deafening.

Stan was stunned. But there was more to come. The twelve councillors looked around at one another, nodded, then rose as one to join in the applause. This sparked louder cheers again from the gallery.

And then came the moment that made the hairs on Stan's neck stand on end. As a reporter for fifteen years, he knew the media were bound to remain impartial. But when he looked over at Mary Slavin at the press table, she saluted him with a closed fist, got to her feet and began banging her hands loudly on the desk. Ivan Coultron, her news editor, was next, and then the girl from the *Londonderry Leader*. Even the man from RTÉ was clapping his notebook against his hand.

Back at the doorway, Gigi McCormack was beaming with pride and clapping up a storm. She knew it wasn't really her victory – or wouldn't be for long. She only had to look at the tears in Letemout Lou's eyes to work that out. Gigi hadn't cried for anyone like that since Dee-Dee lifted his All-Star award three years ago …

As the crowd dispersed from the hall, about half a dozen

men with microphones managed to fight their way through the hordes to doorstep Tommy Bowtie.

'Tommy, why did all the councillors agree to back the senator despite the fact that he's a double murder suspect?' asked one of them.

'It's simple,' said the lawyer. 'There are two groups of us: those who know he didn't do it; and those who hope he did and don't care. I'll leave it up to you to decide which camp I'm in. But get it wrong, you little shit, and I'll clean you out.'

37

The next three nights saw Derry, Strabane and Omagh councils ratify Stan's candidacy at a canter, so by the weekend he was the only confirmed name on the presidential ballot paper. They had tried to kill him within the allocated fortnight but failed.

By Saturday of the second week, the Taoiseach even allowed himself to be photographed with the senator at a Gaelscoil opening in Creggan. And the following day, most of the Southern press, while not exactly slapping Stan's back, were at least starting to suggest that maybe he should be given the benefit of the doubt. All apart, that is, from the *Sunday Irishman*, which ran twelve separate opinion pieces on how Dunavady was a Provo backwater populated by inbred Satanists.

Letemout Lou was expected to join Stan on the ballot paper next. Barring disaster, her nomination would be adopted by four councils – Magherafelt, Newry, Monaghan and Louth – within the next ten days.

The soft left were still toying with the idea of putting up another nominee to shaft the dastardly Shinners. But Fine Gael, who theoretically commanded up to thirty per cent of the popular vote, were looking less and less inclined to run a Blueshirt candidate. Like the rest of the country, they were waiting on Joxer O'Duffy. No one else had come forward from within mainstream Fianna Fáil.

Joxer's mind, however, was on other matters. Jim Wynne had rung him at three o'clock on Monday morning to say he had some very interesting news about Sonny Waterhouse.

'This better be good, Jim,' grunted Joxer.

'Of course it's fucking good, boss – it's three in the morning,' retorted Wynne.

'So give us it,' replied Joxer.

'Too good even for the phone,' said Jim. 'I'll meet you in your Dáil office at half-seven. There'll be nobody about. Sure the culchies never start till ten on a Monday.'

'Make it eight,' sighed Joxer. 'And it had better be worth it.'

'It is, boss,' laughed Jim. 'It is.'

It was.

Joxer got into his office at ten to eight, and had barely taken his Crombie off when his deputy leader banged on the door. Wynne was grinning like he'd just unhooked his first bra.

'Best yet,' he said to Joxer.

'Well, out with it, man,' snapped his boss.

'Patience, Joxer,' replied Wynne. 'There's a bit of a story here – so I think I'd better tell you it as it happened.'

'Okay so,' said Joxer, who was starting to sense the excitement. 'Fire ahead.'

'It starts on Saturday night,' explained Wynne. 'Myself and Majella called into the Haughey Arms for a pint on our way home after the pictures. Normally, I'd avoid the place like a plague, apart from our meetings, on account of the fact that too many politicians use it. But Doheny's was packed, so we head for Haughey's and got a seat upstairs. So I ordered us up a pint, turned round to look for a seat, and who was sitting in the corner but Sonny Waterhouse ...'

'Hardly a shock there,' retorted Joxer.

'Aha,' chuckled Wynne. 'But who was with him?'

'Who?' replied Joxer eagerly. 'Tell me quick, you fucker.'

'A twenty-year-old girl,' grinned Wynne.

'You're kidding,' laughed Joxer.

'I'm not,' replied Wynne, shaking his head. 'She was wearing this little miniskirt that you couldn't blow your nose in, and a blouse cut all the way down to her appendix scar.'

'Well, fuck me,' smiled Joxer.

'There's more,' said Wynne. 'As soon as Sonny saw me, the pair of them drained their drinks and left the bar. So I thought to meself, that's a bit odd. Sonny's eldest child is ten, so for pure craic, I says to the barman, "Is that Mr Waterhouse's daughter?" But, sure enough, the barman says, "It is in his hole. She's a working girl who's been servicing that damned fool for the last three or four weeks now."'

Joxer reached over the table and shook Wynne by the hand. 'You're a fucking angel,' he declared.

'But it gets better,' said his deputy. 'According to the barman, it was Stan Stevenson who actually introduced Sonny to the girl. He says Stan was in a stag party from Derry who hired her for the weekend back at the start of the year. He remembers it well because apparently the senator was the only man in the bar who didn't know Eva – that's her name – was a hooker.'

'Oh that's just beautiful,' laughed Joxer.

'But here's the crunch,' said Wynne slowly. 'I managed to get an address for the girl and called on her last night. And I brought our good friend the Superintendent along with me. As you can imagine, Eva was not a happy bunny at all. In fact she was one bad-tempered little biddy altogether – and left the track of her nails all along the Super's cheek. But when we put it to her that we would personally put her in jail for a long, long time if she didn't help us snare Sonny, she soon came round. So she's agreed to set up another meeting for this weekend.'

'Perfect,' laughed Joxer. 'And will she implicate Stan as well?'

'She clammed up when we mentioned him,' replied Wynne with a nasty little smile. 'Apart from one thing. She strongly denied ever having what she calls professional relations with Stan, but she let it slip that there's a photo of the two of them kicking around Derry.'

'Dare I ask?' asked Joxer.

'You dare,' replied Wynne. 'And in answer to your question, no, neither she nor the senator would be wearing any clothes in this picture.'

'Jim,' declared Joxer, 'I've said this many times before but I'll say it again – you, my friend, are the big dog's bollix.'

'Aren't I just?' smirked Wynne.

The senator's campaign was also the main topic on the agenda for Audrey Grafton's Friday lunch with Harry the Hurler later that week. After a long dark night of the soul, Harry had called off their trip to the Europa Hotel in Belfast and insisted on an open table at the Jack Kennedy instead.

'I'm sorry, Audrey,' he said when he rang her private, untapped line to explain. 'But I can't do it to Lorna. Ten years ago, yeah, when the world was mad and so were we. But not now … And besides, the scandal – if it came out, it would finish you.'

'Don't try and sugar-coat it,' laughed the Super. 'I'm a big girl and know what I'm doing. But I'm warning you, I'll get you in the long grass … And you might just like it.'

'Yes I might,' gulped Harry. 'Hence the open table.'

The conversation at the meal had been a little stilted at first because there were people at the next table. But after the soup bowls had been cleared away, Harry signalled over to Susie Short Shorts who was maître d'-ing, and she quickly found them an empty snug. The point had been proved – no one was hiding anything.

'I was speaking to Letemout Lou last night,' began Audrey as soon as the snug door clacked shut.

Harry smiled awkwardly. 'I take it she's still a little miffed with me,' he said.

'Yeah, like Poland's still a little miffed with Hitler,' retorted Audrey. 'It was one thing supporting Stan out in Dunavady – that was sending out a message. But according to Lou, at least, you rigged the meetings in Derry and Tyrone to make sure he got their backing as well.'

Harry sighed and shook his head. 'I rigged nothing,' he said. 'But yes, I did want to make certain that Stan's name got on the ballot paper. The problem with Lou is that she can't see the bigger picture. She believes she can actually get elected. The rest of us know she can't. She'll do quite creditably – but realistically it's too soon. We're still not quite ready to race in the mainstream. But Stan, if we can clean him up in time, could do very well. Which is why I put the murder stuff out front and centre first day. No last-minute surprises. But between my connections and yours, Audrey, we'll have Stan washed whiter than white by the end of the summer – and that'll allow him a clear run in the autumn.'

'So, either way, you're the puppet-master,' laughed Audrey.

'I prefer to think of myself as a guardian angel,' said Harry.

The waiter knocked on the swing doors and put dishes of spaghetti amatriciana in front of his boss and his girlfriend. Without saying a word, he poured two half-glasses of Chianti, nodded at Harry and then closed the door.

'So I take it the Boys from Armagh have forgiven you for announcing Lou's selection, then?' asked Audrey, spearing a little piece of bacon.

'Course they have,' sniffed Harry. 'I took her down to a meeting of, how can I put this, our, ah, officer board. And she just blew them away. If she can keep that tongue of hers in check, she'll lead the party for a generation.'

'And of course, she has personal experience of how things operate at the sharp end,' said Audrey coldly.

'I don't know what you mean,' retorted Harry quickly.

'Let's just say,' snapped Audrey, 'that Belfast High Court isn't the only place she's been sitting in judgement. Word about my patch is that you and your friends used to draft her in to chair your own private tribunals when things got tricky ...'

Harry shucked back a mouthful of pasta, then put down his fork. 'For the record,' he said, pointing upwards at the imaginary mike, 'could I just say that allegation is complete nonsense. I deny it entirely. But can I also say I think it's a bit rich for a former member of the RUC to be handing me out lessons in morality. It's worse than the Americans telling us they just want to be peacemakers and they don't want the oil.'

Audrey grinned to let Harry know she was conceding the point then drained her glass of wine.

'Talking of oil,' she continued. 'There was another reason I had to see you today.'

'I take it we're not talking baby oil here?' asked Harry, looking up from his pasta warily.

'No,' smiled Audrey, 'though I'll keep it in mind. We're talking about diesel oil. Your brother Jimmy, it seems, has found himself a new pastime out in Dunavady.'

'Oh Lord, don't tell me,' groaned Harry.

'Yep,' replied Audrey. 'We're about to raid a massive diesel-washing plant on the Drumbridge Road. From what we gather, they're rinsing the dye out of about a million gallons of agricultural diesel a month. Problem is, they're not doing the job properly – and are leaving some of the chemical marker in the oil. So when the punters pump the cut-price stuff into their cars, their engines are falling out about a fortnight later.'

Harry covered his face with the palms of his hand and shook his head from side to side. 'How do you know it's Jimmy?' he asked.

'Do you know any other newspaper photographer who's driving a brand new Lexus?'

Harry bit his lip to suppress a laugh. 'I'll sort it out, Audrey,' he said. 'Just give me the weekend.'

38

When Letemout Lou walked into the Monaghan council chamber the next week, a thrill shot right through her as she looked over at the public gallery. It was to be her first formal nomination and was perhaps the first step on a path to greatness. But what really made her night was that Stan had made the effort to be there.

He waved over to her, and as she was about five minutes early, she crossed the room and sat down in the empty row of seats in front of him.

'What brings you here?' she asked, looking at him conspiratorially.

'Just checking out the opposition,' he grinned.

'Your little Orange bedwarmer couldn't make it so,' sniffed Lou.

'No,' mumbled Stan. 'Some pressing business back in Detroit, I think. And to be honest, I don't expect her back. Mary's advertised for a new photographer …'

He said nothing for a moment while Lou stared at him, letting him sweat. Bad idea. Never give your opponent a chance to draw his breath.

'I take it Jimmy Fidget's on his way down,' grinned Stan. 'Or maybe he's here already – and hiding under the table. I hear he does that sometimes.'

Lou blushed and slapped Stan's knee in feigned outrage. '*Touché*,' she chuckled. 'But no. The position of presidential consort is still open.'

'You could always use Harry the Hurler,' suggested Stan.

'As could you, smarty-pants,' laughed Lou.

The council hall was starting to fill up with Sinn Féiners from the border counties. But the newcomers were tactful enough to leave a breathing space around their candidate and her opponent.

'Did you know what he was going to pull in Dunavady?' asked Stan.

'No,' said Lou, shaking her head. She then looked direct into her ex-fiancé's face. 'But to be honest, I wouldn't have missed it for the world.'

'Why do you think he helped me?' pressed Stan.

'He did it for the greater good,' replied Lou. 'It was almost altruistic – except of course with Harry, nothing's entirely selfless. He wants the two of us in the debate so that real Northern issues can be discussed: our isolation; our crappy infrastructure; our deprivation, and the fact that our situation is, at best, an academic debate in the South … And also, Harry needs an unrepentant Northerner in the frame. He doesn't want someone elected who's going to go native Dublin Four, as soon as they get their arse into the job.'

Stan nodded. There's no money in a watchdog who won't bark.

'But,' continued Lou, 'if we're going to be totally honest here, most important of all, Harry doesn't think I'm electable. And he figures you're the next best thing. He also reckons you and I will have sorted out our differences by then …'

'And will we?' interrupted Stan gently.

'I can't see it,' sighed Lou. 'Politically, you might be the golden boy. But privately, you've been behaving like a total flake. You walked out on your job and your family not six months ago. You're going through women like a stag in rutting season. And you're still refusing to answer questions about your possible role in the murder of a man who was blackmailing you – despite the fact you're running for the highest office in the country. I'm thirty-four, Stan. I need a little certainty in my life.'

'You're nearly thirty-six, Lou,' retorted Stan. 'And you should know by now that nothing in life is certain.'

Lou motioned to slap his head and Stan pretended to duck. But her real punch had landed – just as she'd intended.

'So, are you sorry Harry helped me out in Dunavady, then?' asked Stan quietly.

Lou sighed. 'If we were smart, we wouldn't have gone near it,' she said. 'We could have buried you there and then. Rubber John would have spent the rest of the year trying to recover and probably never got another candidate. And, honest to God, we might just have had a chance. But do you know what, Stan?'

'What?'

'I was so proud of you,' said Lou softly. 'Really.'

'As I am of you, Lou,' replied Stan, pointing to his watch. 'Now, go and eat 'em up.'

Sonny Waterhouse knew he was in trouble from the second Jim Wynne spotted him in the Haughey Arms that Saturday night. The next week had been agony as he waited for the axe to fall. But by the weekend, nothing had happened, and he figured he'd escaped. So, naturally, he and Eva staged their own little private reunion. Big mistake.

When the summons came to present himself at Joxer's office the following Tuesday morning, it didn't take him five seconds to work out exactly what had happened. Joxer had given him precisely enough rope to hang himself. And he had. Like the total amateur he was.

As Sonny walked down the corridor to the offices of the Magnificat Seven, he figured it would be bad. Very bad, even.

Which just shows how wrong you can be.

It was fucking terrible.

Joxer and Wynne were sitting on chairs at either end of a conference table when the secretary ushered him through the door.

'You're finished, Sonny,' said Joxer bluntly, pointing Sonny to a remote chair about halfway along the table. 'And to be honest, I'm delighted. All that's left now is for us to discuss how bad it's going to be.'

Sonny sat down at his chair, clenched his fists under the table and glared at Joxer. 'Get on with it so,' he replied.

Joxer opened a manila file on his desk and put on a pair of gold reading glasses.

'We in Real Fianna Fáil,' he began pompously, 'have received information from a reputable source that you, Mr

Waterhouse, have been consorting with prostitutes. The source has forwarded us a sworn affidavit from one such call-girl, a Miss Eva Given, also known as Eva Ready, that she had carnal relations with you on seven occasions on dates during the last month.'

'You bastards,' protested Sonny, pushing himself up out of his seat.

Joxer gestured impatiently to him to sit down again.

'The source has also furnished us,' he said, 'with film footage, which graphically illustrates the accuracy of his, or her, evidence. Our source further says that he or she intends to forward Miss Given's statements to the national press immediately. One newspaper, to my knowledge, has already agreed to publish the story tomorrow. The others no doubt will follow.'

'Fuck you,' shouted Sonny angrily.

'Hang on,' said Joxer. 'That much is a *fait accompli*. You got caught, suck it up. I had to. Now, this is the good part. Our source will then hand over the film footage, which incidentally was shot on Saturday night past in Miss Given's boudoir, to the broadcast media on Thursday. Unless ...'

'Unless what?' snapped Sonny.

'Unless you give us Stan Stevenson on a silver platter,' smirked Joxer.

'Fuck you,' declared Sonny again.

'How bad do you want it to be?' interrupted Jim Wynne, coldly. 'You might just make it back from the scandal if it's quick and clean. You've a day's grace now to sort out things between yourself and Rubber John, and yourself and the wife. But as soon as the pictures appear, you're never coming back. We have you by the sweet-and-sours, Sonny.'

Sonny put his head in his hands and wept silently. Joxer watched his former friend's shoulders shake and grinned over at his new deputy. They owned him, and they knew it.

Sonny looked back up at them in despair, eyes red against an ashen face. 'If I do agree to help you,' he said, 'is there any way you can get me another day's grace from the papers? Marie's visiting friends in England until tomorrow, and I'd rather tell her face to face.'

Joxer looked over to Wynne, who nodded.

'Okay so,' smirked Joxer. 'Anything for you, Sonny. But the story will be out there on Thursday morning. So move quickly. Now. Let's talk about Senator Stevenson ...'

Stan, however, was ahead of the game. That same morning, he'd rung through to his Senate office for his schedule and discovered that a lady called Eva had been looking for him. She hadn't left a message. So he figured it could only be one thing. They'd been caught.

Immediately, he called Sonny on his mobile.

'You couldn't be fucking told ...' he began angrily.

'Don't, Stan,' pleaded Sonny. 'I'm so sorry. So very, very sorry.'

'Save it for Marie,' snapped Stan.

'How did you find out?' Sonny demanded, his voice breaking.

'Doesn't matter,' came the reply. 'Just one question: who knows?'

'Joxer and Jim Wynne,' replied Sonny. 'They say it'll be hitting the papers on Thursday – and that they're going to hand round the video at the weekend. Unless ...'

'Unless you give them me,' sighed Stan. 'Listen, don't talk to anyone. Not Eva. Not Joxer. Not Wynne. And, above all else, not Marie. I'll see if we can square things.'

'But how?' asked Sonny.

'I'll speak to them myself,' said Stan. 'It's me they're looking for – and they're going to get me anyway. But maybe they might go a bit easier on you. Do you think they've tipped off any of the papers yet?'

'I do,' answered Sonny. 'But I don't think they've given them the statements yet – there's no way they could have persuaded them to hold it this long.'

'So we've a bit of time, then,' said Stan, a little more reassuringly. 'One more thing, Sonny. Absolutely no more talking on this mobile. Bye.'

Even his mother would have conceded that Jim Wynne was one of the ugliest men ever to come out of Cork. Not that you could ever tell him that, as Joxer's deputy was also a self-opinionated little windbag. Moreover, his poor eyesight allowed him to blur out the image in the mirror of the dwarf with the buckteeth. And in private moments, he liked to consider himself more of a latter-day Michael Collins. Indeed, for a while he even attempted to mimic Liam Neeson's portrayal of the Big Fellow in the film. 'Riddlin'?' he'd say, pointing his finger into his wardrobe mirror. 'Do you know the price of bullets??? I'll give ya fuckin' riddlin'.'

But it was too much of a stretch. Neeson was six-four at least, while Wynne, by his own admission, had to stand on a box to brush his teeth. So when Joxer appointed him as his number two in the Magnificat Seven, Wynne took on a new starring role. He was Steve McQueen to Joxer's Yul Brynner. A protector of poor natives against the invading barbarian hordes. A man who would ride off into the sunset with Ali McGraw. A cool, smiling, handsome assassin.

Like all film stars, there was nothing Wynne loved more than getting his name in the headlines – except, perhaps, when he was arranging the honour for somebody else. And in this case it was someone who had shat on him and was overdue his comeuppance.

Revenge, Wynne often mused, was a dish best served on the front page.

Unfortunately for Joxer's second-in-command, however, his plans to put Sonny Waterhouse's name in lights had now hit a snag. His vision of seeing his nemesis nailed to a newspaper cross had been delayed indefinitely. And for once, there was no consolation for Jim in the fact that he'd be making the front pages himself.

The two little bullet holes in the centre of his chest had made certain of that.

Sitting in your Dáil office, waiting for Stan Stevenson to come in and grovel for his life, and a motorcycle courier walks in and plugs you. No riddling. Just bang, bang.

Quick as that.

The End.

Who'd have thought it?

39

Stan, typical of his luck, was the first to arrive on the scene after the shooting. Though then again, as he said himself later, at least it was better than Jim Wynne's luck. The senator saw the body slumped over the desk, checked for vital signs, did what he could, then dialled up Security. A Dáil rent-a-cop arrived within two minutes and immediately put Stan under arrest.

'I know your form, you Northern bastard,' the cop had said. 'Now sit in that chair and don't move till the Branch arrive.'

Stan ignored the idiot, lifted the phone and dialled Tommy Bowtie's mobile number.

'Get in your car and drive to Leinster House quickly,' he barked. 'Somebody's shot Jim Wynne – one of the Magnificat Seven. And you'll never guess who got to find the body.'

'On my way,' said Tommy. 'I'll be three hours – barring pit stops.'

'Stick a cork in it,' retorted Stan, 'and get here in two and a half.'

By the time Tommy appeared, however, the senator was off the hook. Well, for pointing the gun at least. There'd never been a murder in the Dáil before, so Special Branch weren't going to miss the chance to show their tight-arsed paymasters just how effective they could be in a crisis. Within minutes, detectives had collected a full set of CCTV pictures of the suspect. They quickly found the footage of him entering the Dáil through the Kildare Street gate, and were able to tail him right up until he produced a German pistol from his inside pocket and knocked on the victim's office door.

Apparently, the young messenger had told the garda on the front desk that he had a 'most urgent' message for Mr Wynne – and had been buzzed right through. Which explained why all the murderer's facial characteristics were completely disguised by a motorcycle helmet.

The good news for Stan, however, was that one sharp-eyed sergeant actually found several frames of film which showed the senator and the hitman passing one another in the ground-floor lobby. Indeed, in one of the stills, the killer appeared to look over at Stan in recognition.

'Probably knew me from my presidential campaign,' said Stan, in an impatient tone that brooked no further argument.

Equally, the senator refused point-blank to discuss the nature of his visit to Mr Wynne's office. But a standoff was averted thanks to the unlikely intervention of Joxer O'Duffy and his good friend Garda Superintendent Conal 'Conman' Donnelly.

'Mr O'Duffy has made me aware of the content of their meeting,' declared Conman pompously. 'It was parliamentary business and shall remain confidential.'

The Branch, however, were less satisfied. 'Just one more thing, Senator Stevenson,' said the lead detective, doing his best Colombo impression as Stan headed for the door. 'Deputy Wynne's tie has been loosened and the top two buttons of his shirt have been undone – any idea why?'

'I did that,' answered Stan sombrely, 'while I was attempting to perform CPR. And yes, I also tried mouth-to-mouth ...'

The cop scribbled quickly in his notebook. And Tommy Bowtie, who'd just arrived, grinned over at his client. 'Gentlemen,' he said to the room, 'I think I'm going to take my client home and fix him a large drink.'

They all nodded, and the Branch man at the door stood aside to let the two Derrymen out.

'Beautiful touch,' whispered Tommy to Stan, as he led him towards the stairwell. 'Give me two minutes on the blower, and there'll only be one headline in the papers tomorrow.'

Sure enough, it only took one call to reset the agenda.

As Wynne had been shot in time for the teatime news, the morning dailies would be screaming for a fresh angle. So Tommy got straight on to the Press Association's Dublin office, while Stan drove them the half-mile or so to his Lad Lane flat.

'Ask the Garda press office to confirm what attempts were made to save Mr Wynne's life – and by whom,' Tommy told the PA news editor. 'And when you want a comment from the senator, ring me back. But don't give the number out to anyone else – particularly RTÉ or we'll be tortured.'

Four minutes later, RTÉ were on the line. 'Can we get an interview with the hero senator for *Morning Ireland*?' asked the late night producer.

'I'll see if I can arrange it,' sniffed Tommy. 'But for God's sake don't give this number to anyone else – especially the *Irish Times*. They'll plague us …'

He punched the Off button on his mobile. 'Five minutes tops before the *Times* call,' he grinned. 'Journalists are worse than old women.'

'You're a marvel,' laughed Stan. And he pulled the car into the little space outside his apartment, where the Hennessy brandy was patiently waiting.

If Stan milked the glory the day after the murder, it was Joxer who stole the show for the following week. Every time you switched on a television or opened a newspaper, there he was, broken-hearted, telling the world how poor Jim Wynne had been shot by drug dealers, animal rights activists, pro-immigrant pinkos – or possibly all three. Most of the papers pointed out that the m.o. was similar to the two killings that Senator Stevenson had been involved in back in Derry. But the gun used in the Dáil was different – and it had been fired from a distance of only six or seven inches – whereas the earlier killings had been from four or five feet, and through car windows. This time, it was up close and personal.

'The senator certainly didn't do this particular one,' Joxer told *NewsTalk 106*. 'But in answer to your next question, no. I'm not prepared to discuss the nature of our party's dealings with Mr Stevenson that day. And can I assure Mr Stevenson that this position will not change. We respect the importance of privacy – and trust he does likewise.'

Stan looked across his desk at Sonny, who had called into his office to listen to the interview along with him.

'You're one lucky bastard, Sonny,' he declared. 'Whoever

did this has scared Joxer so badly, he's dropping all charges.'

Sonny smiled, then glanced over at Stan coyly. 'Does that mean it's okay for me and Eva to appear in public again?'

'Only if you want me to come over to your office and shoot you as well.'

Stan's involvement in the Wynne murder was, of course, huge news back in Derry, where the count in the council elections was getting under way. Letemout Lou, who'd been drafted in as a tallyman-cum-observer, met Audrey Grafton outside the Templemore Complex count centre, and the two of them decided to slip away to Scott's to swap notes.

It was Lou's turn to go up and buy the tea, so the police chief bagged the windowseat with the best view of the Foyle.

'I'm bothered, Lou,' she said, as the would-be president placed the tray down on the table in front of them.

'Why's that?' asked her new friend, pouring out the milk.

'Well, the senator is just a bit too calm for a man who is implicated in three murders,' replied Audrey. 'I've seen guys like that before. They can commit the worst atrocities and then block them out of their mind completely. Like they've never happened. You'll know yourself from the courts that innocent clients live in a permanent state of panic. They're terrified they're going to get done in the wrong. But there's none of that about Stan. He's steady as a rock ...'

Lou chewed over a mouthful of scone, wondering whether or not to take the bait. 'I'll give you this much,' she said eventually. 'Stan was always able to park things and move on. Any time we fought, he'd forget it immediately. He never lets problems prey on his mind. He's a great believer that everything gets sorted out in time, so there's no point in worrying...'

She stopped to take another bite and weigh her words with care. 'So,' she continued, 'whenever someone accuses Stan of murder, I suspect that the little hamster in his brain says to him – "I wouldn't fret – you didn't do that." And he, and the little hamster, just truck on as normal. He just filters out the crap and gets on with enjoying life. It's probably the reason he put up with me for so long.'

Audrey had been holding her coffee cup to her mouth and stared hard at Lou over the top of it. 'I'm not sure you believe a word of that,' she said. 'And there's something else that's annoying me, that maybe you'll want to duck as well ...'

'What's that?' asked Lou mischievously. 'You want to know if he's confessed everything to me?'

Audrey shook her head. 'No – sure you'd only claim attorney–client privilege,' she sniffed. 'No. What's bothering me is this. Why didn't Joxer sink Stan to the gardaí when he had a chance? Why did he acknowledge that Stan was there on legitimate business? He virtually exonerated him.'

'No idea,' answered Lou. Though the copper was right, it was puzzling.

'Have you considered, perhaps,' said Audrey, 'that the nature of Stan's business that afternoon might have been extremely compromising to both Mr O'Duffy and Mr Wynne?'

'I don't follow,' said Lou.

'Well maybe Stan was strong-arming them over some indiscretion,' suggested Audrey.

'I don't think so,' replied Lou.

'Why not?' asked the Super.

'Because that way, Stan would have had them grovelling on his carpet, not the other way around,' said Lou.

'Good point,' acknowledged Audrey. 'Okay, here's another possibility. Maybe they were strong-arming Stan, and they're prepared to drop whatever it was they were holding over him in return for his silence.'

Fuck she's good, thought Lou. She walked me right into it.

'So where does that leave you?' she asked the Super.

'Not in a very happy place,' said Audrey. 'It leaves me with three dead bodies – all of whose owners were at some stage blackmailing the senator.'

'Jesus, Audrey,' laughed Lou. 'Next thing, you'll be suggesting there's a pattern ...'

40

The senator knew when he got the call to go to the Taoiseach's office the next Monday to expect the worst. After a two-week lull, the Sundays were back kicking the shit out of him.

'The *Sunday Times* is calling you the "Grim Senator",' declared Rubber John. 'The *Sunday Indo* has you as "Hitman Stan", while the *Tribune* – my own personal favourite – goes for "President Capone". Chrisht man, it took Charlie Haughey forty years to work his way up to that level of abuse – you've done it in five months.'

Stan sat tensely in the wing-backed armchair, staring at the newspapers strewn across Rubber John's huge leather-covered desk. 'I've never killed anyone,' he said simply. 'I've never fired a gun. I've never asked for anyone to be killed. And I've never paid for anyone to get killed. In fact, I could even go as far as to say, I've never wished anyone dead.'

Rubber John paced the carpet, shaking his head. 'I believe you, Stan,' he sighed. 'But, *ara*, that's not the point. You're a trouble magnet. And the bottom line is you're going to have to go, and go quietly.'

'I didn't do anything wrong,' replied Stan, twisting his head in his seat so he could follow the Taoiseach's pacing. 'And I'm not going quietly. Besides, according to Saturday's *Irish Times*, I'm sitting at fifty-one per cent in the presidential polling – Lou's only on nineteen per cent. That's why the Sundays decided to have a go at me.'

'That and the three dead bodies,' retorted Rubber John. 'You're tainted, Stan. You're finished; I can no longer back you.'

Stan gritted his teeth and stared directly at his boss. 'Before you run away, Taoiseach,' he said, 'I ask you to remember one thing. The dirtiest thing I ever did in politics was at your bidding, when I shafted Joxer ...'

'Are you threatening me, senator?' snapped Rubber John.

'No,' replied Stan. 'But I am asking you to give me to the end of this week. To show you my hands are clean. I think it's the least you can give me.'

'How the fuck did I ever get talked into supporting you?' asked Rubber John, releasing another big sigh.

'Harry the Hurler must have had you by the gonads,' replied Stanley. And they both laughed.

'Okay, Stan,' said the Taoiseach. 'You've got till Friday lunchtime. I promised the Cabinet I'd do it this morning. But sure, I suppose, I promised the country I'd cut taxes ...'

'You won't regret it,' said Stan.

'And that's exactly what I told the country,' grinned Rubber John.

The Taoiseach walked behind his desk and picked up a fax from his in-tray, which he passed to Stan. 'We've one more problem,' he said, as Stan read the headline. 'According to a new poll that RTÉ are going to publish at lunchtime, if Joxer O'Duffy entered the race, he'd poll a solid forty-five per cent. And that's just in the South. Thanks to you, of course, all the unionists in the North would be able to vote for him as well. And what way do you reckon they'll go if they get the choice between an ill-mannered Provo like Lou, a house-trained Provo like you, and a guy saying, "Don't panic – sure, we don't want you in our country, anyway"?'

'Well, well,' smiled Stan, digesting the figures. 'That's interesting.'

'No,' replied Rubber John. 'That's a fucking under-statement.'

Unlike Rubber John, Stan was more than happy that Joxer was effectively entering the race. Ultimately, the senator knew he'd have to face a stiffer challenge than Letemout Lou: there were too many sleeping fascists in the South to allow him a smooth run home. And Stan reckoned that the quicker that Joxer was out front and centre with his intentions, the quicker he could start scoring points back off him.

The senator was also aware that the Real Fianna Fáil leader was privately encouraging the notion that Stan might have had a motive to bump off Wynne. Joxer had thanked him for his heroism in trying to save the deputy's life just one too many times to be sincere. So it was time to play a little poker.

Stan had retained Joxer's mobile number from the good old days – and was able to avoid the battery of secretaries and aides. 'We need to meet, Joxer,' he said. 'And we need to meet now. My office. One hour. Don't be late.'

There was no question but that Joxer would be there. Clever old dog that he was, however, he arrived on the pretext of presenting a framed picture of Wynne to Stan. 'A gift from Jim's most appreciative family,' he said, taking the armchair opposite Stan's desk.

'Thank you,' replied Stan graciously, placing the photo carefully on top of his bookshelf. 'Though I'm not entirely sure I deserve it.'

The senator sat back down in his seat and clasped his hands in front of him. 'I'd advise you, Mr O'Duffy,' he began, 'if you are recording this conversation to stop now, as it will pertain to matters that neither of us will ever want made public. Do you follow?'

Joxer nodded, put his hand in his pocket and produced his office Dictaphone. He turned the little machine over onto its side, and removed two AAA batteries.

'I take it I have a similar guarantee from you,' said Joxer.

'You do,' replied Stan. 'Now, the reason I asked to see you, Joxer, is that we have a little problem. Sonny Waterhouse has got a fit of conscience and is about to go to the Garda over Jim's murder. He's got this crazy idea in his head that the shooting might be linked to the fact that Jim was blackmailing him over a young lady. A working girl, to be precise.'

Joxer was about to interrupt but Stan silenced him by raising his hand.

'I'm sure, for the record, Joxer,' he continued, 'that you had absolutely no idea this awful extortion was happening. But equally, I'm sure you did suspect that the nature of my business with Mr Wynne at the time of his death wasn't parliamentary – hence your very tactful, and timely, intervention.

'But you and I both know that if Sonny Waterhouse blows the whistle on what Wynne was at, people might misconstrue from it that you yourself were implicated.'

Joxer nodded impassively. 'So what do you want from me, senator?' he asked bluntly.

'I need you to help me find the real killer,' said Stan. 'And we've got less than forty-eight hours.'

'I heard the Taoiseach gave you till the end of the week,' smirked Joxer.

'And I'm giving you to Thursday morning,' snapped Stan. 'I don't think I can hold Sonny back any longer. He's up all night every night praying for forgiveness. And besides, if I do drop out of the race, I'm only going to work for Letemout Lou. And I'm far too loose a cannon to have over there – particularly given all the ammunition I'm carrying.'

'What can I do that the Branch aren't already doing?' growled Joxer.

'You've got two superintendents and an assistant commissioner in your bandwagon,' replied Stan. 'The very least you're going to do is completely exonerate me. And publicly.'

'You bastard,' protested Joxer. 'You don't have the nerve.'

'Try me,' grinned Stan. 'Remember, Joxer, the most dangerous people are those who have absolutely nothing to lose.'

Joxer stood up and strode angrily to the door.

'Oh, and by the way, Mr O'Duffy,' said Stan, just as his opponent reached the handle. 'I've been made aware there's a scandalous photo doing the rounds of myself supposedly in bed with a naked woman. I will advise you – just as I advised a Young Fine Gael website that threatened to publish it – that the picture is counterfeit. Furthermore, I'd stress that the two men who forged the picture are both now dead. And my team of very expensive lawyers assure me that if you, or anyone else, ever try to make public this forgery – you will wind up building me so many beach houses in the Caribbean that the Bahamas will run out of sand. Do you understand?'

Joxer pulled the office door open and smiled back at Stan. 'Fuck you,' he replied evenly.

'Yes or no, Joxer?' said Stan. 'Do I hold Sonny back, or do I let him confess his sins?'

'Hold him,' snapped Joxer. And he banged the door shut after him.

Stan grinned. He loved poker. Just give him two jacks for openers, and he'd beat three of a kind any time.

Far from spending his evenings hugging the altar rails as Stan had claimed, Sonny Waterhouse had made a complete recovery from the shock of Jim Wynne's death. And that very night, he decided to sneak back to Eva's Mount Street flat to celebrate. He'd been at a party meeting in Fianna Fáil head offices, just four hundred yards down the road, on Lower Mount Street. And when the rest of the faithful had headed up to O'Dwyer's Bar for a couple of late-night sharpeners, he'd made his excuses and headed towards his car. Only he didn't stop there.

'You're not wise,' was all Eva said, when he buzzed the intercom.

Inside the spacious apartment, the walls were covered with large framed posters featuring black-and-white portraits of Hollywood's most famous goddesses. The shelves, similarly, were filled with books on movies and textbooks from her Film & Drama degree course.

'You'd make a mint doing adult flicks,' said Sonny, eyeing up a very tasteful still of Eva wearing just a long, open-necked shirt.

'No nudity,' replied Eva. 'It catches up on you and cheapens you. Reduces you to a pair of body parts. Flash your bits one time and it's all over the internet.'

'No offence, but ...' began Sonny.

'This is a private business arrangement, Sonny,' interrupted Eva, handing him a chilled Budweiser bottle. 'And given the nature of it, it will always remain private.'

'What about the pictures on Stan's stag night?' he retorted.

'All destroyed apart from the one of me and Stan,' she said. 'And sure that was forged – or rather staged. And by the way, my goodies weren't really visible in any of them anyway. I warned that little shit King Size.'

'You're serious about this acting lark?' asked Sonny.

'Deadly,' replied Eva. 'I think I've got the face for it – and the talent. You get plenty of practice convincing fat, fifty-year-old men that they're the sex god you've been looking for all your life.'

Sonny went red and looked down at his shoes.

'It's simple, Sonny,' she said, answering his next question. 'I do this to pay the bills. This flat, my food, my clothes and my tuition fees. That's all. I don't drink – and I usually bum any cigs I smoke. I don't particularly like this work – but at least I get to do it on my own terms. And I don't work any more than I have to: two, three nights a week tops. At the minute, I've a few euro in the bank, so you're my only client.'

'I'm sorry,' said Sonny. 'I've no right to judge. Not given what I do. And what I'm doing now.'

Eva knelt down beside his chair and stroked his face. 'We all have our own wee ways of going mad,' she smiled. 'Yours is that you want to be twenty-one again and scoring with twenty-year-old girls.'

Sonny sighed deeply and nodded. 'At least I'm halfway there,' he quipped. 'So what's your wee way of going mad?'

'I'm pretty sensible for the most part,' she answered. 'Though I do have a shocking temper. They once threatened to start me on lithium, back when I was in school. I broke a wee fella's arm after he told his mates I'd ... well, put it like this, it would cost you an extra five hundred ...'

Sonny laughed.

'The school shrink said I might have a chemical imbalance in my brain, given my diabetes and all,' she continued. 'And for a long while they were convinced I was suffering from manic depression. The odd time, I admit, I still fire up. He said it was a rare form of aggressive hypoglycaemia – as the sugar level dips in some people it causes chronic mood swings. But just stay on my good side, Sonny, and if you think I'm getting snappy, stick a Mars bar into me.'

Sonny arched an eyebrow and they both laughed. Then Eva kissed his hand, pushed herself up from where she'd been kneeling, and headed for the bedroom. As she reached the door, she yawned, stretching her arms over her head and arching her back just enough to give Sonny a few chemical imbalances of his own.

'Now I'm away for a shower,' she said. 'On my own. But if you sit here quietly like a good boy, I might put on the black boots with the spiky toes when I come out.'

'And what else?' pressed Sonny.

'Baby oil,' she grinned, disappearing into the bathroom.

Sonny stood up to let some blood drain back to his legs. He walked over to the bookshelf at the far corner of the living room and fingered his way through the volumes, before pulling out a glossy hardback on Marilyn Monroe. He'd always had a thing for blondes – must be the gentleman in him.

He opened the book half hoping it would contain the famous *Playboy* shots, but instead he got the shock of his life. The pages had been hollowed out, and a little wooden box about the size of a videocassette had been secreted inside.

He didn't have to look. He knew the minute he saw it. But he flicked the latch anyway. Inside, it was dark grey, German and inscribed with the reference number 'Sig 226'. Oh, and it was the gun that Special Branch said killed Jim Wynne.

41

Finding Jim Wynne's killer had actually been a very satisfying task for Joxer, who once again managed to get himself crowned hero of the hour. And it had proved quite simple too. 'Like stealing candy from a black baby,' he told his new second-in-command, Marta Morgan.

Marta had joined Real Fianna Fáil from the PDs just the previous week, after the party refused to back her proposals to give preference to asylum seekers who agreed to voluntary sterilisation. Joxer – with one eye on the huge women's vote – quickly swept in and appointed her to his inner circle. It also helped that Marta was the doyenne of the Catholic left – and had voted in favour of both divorce and lowering the age of consent. Joxer was delighted to have a seventh TD in the fold again – the Magnificat Six just didn't have the same ring to it. But how long Marta would last after Joxer became president was anyone's guess.

He'd arranged the press conference for the Earl of Kildare Hotel, just round the corner from Leinster House, and the Dublin media were there in force. He told them he was publicly going to name, and shame, a murderer. They couldn't dare miss it. Half of them were there for the gore factor – the other half were hoping Joxer was about to fall on his arse. No matter. They were all there.

Sadly for the great watching public, however, there was little gore – and absolutely no one coming a cropper. Instead, the packed hall got to hear Monsignor George Behan read a brief statement.

'Six days ago,' the doctor began, 'just over a week after Deputy Jim Wynne was killed in the Dáil, Ritchie Reilly, a twenty-two-year-old man who had been attending my outpatient clinic, committed suicide. He had been receiving treatment for acute paranoia and had a history of repeated self-harm. His death, I regret to say, was a shock neither to me nor to his family.

'In the throes of my sessions with Mr Reilly, he had said, at different times, that he believed himself to be in mortal danger from various individuals – including the Taoiseach, the President, the British Prime Minister and, on one occasion, Deputy Wynne. Mr Reilly, it seems, had become quite distressed after Mr Wynne delivered his landmark 'Zero tolerance to drugs users' speech on *Questions and Answers* ...

'As Mr Reilly had shown absolutely no propensity for violence, there was no cause for alarm. Even after Deputy Wynne was killed, I had absolutely no reason to suspect my patient was involved. Likewise, I saw no reason to link Mr Reilly's suicide to the earlier murder. Then on Monday, however, a note – typewritten and in a typewritten envelope – arrived in my morning post. It said simply, "I'm sorry about Mr Wynne," and was signed Ritchie Reilly.'

The priest paused briefly for effect, poured himself a glass of spring water from the bottle the hotel had thoughtfully provided, and drank deeply. The press corps mumbled unhappily. The killer was dead and buried before they'd got a chance to rip him apart.

'I immediately alerted my good friend Joxer O'Duffy,' Behan continued, 'and he in turn contacted Superintendent Conal Donnelly. After a discussion with the Reilly family, I agreed to make the gardaí aware of what Ritchie had said to me while in session. And the gardaí conducted a search of his room yesterday, during which they recovered motorcycling leathers and a helmet, a floor plan of the Dáil, and a catalogue of German firearms.'

The press corps nodded knowingly as one as the final piece of the puzzle was slotted into place.

'Garda Superintendent Conal Donnelly and Deputy Joxer O'Duffy will now answer any other questions you may have,' stated the priest. 'My lawyers advise me I am precluded from speaking any further on this matter. Thank you.'

There was an almost reverential hush in the hall for a few

seconds, as the press privately assessed how far their conspiracy theories had been off the mark – well, the ones they'd printed anyway.

'Just one question before you finish, Father Behan,' interrupted the man from the *Daily Irishman*. 'And it's to do with your specialist field …'

'If you must,' replied the cleric.

'Father Behan,' said the hack, 'would it be fair to say that Mr Reilly was a bandit …?'

'After that,' said Sonny, 'it just got silly.'

Sonny and about forty other TDs and senators had watched the live tele-feed from the conference as it was broadcast into the Dáil bar. Stan had stayed in his office, mindful that they'd only have spent half the time gauging his reaction.

Superintendent Conman had completely acquitted the senator of any involvement 'in this particular killing'. But he dismissed suggestions that Reilly could have been the same courier who shot King Size Barkley in Derry. 'Much more likely that he read about it, and decided to repeat the motor-cyclist disguise,' he explained. He also revealed that the dead gunman had been in full-time institutional care when Barry Magee was shot.

'Joxer was grinning all over his face,' sighed Sonny. 'He was praised by everyone for vindicating you, his political enemy. But he's still left two very damaging strikes against you. So simple too. Hang it all on a dead man.'

Stan stared down at his desk then shook his head slowly. 'For the first time since I came to this place, I feel really ashamed,' he confessed. 'I asked Joxer to help clear me. And he's done that. But he's now gone and sunk some other poor wretch who can't answer back. I didn't care a whit that Wynne got killed. All I was concerned about was how it would affect my career. But now some family's got to live with the fact that their son or brother is a crazed murderer.

'I wonder is there any chance that Reilly actually could have done it?'

Sonny, who'd been absent-mindedly flipping a ten-cent piece in the air, missed his catch. 'You're joking?' he exclaimed.

'It is just possible that Joxer and Behan knew about Reilly and were keeping it quiet up until now to damage me,' replied Stan.

'Jesus,' declared Sonny, astonished. 'You really didn't know. I was sure you were in it with her.'

'In it with who?' asked Stan, baffled.

'Well fuck me,' stated Sonny, closing his eyes, 'I have you all wrong, Stan.'

He picked up an A4 notepad from Stan's desk, produced a Cross pen from inside his jacket and wrote quickly: 'Eva's the shooter. I found the pistol in her flat two nights ago.'

He then tore the leaf from the pad and ripped it into a hundred little pieces.

'Open that cabinet in the corner,' said Stan, pointing past the window. 'I need a drink.'

'Why didn't you report her?' scribbled Stan, sipping hard on the good brandy he saved for emergencies.

'Why don't you think that through?' said Sonny with a grin.

'Okay,' replied Stan, again on paper. 'Why not an anonymous tip? She might have killed three people.'

Sonny took the pad. 'Because,' he wrote, 'she's never shot anyone that didn't deserve it. And secondly, in case you haven't noticed, they've already found Wynne's killer. So it's too late now.'

Stan snatched the pad back impatiently. 'Jesus,' he scrawled, 'I met her on the street recently and she told me she'd been doing a couple of acting jobs up in the North recently. I thought she was just trying to invent a life for herself …'

Sonny grabbed the pen.

'No,' he wrote. 'She showed me the video. It's a promo for Bord Fáilte. Eva is the fine young thing that's supposed to tempt us all to visit Derry's walls.'

Stan grinned and took the pen again. 'Do the dates of her visits to Derry coincide with what happened?' he wrote.

'What do you think?' asked Sonny, aloud.

'So why's she doing it?' Stan wrote.

'She's off her fucking head,' scribbled Sonny. 'Her low

blood sugar turns her clean demented and she's very probably manic depressive to boot. And now it looks like she just doesn't like dirty pictures of her flying about, any more than the rest of us.'

'I hope you've destroyed all yours,' said Stan out loud.

'You bet your furry handcuffs I have,' laughed Sonny.

Joxer's magnanimity saw him leap to fifty-four per cent in the presidential polls – though he was yet to declare he was running. Stan had dropped to twenty-seven per cent, while Lou was holding more or less steady on nineteen. The three men sitting round the table in the *Derry Standard*'s little boardroom were less than impressed.

'We need to narrow the field,' said Harry the Hurler.

'Or organise very tight transfers,' replied Tommy Bowtie.

'It won't happen,' interrupted Uncle Hugo. 'Fianna Fáil won't sanction second preferences to the Shinners. Not officially anyway. Besides, in the Free State second preferences split in all manner of ways. They just haven't got our sectarian discipline.'

'Then somebody has to go,' insisted Harry. 'There's five months to November and our combined vote is still eight per cent behind Joxer's. We need to stabilise quickly and rally behind one candidate.'

'We could always get a new unity candidate,' suggested Tommy Bowtie. 'Somebody maybe like our pal from Dunavady.'

'Too much of a flake,' grunted Harry. 'The wrong man entirely if we want to avoid scandal. Jesus Christ, the only thing scarier than your daughter coming to you to tell you she's got a life-threatening disease is her opening the door and saying, "Daddy, I'd like you to meet Shay Gallagher".'

The three men laughed. It was the first time they'd met up in almost two months. Since they'd decided to run Stan.

To reporters passing the glass-panelled door, they looked like three old fellas just in from the golf course. You'd have been hard stretched to imagine that these harmless-looking gentlemen were attempting to plot a *coup d'état*. Which, of course, was the whole point.

'Okay so,' said Tommy, serious again. 'I vote we lose Lou. She's never going to get more than a quarter of first preferences. The only time the left ever won was with Mary Robinson – and she needed thirty-eight per cent in the first round.'

'I vote we lose Stan,' argued Harry. 'He's dropping points fast – and is still very damaged goods. What about you, Hugo?'

The elder statesmen stroked his chin and paused. 'Let's drop neither for the moment,' he replied. 'We should wait first of all until Joxer declares before we do anything. But I also think we should put our energies into re-establishing Stanley's good name.'

'Okay so,' replied Tommy. 'But how do we explain what he was doing in Derry when Barry Magee got whacked – when he should have been in Dublin? After all, Harry, you're the man who sank him to your new buddies in the police.'

'Everybody hates a tout,' grinned Harry ruefully. 'But Stan was in the Jack Kennedy half an hour before the little Welsh shit got his chips – and I can't deny it. Our real problem is that Stan had motive. For both Barry and King Size. The whole world knows it. But no one will dare say it, or print the picture. Or Stan – and, indeed, you Tommy – will sue their trousers off.'

'In that case,' said Hugo, 'we have to invent another murderer to stop the fingers pointing at Stan once and for all.'

'Like who?' asked Harry.

'I don't know, dear boy,' replied Hugo. 'Do what Joxer did. Find somebody dead, and hang the whole lot on them. My, my, I thought that was your field, Harold.'

'How dare you, Hugo,' sniffed Harry. 'I'm a legitimate businessman. I'll have you know it said so on my last court summons.'

And they all laughed again.

42

The triumvirate reckoned that they'd about a month to turn around Stan's candidacy, after which they would settle for Letemout alone and an honourable defeat. They had to get Stan up by five points – to thirty-two per cent – before the end of June if they were to have a fighting chance. That would leave the combined Stan/Lou total at fifty-one per cent going into the summer break. And Joxer, as the pacesetter, could only stand to lose votes in the autumn – when his own closets would be thrown open for inspection.

It was agreed that Harry the Hurler should handle the first phase of what Uncle Hugo quaintly termed 'Stanley's little makeover'. Harry, thanks to his sins, was the man with the police connection. And the raid on Jimmy Fidget's diesel factory in Dunavady gave him the perfect cover. So he rang Audrey Grafton demanding an emergency meeting in the Jack Kennedy.

'Christ, Harry,' snapped the Super as soon as she sat down opposite him in the snug, 'I warned you three times. And Little Jimmy wasn't even scooped. He was safely away on a job, miles away. So don't be dragging me here to bust my chops.'

Harry just smiled, put his hand inside his jacket and produced a long white lawyer's envelope.

'Hell's cure to him,' he said. 'I hope you bankrupt him – might keep him out of trouble for a while. But that's not why I called you … First, we need to go off the record. Completely. Okay?'

Audrey nodded grudgingly and cursed herself for getting blindsided like this.

'This envelope is for your eyes only,' warned Harry. 'As you well know, someone broke into Barry Magee's house the night he was shot and removed his picture collection and PC. Well, to cut to the chase, a concerned citizen – whose name, incidentally, I do not know – has been working on Barry Magee's computer hard drive for the last few months. The Taffy bastard had a series of passwords protecting his files – all in Welsh of course. But we've finally cracked them … I mean, he has.'

Audrey smirked at the façade.

'He had files on everyone in there,' said Harry. 'Me. You. Father Know-All. You name it. Bit like the police, Audrey. Except, of course, you lot are like Superman and only use your powers for good …'

Audrey pointed to the envelope. 'So what's in it then?' she asked.

'A list of recurring names,' replied Harry. 'For obvious reasons, this man won't give you the hard drive. There's way too much on it. Though he will let you, personally, inspect it, in our presence, to verify its validity. That will be easy enough, as it contains all Barry's personal correspondence, work records, invoices for weddings and so on. You'll also find the templates and access codes for the Derry Underbelly website he used to run … This list, however, came from the directory labelled "Sensitive" – which took us until yesterday to open.'

Audrey reached over the table and took the envelope from Harry's hand. Without opening it, she shook her head and gestured to him to take it back.

'I'm not biting,' she said dryly.

'Just read it here in front of me, then give it back to me,' smiled Harry.

The Super slid a pen under the corner of the envelope and sliced it open. She unfurled the document inside, which appeared on first glance to be the printout from a computer database. She read the top few lines, eyes widening, as Harry looked on.

NAME: Damien 'Skidmark' Gormley
EVENT: Stag party with prostitute
EASE OF IDENTIFICATION: 10/10 (Absolute)
COMPROMISE QUOTIENT: 7/10
RETAIL VALUE: £2,000 (Two weeks' income for DG)
PAYMENT PLAN: One-off purchase.

Audrey scanned the rest of the document in disbelief. There were five pages in total, with around ten victims per page. Some of the 'events' dated back ten years, though about a dozen of them related to Stan's bachelor bash in Dublin in January past. Three of Barry's victims' names were circled.

'Why are these ones marked?' she asked Harry.

'Again, between ourselves?' he countered.

She nodded again.

'They're three people who have contacted us in the past for help in sorting out some delicate problems,' he said. 'And by "us", I don't mean our political department. And by "sorting out", I don't mean arbitration.'

Audrey felt a chill run through her. It was as near an admission as Harry had ever given her as to who he really was.

'And before you ask,' he went on, 'no, this is not a complete list. But it is a list of all the people who had the capacity and the opportunity to kill both King Size and Barry. And they are three people who realise the limitations of due process …'

Audrey reviewed the names quickly.

'The senator's not on it at all,' she said.

'He didn't do it,' replied Harry. 'Nor do you get to see what Barry had on him. But we think we know who did kill the Shakedown Sisters. And I think if you focus on the three names that are highlighted, you'll come to the same conclusion.'

Audrey thumbed through the sheets again.

'Patsy Barkley's already in the clear,' she said after a pause. 'We've a witness putting her in Belfast shortly before her husband got it. And she was in New York with her sister when Barry got his. But thank you for confirming what I'd long suspected – Miss Persil White can get just as dirty as the rest of us. What had she asked you to do for her? Whack King Size?'

'I don't know what you're talking about,' said Harry.

Audrey ignored him. 'I have to admit we didn't look at Shay Gallagher,' she continued. 'Though I'll grant you, he'd a lot to lose – and a ten-thousand-pound bite isn't small change, even for an MLA. Good to know that he'll turn your way in a crisis too. I'd always him pegged for a civilian.'

Harry rolled his eyes in mock despair at the police chief's innocence.

'And then,' smiled Audrey, reading the last name, 'we've Barney Joyce. Yet another victim of the stag-night curse and King Size's digital camera. And of course another MLA. It would be just perfect all round if we turned up something on him, wouldn't it? Given that he killed himself in that car crash a couple of months back and all ...'

Harry shrugged his shoulders then reached out his hand for the envelope.

'No chance I could borrow this?' asked Audrey.

''Fraid not,' smiled Harry. 'But I'd say you've got it pretty much off by heart by now.'

'The stuff on Sammy Muir is interesting too,' said Audrey looking further down the list. 'Fair play to Barry, catching Sammy touting to the Branch man on the Foyle Bridge. Bang to rights, pictures, audiotape and all. More than you lot ever got ... Not that I'm confirming anything mind.'

'You don't have to,' answered Harry. 'So I take it you'd like to verify the hard drive now?'

Audrey had had enough of being played. She shook her head angrily. 'Why?' she snapped. 'There's no point. Let's not fuck about here, Harry, I'm not going to see anything there I'm not supposed to. You've it all arranged to suit your own purposes. You must take me for a halfwit. You got me to accuse an Irish senator of murder – twice. And now you're going to prove it was someone else. Stan gets to become the great oppressed hero and romp home for president. While I'll be the pro-Brit securocrat who tried to destroy a great man's reputation – but failed.'

Harry waved the envelope back towards her. 'Maybe I'll just get this to someone else,' he sniffed. 'Someone who can recognise that you've made a mistake – and that you have to put it right ...'

'You bastard,' snapped the Super.

'We're not that good, Audrey,' said Harry softly. 'You're giving me far too much credit.'

'I know exactly how good you are, Harry,' retorted the

Super. 'You're going to hang all this on a dead man. Same as you did in Dublin.'

Tommy's end of the makeover was a lot easier. He got the number from Sonny Waterhouse after warning him straight out not to lie to him or he'd turn him in. Stan had told him he'd a friend in the Dáil who'd got himself into trouble with a working girl, and Tommy had figured out the rest.

He was prepared for the initial brush-off when he landed at Eva's Mount Street flat and announced himself as Senator Stevenson's lawyer. But after he assured her through the intercom that he was here as a friend – and that Stan was in trouble – she eventually let him in.

'What do you need from me?' she asked him, pointing to an armchair.

'We need you to help clear Stan of murder,' replied Tommy.

Eva blanched. She sat down on a director's chair opposite the lawyer and covered her face with her hands. 'I know nothing about it,' she said.

'We think you do,' continued Tommy, taking careful note of her discomfort. 'We think the man who killed both King Size Barkley and Barry Magee was being blackmailed after he got photographed with you. We just need you to confirm his identity.'

Eva exhaled slowly and let her shoulders sag. They weren't trying to pin it on her. There was a chance she could get through this.

'Go on,' she said cautiously.

'We need two things,' explained Tommy. 'We need you to give a sealed statement to the police in which you confess that the picture of you and Stan was staged.'

'But it was staged,' replied Eva. 'King Size made me pose for it after Stan fell asleep. Stan refused his stag night special point-blank – despite the fact the others were paying.'

'You're joking,' declared Tommy, giving Eva a very approving once-over.

'Nope,' she said, 'he's a lovely gentleman. Really. That's why I'll help him if I can. It's the only reason you got in the door.'

'Okay,' smiled Tommy. 'Well, here's the tricky part. We believe a man called Barney Joyce threatened to kill King Size Barkley for taking his picture with you. And we think it's possible you may have heard him say so …'

'Which one was Barney?' asked Eva.

'This one,' said Tommy, producing his picture. 'Mr Joyce's temper was legendary. Unfortunately, however, he has since been killed in a car accident, so we're left trying to piece things together without him.'

'Gotcha,' nodded Eva, not quite believing what was happening. 'I might have heard him say something, all right. But how do I know the statement I give will remain sealed?'

'I'll retain the only signed copy,' answered Tommy. 'And I'll give a redacted version – with your name blacked out – to the police.'

'But if I'm the only evidence …' began Eva.

'Not even remotely,' interrupted Tommy. 'You're just the final bolt on a triple lock. The police have already established that Barney had motive – and they're looking hard for his weapon, which I'm pretty sure they're going to find. The bottom line is the police won't be relying on your statement and they're not going to challenge it. As I say, it won't have your name on it – but I will get it co-signed by two other witnesses – one a newspaper owner, the other a priest. And that should convince them it's genuine.'

'How do I know you're not setting me up?' pressed Eva.

'You don't,' replied Tommy. 'But talk to Sonny Waterhouse. He'll vouch for me.'

'Okay so,' said Eva. 'I'll text him tonight. And if he okays it, ring me tomorrow and we'll talk again.'

Tommy left the flat confident he'd got his result. But as he walked down the stairs, he couldn't help wondering if it had been just too simple. Eva had volunteered to help Stan out of the goodness of her heart. And the five grand sweetener Hugo had given him before leaving Derry had remained in the envelope tucked inside Tommy's breast pocket.

'Something not quite right here,' said Tommy to himself, as he strolled up towards O'Dwyer's Bar. 'She knows who really did it.'

43

Lou wasn't sure who was more livid, herself or Audrey Grafton. She'd called her a few minutes after Assistant Chief Constable Peter McLoughlin appeared live on *Sky News* to announce he'd caught the double killer – and that the police would be making a full apology to Stan Stevenson. Audrey, however, was so incensed she could hardly speak, so Lou said she'd ring back the following day.

The ACC – who incidentally was Audrey's line manager – had breathlessly revealed how he, personally, acting on a tip-off, led a raid on Barney Joyce's outhouses and discovered a pistol inside an old stereo speaker. The gun was a rare Russian weapon – the same make and model that had been used in the Derry murders. A ballistics test wouldn't be possible, as the barrel had been damaged – but the police didn't need it anyway. They had motive. They'd found computer records showing the former MLA was being blackmailed by Barry Magee, and an eyewitness had come forward to say she'd heard him threatening to kill King Size.

It was neater than a row of teeth. Audrey had refused to play another round of Hang the Patsy, so Harry had found a sap who would. Her Boss.

Lou rang Audrey again the following morning at her office, and they arranged to meet for a private lunch at the Kennedy Inn. The policewoman arrived first, and by the time Lou entered the little room she was already halfway down the first bottle of Chardonnay. There would be two more.

'Are you going to quit?' asked Audrey, defying her to agree. The *Irish Times* had done a snap poll the previous evening after the police announcement. Lou had dropped four points to fifteen per cent; Joxer had dipped six to forty-eight, while Stan had shot up ten to thirty-seven.

'I just might,' replied Lou sombrely. 'Ten points in one day. Jesus, another two or three per cent swing and he'll win this race ... At the moment, I'm effectively working as a kicker for Stan – I'm guaranteeing him second preferences. There's no way our people will vote for Joxer. In fact, they'll give their number twos to Stan *en bloc* to keep Joxer out.'

Audrey nodded. 'So what would happen if it were a straight head-to-head between Stan and Joxer?'

'That's the rub,' sighed Lou. 'Stan would almost certainly lose. For my money, the Free Staters won't hack another Northerner. Not one who'll refuse to go native, anyway.'

Audrey filled her friend's glass again then replaced the bottle in the cooler. 'So,' she smiled, 'I take it you're tempted to drop out then – to spite Stan?'

'Not Stan,' retorted Lou. 'Harry. He's taking the hand – playing favourites with Stan after begging me to run.'

'I can see your problem,' said Audrey. 'Harry shafted me royally as well. But I'm surprised at you taking it like this. You've far too much sense to be bending over like a good girl ...'

'And there was me thinking you liked it like that.'

'No fool like an old fool,' grinned the cop. 'You know, I actually thought Harry could have had a thing for me. Christ, they're good, Lou.'

'No, they're not,' countered Lou. 'Harry flies by the seat of his pants – just like the rest of us. And by the way, I assume you've heard that Mrs Hurley has flown the coop.'

'Lorna?' replied Audrey, just a little bit thrilled. 'What got into her?'

'A visiting Sicilian law lecturer is what's got into her,' smiled Lou. 'But Harry won't touch him, because he's heard he's connected back in Palermo.'

'You're joking,' said Audrey, laughing for the first time in about a week.

'I'm not,' replied Lou. 'So don't be taking that mobile number off the speed dial just yet. Now, let's open another bottle.'

Back in Dún Laoghaire, Joxer O'Duffy had summoned Marta Morgan and Father Bend'em-Back to his Northumberland

Street constituency office for a council of war.

The three sat themselves around the kitchen table, on which stood a twenty-glass bottle of Paddy, three glasses, a large jug of water for the woman, and two tubes of Pringles.

'It's time to move on, Joxer,' said the priest, by way of an opening. 'If you try to bring the shootings back into the campaign after everything that's happened this week, there'll be public uproar. He's an innocent man – you said so yourself. Jesus, and now he's spinning himself as some sort of wronged saint.'

'Father Behan's right,' nodded Marta. 'And besides, every newspaper that's backing us will be referring to him as *former* murder suspect until the end of the campaign. The shit might be gone, but we'll make sure there's still a stench.'

'Bollix to that,' snapped Joxer. 'Somebody shot Jim Wynne and it sure as hell wasn't Ritchie Reilly. We can't let him away with it. Jesus, Marta, he's laughing at us. That stroke they pulled in Derry with Barney Joyce was just rubbing our noses in it. Stevenson has to pay.'

'Do you want to be president, Joxer, and run the country?' asked Father Behan. 'Or do you want to fuck about on the margins all your life, fighting stupid fights you can't win?'

Joxer pounded the table as if in anger, then smiled disarmingly. 'I want to fuck about on the margins – isn't it obvious?'

His companions laughed, and Marta reached for the bottle. She professionally poured out three doubles. Then she added a splash of water to her own to please Joxer. 'There is one thing we could do to turn the tables back on Stan,' she suggested, raising her eyebrows mischievously.

'Go on,' said Joxer.

'The police in Derry got the gen on Barney Joyce after a quote unquote burglar took a fit of conscience and handed them the blackmail list.' She grinned. 'What if someone were to break into Father Bend'em-Back's office and steal Stan's file? Stick that along with the prostitute's story that the senator refused to sleep with her, and the whole country will be thinking that he prefers his pillows scented.'

'Absolutely not,' yelled Father Behan, furious.

'She's a stunning girl too,' continued Marta, ignoring him.

'There's no way any hot-blooded male could turn her away. And we have some very publishable pictures of her, courtesy of the Sonny Waterhouse video. Though, obviously, we'd have to cut him out of them.'

'Jesus, Marta,' laughed Joxer, 'and you such a good Catholic girl too.'

'I know,' she said with a mock sigh. 'The lengths we have to go to, to protect our faith.'

'You cannot do this,' shouted the priest forcefully. 'My files are sacred.'

'Tell that to Ritchie Reilly's parents,' retorted Joxer menacingly. 'You bought into this, George, because you want a red hat ...'

'He wants a red hat?' interrupted Marta, confused.

'Yeah,' grinned Joxer, gesturing with his thumb to the priest. 'Our friend there would like nothing better than to become Cardinal Benders ... Seriously though, Marta, I like your plan. Though we'll save it to the last week of the campaign. If we keep it until then, there'll be no way back.'

The priest closed his eyes and gritted his teeth. 'Be very, very careful, Joxer,' he warned. 'You're messing with dangerous people.'

Joxer grinned, then put his giant paw over Marta's tiny hand and squeezed it affectionately. His number two pulled away. A little too quickly.

'What age are you, Miss Morgan?' asked Father Bend'em-Back quickly.

'Thirty-seven,' replied Marta.

'And yet you've never married,' said the priest coldly. 'Any reason for that ...?'

Three miles across the city, Sonny Waterhouse was also eating Pringles and drinking whiskey. Though unlike Joxer's coterie, Sonny was stark naked and he wasn't lapping his booze from a glass.

Sonny, as any mathematician worth his salt could tell you, got married at the point of a shotgun. But, like most Irish politicians, he was too old-school to consider divorce, and instead he preferred to find ways to make the misery bearable.

Above all, however, he was a pragmatist and reasoned that wherever there were restraints, there must also be release mechanisms.

'Is that what I am?' asked Eva, glancing up from the pillow at him. 'A release mechanism?'

'No, no,' he protested, sensing the danger. 'You're much more than that. You're a fully equipped escape module. James Bond style. A custom-built bubble that can provide lavish comfort through heavy fire and high seas. You've even got the six-foot bed and silk handkerchiefs.'

'Very cheesy,' laughed Eva, forgiving him. 'And well done for digging yourself out of that hole.'

'Thank you,' said Sonny. 'And I have to say I'm flattered that you care enough to fight with me.'

'What lady could resist Double-O Seven?' smiled Eva, pulling the sheet back to expose her negligée and winking theatrically.

'I just hope you're not an enemy agent,' said Sonny gently.

'I don't follow you,' replied Eva, puzzled.

Sonny looked her straight in the eyes and took a deep breath. 'I found your gun, Eva,' he said. 'Please don't shoot me with it ...'

'So how did you know she wasn't going to make you number four?' asked Stan when he hooked up with Sonny at Doheny & Nesbitt's later that night.

'I've good instinct,' replied Sonny, nodding his thanks for the pint. 'Eva only harms people who threaten her. And I'm as soft as a sockful of shit. Oh, and I took the firing pin out of the pistol the last day I was there. The old FCÁ training.'

'So was she angry when you told her?' pressed Stan.

'No. As soon as I asked her about it, she started to cry. She must have cried for a full hour, she was so ashamed.'

'But what possessed her?'

'Pure fear,' explained Sonny. 'King Size was trying to force her to sell her story about your stag do to the papers. He was holding the pictures over her head. So, when she got the acting job in Derry, she thought she'd pay him a visit. But first she visited her uncle in Tallaght – the only man in her family who knows what she does for a living – and asked him for some personal protection. Finding King Size in Derry wasn't hard, but he just laughed in her face and told her to take a hike. So she followed him in a black rage from the Jack Kennedy, on a motorbike, to the traffic lights on the Strand. Then bang, bang, night, night Mr Barkley.

'A couple of weeks later, Barry Magee made the mistake of trying to use King Size's archive to continue the shakedown on you and your pals. Eva got wind of it when Barry posted a photo of herself and Dumpy Doherty on his Derry Underbelly website, just to show you all he was serious. Faces blacked out – for the time being. So when Eva came back to town to retake a scene for the ad, she tracked Barry down and asked him to leave her out of it. But he just told her that quote unquote "no damn Dublin hooker" was going to stop him making a living, and hit her a slap. So she bided her time, returned quietly to Derry three days later and bang, bang, night, night Mr Magee.'

'And Jim Wynne?' asked Stan. 'How did she know where to find him?'

'Ah,' said Sonny, avoiding the senator's eye. 'That's a little more complicated. Between ourselves, Stan, the first night I met Eva, she persuaded me to give her a late-night tour of the Dáil. She really enjoyed it and was most appreciative. So now and again we would go back there – though always late on. Constituency business, you know.'

'I'll bet,' said Stan. He necked about three inches of stout and rifted happily. 'Remind me never to eat anything off your desk ever again.'

Sonny grimaced, half embarrassed, half proud.

'So how do we know she isn't a loose cannon?' pressed Stan.

'We don't,' said Sonny. 'But she knows how lucky she's been – and just wants the whole thing to go away. So she gave me her guns – both of them, she stole the other one from Barry Magee's car of all places – and swore to me that her Annie Oakley days were over.'

'And are they?' asked Stan.

'Well, for Joxer O'Duffy's sake, I sure to fuck hope so,' grinned Sonny.

44

It wasn't necessarily the most diplomatic move for Uncle Hugo to demand that Stan be his best man – given that Letemout Lou was to be Mary Slavin's bridesmaid. Particularly as it would entail the jilted groom and the jilting bride standing together at the altar they should have been married at. But, as Mary said, it was her day, not theirs, so they could shut their damned mouths for once, and do as they were fucking well told.

The ceremony took place in the Long Tower chapel with just the four of them present. And Lou cried. And so did Stan.

'Any other takers?' said the priest, as Stan handed him a little envelope. 'I'd happily do two for the price of one ...'

'That's very generous of you, Father,' sniffed Lou, aware that this was only the start of the ribbing for the day. 'But we're not together any more.'

'Course you're not,' grinned the curate mischievously. 'And I never once looked at a naked woman and had impure thoughts ... But I thought I'd better chance my arm anyway. If I leave it until after one of you is president, the bishop will pull rank and cut us mere mortals out of it altogether. But anyhow, from what I hear, Stanley's turned the other way ...'

Lou's face went puce, and she was on the point of asking him if he'd worked out why people don't go to fucking Mass any more when Stan took her arm gently and winked at the priest.

'When the time comes, I promise we'll not pass you by,' he laughed.

The Kennedy Inn had been pre-booked, so Stan had arranged a reception in the banquet room of the Tower Hotel for about fifty of the bridal party's close friends and relatives.

So after they'd taken the statutory four hundred photos in the grounds of Thornhill School in the warm August sun, the party of four headed back into the city centre.

'What did he mean?' hissed Lou to Stan as they followed Mary and Hugo into the lobby.

'What did who mean?' answered Stan, kicking for touch.

'The priest – he said you'd turned the other way,' snapped Lou. 'You're not thinking of becoming a Protestant, are you?'

'Okay, so I've thought about it,' Stan lied. 'But for God's sake, that's confidential, Lou. Everything today is off the record.'

Stan breathed out again. Christ knew what she'd do if they heard about his sessions with Monsignor Behan. She'd either denounce him as a complete fraud and then kill him, or alternatively just kill him outright.

Lou stopped at the door of the banquet room to adjust the neckline of her blue chiffon dress. It was the first time Stan had noticed how well it showed off her slender figure. He'd been so busy up until then trying not to stare at the beautiful curves of her long legs, or breathe in her sweet apple-musk. Lou smiled, then trembled slightly, as she caught Stan watching her. Admiring her. Missing her.

'Breathtaking,' he said quietly. 'I'd nearly vote for you myself.'

Audrey Grafton had, quite sensibly, sent Hugo and Mary her regrets, along with a very expensive antique letter-opener as a gift. She was still too sore. So sore in fact that, in conjunction with Her Majesty's Customs, she had raided no fewer than seven different divisions of Harold Hurley Inc. over the past six weeks. They had impounded all eighteen cigarette machines from his bars after finding one solitary smuggled pack of Marlboro – in a barman's coat behind the counter of the Jack Kennedy. They then closed down Harry's taxi depot for a week after one car from 135 showed traces of red diesel. And they suspended trading at both his off-licences, following a very successful sting operation to stamp out underage drinkers. Pointedly, no other licence holders in the district were targeted.

No. Audrey had prudently voted to give the wedding a

miss. Until, that is, Mary rang her personally at the station to warn her that if she wasn't at the Tower at the appointed hour, the letter-opener would be returned immediately, and in a manner that would cause Audrey considerable discomfort. So here she was, parked at a table for four, with Harry the Hurler, and Mr and Mrs Tommy Bowtie – both of whom were late.

'Lorna not coming so?' gibed the Super, as Harry studied his fingernails.

'Weddings aren't her thing,' muttered Harry cautiously.

'Once bitten and all that ...' grinned Audrey.

'No,' Harry lied, 'if you must know, she's on a diet. She's very careful about what she eats.'

'Yeah.' Audrey grinned. 'Unless it's Italian ...'

Surprised, Harry blanched, but immediately realised there was nothing else but to take it on the chin. 'Okay, you got me,' he laughed, putting his two hands in the air. 'Lorna's gone. Sicily actually. So let's have the Godfather jokes: He made her an offer she couldn't refuse, or, She thought it had been too long since we hit the mattresses, or, even, The Hurley family has a lot of buffers ...'

Audrey winced in mock sympathy. 'Ah,' she teased, 'but didn't Michael Corleone also say that if history teaches us anything, it's that we can kill anyone?'

Harry grinned, relaxing a little. 'I'd forgotten that one,' he said. 'But I'll certainly use it again ... The quote, I mean – not the advice.'

They paused to sip their champagne and look around at the other guests, none of whom seemed remotely interested in joining them.

'Got any smokes?' asked Audrey at last. 'Weddings make me nervous.'

'Nope,' smirked Harry. 'I'm all cleaned out ...'

They both laughed.

'And what have you to be nervous about, anyway?' asked Harry. 'I'm the one Mary Slavin stuck at a table with the cop who's trying to close him down.'

'You want me to believe you're scared of me, Harry?' declared Audrey, incredulous. 'You're running two candidates for president of Ireland.'

'I'm helping – not running,' interrupted Harry. 'And it's minor stuff. For Lou only. Stan's a totally different party.'

'What percentage of Lou's number twos will go to Stan then?' pressed Audrey.

'If it's not ninety, then I'll be demanding a recount,' conceded Harry ruefully.

'Well, there's a coincidence,' retorted Audrey.

'Look,' said Harry gently, 'you have me figured for some mastermind, Audrey. You think I have this grand plan. But truth is, I'm just a guy struggling to keep up. Same with my business. I've got the taxman with a loaded gun going out one door, while my sleeping partners – who thank God are no longer allowed to carry guns – are coming in the other. And then you bust in, in a big, stroppy huff and try to close me down.'

Audrey grinned. 'When you put it like that, I almost feel sorry for you,' she said.

Harry ignored the gibe. 'I make no apologies for trying to make a good life for myself,' he continued. 'And yes, I'm a very good organiser. And yes, I can get things done. But do you think I enjoy what I do? Honestly?'

He paused and looked directly into her face. 'The truth is, Audrey,' he said, 'I hate it. Really hate it. Hate the people. Hate the job. You know the last time I had a conversation with anybody I actually liked?'

'When?' asked Audrey, curious.

'Eight weeks and three days ago,' he replied. 'When you threw your cup of coffee over me and walked out of the Jack Kennedy.'

Jimmy Fidget had also declined his invitation to the reception, proffering a John Rocha crystal vase in his place. He'd been behaving himself for two months now – ever since the diesel plant was shut down – but reckoned it still might be a bit early to revisit polite society. Besides, if there were ever a day in which he could be guaranteed a smack in the mouth, this was it. Stan Stevenson, Letemout Lou, Audrey Grafton and his brother Harry all in the one room. He'd be lucky if Barney Joyce didn't rise from the grave and finish him off.

Uncle Hugo, however, had been kindness itself to Jimmy

since he started at the *Derry Standard* – and long before. Eighty per cent of Jimmy's misdemeanours had never made the paper. And there weren't three people in Derry who would have hired a schizophrenic – not one with Jimmy's record anyway. So when Hugo rang him up and pleaded with him to come to the party as a special wedding-day favour to him, and to bring Susie Short Shorts along, he cancelled his weekend away and got fitted up for the tux.

'He seems to be in great form,' Letemout Lou said to Susie as Jimmy disappeared off to take some pictures. 'I've never seen him more at ease. When I was, ah, friendly with him, he was wired to the lights. What's your secret?'

'Between ourselves?' asked Susie.

Lou nodded.

'I've told him if he stays out of bother for a full year, I'll marry him,' answered Susie.

Lou arched an eyebrow. 'You're kidding?'

'No, not at all. I know it sounds strange, but it's relaxed him. He doesn't feel the need to keep proving himself – to keep impressing me. He's stopped trying to compete with the rest of the world. And when he does that, he's the sweetest guy on the planet.'

'What about his illness?' Lou asked. 'Aren't you worried it could worsen?'

'Look, Lou,' replied Susie, 'the short answer is, we're all nuts. Me, I'm a thirty-five-year-old MBA who spends her days serving beer to gangsters. Mary up there kept Hugo waiting for thirty years. You, you're wasting your life chasing rainbows because you're too proud to make up with your boyfriend – who, by the way, is far too good for you.'

Lou reddened slightly but said nothing.

'There's not one of us who's not certifiable,' continued Susie. 'Even the likes of Stan. The only reason he's running for president of the country is because he's bored and has too much money. Oh, and he also wants to poke you in the eye … And as for Harry the Hurler over there, the poor sap can't keep his eyes off a woman who's trying to put him in jail. No. We all have our own ways of going mad. The only difference is, Jimmy's never bothered to hide it.'

Lou laughed at the speech – but she was needled. 'What do you mean, Stan's far too good for me?' she pressed, trying to sound light.

Susie pointed over to a table in the corner where Stan was busily flirting with two eighty-year-old cousins of Hugo. They were hanging on his every word. 'Just watch him now,' said Susie. 'He's working the room, taking care of all the loose ends. Later on after the meal, he'll make certain everyone has someone to talk to or dance with. And he'll also make sure no one drinks too much – and won't touch a drop himself until he tucks everyone safely into their taxi home at the end of the night …'

Lou grinned. Stan had been doing that all their lives, so much so that she'd never really noticed it.

'As for his best-man speech,' said Susie, 'according to Harry, Stan's spent two days working on it. And apparently it's the best thing Harry's ever heard – presidential debates included. Though of course, Stan will never let Hugo think that it's anything but off-the-cuff. Because that's his style. If Stan does you a favour, he doesn't want you to know a thing about it … And finally, for a man with a reputation for being close with a dollar, Stan has spent, I'd guess, at least five hundred pounds on the little orchid arrangements for the tables – after he got me to find out Mary's favourite flower.'

Lou acknowledged her defeat with a graceful bow. 'So if I can cut to the chase here, Susie,' she said, 'you don't think I deserve him?'

Susie smiled and looked up towards Stan who was getting an order at the bar. 'Do you see what colour tie he's wearing?' continued Susie.

'Not from here,' replied Lou. 'I can't say I noticed it.'

'Nor me,' answered Susie. 'But I'll bet you a thousand pounds it's ocean blue – the exact same shade as your dress. He'll have had it made specially.'

'You're joking,' retorted Lou, genuinely surprised.

'He's a star, Lou,' said Susie simply. 'And in case you missed it, he looks like a million dollars. Like a man who should be president. Jesus, if you don't bag him quickly, you'll regret it.'

Lou looked directly at Susie and shook her head. 'It's not that simple,' she sighed. 'One question for you – where was Stan when Barry, who he absolutely hated, was shot dead in the Baywater Estate?'

Susie stopped short. 'You mean no one's told you?' she replied, failing to hide a grin.

'Told me what?' snapped Lou impatiently.

Susie looked over her shoulder to make sure that Stan was out of range. She took Lou's arm and pulled her closer. 'Strictly between ourselves?' she whispered.

Lou nodded.

'Okay,' continued Susie. 'You remember when Stanley first fell in with Joxer O'Duffy and that crew?'

'Yes,' nodded Lou. 'It was about the time the pair of you were friendly.'

'Friendly like limpets,' countered Susie, with a dirty laugh.

Lou scowled but bit her tongue for once. 'Continue,' she told Susie coldly.

'Joxer wasn't happy that Stan was still single, and was trying to get him married off,' explained Susie. 'Now Stan certainly wasn't going to marry me, but he didn't want to tell Joxer he was only in it for the, ah, friendship. So instead he told him that he actually preferred men – but was living his life in the closet …'

'No way,' interrupted Lou.

'Way,' grinned Susie. 'Now Joxer, for want of a better term, swallowed the story whole. And he sent Stan to that priest – you know, Bend'em–Back Behan – to get straightened out …'

'This is just too good,' laughed Lou. 'Please promise me you're not lying.'

'And it gets better,' continued Susie, smiling broadly. 'The day Barry Magee got whacked was supposed to have been the day of Stan's first session. But Stan, being Stan, couldn't go through with it. He lost his nerve. So instead he went for a drink on Parnell Street where, lo and behold, he was immediately chatted up … by a man.'

'You're kidding,' gasped Lou. The media were going to lap this up.

'His head was spinning,' said Susie. 'And he actually started to convince himself that he must have been giving out gay vibes. So he got a taxi to the Derry plane, flew home and came straight to the Jack Kennedy, which is where Harry the Tout spotted him.'

'But why did he go to the Kennedy?' asked Lou, baffled.

'To see me,' grinned Susie. 'There was something he had to check. Urgently ... You want me to paint you a picture?'

Lou's eyes widened and she shook her head in utter disbelief. 'I'll kill him,' she giggled. 'No wonder he wouldn't tell me.'

The two women burst out laughing, and Lou hugged Susie in delight. Hugo watched them from the top table. Mission accomplished.

'Of course if you are going to kill him ...' said Susie, with a serious edge to her voice, '... you're going to have to catch him first.'

With that, Lou turned around and saw Stan approaching with two glasses of Veuve Clicquot, neither of which was for him.

Susie was right. He did look like a million of dollars. And, when he lifted his arm to pass them their glasses, Lou smiled happily at the thought she'd just lost a thousand quid. Stan's tie, of course, was ocean blue.

45

The next morning Lou was dabbing with a damp napkin at a tiny spot on her chiffon dress when Stan sat down beside her.

'Give me one good reason I shouldn't use the Behan stuff against you?' she demanded mischievously.

'Because Harry the Hurler won't let you,' replied Stan. 'Our combined vote is what he's counting on. You're only allowed to attack Joxer – not me.'

'True, of course,' answered Lou quietly. 'But that's not my reason.' She looked sideways at him, coyly.

'So what is it?' asked Stan.

She closed her eyes and took a deep breath. There was no backing out now. She had waited too long. 'This had better never leave the room,' she said quickly, 'but I don't want to fight with you any more. I'm worn out – and it's all become so pointless. Please don't think I'm getting soft, Stanley, but I'd much rather be your friend.' She stopped. 'Your best friend …'

Stan smiled and took her hand gently. 'You were always my best friend, Lou,' he said. 'Just sometimes we didn't tell one another enough. And don't worry. I'll not tell anyone you're getting soft. It'll be our little secret. That and the photos of yourself and Jimmy Fidget….'

'You wouldn't dare,' Lou gasped, trying not to laugh.

'God no,' grinned Stan. 'I mean, what man would do that to the woman he wants to marry. If she'd ever have him again that is …?'

Lou stopped suddenly, looked up into his face and beamed. 'She might, you know – if she were asked nicely …'

Stan cupped her chin in his hand, stared approvingly at the summer freckles on her little nose, and then kissed her lightly on the forehead. 'Louise Johnston, I love you more than life,' he said. 'I want to spend every day with you, and every night with you. I never want to leave your side. Then, when our days here are all done, I want to spend eternity with you.' He paused. 'And I want to start now ...'

Lou nodded, almost shyly, and quickly wiped her eye with the napkin she was holding in her hand. She then looked at him dead centre and nodded. 'I accept,' she replied, '... and I want to start now too.'

She threw her arms around his neck and hugged him tightly, half hoping that it might shield him from her big broad grin. But he caught sight of her face in the bedroom mirror and started to laugh.

'As proposals go,' she sniffed, 'that wasn't bad at all, Stan.' She waited a beat. 'For a big pansy ... Now, help me zip up this beautiful dress, and we'll sneak out the back door. I wonder is there any chance no one saw us slip off last night.'

Already seated in the darkest corner of the Tower's dining room were three red-faced men who looked more like hardened brandy drinkers trying to piece together the events of the night before than plotters attempting to pull off a *coup d'état*.

None of the men was quite up to eating – not until the coffee had done its job, although all three had scrambled eggs and toast in front of them.

'It's time to pull Lou out, Harry,' said Tommy, hand shaking slightly as he put down his cup. 'The punters know she's only running as a help-me-up for Stan – and your vote's going to suffer because of it. As will Stan's.'

'Problem is,' replied Harry the Hurler, patting his pockets for Nurofen, 'if we pull her, the North's no longer on the agenda. Joxer will have Stanley debating tribunals, immigration and tax policies. And let's face it, he'll kick seven colours of shit out of him. As long as Lou's there, Joxer can't avoid the one thing he's trying to avoid.'

They both looked at Hugo, who was staring hard at a forkful of egg, wondering if he should dare.

'Have to agree with Mr Hurley here,' he said at last, putting down the fork. 'Though not necessarily with his reasoning. For my money, a large part of Stan's appeal is that he's an alternative to both the loony left, no offence Harold, and the loony right. If we were to pull Lou, Stan immediately lurches leftwards. But at the moment, she's covering his flank.'

The trio nodded soberly as one, disappointed it had come to this for Lou.

'Any chance she could make some inroads into the women's vote?' asked Tommy.

'Not really,' sighed Harry. 'The feministas will vote for her – but they were always going to the left anyway. Joxer has sewn up the Old Biddy vote, and the younger dolls like Stan. He's a good-looking boy. No offence, Hugo ...'

Hugo grinned. He didn't care that he was ugly. He was rich.

'Any more poisoned arrows waiting for Stan?' he asked Harry. 'Have your people dug up anything that Joxer might find?'

'Not really,' sniffed Harry. 'I mean he likes the ladies. But he's not married, and most people accept he plays them one at a time. The one thing that he could get flak over is his dealings with Bend'em-Back Behan. Jesus knows why he was going there for private counselling – he's refused point-blank to tell me. But that'll all remain under wraps. Doctor–patient privilege.'

Hugo took up his fork again, stared at the egg uncertainly, then gave Harry a sideways look. 'And what about the three people your men shot – that's not going to come back on Stan again?' he asked.

'Jesus, Hugo,' protested Harry, 'not even the cops are saying I did those ones.'

'Well, who whacked them, then, to use the vernacular?' pressed Hugo.

Tommy Bowtie smiled round at his two friends. 'I think I might know.'

Out in the lobby of the Tower Hotel, Audrey Grafton was exiting the lift and heading briskly for the front door. But it was no use. Mary Slavin was at the reception desk, leafing through a stack of congratulations cards, and she wasn't going to let the chance go a-begging.

'Good morning, Superintendent,' she announced at the top of her voice, turning just about every head in the room. 'I trust you slept well.'

'Good morning, Mrs Stevenson,' replied Audrey through gritted teeth. 'Yes, under the circumstances I thought it would be more sensible not to attempt to drive. So I booked a room and crashed out.'

'So wise,' said Mary.

'Indeed,' said Audrey, 'it wouldn't do for a police chief to get caught under the influence.'

'No it would not,' agreed Mary.

'And a woman wouldn't be safe going home on her own in a taxi at that hour of night,' continued Audrey.

'Definitely not,' grinned Mary, 'even a police chief. Unless, maybe, she'd Harry the Hurler in the back seat of the car along with her …'

Audrey pointed her finger in warning at the new bride. 'You think you're so smart,' she shot back. 'You and your seating plan. You knew damn well Tommy Bowtie and his wife wouldn't be at the meal.'

'I think what you mean,' interrupted her friend, 'is, Thank you, Mary.'

Audrey shook her head in mock remorse. 'Bang goes my promotion,' she groaned. 'They're going to bust me back to the Late Night Loonies' Desk. I'll end my days ferrying sober-up coffee to Danny Aftershock and Bite Me O'Boyle.'

Mary pointed over to the lift, which had just opened again to reveal Stan and Lou. 'If you think you're in bother, Audrey,' she grinned, 'just where do you think Rubber John is going to bust Stanley back to?'

'Well, well, well,' whistled Audrey. 'And I do believe that dirty trollop is wearing the same dress as last night.'

'I don't think they see us,' said Mary. 'They look like they're heading out the back way. I think I'd better shout out after them …'

The *Daily Irishman* had got permission to send a photographer along to the Tower to take one shot of the 'Media Marriage of the Year'. And they duly featured a front-page photo of the two presidential candidates toasting Hugo and Mary with champagne.

Normaltimes, this would have been no bad thing for Stan and Lou. But while they were partying up in Derry, Joxer O'Duffy had been spending the week with the Irish Army distributing famine relief in Central Africa. And so a Blueshirt bastard of a Free State sub-editor (Lou's words) thought it would be a clever idea to juxtapose a photo of Joxer, cradling a dying child, with the party snap.

Sonny Waterhouse, whose job it was to stop such things, took consolation in the fact that Rubber John was on a fishing holiday in Ballina, and so not physically able to give his new telescopic rod its first rectal test-run – as he was promising to do on his return.

'How the hell is this my fault?' Sonny pleaded.

'For one, they should never be fuckin' pictured together as besht of pals,' yelled Rubber John. 'We all know they've a hishtory. But it's now looking like us and the Shinners are gangin' up on Joxer. They are not to be photographed together – other than at debates – between now and the election. Do you understand, you fuckin' *amadán*?'

'I do, boss.'

'Now,' continued the Taoiseach. 'We need to do some damage control. As soon as Joxer gets back home, get a picture of him tucking into a big dinner somewhere – it doesn't matter where. Shteak preferably. Then we'll run it in one of our papers, the *Dublin Daily* maybe, with another picture of the little black fella – or, better still, his grave. In fact, it could be any grave. Who's going to know anyway? Give it a big fuck-off headline – something like: "How quickly we forget".'

'Shouldn't be a problem, Taoiseach,' replied Sonny obediently.

'One more thing,' said Rubber John slowly. 'And you cannot let Stan know this. We're going to have to hit Lou with a hatchet – and nobody can know it's coming from us. Leak it to Joxer that Lou was seeing that psycho child-killer Jimmy Fidget after she broke up with Stan. It'll not be our proudest hour, but it's worth two or three points to us. Now get to it — and no more falling asleep at the wheel.'

'No, no more, boss,' stuttered Sonny.

'Oh and in case I forget,' said Rubber John, with a softer edge to his voice, 'if I catch you back in Mount Street again, it had better be on party business. Do you understand me, Don Juan?'

'I do indeed,' answered Sonny sharply. 'I wouldn't want to be lowering the tone of her neighbourhood.' And he rang off.

46

Timing is everything in cards and in politics. There is no point in playing your ace to take out a jack, when you have a queen in your hand. Aces are made for taking out kings, as Joxer O'Duffy, a lifelong bridge player, knew well. So, with the ace safely tucked inside his pocket waiting for the senator, Joxer played his queen against Letemout Lou. It was three weeks before D-Day and just three days before the big RTÉ debate.

'The Judge and the Baby-Butcher' screamed *Sunday Ireland*. 'Lou's lover bombed sleeping child,' replied *Dublin on Sunday*. But it was the headline in the *Sunday News* that hurt her most: 'Do we want a president who slept with a child-killer?'

By Tuesday, Lou had dropped six points to nine per cent. Her vote in the North was still holding up solidly, but it had fallen through the floor in the South. Stan was down a little, by association, on thirty-five per cent, while Joxer was cruising towards the title on fifty-six. The Northerners' combined vote was now twelve per cent behind the Real Fianna Fáil leader.

'Uncloseable,' lamented Harry, shaking his head sadly.

'It just needs a six per cent swing,' replied Hugo.

'Or a big fucking rock to fall on Joxer,' quipped Tommy Bowtie. And all three of them laughed.

RTÉ had plumped to hold the hustings in Galway, in the university's five-hundred-seat O'Flaherty Theatre. Joxer had tried to push for UCD, his old alma mater. But the Taoiseach wanted to take it to his home turf, and the programme producer, who was dating an immigrant and hated Real Fianna Fáil, agreed.

On Wednesday morning, the day of the debate, Stan was in

Galway's Eyre Square Centre, working the shoppers, when Lou rang him on the mobile. He'd been expecting it.

'I've had enough,' she said. 'I'm withdrawing. I'm going to announce it this evening – at the end of my speech. I'm going to call it as I see it – and blame Joxer's dirty tricks. I just want to make sure you're ready for it. You could make quite a bit of hay.'

She rang off abruptly. Instinctively, Stan grabbed the Chief Whip, who was at the front of the cortège, and pulled him to the side.

'Get Harry the Hurler,' he hissed. 'And damn quickly.'

The gardaí were of course tapping Lou's phone, so the Real Fianna Fáil camp knew she was quitting less than twenty minutes after she called Stan. Conman Donnelly called to Joxer's Dáil office personally with the news.

Marta Morgan was not impressed. 'This is going to burn you,' she told her boss. 'Campaigns, believe it or not, should not be about who you sleep with.'

'I know that, dear,' smirked Joxer, 'otherwise you would never have been elected in Catholic Drogheda. Now, would you? But at this level politics is all about who you're friendly with. Now let's face it, would you rather your president was married to a kiddie-killer or to an upstanding Christian like my wife?'

'I'm not sure,' replied Marta unimpressed. 'If by "Christian" you mean a beaten shell of a woman who needs four different types of anti-depressant to get her through the day, then I'll take my chances.'

'We haven't got time for this, Marta,' snapped Joxer. 'The helicopter to Galway is going in half an hour. I need you to cover my back when this blows up. You're going to issue a statement saying it's revolting how Lou is trying to elicit sympathy just because she's a woman. It demeans her and all women. All candidates, male or female alike, must be subject to the same levels of scrutiny ... I know I might take a small hit, Marta. But you have to limit it. And you'll do it, by the way, because as soon as I'm president, who do you think's going to be running our party in the Dáil?'

Marta smiled like she believed him. Not that she did for one moment. But he was right. They hadn't got time for it, now. She'd cash in her IOUs another day.

Stan was talking to Leaving Cert students at the Jesuit College on Sea Road when Sonny's call came through. Stan excused himself and stepped out into the corridor.

'No dice,' said Sonny simply. 'Rubber John said you've got to slate Lou's character from a height – every bit as hard as Joxer does. You have to put clear water between you and her. When the Shinners fuck up, it's an unwritten rule that you have to hammer them twice as hard. I mean, the temerity of them, running for the presidency of the country, and all.'

'Tell Rubber John that she's my friend, and I'm going to bat for her,' replied Stan bluntly.

'He'll pull his support,' said Sonny.

'No he won't,' retorted Stan. 'And I know he won't because that would be disloyal. Which is precisely what I'd be, if I don't take on Joxer.'

'Kiss goodbye to the Áras so,' said Sonny.

'Do you really think I'm bothered?' asked Stan enraged. 'My best friend of more than twenty years has spent the past two days putting over a nervous breakdown in her bedroom because somebody – and I'm certain it's from our team – told Joxer dirty little stories about her. And I'm not even allowed to go and see her in case someone might find out?'

'Ah that's not fair, Stan,' protested Sonny.

'It's fucking true,' countered Stan. 'I thought us Northerners were cold-hearted bastards – but at least we do it in the open … And by the way, Sonny, in case you've forgotten, I actually employ Jimmy Fidget as a photographer at the *Derry Standard*. He works for me. So how in the name of Christ am I going to get up there tonight and tell the world he's not a fit person for society? Do you really want me to be a hypocrite on top of everything? Sorry, mate, but this cannon's just worked its way loose. Now watch this fucking space.'

'How did it go?' asked Rubber John when Sonny had finished.

'Better than I thought,' replied Sonny, smiling over the desk at the Taoiseach. 'He's madder than hell – ready to flay Joxer alive.'

'Perfect,' laughed his boss. 'We need a bit of passion tonight. Stan's too damn fair-minded. You have to fire him up sometimes.'

Mary Slavin had got to make the Good Cop call to Lou. She understood exactly why she was pulling out and supported her decision entirely.

'It's a real pity, though,' she told her. 'You're exactly what I want in a figurehead for the country. Young, dynamic, a great speaker, and so, so smart. Not to mention somebody who'll loan me their old dresses.'

Lou's teeth grated as she listened. She didn't have to have it spelt out. She was letting the side down.

'Stan's a lovely guy,' continued Mary, 'but he hasn't got your sharpness. It was always going to be Joxer anyway, so we might as well get used to it. You had a good run.'

Thanks a bunch, said Lou to herself. And you're right, quitters never win.

Half an hour later, Audrey Grafton, as so often before, got to be Bad Cop.

'You're being spoilt and self-indulgent,' she told the candidate. 'Let's face it, it was the reason Stan ran away from you. And now you're doing it again – though this time the whole world knows it. Simple fact is, Lou, you've dished out some pretty hard knocks in your time, and now you're getting one back. And I have to say I'm shocked. I always figured you for someone who would get straight back up and into the game again.'

Disappointment, guilt and abuse in the one sentence, thought Lou. It's like listening to my mother.

'You didn't get to be a High Court judge and an MLA by whinging every time you got slapped back,' Audrey told her. 'You took it on the chin, then tried again. And that's what you have to do now. The only shame, Lou, is lying down and letting them do this to you … You're better than them.

Remember that. Suck it up, stay in the race, and I'll vote for you myself.'

Lou looked out the window of her room in the Skeffington and down onto Eyre Square, where a couple of students were sitting on a backpack smoking a reefer. She and Stan fifteen years ago.

She grinned. Stan had turned her round, and he hadn't even spoken to her.

'How did it go?' asked Harry, when Audrey had finished.

'She's back in it,' smiled the policewoman, handing him back his mobile. 'She's going to go down fighting.'

Harry pushed open the door of the little snug and signalled over to the barmaid for his tab. The drink bills had thankfully got a lot lower since they'd started lunching on a daily basis.

'If Lou left now,' said Harry, 'she'd never return. This way, at least she'll fight another day. And boy, I hope I'm around to see it.'

'And what about Stanley?' pressed Audrey.

'No,' sighed Harry. 'I think he might just get within a few points of Joxer. But you can bet your eyeteeth that Joxer's got one up his sleeve to spring on Stan before poll day. Still, a lot could happen between now and then.'

'You're right,' said Audrey, 'and, given the form Lou's in, a lot could happen tonight.'

47

In the late afternoon, the three candidates were taken on a tour of the campus by the students' union president, Pascal Lynch. A film crew and two or three journalists tagged along, so Pascal the Rascal, as he was known by the governing body, put on a show.

He started by walking them around the classical Victorian quad. It was the oldest and most impressive of the campus's ninety buildings – and, as it was autumn, the ivy covering the Aula Maxima in its centre had turned dark purple. Pascal was a native Galwegian and had all the gen.

'The college,' he began, 'was opened by the Brits back in 1849. And it is without question the most beautiful campus in Ireland. The reason we know it's the most beautiful is that it was built at the exact same time as Queen's University in Belfast, and we were sent their plans by mistake. So we held onto them.'

Pascal took the salutes of a couple of freshers as they walked out of the quad past the old porters' desk. He then pointed up at the new sign adorning the front of the building. 'The university,' he said, 'was actually known as Queen's College Galway until the start of the twentieth century when a few of Letemout Lou's ancestors managed to get the link to the occupying forces dropped, and it became University College Galway. Then, a couple of years back, a bunch of civil servants decided it was time to go even more upmarket, so we became National University of Ireland, Galway.'

The student continued with his alternative history as the group ambled slowly down past the tennis courts to the new students' union block. As they reached the building, he pointed them into the college bar and guided them towards a table of wine and sandwiches which had been left out for them.

'Who'll you be voting for, Pascal?' asked one of the hacks.

'Naturally, I'll be voting for Letemout Lou,' he grinned. 'You know us student types – we can't resist a lost cause. Though my deputy, Jenny Carr, to her great shame, is going to be backing Mr O'Duffy. She even decked out her office with several of his posters, until we passed a motion ordering her to draw little Hitler moustaches on them.'

The journalists, and the three candidates, were lapping this up. 'So I take it, then,' said the RTÉ man, 'you'll be giving Senator Stevenson your number two.'

'Absolutely,' said Pascal, slugging back the free wine. 'I mean, let's face it, we all know he'd much rather be a Shinner, he just hasn't got the balls for it.'

Joxer laughed out loud. 'I think I'm going to quote you on that tonight,' he said to Pascal.

The student's smile froze, and he stared directly into the face of the Real Fianna Fáil leader. 'As long as you also say that I think you're a racist prick,' he said icily. 'And that you should go to jail for what you did to Ms Johnston.

'Now, ladies and gentlemen, let's move on to the Engineering blocks …'

The three speeches were limited to eight minutes each which, as Stan pointed out, was roughly eight times as long as was necessary. The real money would be in the Q-and-A sessions.

The only real surprise in the candidates' presentations was that while Joxer, who spoke last, tore large strips off Stan over everything from immigration to education, he didn't attack Lou at all. Indeed, he went so far as to praise her 'dignity' in the face of 'appalling smears'.

Stan twigged immediately. 'They've tapped your phone,' he whispered to Lou. 'He thinks you're going to pull out at the end of the night and doesn't want to get the blame for it. You've got a free licence to beat the tar out of him on live TV …'

'Haven't I just?' she whispered back. 'Just don't think I'm going to go soft on you, either.'

The first question, as they were in Galway, centred on funding for Irish-language TV – and was asked in Irish. The trio all knew it was coming and read carefully from their notes, while the viewing public at home flicked over to the football on Sky Sports. The next contribution, however, was from the secretary of the college's Labour Society, a straightforward individual who, unusually, wasn't known to be following anyone's agenda.

'The media treatment of the candidates,' he said bluntly, 'has it been justified?'

You could have heard a pin drop. The game was on. Stan stood ready and fired up beside Lou. But he wouldn't be needed.

Lou was first – and stared over at Joxer as she stood at the mike.

'I'll be making a fuller statement on the media's treatment of me after the debate tonight,' she began, noticing her nemesis shift in his chair. Stan was right. He was convinced she was going to pull out. Time, so, to take him to the fair. 'For the moment,' she continued, 'can I just say that where the media, in general, have failed is that they have allowed wild gossip about sex, and unfounded rumour about murder, to replace any coverage of real electoral issues. Debate and dialogue have been replaced by dirty deeds and dirty pictures.'

She stopped and looked out at the four hundred and fifty assorted students and fifty dignitaries who'd been allocated seats.

'I understand there's about forty overseas students in here tonight,' she said. 'Could you all please stand up? Now, anybody's who's from the EU or the United States can sit down.'

About thirty, mostly black and Asian, remained standing.

'Okay,' she said, pointing at Joxer. 'This man is trying to introduce a law which means your brothers and sisters will never be allowed into this country to study – and you yourselves will be deported as soon as your courses are over. No exceptions.'

Joxer raised his hand to interrupt but the RTÉ chairwoman just shook her head and signalled that Lou had the floor.

'Stay standing up for a moment please, if you could,' said

Lou to the little group. 'Now, could everyone else in here whose parents' income is taxed at source please stand up. Or, indeed, any of you who actually earn money yourselves which is pre-taxed.'

The theatre began to buzz with excitement as about one hundred and fifty more people got to their feet. The RTÉ director, sitting in a makeshift gantry at the back of the hall, rubbed his hands together in satisfaction. This was going to be one doozy of a show.

'Thank you,' grinned Lou, as silence fell again. She pointed round again at Joxer. 'Another issue no one has mentioned up to now is Mr O'Duffy's No Payment Amnesty Bill. This new law, if it's passed, will mean that you and your parents should pick up the cheque for this very rich man and his very rich friends, who bled the country dry in the seventies and eighties. These men and women, by the way, paid on average about a tenth of the tax, in real cash terms, that you and your families did. The Amnesty Bill will wipe all their slates clean. So, if he's elected, don't come crying to me when he rolls you over in the bed to give you a schlacking.'

'And that man,' she stated, nodding down at Stan, 'and his party are going to help him do it.'

'You go get 'em girl,' shouted a voice, Oprah-style – and everyone laughed, including Lou.

Back in the gallery, the RTÉ director was biting his nails excitedly. This could be better than the *Late Late Show* when Gaybo unravelled the condom. All he needed was for someone to say 'fuck' and he'd be putting it in for an award.

'Now,' continued Lou. 'Could all of you who are on your feet stay standing for a moment, please. And could I ask all the remaining women in the room to get up as well.'

Another hundred and fifty members of the house rose to their feet, most of them smiling. This was a lot more fun than they'd hoped.

'This man,' declared Lou, looking straight at Joxer, 'wants to sterilise immigrant women so there'll be no black babies in Ireland. At the same time, he wants an end to the Freedom of Information on abortion, and he wants a twenty-year ban on the pill. He wants an abolition of all tax breaks for working mothers – including crèche care – and he wants maternity leave, for women who do work, cut back to twelve weeks, in the hope that more of them will give up entirely. This is all on the record. Some of you might even agree with him – and that is your right. This is a free country. Just about.'

The hall went silent as Lou turned back round to face Joxer directly.

'But most important of all,' she said, eyeing her opponent coldly, 'and where Mr O'Duffy crosses the line, is that he wants us women, all of us, to be held accountable for the mistakes of our partners. Our boyfriends. Our husbands. Our girlfriends, perhaps. Bad enough we have our own failings, but we've now gotta answer for other people's as well.'

She stopped and looked round again at the audience. She didn't have to spell it out any further. 'What I want to ask you now is this,' she said softly, 'anyone who's only ever gone out with men – or women, who are perfect in every respect, please sit down now.'

Nobody moved. Not even Joxer's champion-on-campus Jenny Carr.

'They mustn't have understood the question,' smiled Lou, grinning over at Joxer again. His face was dark red with anger.

'Okay, I'll make it a bit easier,' she went on. 'Anyone who's never had a bad date can sit down.'

Again, nobody budged. But there was more laughter when a voice at the back shouted up: 'Are we allowed to stand up on the desks?'

Lou looked out at the crowd. There were now fewer than two hundred men sitting in the lecture theatre.

'One final question,' said Lou. 'Trickiest of all perhaps. And I want you to be honest here. Could I ask all you remaining men who think Northerners are a bunch of whingeing troublemakers, who would wreck the Republic if you let them in, to stay seated – and the rest of you to stand up please.'

About half the men got up, leaving about a fifth of the hall still sitting down. Some of them looked quite shamefaced.

'But I'm not a Joxer supporter,' shouted one seated student, in a panic.

'No,' said Lou, 'but you're one of about only a hundred

people left in this room who'll be able to vote for him with a clear conscience.'

The student gave Lou a stage bow, then rose to his feet. The crowd began to clap slowly. Four more students in the front row stood up, then three in the row behind them. The applause grew. Then another two rose on the side aisle, and a group of three at the back. In ones and twos, they kept rising and rising, until in the end only about thirty people in the hall were seated. The noise of cheering and clapping and shouting was immense. Even Stan was on his feet, whistling and banging the table in front of him at Lou's performance.

The ovation lasted a full three minutes, until the convenor finally managed to get some order. 'Mr O'Duffy,' she said, raising her hand to hush the crowd. 'Your rebuttal please.'

Joxer stormed up to the podium in a black rage. 'This is a fucking fix,' he screamed, spit shooting from his lips. 'A total fucking fix. And RTÉ should be fucking ashamed of themselves for letting it happen ...'

The programme director in the gantry leapt to his feet and shadow-boxed the air in delight. Three fucks in the one breath – in a presidential debate. He was made for life.

'If Lou doesn't win,' he grinned to his soundman, 'I wonder would she come and work for me ...'

48

It was good. Very good even. But it was never going to be enough, and Lou knew it. By the weekend, her numbers were peaking at an inflated twenty-eight per cent. But by the following Thursday, they'd dropped back to twenty – a creditable but more realistic showing for a candidate from the left who wasn't in bed with the Labour Party. Joxer had stopped the rot by alleging that Pascal the Rascal had given seating preference at the hustings to Sinn Féin supporters – and then produced video footage of the audience to show how the students' union president had personally started the ovation at the end.

No, it was never going to be enough. Fickle and all as the free press were, they weren't going to desert the Only True Irish Candidate in his hour of need. Much more interestingly, however, Stan's vote had remained fairly stable in the mid-thirties. So there was growing speculation that if he could command three-quarters of Lou's second preferences – which pollsters agreed was possible – he could just pip Joxer on the final tally.

For the last three weeks before Super Thursday, the candidates took to the streets 'kissing flesh and pounding babies', as Stan remarked. But as every day passed, the senator was growing more and more nervous. At least Lou had the luxury of being out of contention and could enjoy herself.

'Joxer's getting ready to hit me with a metal bar,' Stan told her when they hooked up for a private dinner at his Derry flat on the long Halloween weekend. Harry had posted plainclothes sentries along the street and around the apartment block to make sure no one could see them together.

'You could always hit him first,' suggested Lou.

'I'd love to – but his head is made of concrete,' replied Stan. 'And besides – everything bad there is to know about him comes out of his own mouth. But people forgive him because he's their cuddly old fascist uncle. Only difference is when your uncle says that all wogs should be sent back to Africa on the banana boats they came in on, he's not speaking on behalf of the Irish nation … Why aren't more people up in arms?'

Lou forked up a piece of apple pie and chewed slowly. 'Familiarity,' she said after a pause. 'They understand his bigotries and feel safer with them. He's not asking them to change. Better still, he's managed to make change – even change for the better – the enemy. It's classic Tory bullshit. The old ways were always best.'

Stan drained his coffee and reached across the table for Lou's hand. 'Maybe Joxer's right,' he grinned. 'Maybe the old ways are the best. Maybe it's time we started adopting a few old ways of our own. After all, you're in just the right party for it. Their old ways were certainly effective …'

Lou lifted his hand to her mouth and nibbled gently on the side of his thumb. 'Now, now, senator,' she scolded him. 'You know you don't mean that. You're just a little bit uptight. But if you go and tell the man guarding the front door to go and take his tea break, we'll see what we can do about that. I think I know just the cure.'

The following Friday, six days before polling day, Conman Donnelly, Joxer's old friend in the gardaí, rang Stan personally to deliver the first slap.

'There's been a burglary at a psychiatrist's offices on Dominick Street,' he said, his soft Kerry accent oozing concern. 'It was Monsignor George Behan's clinic – I believe you may know him. Some documents have been stolen; we haven't yet established how many … The reason I called you is, well, I asked for a full client list – and have just got it. And I'm afraid your name's on it, senator, and we can't find your file. The monsignor is very distressed. I can assure you, we will be moving heaven and earth to ensure its safe return …'

Stan, who'd been sitting at his desk in Leinster House trying to get his head around a speech on cattle levies he had to give

270

at the RDS, closed his eyes and nodded slowly. His gut felt empty, his head light. He was finished. They'd done him.

He took a breath and counted silently to ten before speaking to the policeman. 'I take it,' he said, 'that none of the press is aware of the priest's client list as yet – and that you're not commenting about any of the names on it?'

'Sorry, Stan,' came the blunt answer. 'It's already out there. They know. But let's face it, it's your own fault. No one forced you to become a pillow-muncher.'

'No indeed,' retorted Stan angrily. 'Thank you, Mr Donnelly, for taking the time to call me. And can you thank your boss, Mr O'Duffy, for having you pass on the message? I trust you'll have a long and distinguished career as his new Garda Commissioner …'

Conman sucked in air, as if in pain, then laughed. 'Now, now,' he said, 'don't be sore, Stan. You Northerners have to learn how to lose with a little grace.'

'You're right of course, Mr Donnelly,' replied Stan, calm again. 'We've a lot to learn from our Southern brothers and sisters.'

The Dublin papers were particularly unkind, even by British standards. Three of them got psychiatrists of their own to confirm Father Behan's suspicions that the senator was a bisexual schizophrenic – citing his many 'unfulfilling' relationships with women and his 'sordid' affairs with 'numerous' unknown men.

The *Sunday Irishman*, of course, wet their pants with joy – and had no fewer than seventeen separate articles on why Northerners, particularly nationalist ones, shouldn't be allowed to run for president.

The *Sunday News* went straight for the money, however, and compiled a list of the ten Dáil Members the Senator Might Fancy Most. Only one of them was a woman – and as you'd expect, it was Marta Morgan. But even Stan – who had handed out quite a bit of stick during his own newspaper days – thought it was a bit tasteless to stage the How They Might Look Together photos.

By Monday, the *Irish Times* had the senator's numbers at

eighteen per cent and dropping – and were citing his refusal to comment at all on the files as part of the reason for his collapse.

'Why don't you speak out, so?' asked Harry the Hurler, who had flown down to Dublin with Audrey for the last few days of the campaign. 'I mean, you were acting on behalf of Rubber John. And by protecting him now, you're damaging yourself. As far as we're concerned, it's over. It doesn't matter any more. We've had a good run. We'll be better prepared next time.'

Stan shook his head. He'd spent the past three days studying the chessboard. 'It's too late,' he said. 'They've timed it perfectly. If I spoke out now, I'd only hurt Rubber John and do myself no good whatsoever. I'd look like a coward, blaming other people. I'm much better off taking the hit for him and storing up the brownie points for later.

'Truth is, Joxer is a much better operator than we gave him credit for. When you come back – and let's be honest, I'll not be in the field – you need to be a lot sharper. The old hands know how to play the long game.'

'True,' grinned Harry. 'But never forget, we've a few old hands on our team as well.'

Rubber John appreciated the silence. So much so that he arranged a press conference for the steps of the Dáil on Monday night, where he stood shoulder to shoulder with his candidate to denounce Joxer's dirty tricks. He even accused Joxer of staging the burglary with Father Behan's assistance, specifically to target the senator. Ultimately, however, it would be too little too late.

'It'll make a nice picture in tomorrow's press – if they use it,' said Stan.

'Yeah,' said Rubber John, shaking the senator's hand for the battery of cameramen. 'It'll certainly be a lot nicer than the one they printed of us together in yesterday's *Sunday News*.'

Stan laughed, then watched as a party officer passed around a press statement to the thirty or so reporters.

'Do you mind if I say a few words?' he asked Rubber John.

'Fire ahead,' said the Taoiseach. 'It's the least we can do.'

The senator clapped his hands together and walked two

steps down. 'I've a brief announcement to make.' He smiled. 'If you could form an orderly swarm ... Some of you might be aware that I've taken a bit of a tanking over the past few days. Indeed, some of you may have even been the tankers involved. That's tankers with a "t", for the benefit of the tabloids ...'

The press corps loosened up at that, and most of them smiled. Apart from the *Sunday News* hack, who asked his pal what the senator meant.

'Can I just say,' continued Stan, 'that I accept it's all part of our open political process, and I don't resent it – not a bit. As a newspaperman myself, I know the ease with which lives and reputations can be destroyed. But I'm also aware that you all know that, and would never act outside the bounds of your integrity. No one likes doing dirty work – but you have to serve the public interest. And you have done so well. Far too well for me, I must add.'

He grinned down at two or three reporters who were nodding apologetically.

'I also know that there is a resistance to change,' said Stan, 'particularly with regards to the role that us Northerners can play in politics on the island. And it's for precisely that reason that I agreed to go forward in this election. But the one thing I failed to do was to explain to you just why it's so important for us to have the link with you.

'I know you think we're stuck in a time warp – truth is we are. And I know you think we're all cracked – Jesus, I've pretty much proved that myself over the last week. And I also know that half of you want to bolt the doors when you see us coming. But the simple truth is, people like me – and there are huge numbers of us in the North – greatly admire you in the South. We envy you, even.

'We love your openness, your friendliness, and your laid-back attitude to life. We love the fact that you govern your country in a fair and sympathetic way. That your decision makers are accountable to the people. That the rights of the public are always protected. That what the people say counts. That you don't split and divide – but unite for the common good.

'We look at how you've turned a small rural nation into one of the most successful in the world, and we take our hats off to you. We look at your initiative, your determination to succeed, and think to ourselves, if only we could bottle that and drink it.

'We love your culture and history and heritage – in fact many of us like to believe that it's a common heritage. In short, we want to be part of it. To be like you.'

He paused to look round, to let them form the question in their heads before he answered it.

'Now, not all of you want us,' he said. 'Let's be frank, a whole big bunch of you don't want us. But you can't stop us dreaming, and you're not going to stop us hoping. Just occasionally, maybe once in a lifetime, the ugly frog gets to kiss the good-looking princess. Or kiss the good-looking prince – depending what paper you believe ...'

This time there was loud laughter.

Stan took another breath and steeled himself.

'For my part, I believe I am now standing in the way of that dream,' he said. 'So I spoke to the Taoiseach earlier this evening and asked him to withdraw my nomination. But typical of his loyalty, he refused.

'More important, he told me – very wisely, I have to say – that it would be a cop-out. If you're arrogant enough to ask the people to let you lead them when things are going well, you must also be tough enough to let them reject you when things get bad. They deserve no more.

'I am very aware of my frailties. Indeed, thanks to you lot, so is everyone else. But to those I've let down – and in particular the Taoiseach here, and those people in the North whose dreams I trod on – can I just simply say sorry. Thank you.'

The final words were barely out of Stan's mouth when a spontaneous round of applause erupted from the pack. The Taoiseach, who was a great believer in getting out when the going was good, put his arm around the senator's shoulder and led him back into the lobby. 'They'd only fuck it all up by asking stupid questions,' he whispered, grinning.

The two men walked into the Dáil lobby and shook hands. 'Jesus, I wish you'd got to give that speech last week,' said Rubber John.

'Maybe next time,' quipped Stan, hoping his boss wouldn't, for one minute, think he was serious.

'Not in this life, Stan,' laughed the Taoiseach. 'Not in a million fuckin' years.'

49

Joxer hadn't been in Mount Street since the day he'd been expelled from the party by Rubber John. On that occasion, the security men had actually bodily lifted him from the front office and turfed him out into the front street. Though, truth be told, he shouldn't really have slapped the General Secretary in the mouth like that. It wasn't her fault. That Galway bastard had put her up to it.

Tonight, however, Joxer was delighted to be back taking care of a little business on his old stomping ground. Not that he was revisiting the office, mind. No. His business was with another nasty little fucker, who lived four hundred yards further down the road. A fucker, who, he'd just learned, had put two bullets into his best friend.

Georgie Behan had just got the full story from a client. In total confidence, of course. But typical priest couldn't hold his water. Confessional seal, his arse. He couldn't fucking wait to tell him. He was shaking like a puppy on his first warm leg. Funny thing was, Joxer was actually delighted. He'd always assumed some Derry headcase had shot Jim Wynne as a favour to Stan Stevenson. And there was no fucking way he was crazy enough to start butting horns with those guys. But a twenty-year-old streetwalker with a purse gun? That was a different matter.

As he approached the stairwell, he tapped his hip gently to check the automatic was secure in its holster. Back when he was a detective sergeant, he'd been fined fifty pounds for 'losing' it and banned from carrying a pistol for a month. It must have been the cheapest untraceable weapon ever bought.

Poor Jim. Poor, poor Jim. The little rabbit-toothed bastard had only been doing his duty as a patriotic Irishman.

Defending his boss – no, defending his *country* – against those Northern fucking savages. And he'd been gunned down by a back-entry prozzie. How fucking dare she?

That's why she had to know it was him. This is what happens when you mess around with the big boys. With the country's president-elect. Let it be the last lesson you ever learn. We take it fucking personally, Missy.

Stan and Lou, meanwhile, had returned to Derry and planned to cast their votes together the next day. In the final *Irish Times* poll of the campaign, published that morning, the two Northerners were tied on eighteen per cent each, while Joxer was sitting in complete command on sixty-four per cent. Unassailable.

The pair had arranged to hold a brief photocall at the polling station on Northland Road shortly after the boxes opened at eight o'clock. Though the way Harry the Hurler was pouring drink at supper in the Jack Kennedy, they'd be doing well to make it by midday.

'We're going to walk up hand in hand,' Lou told Audrey. 'I'm going to wear my shortest skirt, my new Jimmy Choos and, if there's a cameraman from the *Irishman* there, I might even stick my tongue down Stanley's throat.'

'Revolting,' grinned Audrey.

The waiter came into the snug with another three brandies and a glass of white for the boss's girlfriend.

'So what now for the two of you?' asked Audrey, lifting her Chardonnay.

'Well,' said Lou, 'we're going to head off for a brief, ah, holiday to Cuba, after which I'm going to take the chair of the Assembly's Judiciary Department. And next year I might just go for a ministry.'

'And what about you, Stan?' said Harry.

'I think I'm going to call it a day,' he replied, with a smile that might have been just a little bit sad. 'I'll finish my senate term in deference to Rubber John. But I've achieved what I set out to. Someone else can take the Stan Plan to the next level … To be honest, I'm not sure I could hack day-to-day politics after all this. I mean, how do you top being pictured naked with the Taoiseach, the Chief Whip and Marta Morgan?'

They all laughed.

'No,' he continued. 'Hugo's retiring as MD of the papers at Christmas to concentrate on his drinking. And he reckons it's time I took over ... Let's see that oul bitch Mary Slavin try to send me to a council meeting now.'

Lou punched his arm in reproach, while Audrey looked horrified.

'Can I quote you on that?' grinned Harry.

'Jesus, don't you dare,' retorted Stan. 'She'd boot me round the office – and send me back out to Dunavady. Boss or no boss ... The other thing we're planning is a wee project with Sonny Waterhouse. He wants me to link up with him to produce a new North Dublin newspaper – that's if his wife doesn't clean him out first.'

'Or Eva,' said Lou. And they laughed again.

Outside the snug, the crowded bar went quiet as the first bong from ITN presaged the late-night headlines. It was a hangover from the days when Derry automatically dominated the world news.

'I wonder will they have any word on the final RTÉ poll?' muttered Harry.

'Aren't you a bit old to start believing in miracles?' said Audrey.

But before anyone else could speak, there was pandemonium in the outer bar. A tumultuous cheer went up from the crowd followed by deafening applause. Then amid the frantic roaring, a chant broke out. To Stan's slightly befuddled ears it sounded like: 'Dig a hole for Joxer! Dig a hole for Joxer! Na, Na, Na, Na – Na, Na, Na, Na! Dig a hole for Joxer! Dig a hole for Joxer! Na, Na, Na, Na – Na, Na, Na, Na!'

The bar lights started to flash on and off in time to the conga, just as Jimmy Fidget bombed his way into the snug.

'Come out quick,' he shouted at Stan and Lou. 'Come out. Come out. The pair of you. You're back in it!'

'What do you mean?' asked Lou, yelling to be heard over the noise.

'It's on the TV,' whooped Jimmy, beaming. 'Joxer's been

shot. No word yet who did it. But he's deader than the devil's heart ...'

All heads turned and looked at Harry. 'No way, no way,' he protested. Then he relaxed again as he realised they were teasing him. 'I'm just out having a drink with the chief of police and a High Court judge,' he grinned.

Three pairs of eyes then switched to Lou. 'Typical,' she sniffed. 'You're in Sinn Féin five minutes and you get blamed for everything. Sorry to disappoint you, but I got my pound of flesh in Galway.'

They laughed and looked round at Stan.

'Absolutely not,' he declared. 'Jesus Christ, there has to be one murder in this country I didn't do.'

'So who then?' asked Harry.

'Probably mistaken identity,' replied Audrey. 'You know Dublin – full of drug dealers. Terrible place altogether ...'

The Garda Support Unit had raided the apartment within twenty minutes of the neighbours reporting screams. But it was too late. When they arrived, Joxer was lying dead on the four-poster bed, a naked limb tied to each corner. Other than that, the scene was unremarkable. Apart, that is, from the unpeeled bananas protruding from his two main orifices.

The attending doctor, who by sheer dint of luck happened to be an Indian immigrant, couldn't suppress a smile. 'You really should vary your diet a little,' he muttered, looking down at the corpse.

Eva was in the corner of the bedroom, being comforted by a passer-by who'd broken into the flat after the second gunshot. She was crying hysterically, breaking off only to retch and vomit into her hands. Her two eyes had been heavily bruised, and her beautiful little nose broken, in the pistol-whipping. She'd also lost most of her front teeth, and her swollen mouth was bleeding like a pump. The Guards had gently taken the gun off her and stashed it in a sealable bag.

Eva clearly wasn't fit to be questioned, so the doctor jabbed her with a sedative. And as soon as her eyes closed, he sectioned her to the secure wing of St Mildred's Mental

Health Clinic for seventy-two hours. Enough time, he figured, to let a little dust settle.

'She's one strong lady,' he said, gesturing towards the bed. 'She dragged that fat bastard from out there right up onto the bed.'

The inspector-in-charge peeled away from the little group of plainclothes men at the door and approached the medic. 'So was he killed by the first or the second shot?' he asked.

The doctor grinned at the detective's coyness. What he was itching to say was, Tell me, Doc, was it murder or self-defence? 'Ultimately, that's up to the pathologist to decide,' he replied, thinking quickly. 'But I'm almost certain the first bullet — the one that hit him in the head in the living room — killed him. The second one — the one he took in the heart when he was lying on the bed there — was just out of bloody-mindedness. I've no doubt he was dead already. He'd probably have bitten through the banana otherwise ... Oh, and for Christ's sake, leave that other banana where it is, until you get him to the morgue.'

'So why did she strip him and fix him up like this?' pressed the inspector.

'No idea,' sighed the doctor. 'But if that photo of her on the dresser is anything to go by, it looks like Joxer did some serious damage to a very pretty face. Maybe it was the only revenge left open to her. Let's be honest, who's going to remember he was nearly president after this ...?'

50

By lunchtime the following day, the outgoing Commissioner had issued a blanket ban on detectives carrying
videophones during working hours. The front pages of the
Irishman and *Dublin Daily* had ensured that. Not that he could
have blamed whoever did it. I mean, who's going to believe
that you found the next president in a working girl's flat with
half a fruit-bowl up his arse? Unless of course you manage to
get it on the front page of a tabloid.

Conman Donnelly had ranted and raved in the
Commissioner's office for about twenty minutes, and Father
Behan had rung in demanding a full inquiry. But they both
knew it was pointless; they were finished – as were any
chances of the poll being called off. The High Court had sat
in special session at 6.00 a.m. to hear the arguments for a
postponement. But as soon as the Real Fianna Fáil barristers
saw the first editions, they realised it was futile. There were
just too many variations of the 'Banana Republic' joke for the
party ever to recover. In the end, all were forced to agree that
Joxer's name would stay on the ballot but any votes he
received would be discounted.

The prostitute, however, still presented them with a
problem. Before the doc had knocked her out, she'd confessed
to the entire room that, yes, she had killed Joxer – just like
she'd killed 'that ugly little Cork man'. And if that meant what
the Commissioner thought it meant, things could become
very tricky altogether. Indeed, Pandora's box would look like
a fucking picnic basket.

Her solicitor was a wily sort, though, a Northerner called
McGinlay. Very old-school – still wore a bowtie. He seemed
like a dealmaker. And there was just a chance he could

persuade her to cop a plea and avoid a most embarrassing trial.

Stan had refused the summons to Dublin. There was no reason for him to fly south again, not when there were last-minute votes to be scored in Derry. He was a great believer in Tip O'Neill's first rule of thumb – all politics is local. And besides, Rubber John was only going to browbeat him into appearing at the RDS count centre the following day. Now that they'd a shot at actually winning the thing.

Only two days before, the Taoiseach had whole-heartedly agreed with Stan's assessment that it wouldn't do a damn bit of harm to miss the declaration. 'It's not very mannerly to your voters, Stan,' he'd said. 'But you're right. It'll annoy Joxer something awful if we're not there. He'll have no one to crow over. He'll look like president of fuck all.'

Harry likewise had given Lou a pass from the count. But again, that was when he was sure she was a loser. So when he caught up with her on a door-to-door canvass in the Brandywell that afternoon, he told her to go pack her overnight bag.

'No fucking way,' she snapped matter-of-factly. 'I'm sure the cameras can find the two of us in Derry. There are other cities in this country other than Dublin.'

'You're a coward,' retorted Harry. 'You're only ducking it now because you're afraid you might lose. Look, the first exit polls have us neck and neck. Some even have you a shade ahead. You could be our first ever president. You have to be there.'

'Maybe,' said Lou, walking quickly towards the next block of houses, 'but if you'd taken the hammering I had over the past two weeks, Harry, you might understand ...'

'Don't pull the sympathy card with me,' countered Harry angrily. 'You signed up to this, now you can fucking see it through to the end.'

Lou, who was just about to open a garden gate, stopped dead in her tracks. She clenched her two fists, turned round and stared directly into Harry's face, eyes narrow with rage.

Harry swallowed. He'd crossed the line. 'I'm so, so sorry,'

he stammered quickly. 'Really. It's just the pressure getting to me. I didn't mean it. Please forgive me ...'

'Go,' hissed Lou, through gritted teeth. 'Go now. Don't look back. And don't say another word. And if you ever fucking speak like that to me again, you'll wind up thinking Joxer O'Duffy got off light.'

'So where is she now then?' asked Audrey when Harry finished giving her the update in their suite in the Jack Kennedy later that evening.

'She and Stan hooked up at St Anne's polling station, immediately after the boxes closed, and headed off in his car.' He sighed. 'Somebody said they were heading for a late supper in the City Hotel. All I know is that I sure as hell wasn't invited.'

He looked deflated, so Audrey went over to where he was sitting on the leather sofa and kissed his cheek. 'Poor old Machiavelli,' she laughed. 'Nobody appreciates all the hard work he puts in.'

'It's just that this is maybe the only chance we could ever have of doing it,' he moaned. 'The last exits have us at fifty-one per cent. We should be savouring the moment. It's history.'

Audrey shook her head slowly. 'It's not going to happen, Harry,' she said. 'Not this time. They're not ready for her – nor for you. And besides, every Northern Prod, except maybe myself and a couple of those commies from the universities, will have voted for Stan to keep her out.'

Harry stopped and smiled at her. 'You voted for us?' he said, taking her hand, delighted.

'Yes I did,' she replied. 'But, well, it was the singer not the song ...'

He squeezed her wrist gently. 'Which singer?' he asked.

'You, you jackass,' she retorted, laughing. She raised her eyes to heaven, as if regretfully. 'But it doesn't matter – you're still going to lose.'

'I don't think so,' sniffed Harry. 'In normal circumstances – if I hadn't fallen out with Lou – I'd be hugely excited. In fact, I really think my luck is just about to turn.'

'That's because it is,' whispered Audrey, taking off her earrings and raising her eyebrows at him. 'But let me assure you, it has nothing to do with elections.' She smiled and pushed him back flat on the couch. 'I'm trusting, of course, that politics isn't the only thing you can get hugely excited about ...'

Back at the City Hotel, Tommy Bowtie had just arrived in the dining room, where he hoped to catch up with the two candidates. He'd spent the day in Dublin and had only barely got home to Derry in time to vote. There was no sign of either Lou or Stan, however. But Hugo and Mary were sitting down at the corner window facing the Foyle and they bade him join them.

'The pair of them have skipped off back to my house for a bit of peace,' explained Hugo. 'I gave them the key. They weren't in the door here thirty seconds when a camera crew arrived outside, so they sneaked out through the kitchens.'

A waiter arrived and quickly arranged a place for Tommy at the table. He then scooted off to fetch a pint of stout and a chilli chicken sandwich.

'How did you get on with the gardaí?' asked Mary.

'Very well, all things considered,' replied Tommy. 'But God love that poor wee girl. She's in a shocking state – physically and mentally. Her little face is really mashed up.'

'You saw her so?' interrupted Hugo, surprised.

'Yeah,' nodded Tommy, 'they let me into the clinic to see her for about thirty minutes this afternoon. The Guards arranged it for me. I spent an hour with their head man this morning and then another late this afternoon, after I got back in from the hospital.'

'So what did she tell you?' asked Hugo.

'More or less what we'd suspected,' said Tommy. 'Joxer dropped the gun when he was beating her with it, so she picked it up and shot him.'

'Clear-cut self-defence, I would have thought,' declared Mary.

'Except,' replied Tommy, grimacing slightly, 'Eva's next-door neighbour is still insisting that the last screams he heard were male ...'

'I thought the doctor said the first bullet killed him?' said Mary.

'They're not really sure,' answered Tommy. 'Not sure *yet*, that is. There's still some doubt. And, well, the pathologist's report could, ah, depend enormously on whether Eva accepts the deal they're offering her ...'

'Which is?' asked Hugo, leaning forward.

'Three years in the clinic, in return for a qualified insanity plea,' said Tommy flatly. 'It's basically half insanity, half self-defence. Apparently she suffers from aggressive hypo-glycaemia, which can make her turn violent. And they're also testing her for manic depression. They wanted to give her six years, but I beat them down. They actively don't want a trial. Christ knows what would come out. As part of the agreement, of course, everyone accepts that anything she said in the room after they found Joxer was just her hysteria. I could possibly even have got her less but ...'

'But what?' Mary said.

'But,' continued Tommy, 'she really needs help, and for the moment that's the best place for her ...'

'Says you, maybe,' countered Mary, a little indignantly.

'Yeah,' sighed Tommy. 'Me and four dead bodies.'

51

R TÉ was particularly incensed that it was being forced to fly two presenters, two production crews, a newsreader and three roving reporters to Derry. But the programme editor was damned if he was going to hire the conference room at the Jack Kennedy as his studio.

'It's a deal–breaker,' said Harry. 'The only place the candidates are going to do public interviews today is at my hotel.'

The editor stared into his phone and slowly counted to ten. 'How much so?' he asked, clenching and unclenching his free fist.

'Twenty grand,' replied Harry. '… For a world exclusive.'

'You're off your fucking head,' yelled the editor. 'No way. That's extortion. I'm going to report you.'

'Oh yeah?' said Harry calmly. 'To who? Now go off and lick your wounds, then ring back in half an hour, or I'll sell the whole thing off to TV3.'

Harry clicked off his cellphone and grinned across the breakfast table at Audrey.

'That,' she said, 'was very naughty. And very, very dangerous. Twenty grand to rent a room for one day? What if they refuse to turn up and announce on air that you're screwing them? Or, worse again, what if they try to suggest that Stan and Lou are behind it?'

Harry bit down on a piece of toast, then washed it back with a mouthful of cappuccino. 'You weren't listening properly, Aud,' he smiled. 'Nobody mentioned anything about rent. I'm offering to sell RTÉ an exclusive story for what I believe is a reasonable sum of money. And trust me, by lunchtime they'll be paying it – and paying it happily.'

'What's going on, Harry?'

'Swallow back your coffee, put on your suit and I'll tell you …'

The initial declaration was expected at around one o'clock, but in the event of recounts, there was no saying how late the announcement would be. Both challengers had full teams of sixty tallymen at the RDS count centre. Stan's crew were led by the Chief Whip and Sonny Waterhouse. Harry's younger brother Gerry and Chris Caddle from Dunavady were heading up Lou's squad.

'It's bad form that they're not down there,' said Audrey, as she climbed into the passenger seat of Harry's Mercedes.

'Actually,' he smiled enigmatically, 'it's not.'

Audrey looked across at the man who was slowly wrecking her career and waited.

'Lou phoned me last night while you were grabbing your shower,' he began. 'She was just as upset as I was about our row and wanted to explain …'

'Explain what?'

'Well, why she was so uptight. And after hearing her out, I agreed that she'd every right to be annoyed. So I apologised.'

'Good to hear. I trust she accepted it.'

'Yes,' continued Harry slowly, 'but there's a condition. We have to do her a favour. So strap yourself in there, till we get moving …'

At eleven, the word from the count centre was that the race was still pretty tight. Lou was ahead by a couple of points but they'd yet to open the bulk of the Northern boxes.

'Nervous?' Stan asked her.

'I've butterflies the size of bald fucking eagles,' she whispered. 'But I love the new suit, by the way.'

'Got to make the odd effort,' he replied, sneaking a sideways gleek at her. 'You're looking very tasty yourself. In fact I've never seen you tastier …'

Lou laughed. 'You're just saying that to get yourself a little presidential loving later tonight.'

'Hmmph,' snorted Stan indignantly. 'Maybe, I'll be able to get a little presidential loving all by myself …'

Lou lifted his hand, which she'd noticed was shaking. 'Are *you* nervous?' she asked, a little surprised.

'A small bit,' he admitted. 'But it's more the anticipation. I know it's a great thrill and everything, but I can't wait until it's all over.'

'Me too,' she confessed. 'The pressure will be all off us in an hour or so.'

'That's if Harry and Audrey show up,' said Stan, looking anxiously at his watch. 'Now where the hell are they?'

'Right behind you,' grinned Lou. And she pointed back down the aisle to where their two friends were coming through the chapel doors.

'They're where?' barked the Taoiseach.

'They're at the Long Tower chapel in Derry getting married,' replied Sonny Waterhouse, grinning broadly. 'He swore me to secrecy. He reckoned you'd throw a fit ...'

Rubber John, who'd just arrived at the count centre, raised his fists as if he were about to mill his Meath TD but then started to laugh.

'They planned it the night Georgie Behan's files became public,' said Sonny, 'when they realised they were both out of the reckoning. I suggested to Stan yesterday that he might postpone it for a little while, but he told me in no uncertain terms that he'd already wasted twenty-five years of Lou's time and he wasn't going to waste another fucking day. He then said something about getting his priorities straight and busting my bollocks if I spoke so much as a word to you ... So we never had this chat.'

'The sneaky bashtard,' smiled Rubber John, shaking his head. '*Ára*, I thought he was just being thick-headed – refusing to dance to the Dublin tune. Well, fuck him for a dark horse.'

The Taoiseach stood staring at Sonny, drumming his fingers on his hips, as he always did when he was thinking. After about ten seconds, he snapped his fingers and pointed to his cousin Marky, the Chief Whip.

'Ring the office and get them to send the helicopter,' he ordered. 'They can land it on the old pitches outside there. Sonny boy, we're off to Derry.'

The Chief Whip smiled and immediately pulled his cellphone out of his trouser pocket.

'By the way,' interrupted Rubber John, remembering where he was, 'we're sure how this thing is going to swing?'

'It's pretty much as they predicted, Taoiseach,' answered Sonny soberly. 'You know Fianna Fáil tallymen – they're the best in the business. But Marky'll patch the result through to the chopper, as soon as it's confirmed. They're not going to give the declaration anyway until they've got your face live on camera.'

'Exclusive access?' asked the RTÉ man.

'Completely,' promised Harry.

'For twenty grand …?'

'No,' said Harry slowly, as he looked at his watch. 'You're late. It's now going to cost you thirty – and that's our money.'

'Deal,' said the RTÉ man quickly. If he missed this one he was finished.

'Who told you the news?' grinned Harry.

'Sonny Waterhouse. But the little fucker put the bite on us for two grand first.'

'Great,' said Harry. 'Look, we'll catch up later. The priest is about to throw my mobile in the font. Oh, one last thing. Cash up front, of course.'

'Of course,' laughed the RTÉ man, thanking God that he'd had the wit to tell management it would cost fifty.

Harry, however, was only spinning the RTÉ man a line to get rid of him. The priest hadn't yet started as, at the last minute, Lou insisted on wiring off Mary and Hugo. And the pair were just getting settled into their front-row seats in the next-to-empty chapel.

'You're nothing but a dirty tramp, Johnston,' sniffed Mary, readjusting her hastily donned hat.

'Ah now, Mary,' said Lou, placating her. 'I couldn't have told you. You just can't help yourself. It'd have been front page news thirty seconds after you found out.'

'No, it wouldn't,' insisted Mary crossly. 'I can keep my mouth shut.'

'How many people did you phone from the car on the way here?' interrupted Stan.

'None of your fucking business,' retorted Mary. '... Sorry, Father.'

'At least six,' grinned Hugo. 'Including two national newsdesks. Fair play to you for doing it like this, Stan. And thank you. I'm thrilled to be here.'

'Shall we get started so?' said the priest. 'If we delay it any further, the bishop will land down and do me out of a job.'

'Absolutely, Father,' said Stan. He took Lou's hand again. 'I've waited way too long already.'

Despite Mary's huff, there were no objections to the couple being united in holy wedlock. Nor had Lou any problems about agreeing to love, honour *and* obey. (She had her own opinions on the value of oral contracts.) And, to cap it all, Harry had somehow managed to purloin two perfectly fitting rings.

As Lou lifted back her white veil and kissed her new husband for the first time, the four witnesses smiled and clapped approvingly. Then each quietly wiped their eyes when they were sure no one else was watching. Stan took half a step back and stared at his new bride with a mixture of pride and devotion, before reaching into his pocket for a silk hankie to dab her cheek.

'Always taking care of me,' she smiled.

'And always will,' he whispered, kissing her again.

With that the beeper inside Stan's jacket went off, and every head turned towards him indignantly.

'Answer it,' said Lou.

'I will not,' he replied, turning the little machine off.

'I really hope it's what you want,' she told him. 'You deserve it.'

'It's what you want too,' he smiled.

'No,' said Lou softly. 'The only thing I want in the world is standing right here beside me.'

52

Stan was right. Lou had never looked better. And a good job too. Because half an hour later, when the six-strong bridal party stepped outside the chapel for photos, the entire town was waiting. Along with half the world's media. And the roar of approval that broke out when they appeared in the doorway nearly lifted them off their feet.

'Any chance of a few words?' shouted a reporter from the *Irishman*.

'Later on, at the Kennedy Hotel,' the best man replied. 'Though I think RTÉ will be taking up a collection on the door ...'

'Where did you get the gorgeous dress, love?' called out an older woman in the crowd.

'Handmade here in Derry,' grinned Lou, who knew better than to admit she'd bought it off the rack from House of Brides in Kensington.

'Which one of you will be sleeping on the presidential side of the bed?' yelled another hopeful journalist.

The happy couple laughed and surreptitiously pointed at one another.

'I can answer that one,' boomed a Southern voice, as a small team of suits pushed their way through the throng.

'Oh fuck no, it's the Taoiseach,' groaned Stan as he watched the advancing posse. 'How the hell did he get here?' He then spied an apologetic-looking Sonny Waterhouse in the pack. 'Never trust a Southerner,' he sighed.

But there was no time for recriminations, as Rubber John was already bounding up the dozen or so steps towards him. 'You ungrateful rat,' he shouted, grabbing Stan in a bearhug. 'I should have you shot.'

The Taoiseach then turned towards the bank of TV cameras and announced: 'What do you think of this fella? I make him president of the country and he doesn't even invite me to his wedding …'

There was silence for about half a second while Stan and the watching crowd let Rubber John's words sink in. Then a deafening cacophony of cheering and clapping erupted, so loud and so prolonged that the small group at the top of the steps were forced to cover their ears.

Stan immediately glanced over at his new wife. But he needn't have worried. She was smiling more broadly than he was. She pulled him close to her and put her mouth up to his ear.

'I already knew,' she hollered, producing a pager out of her little white purse. 'I cheated. I told Harry's tallymen to page your machine if it was you – and mine if it was me. But I have no messages …'

Stan pulled out his own machine and read the text, which said simply: 'U – by 2 %.' He then went to hug Lou again but was elbowed out of the way by the Taoiseach, who grabbed her round the waist and kissed her warmly on the cheek.

'Commiserations,' he said.

'No need,' she laughed. 'The other's just a job. This is my life – and I couldn't be luckier.'

'You're very wise,' nodded Rubber John solemnly. 'It's the only thing that matters. May the two of you wander ever with woven hands …'

Lou stopped and looked at him, impressed. 'Yeats,' she grinned, recognising the quotation. 'And I always figured you for a know-nothing bogman, Mr Blake …'

'Yeah,' retorted the Taoiseach, 'a few other people have made that mistake too. How do you think I ended up leader of the party? … Now, grab that man of yours till we get out of here and open a few. Big Harry tells me he's buying.'

THE END